Nation of Enemies

Nation of Enemies

A Thriller

H.A. RAYNES

WITNESS
IMPULSE
An Imprint of HarperCollins*Publishers*

This is a work of fiction. Names, characters, places, and incidents are products of the author's imagination or are used fictitiously and are not to be construed as real. Any resemblance to actual events, locales, organizations, or persons, living or dead, is entirely coincidental.

EPub Edition AUGUST 2015 ISBN: 9780062417695

Print Edition ISBN: 9780062417701

10 9 8 7 6 5 4 3 2 1

To Beatrice
Who planted the seed.

April, 2032

Chapter 1

London, England

So, THIS IS freedom. No sirens pierce the air. Buildings in the distance are whole. Yet the ground beneath his feet feels no different. Dr. Cole Fitzgerald glances past their docked cruise ship, to the horizon. The sky blends into the ocean, a monochromatic swatch of gray. A chill in the air penetrates him, dampens his coat and makes all the layers underneath heavy. When they left Boston, pink-tinged magnolia petals blanketed the sidewalks, blew across overgrown parks and the burnt remains of brownstones. He'd reached up and touched a blossom, still hanging on a limb. It's remarkable to see beauty amid war.

The din of discontent is constant. On the vast dock of England's Southampton Cruise Port, a few thousand passengers stand in line, all on the same quest to flee the United States. He's heard that three million citizens emigrate annually. But no one documents whether those people are more afraid of the lone wolves and militias, or of their government bent on regaining control. Cole isn't sure which is worse. But London is a safe place to start again. They have family here, built-in support. No point in dwelling.

Beside him, Lily's usual grace and composure are visibly in decline. He reaches out and gently strokes the nape of his wife's neck, where pieces of her dark hair have strayed from her ponytail. The coat she wears can't hide her belly, now twenty-nine weeks swollen with a baby girl. Cole wishes he could offer her a chair. Instead she rests on one of their enormous suitcases.

Their son Ian sits cross-legged on the asphalt and reads a paperback. Throughout the journey, he's gone along with few complaints. Ten years ago he was born the night the Planes Fell, the night that changed everything. Living in a constant state of fear is all he's ever known. The joy and devastation of that night was so complete. To become parents at the same time terrorists took down fifty passenger planes . . . there were no words. It was impossible to celebrate while so many were mourning.

The mist turns to rain as night comes. Every fifty feet or so instructions are posted: *Prepare left arm for MRS scan; Citizenship Applications must be completed; Use of electronic devices prohibited.* Finally they cross the threshold of the Southampton Port Customs and Immigration building. The air is sour with sickness and stress and filth. Dingy subway tiles cover the walls of the enormous hall. Ahead, above dozens of immigration officer booths, a one-way mirror spans the width of the wall. Cameras, security officers, judgment. Cole's skin prickles.

In one of numerous queues they finally near the end. Lily elbows him and juts her chin toward the front of the line. People are scanned and then directed to one of three signs: *Processing, Return to Country of Origin,* or *Hearings.* Bile stings Cole's throat.

He calculated the risk of this trip, turned the possible outcomes in his mind endlessly. But thanks to Senator Richard Hensley and the biochip he legislated, it's all about genetics, DNA. Black and white.

They shuffle forward. Cole takes Lily's hand in his. It's comforting, despite the sweat coating her palm. He only wants to live a normal, safe life with his wife, with their children. It doesn't seem too much to ask.

The immigration officer at desk number 26 does not smile. The man's shorn, square head sits atop a barely discernible neck. Without glancing up, he shouts, "Next."

They move quickly. Cole hands him their citizenship applications.

"Prepare for scanning," the officer says. Wearing latex gloves, he holds the MedID scanner aloft as Cole lifts his left arm. The officer scans the biochip, barely discernable under the forearm skin. The process repeats with Lily and Ian.

"Mrs. Fitzgerald, please come forward again," the officer orders.

She trades concerned looks with Cole. "Yes?"

The officer rifles for something under the desktop and his hands return with some kind of an apparatus. "Excuse me," Cole says. "What is that?"

"IUMS," the man says.

"I don't know what that is," Cole says.

"In Utero MedID Scanner," he explains. "It's just another version of the MRS."

"What are you going to do with it?" Lily asks.

"Ma'am, I need you to lean forward." He gestures with the scanner in his hand.

"We don't have those in the U.S.," Cole says quietly. His mind spins. They opted out of prenatal testing, wanted to enjoy their baby girl before knowing what her genetic future might hold. Despite his research, he's never read about this technology.

"New protocol." The man smirks. He aims the scanner at Lily's belly. "Handy device that'll shed light on the fetus."

"You don't need a MedID? A blood test?" Cole presses.

The officer shakes his head. "It's an estimation but it's good enough for our purposes." He swipes the wand across her sweater-covered belly and once again regards the small screen.

With wet eyes, Lily wraps the coat tightly around her. Ian leans into them and the three meld in anticipation. They watch as he stamps each application. From this angle, Cole can't read it, but he knows. Lily's MedID number of 67 is eight points from the clean benchmark of 75. There's a thirty-percent chance she'll develop leukemia. A fifty percent chance depression will strike. And a ten percent chance she'll be diagnosed with early Alzheimer's. Fortunately, both Cole and Ian are in the clear with MedID scores of 84 and 78 respectively. They have virtually no markers for disease. In the eyes of England's society, Lily will be a drain on public resources. But what about the baby?

Wearing the same bored expression, the officer says, "Cole and Ian Fitzgerald you've been approved and may proceed to the Processing line. Lily Fitzgerald, you and your unborn child have been denied and will immediately return to the United States. Do you wish to make a plea?"

"We do." A wave of nausea hits Cole. "What's the baby's number?"

"The estimate is seventy-four." The officer taps his device and reaches below his desk to retrieve a piece of paper from a printer, the medical summary for their family. He hands the paperwork back to Cole and directs them to the Hearings line.

"Seventy-four," Lily whispers. Her skin is ashen.

One number away from being a clean, cherished 75. It might as well be twenty. Denied is denied. Still, they're prepared to fight. The rumor is that immigration judges rarely turn away individuals with specialized degrees.

They head down the corridor and enter another section of Immigration as Cole rehearses his speech silently. They join one of the lines, each ending at a glass-encased booth. A digital monitor hangs atop each one with the name of a judge.

"How do you feel?" Lily asks.

"Like I'm about to kill someone on the operating table." Cole reads the name on the booth ahead. "Let's hope Judge Alistair Cornwall is having a good day."

They will have five minutes. Plea guidelines are posted above each booth:

- *03:00 per Plea*
- *01:00 Judge Review and Decision*
- *00:30 Final Arguments*
- *00:30 Final Judgment*

Gavel-like sounds punctuate the hearings as the lines move ahead simultaneously. Cole's heart pounds as he clings to his CV, Harvard and Yale doctoral certificates. *Sell, sell, sell. I'm a commodity. My family is worth more than numbers.*

The gavel sounds. It's their turn. Cole slides the stack of papers through an opening to Judge Cornwall. Wiry gray eyebrows fan out over the judge's dark eyes. He glances briefly at Cole, then turns his attention to the documents.

"Proceed," says the judge.

"Your honor, I'm Dr. Cole Fitzgerald, Chief of Emergency Medicine at Massachusetts General Hospital in Boston. For the past six years I've been on the Bioscience Board there, which has led the world in testing protein-based drugs targeting cancerous cells." Cole coughs, glances at Lily. "For five years my wife, Lily, has been on a prophylactic course of medication used to delay or completely stop the onset of Alzheimer's. Your new scanning system has just informed us that Lily's carrying a baby girl with an approximate MedID number of seventy-four. But with eleven weeks left in the pregnancy, there are still opportunities to gain that one point needed to give this child a clean number. We'll make it our priority. I realize the immigration safeguards are in place to insure England's physical and economic health. And I assure you that the four of us will contribute to the well-being of this country."

The timer sounds. The judge leans to the side as he peers over Cole's shoulder at Lily.

"Mrs. Fitzgerald," Judge Cornwall says. "You've brought quite the trifecta with you."

"Excuse me, sir?" Lily slides beside Cole.

"Cancer. Alzheimer's. Depression."

Her mouth opens, closes.

The judge continues. "Fortunately, cures seem to be on the horizon. But they're not here yet." He flips through the paperwork. "After reviewing your case and considering your statement, my decision is to grant you, Dr. Fitzgerald, and your son Ian, temporary visas. However, I am unable to grant both Lily Fitzgerald and the unborn child the same. Mrs. Fitzgerald, your health is cost-prohibitive, and as for your fetus, there is already an endless line of children in our medical system."

Lily leans heavily into Cole. The timer sounds. Thirty seconds to argue.

"Please, sir." Cole's chest tightens. "My son needs his mother, and I need my wife. Our new child needs a chance. My services to your health-care system will be of great benefit and I'll work tirelessly to make sure your investment in me is a wise one. Ian will thrive in your schools. And we'll treat our daughter in utero, as I mentioned. She'll grow up and contribute to your society. I swear she will. Please."

The final timer goes off.

"But you can't guarantee it, can you?" Judge Cornwall slides the papers back through the slot. "No one can predict the future and many a parent has been disappointed in the outcome of children. One never knows. I regret to tell you that my decisions are final."

The gavel sounds. People behind them in line push past to get in front of the judge. In silence, the Fitzgeralds gather their things and move along the white tile floor, marred by a continuous gray smudge. At the entrance to the two final corridors, Lily moves toward the *Return to Country of Origin* sign. She says, "I want you and Ian to stay."

"No," Cole says. "We tried. We did our best. It didn't work."

"It worked for the two of you. You can be safe here."

"It's not an option, Lily."

"I'll go back. Have the baby. Maybe Kate or Sebastian can help us get visas."

Cole shakes his head. "You can't ask an FBI agent to help you do something illegal."

Ian watches them wordlessly.

"This isn't forever." Lily reaches for his hand and presses it between hers.

"What if Ian stayed here with your cousins?" Cole suggests. "He'll be safe while we work things out at home."

"No way," Ian interjects. "I don't know the cousins. And what if you don't come back?"

A river of people flows around them, arms and suitcases jostling them. The faces around them display raw emotion, nothing hidden: joy, angst, fear, relief. A security officer stationed a few feet ahead of them signals people forward with a waving hand.

Finally Lily nods. Defeat burns in Cole's gut. The three of them wrap arms, touch hair, kiss cheeks, and hold on as they savor the one moment they have left in this safe haven. And then it's time to go. Once again they pick up their belongings and head in the direction they no longer want to go. Back home.

Chapter 2

Washington, D.C.

A WAITER SWINGS by and hands Senator Richard Hensley another scotch on the rocks. It helps to override the anger that has settled in Richard's gut, loosens him up enough to mingle at this fund-raising gala. Between tuxedos and gowns, he watches fellow senator James Gardiner, the newly nominated Liberty Party presidential candidate. Richard runs a hand through his thick white hair. Gardiner is ten years his junior and has barely dipped his toes in politics, yet somehow he may lead the country in a matter of months. It's tough for Richard to stomach.

Second place is unacceptable, and yet here he is. A month has passed since he lost the nomination to Gardiner by a handful of votes. After years of public service—years of ushering through the MedID to protect these evidently ungrateful citizens. The wealthy hide out in Safe Districts, and the middle class has fled to the countryside, while the low-income population remains in what's left of city housing. Agriculture is the only sector that's seen a boon in a decade. Fortunately, the largest corporations have survived by increasing security to keep their buildings and employees safe. But for the most part Richard's hometown of Boston has been reduced to piles of bricks. And though the New York City buildings still pierce the sky, firefighters can't keep up with the blazes that are set daily. Chicago is burning as well, and from the air, Los Angeles sparkles, the sun glinting off the shards of glass from incessant looting.

After the Planes Fell, every religious fanatic and mentally ill citizen was emboldened. They come from all sides, with different agendas—though one of the shared themes is restoring their lost civil liberties. If it was just one effort, it would have been more predictable, easier to fight. But the attacks don't stop and law enforcement can't keep up. The lack of courage in the citizenry is disappointing. If it wasn't for Richard's MedID program, all hope and control would be lost. He'd been foolish to expect gratitude in the form of the nomination. He drains his glass, enjoys the burn that travels down his throat.

For two weeks following the results, he shut himself away from the world and considered his options. But the private sector doesn't appeal to him and he's far too young to retire. Politics course through his veins, a calling passed down from a father and a grandfather who were senators until their dying days. To walk away is unthinkable. So when he received the call, he had no choice but to accept.

His rival appears to have similar style and grace, floating seamlessly through the sea of party supporters. They lock eyes. Richard smiles and holds up a hand in greeting. After all, they must appear cordial now that he's Gardiner's running mate.

Couples crowd onto the dance floor. An old pang grips him

as he feels for the ring he still wears, turning it around his finger. Norah would have shone on that floor. She would have propped him up tonight, slid her arm into his and fortified him. He drains his drink, checks his watch. A familiar hand swoops in and plucks the empty glass from his hand.

"Did they teach that at Yale, Carter?"

"No sir." Carter grins. "When I was President Clark's personal aide, I became intimately familiar with the importance of refreshments at such events."

"I won't argue with that."

Landing Carter as his chief aide was a godsend. It came as a surprise that the President was willing to part with him, though he obviously realized it was for the good of the party. Now, Carter rarely leaves Richard's side. He's a constant, competent presence who has been steeped in this world for over ten years, since he was a White House intern. Carter's eyes stray over his shoulder. "Senator, the President's heading your way."

Turning, Richard regards President Clark. He's an imposing presence, standing at six-five, with broad shoulders and a shaved head. His face softens when he smiles, but that's the only softness he displays. In his two terms as President he's provided great strength to the country in the face of the war, a true Commander-in-Chief. Richard extends a hand and the two men shake in greeting. "Mr. President. Are you enjoying yourself?"

"Always." President Clark says it with a charming grin, but it falls away quickly.

"Evening, Mr. President," Carter says.

"Good to see you, Carter." The President raises his glass to them and drinks.

Richard's aide excuses himself and disappears into the flow of partygoers. Secret Service agents for both men linger a few feet away, their eyes on the crowd.

"You should have won the nomination," President Clark says.

"That was certainly my opinion, Mr. President."

"Everything can change in an election year. For better or for worse."

"I'm sure James Gardiner will be the man to make those changes. For the better."

"Don't be so sure." President Clark glances around them. "Up to now it's all been campaign rhetoric. Bipartisan bullshit. Promising an end to the war."

"It's all anyone wants."

"Indeed. But this is no time to change a system that's in its infancy. If he has his way, Gardiner will phase out the MedID."

"I'm well aware." Richard's cheeks flush and he sips his scotch.

"Polls indicate people believe our country has changed for the worse in the past four years. That the War at Home has gone on too long. But after almost eight years in the Oval Office, I can tell you honestly, the country has never been stronger. And that's in great part because of your efforts."

"Thank you," says Richard. "Truth is, I expected more voter support after introducing the MedID."

"People are shortsighted," President Clark says. "They can't see potential."

Several religious groups have labeled the MedID the "Mark of the Beast," the beginning of Armageddon. But it's meant to root out terrorists and individuals who have a reason to stay off the grid. Of course, they're the only ones who don't have MedIDs! A decade ago, with the wave of random school shootings, suicide bombings, and Christian martyrs, citizens were clamoring for the government's help. Richard delivered. And After the Planes Fell, those same citizens felt reassured by the MedID. Over the years, they've spent billions on the system, and there's quantifiable proof that MedID works. Law enforcement uses it to track suspects and to identify those who don't want to be found. Because of the mandated physician chip updates, health care has become streamlined. The workforce is strong. Ever since employers started hiring contract workers and scanning their MedIDs, productivity rates have spiked. No one takes sick days anymore. Those with clean MedIDs praise the system, and anyone with a score below a 75 cries foul. They're angry, desperate. But for things to change, a segment of the population will suffer. It's no different from any other war.

"Gardiner will turn on us," the President says.

"I know, sir." He bristles at the thought of James Gardiner's lack of respect or understanding of the MedID. It may not seem it now, but it will be the glue in their society. The two men stand in silence as the orchestra strikes up a new tune.

"I hear it's beautiful in Boston this time of year," President Clark says.

An odd non sequitur. "My favorite time at home."

"I hear the tourism office is kicking off a national campaign."

"Yes. It's on my agenda to attend." His thoughts go to his daughter, Taylor, who lives in Boston and hasn't spoken to him in over a year.

"Persuade James Gardiner to join you." President Clark gazes into the crowd. "I'm sure a few words from our presidential candidate would go a long way to encouraging the average American to vacation in the States."

"With all due respect, Mr. President, I'm quite capable of amping up the crowd alone."

"Yes, but he ought to join you at the event. See that he does." President Clark looks pointedly at him and pats a heavy hand on his shoulder before moving into the crowd.

The air is suddenly thick and soupy, the tie at Richard's neck snug. A waiter appears with another drink. He swallows the remaining contents of his glass and takes the new one. The rest of the night passes quickly, though Richard is distracted by this task of convincing James Gardiner to join him in Boston. Something in his gut tells him the President's order is about more than promoting tourism.

May, 2032

Chapter 3

Safe District 149, Massachusetts

It's hard for Lily Fitzgerald to believe that only a month ago they were on a ship to London, only to be denied entry. Now thirty-four weeks pregnant, she rests her hand atop her belly and sets her feet on an unpacked box of pots and pans. Early morning sun fills the room as she sits at the kitchen table checking email on her tablet. She shifts uncomfortably in the maternity jeans she's come to loathe. The baby moves and a bit of Lily's belly juts out. An elbow? A foot?

Their failed attempt to immigrate brought her to a dark place. Since the moment they scanned her belly, she's questioned everything. If it weren't for the baby, they might be living in England. And though she wants this baby with every thread of her being, she knows it's selfish. After Ian was born, they debated having another child. It seemed wrong, knowingly bringing a child into war. But it didn't stop her yearning. Finally, they decided to leave it up to Fate. Fate waited ten long years. Despite everything, she can't wait to meet her daughter.

She's promised herself not to cry anymore, and she needs to be strong for Ian. Cole says he'll find a way around the MedID system, but she can't imagine how. He also swore to keep them safe. When they'd disembarked in South Boston, he surprised her with a self-driving, bulletproof Land Rover waiting for them in the harbor parking lot. And instead of going to their wilting Victorian in Brookline, he'd taken them to a Safe District just west of the city. They'd been fighting this move for years, clinging to an old way of life in a beautiful, but decaying, neighborhood. Now they live in an unimaginative, mind-numbing, prefab house. Still, she has to admit that driving through heavily guarded gates into a community surrounded by twenty-foot walls is comforting. She actually lets Ian ride his bike down the street now. And Cole has abandoned his treadmill, his runs finally infused with fresh air. He must've spent most of their savings for their new life-in-a-bubble. The exclusivity of it all bothers her—most people can't afford to live this way. But her children are safe here. So to hell with her guilty conscience.

The next email fills the screen with video of an animated woman. Her voice is eerily friendly. "Lily Fitzgerald, your daughter has a forty-eight percent higher chance of securing a clean MedID number if you address issues in utero. New life equals new opportunity. With embryonic intervention, your daughter won't need to worry about major medical issues. Though you've entered your third trimester, there are still options available. Don't wait until it's too late. Call now to give your baby a healthier future."

With an edge of anger in her voice, she commands, "Delete." Goddamn them. These infernal governmental messages torment her. It's becoming the norm, choosing sex, eye and hair color, musical and athletic abilities, along with gene editing to cull "abnormalities." But it's not natural, and shouldn't having a baby—of all things—be natural? Her hand shakes as she reaches for her bagel, knocking into her orange juice and sending a splash over the edge. "Shit."

Orange drips pool on the laminate wood floor. In her mind she hears the judge denying them again and again. Cole enters the kitchen and kisses the top of her head. She doesn't move as she watches him mop up the juice with a towel.

"What's wrong?" he says.

"Another email from Government Health."

He sits next to her. "You all right?"

"She's a seventy-four, Cole. What if we missed an opportunity to change her life? To give her a healthier existence?

"You're a sixty-seven and I think you're perfect."

"Don't joke."

"I'm not." He sighs. "Listen. We had ultrasounds, did all the same tests when you were pregnant with Ian. It'll be okay. She'll be happy and healthy and that's it."

This is one of the many reasons she married him. He has a way of calming her. She shakes her head. "Every time I get one of those emails it throws me. Sorry."

"Don't be. People in Government Health know how to guilt people into action."

Lily taps his smartwatch with her finger. "Don't forget your gig this morning. The fourth grade waits for no one."

It takes a moment to register and then Cole remembers. He rushes down the hall.

The door to Ian's room is open, voices emanate from the computer. Quietly, Cole enters and sits on the unmade bed. His son's back is to him, seated at his desk in a corner of the room. Like every other room in the house, his is filled with unopened boxes.

A large monitor features the heading *Social Studies, Miss Johnson's Class* along with nine video feed windows with his classmates and his teacher. Ian spins around in his chair, and Cole gives him a thumbs-up. His son grins the same grin as his mother, though Cole doesn't see Lily's quite as often anymore, especially since London. Ian is a good physical mix of them: her smile, his eyes; her hair, his physique. He's always been a good boy, kind to others and very gentle. Perhaps too gentle for this world.

"Miss Johnson, my dad is here," Ian announces.

On cue, Cole walks over and waves into the camera.

"Class, this is Dr. Fitzgerald," Miss Johnson announces.

"Good morning, Miss Johnson. Class."

The students return the greeting in monotone unison.

"As we begin our unit on the MedID, I thought it would be helpful to have an expert answer some of your questions," Miss Johnson says. "Dr. Fitzgerald works at Massachusetts General Hospital in the emergency room, so he knows a lot about this subject. How would you like to start, Doctor?"

"I'm sure everyone has questions," Cole says. "Who wants to go first?"

The kids are hesitant, looking away from their monitors. The teacher says, "Why don't I get the ball rolling. As someone who works in a hospital, can you share what the MedID law has changed over the past several years?"

"I don't think we have enough time for that." He smiles. "But hospitals can better treat patients who have a MedID. Being able to quickly identify a patient's medical history is essential in the treatment process. It saves lives."

"Some people don't get MedIDs," one of Ian's classmates says. "How come?"

Cole hesitates, considers his words carefully. "Every U.S. citizen is required to have one, but yes, some people choose not to. The chip was originally meant to streamline health care. But it also allows the government to see personal information. Some people don't agree with that. They want their private lives to stay private. But the government thinks they can protect citizens better if they have access to certain areas of our lives. After the Planes Fell, they changed the MedID system. Law enforcement started using it to narrow the suspect list for terrorists. Criminals don't want to be tracked by being scanned, right? So that's one reason. But even some good people don't want the government to know their personal business."

"So they go to jail?" a dark-eyed girl asks.

"That's up to the police and the FBI. But they're breaking the law by not having one."

"So it's not just our medical records?" the girl continues.

"No, MedIDs are also tied to driver's licenses, social security cards, passports, bank accounts. Employers and insurance companies also use MedID information."

A blond boy asks, "Do visitors from other countries have to get our MedIDs?"

"Good question. If they're just visiting, they're given a temporary locator chip. It's like a MedID, but the only information on it is the person's name, country of origin, and contact information. The system tracks visitors who stay longer than four weeks. But all people entering the U.S. on visas, work permits, or those attending college are given MedIDs. When they go through customs, there's a MedID clinic right there at the airport."

Another girl raises her hand. "Do other countries make people wear MedIDs?"

"Japan is the only other country participating in a MedID program," he explains. "But the chips and technology are available worldwide. Other countries can deny people entrance based on MedID numbers. They're more apt to allow in only people with clean chips. Many countries are happy to take our healthiest citizens who'll be productive in their society."

The same girl asks, "How do doctors get new information on the chip?"

"I bet you remember this from checkups with your doctor. We use an MRS—a Medical Record Scanner—and the information is sent wirelessly. Parts of the chip are encrypted, which means they can't be changed. Things like your name, birth date, social security number."

There is a lull in the questions. Miss Johnson says, "Well thank you for your time, Dr. Fitzgerald. That was very informative."

Cole nods, pats his son on the shoulder. Ian beams and returns his attention to his class. At the door, Cole lingers. School should mean recess and lunches with friends, team sports and field trips. It pains him that his kids will miss all of that. But at least they won't be sitting targets for rogue students and radical groups.

Back in the kitchen, Lily's reading a book. Cole takes a seat at the table, moves his chair next to hers. Placing both hands on her belly, he leans over and kisses her passionately, something he hasn't done in far too long. When they part, she has tears in her eyes.

She looks down at his hands. "I can't bring myself to unpack the boxes. To put up pictures and artwork."

"I know." He leans back in his chair and stares at the bare white walls that bring the word sanitized to mind. "But seeing our things again might make you feel better."

He knows she wants out of this country more than he does. There must've been a moment in London when she wondered if he'd emigrate without her. Their MedID point inequality heightens her anxiety, makes her worry he might leave her. It's ludicrous, of course. But it's happened to friends of theirs. All he can do is reassure her.

"I should get going." Cole kisses her check on his way out.

"You wearing your skins?" she calls.

Pulling down the collar of his shirt, he reveals the gray, skin-tight material that serves as a ballistics shield. When they returned from London, he'd bought skins for the whole family. The bodysuit was uncomfortable at first, but he's gotten used to it. With hospitals a constant target, he'll take all the help he can get.

Chapter 4

Boston, Massachusetts

THE DRIVER JUTS his middle finger into the air at the sound of a car horn. The windows of his Mustang are down, the air whipping his hair chaotically as he passes abandoned Victorian mansions with overgrown lawns and peeling paint. Graffiti winds like ivy from house to house, from fence to sidewalk. Cruising by dilapidated Fenway Park, he shouts, "Go Sox!"

A death metal song screams from the car speakers, his head bouncing to the thrashing beat. He knows his fellow Brothers and Sisters in Arms—BASIA—are with him in spirit. These last few minutes make the hairs on his arms stand up. This is it. Salvation.

A ring tone sounds, an image of a blond boy appearing on his windshield.

"Answer call." The music halts and there's a click. "Hey."

"Hi, Scotty." His brother's voice is just beginning to crack. "What're you doing?"

"I can't talk now. I left a note for you guys." He lifts his foot slightly from the accelerator, his heart pounding.

"Where are you?"

"Listen to Mom, okay? Do your homework, clean your room. Don't make her cry."

"You made her cry."

He shakes his head. "You're not me."

"Can we hang out later?"

"Be good, Leon. I love you, little man."

"Jeez, why're you saying that?"

"I gotta go. Take care, buddy." He shuts off the phone.

The music screams once again as the car careens past crumbling and charred buildings. Blowing through lights, he swings onto Newbury Street. Looted storefronts are a grayish blur. A smattering of suits stride down the street. At a red light, he pulls to a stop and stares at his destination, a brownstone building one block down. His whole body trembles.

"BASIA is eternal life!" On the passenger seat is a crude bomb, wrapped with wires and duct tape. He presses a button and instantly shoves the gas pedal to the floor. The wheels spin, burning tire treads that emit a high-pitched shriek. People scatter.

"The Lord is my shepherd, I shall not want . . ."

Outside the Liberty Party headquarters, two armed guards flank the glass doors, raising their semiautomatic rifles. A flash of Leon appears in his mind.

"He leadeth me beside the still waters. He restoreth my soul."

The Mustang jumps the curb. Bullets shatter the windshield. The guards dive out of the way. He closes his eyes against the glass shards but keeps his foot glued to the floor.

"He leadeth me in the paths of righteousness for His—"

The car smashes through the doors and explodes.

A FEW BLOCKS away, stained-glass windows tremble, dust floats down from ceiling moldings.

In the Patriot's Church office, behind a sleek glass desk, Reverend Charles Mitchell reclines in his chair. The thumb on his left hand presses into his right palm, traces the tattooed, imperfect cross that follows the creases in his lifeline. It's been a habit for as long as he can remember. As a boy, in his first foster home, he'd noticed the cross there, with him always. As though he carries God in his hand.

Across from him on a sofa, Hannah sits curled up on the cushions. Her green eyes are wide, her tangle of red hair loose down her back. A beautiful child, though at eighteen, a child no longer. She's been with him ten years, since the Planes Fell. It's hard to believe she'll soon be his bride, but forty-five seems a good age to marry. He follows her gaze to the large wall monitor. The audio is muted, but breaking news streams live from a bombing. Ambulances and fire engines are parked behind a reporter as people in uniform run this way and that. Yes, this morning God was with Scott Durgin, the evidence a blackened crater in Boston's Liberty Party headquarters. It reminds him of the tomb from which Jesus emerged, born again. He closes his eyes in a silent prayer of thanks.

"You send him, Charles?" Hannah's voice still has a southern lilt despite elocution lessons.

He shakes his head. "No one could tell that boy what to do."

Though he acted alone, Brothers and Sisters in Arms was in Scott's heart. BASIA's victory is shared with other groups who fight in the resistance. Across the country, people are on their knees in thanks. It's what Charles has worked for. A headache suddenly and swiftly stabs at his temples, making his eyes water. It happens sometimes, after these events. He believes it's brought on by grief—he doesn't *want* people to die. But this is war. This is Armageddon.

Charles's voice commands, "Power off," and the monitor goes black. He retrieves a prescription bottle from his desk drawer. Without water, he swallows a pill that should erase his pain by the time he takes the stage.

Hannah stands and slips into her black flats. "You feeling all right?"

"Fine." From his suit jacket pocket he pulls a lavaliere microphone and pins it to his lapel. In a corner of the room his bodyguard stands at attention. With or without his holstered gun, Henry is an imposing presence.

Charles rises, straightens his suit. "I must admit, I didn't think he had it in him."

On cue, Henry opens the office door.

"He was quiet, I remember." Hannah's brow furrows, a vertical line forming on her freckled brow. "He brought a little boy to service one day."

"His mother wasn't too happy about that," Charles says. "But Scott turned out to be a fine soldier of God."

"Like my father," Hannah says, her voice soft.

"Yes, he was one of the best. A minister and pilot wrapped up into one. Meant for greatness." He remembers her father well, a devoted leader, willing to give up his family in the name of God. "All right. Let's get this show started."

Every pew in the cavernous, circular nave is full. People line the aisles and crowd together along the walls. Hannah enters first, takes a seat in the row designated for Charles's family, orphaned children and teens of every age and race. Charles comes in after her, his hands clasped humbly as he makes his way to center stage, slightly raised above the seats in his very own theater-in-the-round. Upon seeing him, voices hush, bodies settle. A thousand pairs of eyes follow him. The energy in the room is electric. Their faith has carried him far.

"Good morning." He turns slowly, taking in his flock.

"Good morning," they say in unison.

"God bless America," he says.

"Amen," they say.

One last rotation and he faces the portion of the wall on which is painted a massive mural of a palm—his palm—with the tattooed cross. "Whether you came today for God or country or family—or all three—you are here to be saved. No one on the other side of that door," he points to the church entrance, "is fighting for you. Do you think they're fighting for you?"

"No," they answer. Affirmations from the crowd invigorate him.

"They don't care about your God-given rights. The civil servants no longer serve—they play God. They give orders. Tell you what to do, what not to do. They deny you your dreams."

"That's right!" the crowd says.

"One nation under God." Charles grips the Bible that rests on his podium. "Make no mistake. This is, has, and always will be, one nation under God. The day the courts removed that phrase from our national pledge of allegiance, I knew it was a sign." That news had hit him viscerally, took his breath away. In response, he'd spent that day in a tattoo parlor. The pain in his newly inked palm had soothed him, for no good comes without sacrifice. "And God is angry. Angry at the politicians and the government. At our supposed representatives who serve only themselves. For if they truly served us, would they make a dying child wait to see a doctor?"

Shouts of "No!" fill the hall.

"They turn their backs on those of us without jobs when it's their own laws that have put people out of work. They feed off our desperation. Can't support yourself? Good. Can't care for your children? Even better. They want you to depend on them. They want you fearful. Hungry. Dependent."

People shout out in agreement. Charles lets the clamor build as he makes eye contact with parishioners. Finally he sees the face he's searching for. Senator Richard Hensley's daughter, Taylor. Only child of the future vice president of the United States. Henry had told him she'd come. Of course, in her wake, news vans are lining the curb outside. She's in the back, on her feet with the others. What brought her here today? Does she share their passion?

"We are hungry to be free," he continues. "Hungry for change. Well let me assure you, change is coming. Change starts right here. Your strength and spirit has carried you to Patriot's Church. Our children deserve a bright future in God's country. This land, our home, should be a place of dreams. Many of us can still remember the time before. We know it's possible. But the leaders of our great country have forgotten what America means. They instill fear and they rule without our support. Without people of faith. But here, we know the truth. Slowly, steadily, we're gaining on them, taking back our country. Because this is *our* country. This is our war to win. And we *will* win!" Charles raises a fist in the air.

Cheers as a thousand fists punch the air. Charles beams. After a few seconds, he lowers his hand and the believers do the same. His mood darkens with the seriousness of this sermon. He waits until he has silence.

"I don't celebrate the lives lost in this battle. But even as those souls, God willing, ascend into everlasting life, we are gaining ground here on earth. They will be remembered for making the ultimate sacrifice for our freedom." A sharp pain stabs at his temple, his eyes water. He breathes through it and continues. "One of our own gave his life this morning in service to God and his country. Scott Durgin was a man of conviction. A fine soldier. Of his own volition and fierce beliefs, Scott made a bold statement by demolishing the Liberty Party headquarters. I don't condone the slaughter of innocents, but Scott sacrificed himself for his beliefs. He's a hero who'll forever live in our hearts." Gasps and whispers fill the air. "Our enemies heard us loud and clear on this beautiful spring day. Do you think they're listening to us now?"

"Yes." Every head nods, every pair of lips mouth *Yes.*

"Do they feel our power?"

"Yes."

"As well they should. Now. Every day we're blessed with new members. If you're new today, welcome. Please stand and introduce yourself." He locks eyes with Taylor. She is striking despite her short hair and lack of makeup. Prettier than in the tabloid pictures.

Her cheeks blush as she looks around the room. As others rise to their feet, so does she. The room quiets in anticipation. He extends a hand in her direction.

"Please," he says. "Don't be shy."

Taylor holds up her right hand in greeting. "My name is Taylor

Hensley. Please don't hold my last name, or my father, against me." Laughter from the crowd. "As a widow, a mother, and a citizen, I've felt lost and in limbo for a long time. I haven't been to church in years, but I believe in God. And I believe in freedom. Thanks for the welcome. I'm happy to be here today."

The crowd claps one time simultaneously and in unison extend their right palms to him—many revealing cross tattoos.

Charles nods in acknowledgment and says only, "Welcome, Taylor." With her as one of his flock, the possibilities are great. But in the beginning, he must treat her like all the rest.

Chapter 5

Boston

In front of Massachusetts General Hospital, throngs of people and press crush against one another, desperate for information. No names have been released so far, no number confirmed dead. FBI Special Agent Sebastian Diaz winds through the revolving glass doors of the hospital on his way to interview bombing victims.

When headquarters called with the news, his body grew leaden. His fiancé, Kate, has been working with the Liberty Party. He called her, got voice mail. Texted. Called again. Called her sister Lily, to no avail. Kate's family—her sister, brother-in-law, Cole, and nephew, Ian—have become his own in the past year. As he tried the numbers over and over again, his hands shook. "She's okay, she's okay," he repeated out loud to himself. But service was jammed. Finally a text from her: *I'm safe, home. Go to work. xo.*

And he did, eagerly. There's no sign of his partner, fellow agent Chris Renner, but Sebastian can't wait. It's crucial that the

Counterterrorism Taskforce interviews victims immediately. Ahead, an eight-member security team guards the Mass General entrance. Four burly men dressed in dark suits are armed with guns and expert martial-arts skills. Dressed in business attire, another man and three women round out the group, sitting at touch-screen desks. Their job is to identify potential terrorists in the steady stream of hospital visitors and outpatients.

The line moves forward, each person passing through safety screening stations. Despite his FBI credentials, Sebastian is treated no differently. As the soles of his leather shoes press against the smart carpet, he watches a security analyst up ahead. He knows that when she swipes her index finger across her tablet, a biometric measurement on him appears. A few more steps and he encounters one of several screens with the outline of a hand, prompting him to hold his right palm about an inch away. When it beeps, he removes his hand and walks a few more steps until an interactive board prompts him to enter the name of the patient or doctor he is there to see. Sebastian can't see the subliminal flashes—images of known terrorists, words such as Taking Back the Country, photographs of government officials—but he knows they're there. By the time he reaches the analysts and armed guards, his body temperature, heart rate, and respiration have informed security that Sebastian Diaz does not harbor malicious intent and poses no immediate threat to the hospital. He passes through the final door to the ER.

The frenetic energy makes Sebastian stand still. An antiseptic scent coats the air. It triggers his memory of the last time he'd made a call like the one he made to Kate. But that day, his father died on a gurney behind one of the pale blue curtains. He'd just been doing his job, working at a desk job at an investment firm, when a disgruntled ex-employee walked into the office and set off a bomb. After Sebastian's father was buried, his mother and brothers returned to Buenos Aires to be with family. With them safe and far from the war, he can focus on his job.

Through the chaos, he sees his future brother-in-law, Dr. Cole Fitzgerald. The chief of Emergency Medicine is consulting a floor plan of the ER displayed on a smart wall. His fingers sweep across the electronic diagram, moving physician and patient names to correspond with beds and operating rooms.

Sebastian steps alongside him. "Welcome back."

Cole glances at him, sniffs. "It's good to see you."

They shake hands. It's the first time Sebastian's seen him since he and Lily got on the ship, headed to London. He wasn't sure he'd ever see Kate's family again.

"Busy morning," Sebastian says.

"Aren't they all." Cole looks toward the entrance. "You alone?"

"Renner's on his way." Sebastian scans the faces in the beds. "How many dead?"

"Eleven. Seventeen are critical."

"Mind if I start the interviews?"

"No problem." Cole gestures toward a middle-aged man wearing a johnny and sitting on a gurney. Bandages cover half his face. "Start with him."

Sebastian heads in the man's direction, glancing back at Cole. "We still on for tonight?"

"Yeah, of course."

"We'll bring the wine," Sebastian says. "Kate can't wait to see Lily."

Everything has changed in just a year. Sebastian had always thought he'd stay single, especially with the long hours he puts in at work. But Kate reminds him there are still reasons to be happy, despite the terrible shit he sees daily. He had no idea how much he needed to forget.

Sebastian hears his name being called. Renner catches up with him and together they approach the patient with the bandaged face.

DR. COLE FITZGERALD's attention is quickly drawn back to the bloodied and broken patients being wheeled this way and that. The choreography of his staff and how the teams work within chaos always impresses him. When he took his family to London, he'd told the hospital he was vacationing for two weeks. He'd hoped never to return.

"We have a problem." It's Nurse Huberty, her voice low. She is his eyes and ears on the floor. Nodding her head to a curtained bed across the room, she explains, "Your new hire, Dr. Riley, is refusing to update the chips."

"I'll take care of it. Thanks."

At the partition, Cole opens the curtain and enters the tight space. Inside, Dr. Karen Riley speaks to the parents of her patient, a girl of seven or eight years, who sits on the bed. Her two front teeth are missing and her brown hair is in a braid down her back. The girl's johnny has been discarded on the floor and she's fully dressed. The mother grips Dr. Riley's arm. The father rubs a hand over his daughter's back. The Medical Record Scanner rests on the side table, untouched. Dr. Riley has only been at the hospital a month, so Cole doesn't have a read on her yet. Her petite build and unruly curls give her a mousy appearance. But he senses strength underneath.

"Excuse me, Dr. Riley," he says. "A moment, please."

Riley excuses herself and follows him. It's hard to find privacy with all the activity, so he leads her to a supply closet. The voices and machines fade into white noise when the door closes behind them. On either side of the narrow space, shelves are filled with bandages, syringes, bed pans, and countless other items. Riley pulls off her latex gloves and drops them into a receptacle. He watches as she methodically touches each finger on her right hand to her thumb and repeats this action. A nervous habit he noticed during her interview.

"It's part of your job to update the chips," he says. "There's no choice in the matter. You have to do the scans."

Though her cheeks blush, Riley steps toward him, her eyes meeting his. "With all due respect, we're here to help and heal people, not to subject them to laws that violate their civil liberties."

"You knew the job when you signed on. This is a state-run and -financed hospital. Neither of us would be here healing people if it weren't for government support. And whether or not you like it or agree with it, you will update the MedIDs."

"That family is planning to move to Finland next week. If I update Tess Connelly's chip, it'll ruin those plans. It will take away their chance to—"

"Not our problem," he says. "You won't make it in this field if you can't separate your emotions from your work. Believe me, I know that's hard to do sometimes."

Red blotches appear down Riley's neck. "How can we save people and then condemn them? What we write on MedIDs impacts lives forever."

Not mousy at all. Feisty, even. Of course he agrees, but he can't say as much. "This isn't a debate, Dr. Riley. I'm not in charge of this country—I'm in charge of this ER. When I'm here, I don't have political opinions. And the MedIDs are part of our job."

"I just think—"

"Think about this. I hired you because you're a talented doctor. But I'll replace you if you can't do what's required." He turns and opens the door. "When you finish your shift tonight, let me know if you're on board. In the meantime, Nurse Huberty will do your scans."

On the floor, he passes a packed waiting room. People shout over the loud volume of the TV. Cole recognizes the advertisement for Hudson's Funeral Homes. The owner is selling a service that doesn't need to be promoted. He imagines they'll be just as busy today as the ER.

Chapter 6

Newton, Massachusetts, suburb of Boston

WEARING A WHITE bathrobe, Steven Hudson sips coffee at the kitchen table. A monitor in the wall entrances him as he watches himself on the Hudson's Funeral Homes commercial. Unconsciously, his hand goes to his graying hair, moving lightly across the waves, stiff with styling product. Despite the makeup, he can see the childhood scar on his forehead. It folds into a horizontal wrinkle when he lifts his eyebrows. He moves his lips along with the script, matching his own voice projected from the speakers.

"The world we live in has so many uncertainties these days. The War at Home means casualties in our neighborhoods, and sometimes, death on our doorstep."

He appears somber and honest, a trustworthy partner in death. The intro segues into a montage of bombed schools, men weeping, mothers clutching babies amidst destruction. Once again he appears onscreen. "Hudson's Funeral Homes provide stability when you need it the most. I guarantee a compassionate staff, twenty-four-hour support, and most importantly, respect for you and your loved ones when you choose Hudson's in your time of need. Call 999-HUDSONS for the location near you."

Steven commands, "Monitor off." If his parents were alive, they'd be proud to see how he's grown the business. He and his family live in the first Hudson's location, a stately mansion converted by his father fifty years ago that's now the national headquarters. When the war began to creep into the suburb of Newton, he built his very own Safe Wall around the property, encasing the house so that his family—and the families they service—would be protected. He must admit, he sleeps better with the bulletproof lacquer on the wall's smooth surface.

Aside from the living areas, there are two visitation rooms and his office. Each piece of furniture and every drape was handpicked by him and his wife, no expense spared. In the basement are the preparation rooms, though with the tremendous success of the business, he no longer needs to prepare bodies himself. However, on occasion he'll disappear into a prep room. The process is peaceful, and he still enjoys the work. The converted carriage house on the property contains two chapels. Hudson children were never allowed a swing set on the sprawling green lawn because it might seem inappropriately playful to mourners.

Wearing a matching robe that appears gray in comparison, Sarah walks into the kitchen. His wife doesn't acknowledge him. Mascara is smeared under her red-rimmed eyes and roots of gray part her black hair down the middle. He watches her as she pours a cup of coffee. The other night he caught her smoking marijuana. If it was only the pot, it wouldn't bother him.

"Liberty Party headquarters was bombed this morning," he says. "Just awful."

There's no reaction from her as she sits at the table.

"We should pull in around ten," he continues. "Not bad for a Wednesday."

She ignores him. It drives him crazy when she's like this. He slaps the tabletop hard. She jumps, making coffee slosh over the side of her cup.

"Hello?" He leans closer. "Anyone in there? You're like the walking dead, Sarah."

"You wish."

He shakes his head. "You gonna get out of that robe this month?"

"What's the point?"

"You should start painting again. You need another . . . vice."

"Fuck off."

"What fun banter we have these days." He takes a deep breath. "Hey, why don't you help me out downstairs today? I bet we get slammed mid-afternoon."

"No thanks." Sarah closes her eyes. "House, what time is it?"

From hidden speakers an automated female voice announces, "The time is ten thirty-five. The temperature outside is sixty-eight degrees. A good day for gardening."

"Is Jonathan awake?" Sarah suddenly seems alert.

Steven shrugs. "Haven't seen him."

She stands and glares at him. "You didn't wake him up for school?"

"He's your son. You wake him up."

For a moment it seems she might cry, but then she bites her lip. "You've been his father for eight years. Would it kill you to take an interest?"

He drains the rest of his cup, the time helping to calm

him. "That kid goes days without talking to me. He hasn't been in a good mood since 'twenty-two. I tried to bond with him last year when I took him to the National Funeral Home Convention. You know what happened. Every time I make an effort, he runs in the other direction, which usually involves the police. I'm done. Done."

"He's just a kid, Steven. You think it's easy for him to live around death day in and day out? No wonder he doesn't want to get out of bed."

"Death pays for his video games. It pays for his goth wardrobe, his food, and for this beautiful house." The kid is ungrateful, and if it wasn't for Sarah, he'd toss him out on his ass. "He needs to respect death. He needs to respect me. He's seventeen. Time to grow up."

Sarah strides out of the kitchen, down the hall, up the stairs, to a door at the far end of the second floor. She knocks. No response; she knocks again. Finally she turns the knob.

Jonathan's room is an assault on the senses. Bloodred paint covers the walls. The antique furniture has been painted black. Metal band posters serve as wallpaper, with visuals that scream as loud as if their music was playing. It's hard to tell, but a professional decorator created this "look" based on her interview with Jonathan. Sarah had told the woman she didn't care what it looked like, she just wanted him to be happy and feel at home in his space. He rarely leaves it, after all. Kids don't seem to hang out anymore. The war put an end to afterschool activities, loitering in malls, and going to underage clubs. Poor kid has never even met his classmates in person. It's like solitary confinement. And the darkness she sees in him is troubling.

A long, skinny lump is buried under the covers of the bed. On the pillow, a tuft of brown hair peeks out. She reaches down, her fingers running through the soft strands. It's the only time he allows her to touch him anymore.

"Jonathan?" Her voice is soft. "Jonathan. Wake up. You're late." She pulls the duvet down. Underneath the mop of hair and through the piercings in his ears, eyebrows, and lip, is an attractive boy. Thick black eyelashes twitch as he struggles to open his eyes. She gets in one last stroke before he bats her hand away.

"Cut it out." He pulls the blanket back over his head.

"You've already missed your first two classes. Get up." Playfully, she smacks a lump that must be his butt. "I thought you liked chemistry. Isn't that your next period?"

"Yeah. They're teaching us how to make a homemade bomb."

"That's not funny, you know."

"It's a little funny."

"Trust me," she says. "School was a lot more fun before kids learned how to make bombs. Now you're stuck here."

With an exasperated sigh, he sits up and swings his legs out of bed.

"You want a quick breakfast?"

"Is he down there?"

She nods. "I'll bring something up." She leaves, closing the door behind her.

Jonathan grabs a crumpled black T-shirt from the floor and pulls it over his head as he sits at his desk. School. Waste of time. At his command, the computer comes to life. Playtime. His fingers fly over the keyboard, bringing up his official school site. In minutes he gains access to the server, hacks the system, and disables the site. It's like giving his classmates an old-fashioned snow day. Much easier than crashing the U.S. Department of Education's site. He did that when he was twelve. Should've been more careful, though—the Feds tracked him in less than twenty-four hours. But being in sixth grade had worked to his advantage and he'd gotten off easy. He's on a watch list now. Whatever. He likes the challenge. Leaning back in his chair, he yawns. Laughs. It's a beautiful day to play some video games. Maybe go boarding. Fuck school.

Chapter 7

Boston

FBI Special Agent Sebastian Diaz runs through details from the attack as he prepares for the brief. In a glass-walled conference room of the Bureau's Boston office, twelve men and women wearing various shades of gray and navy sit at an oblong table. To his left is his partner, Chris Renner, to his right an empty chair at the head of the table, intended for the Special Agent in Charge of the Counterterrorism Unit, Ron Satterwhite. The fifty-year-old's solid, compact frame reaches only five-six, and he rarely sits, lest he be looked down upon. At the front wall, he brushes a hand repeatedly over the electronic display of devastating images of today's bombing.

Satterwhite's eyes are slits. "It's our job to be ahead of these situations. The deputy director is demanding to know what happened." No one speaks or moves. He shouts, "What happened? Is anyone taking credit?"

"They're not taking credit, but the driver was a BASIA militant." Sebastian swipes a finger across the table in front of him. Instantly, a new window appears on the main wall. Covertly taken photos show people entering Reverend Charles Mitchell's Patriot's Church.

"Scott Durgin disappeared from the church a few weeks ago," Renner says. "He was off our radar. We profiled him several months ago and determined he was a follower, not high-risk for making a strike. I spoke to my informant, who says Mitchell was surprised by the attack."

"Your informant is worthless, Renner. As is your profiling." Satterwhite slams his hand on the table. "If you think for one second that bastard is ever surprised, then maybe you should sign up for his congregation, since it seems you're buying his bullshit now."

Renner's cheeks flush. Though Sebastian doesn't know his informant, he knows Renner's grown to trust the person over the years. He gets personally offended if and when someone questions his informant's validity.

It's Sebastian's turn. "NSA and Homeland Security are mining data on communication between Mitchell and his followers. But as we all know, the Reverend hasn't owned a cell phone in twenty years and doesn't appear to use computers."

"Mitchell's security team, then," Satterwhite presses. "The men and women closest to him. You telling me none of them use electronic devices?"

"They've been trained well, sir," Sebastian says. For years, anyone could be tracked via their MAC address—a unique identifier emitted by every electronic device. But once word of the NSA's surveillance capabilities leaked out, many citizens went off the grid. There's even a new trend of writing letters. "Mitchell's people dump disposables after a few uses. They switch email addresses and computers constantly. When they do communicate electronically, the emails and texts are encrypted and self-destruct before we can hone in."

"Unacceptable." Satterwhite gestures to the wall of information. His lips press into a thin line as he paces. "There are over ten thousand radical militias and antigovernment groups spread across this country. Add to that lone wolves and kids with chemistry sets. That's tens of thousands of enemies of the state stacked against our fifty-six field offices. Do the math. Our manpower and resources are at capacity, and that's not changing anytime soon. I realize you're stretched. I also realize there are casualties in war. But we have to work harder. *You* have to work harder. Give more. 'Cause what you're giving isn't enough."

It's an old speech. After every attack, Satterwhite berates them and reiterates their mission. But despite the growing list of terrorists, Mitchell and his Brothers and Sisters in Arms remain enemy number one with their nationwide following. The Bureau had never even heard of BASIA until a quote from one of the Fallen Planes' black boxes was determined to be an integral part of Mitchell's sermons, a revised portion of the Declaration of Independence. That heretic is after One Nation Under God, a theological state. But with only circumstantial evidence, there's no proof, no clear connection, between Mitchell and the Fallen Planes. Or any other attack, for that matter.

On the wall, Satterwhite displays a photograph of Mitchell at the top. Branching off from him are lines that lead to known terrorists who have successfully carried out attacks.

"This is our guy." Satterwhite jabs his finger at Mitchell. "Thousands of families email me weekly for a status report on the Planes investigation. Some of you were in braces, maybe don't remember it well. So if you need a refresher on the mass murder that man caused, you're all welcome to review the case file. He's the leader of the nation's largest antigovernment church. We have loose threads tying him to twelve of the fifty suicide pilots. To be clear. Mitchell's never surprised. Mitchell's pleased as fucking punch."

The last zinger hits Renner, whose hand creeps to a patch of the tightly curled dark hair at the back of his scalp, pulling and twisting a piece.

"Depending how we look at it, there's a new opportunity—or a new complication—at Patriot's Church." Sebastian pulls up an image and adds it to the Mitchell graph. "The Mind's Eye surveillance flagged Taylor Hensley at a church service this morning."

Satterwhite sniffs. "Mind's Eye was scooped by the local news."

"Right. Well, the senator's daughter tends to bring the news vans wherever she goes."

"That's one hell of a complication. Mitchell must think he's hit the goddamned lottery. There's no room for a misstep here. You have a plan, Diaz? Renner?"

Renner displays images of Taylor Hensley's famous graffiti. Much of it is antigovernment with a decided prejudice against the MedID. He says, "Based on her very public artwork, we could detain and question her. Possibly get a warrant to monitor her calls. But with her father as a vice presidential candidate and her newfound affiliation with Patriot's Church, we'll be stirring the pot. You don't get more high profile than this."

"Taylor's a single mother," Sebastian adds. "That could make her vulnerable. If Mitchell gets close enough to her, it poses an obvious risk to her father."

"Clear out." With an angry wave of his hand, Satterwhite dismisses everyone except Sebastian and Renner. The last person files out and shuts the door. Finally, Satterwhite takes his seat at the head of the table. "Go on."

"The Mobile Surveillance Team assigned to Mitchell has gotten nowhere," Sebastian says. "They tail him to and from his home, the church, and the BASIA compound. He never goes into businesses or makes home visits unless it's to a sick member of his church. The MST placed a couple operatives in the congregation, but we already know his rhetoric and that's all he's giving up in a public forum. It's not against the law to slam the government."

"Maybe it should be," Satterwhite mumbles.

"Anyway it's not enough," Renner says. "We need a new strategy."

"All right," Satterwhite says. "We'll divert those funds elsewhere."

"We have to get in. The closest we've gotten is Renner's informant," Sebastian says.

"Will your informant take more risk?" Satterwhite asks.

Renner shakes his head. "Depends, sir."

A tense moment passes before their SAC continues. "Recruitment skyrockets after an attack, so the timing is right to send someone in. The informant is a potential cooperating witness that can smooth the way. Renner, you'll need to do some handholding to ensure he or she feels safe. Make promises. Say whatever you need to say to make it happen."

Once again Renner twists the same piece of hair as he nods. They wait. Suddenly Satterwhite looks pointedly at Sebastian. "Are you ready, Diaz?"

Shit. Under the table his hands clench tightly together. "Sir?"

"Renner needs to secure our one and only direct access to Charles Mitchell. He's built that relationship going on a decade now. We can't compromise that. He's positioned perfectly to be your handler."

"Right," says Sebastian.

"So that's a yes?"

A flash of Kate trips his tongue. He straightens. "Yes. Of course."

Satterwhite leans in. "Excellent. This operation stays between the three of us. You'll receive a legend, Diaz. Our techs have a line of aliases that are alive and kicking with steady credit histories and social media interaction. We just need to find you a match."

"How long will it take?" Sebastian asks.

"A month maybe. There's no room for error. This is our one shot. Work on wrapping up your life. Renner will help. You'll relocate locally. Your fiancée needs to know you'll be out of touch. That ring on her finger should make her feel secure."

He nods. This was not in his plan. He's supposed to get married next year. What's he going to tell Kate? Though she knows what she's signing up for as an agent's wife, there's no way to prepare for this.

"You're in the unique position to protect the future vice president and his daughter. If any harm comes to them because of Taylor's affiliation with Mitchell, the blame will fall on this office. I can't protect you if this blows up, Diaz. But we're on this early. Let's get to work."

They leave the conference room, and Sebastian ducks into the men's room. He grips the counter and stares at himself in the mirror. Undercover. He's been trained for it. Used to keep up with reports to glean tactics and to learn from others' mistakes in the field. It's a once in a lifetime opportunity. If this had come three years ago he would've jumped at it. But he has Kate now. An actual shot at a future. Renner tells him he's gone soft. He's joking, but maybe it's true.

Sebastian thinks of his partner. Renner's younger, has no family. Just a dog and an informant who's more like a sibling. It should be him.

Chapter 8

Safe District 149

"OVEN, PREHEAT TO four hundred," Lily instructs. "House, play acoustic channel." The oven's digital screen lights up and hidden speakers infuse the room with soft guitar music. This house's modernity makes her grieve for the charm of their old home with its winding staircase and wide floor planks. Maybe she should hang some pictures.

Finished with dinner prep, she sits down at the kitchen table and rests her feet on an adjacent chair. Cole should be home from his shift any minute. Suddenly, the front door opens and laughter travels down the hall.

"It's us!" Kate's voice.

"Down the hall, in the kitchen," she calls.

The smooth tenor of Sebastian's voice carries, but she can't make out what he's singing. At first, she hadn't trusted him—all cheekbones and charm. Even a scar across his chin seems aesthetically placed. And the FBI isn't a selling point. As Kate's only living family member, she had to be skeptical. Then, about a year ago, she'd asked him about his family. His voice had quavered when he told her about his father, killed in a senseless bombing. It was a glimpse into a different side of him, vulnerable and genuine. Finally she stopped judging him. It's a good thing, since he and Kate are now engaged.

They're all smiles as they enter. Lily hugs Kate. The touch of her sister makes Lily's eyes water. It's only been a few weeks, but she hasn't seen her since they left for London. Sebastian hugs her warmly, kisses her cheek. In silence, they take in the new house. Under her shirt, heat rises on her chest, her face grows hot. The Safe District house, the bulletproof cars. Surely they think she and Cole have gone to extremes.

"I've always wondered what these houses looked like," Sebastian says.

"Not exactly your style, Lil," Kate adds.

"Style has moved down on our list of priorities."

"It's nice." Kate wraps an arm around her. "Just a little stark. With some paint and artwork you can make it your own. I can help you unpack."

In search of wineglasses, Sebastian tries different cabinets until he finds them. He places four at the table and they all sit. Kate reaches a hand over and gently squeezes Lily's arm. Since they were kids, they could say much without uttering a word. Lily's only solace after their failed journey is being with her sister again. Lily watches as Kate twists her waves of blond hair into a messy bun. She's always been envious of it. Both have blue eyes and a multitude of freckles. Other than that, they're night and day.

Sebastian selects a bottle of red and pours liberally, with a half glass for Lily. Everyone seems to take a deep breath.

"Cole had his hands full this morning," Sebastian says.

"I imagine you were just as busy," Lily says.

Seemingly lost in thought, his gaze rests on the table. He nods absently.

"Seb, honey, you okay?" Kate reaches a hand over, rests it on his arm.

"What? Yeah, of course." He sips his wine. "Sorry. Long day with not enough resources."

"You'd think there'd be ample funds in counterterrorism," Lily says.

"We're casting a wide net during a war, a recession, and a mass emigration. All in an election year. Money's spread pretty thin." His tone is frayed, with an unfamiliar edge.

"National Tourism seems to have plenty of money." Lily strokes the stem of her wineglass. Since she stopped working, she's both admired and envied Kate's career track, from office assistant to director of the Northeast Division for National Tourism.

"I don't know how he did it, but Richard Hensley almost doubled our budget this year," Kate says. "I met with him today to go over the event we're having at the State House."

"Is Hensley your speaker?" she asks.

"No, James Gardiner." Kate's face wrinkles in distaste. "He's a hypocrite. Just a few months ago he publicly came out against increased funding for tourism. But now that he's the face of the Liberty Party, he's apparently doing what he's told."

"Maybe he thinks international visitors heighten the threat level," Sebastian adds.

"Actually," Kate says, "starting with this event, we're solely focusing on U.S. citizens. For Americans traveling within the fifty states, there's no bureaucracy with MedIDs and travel costs are relatively cheap."

"Fantastic." Sebastian brightens, leans in closer to her. "Take me on vacation."

"Who's going on vacation?" Cole appears from the darkened hallway. He kisses Kate on the cheek and shakes Sebastian's hand. "Great to see you guys."

"I didn't hear you come in," Lily says. He stands behind her, placing his hands gently on her shoulders.

"So where are we vacationing?" Cole asks.

"Can I entice you to visit beautiful Bar Harbor?" Kate fills his glass.

"No offense—I love the Northeast—but I'm thinking Florida Keys," he says.

"White sand, turquoise water." Lily closes her eyes.

"They're heading into hurricane season," Sebastian adds. "Not to spoil your trip."

Lily pats her belly. "We're heading into our own hurricane soon."

Cole grins. She gestures to a cheese and crackers platter on the counter and he retrieves it, sets it in the center of the table. Silence creeps in as everyone sips and eats. Lily strains to think of a neutral subject; she doesn't want to talk about the obvious.

"Speaking of travel," Kate says. "We haven't had a chance to hear about—"

"Not now," Lily interrupts.

"Let's just get it out there," Kate insists. "When we said goodbye at the port, I wasn't sure I'd ever see you again."

"That's dramatic." Lily shoves a cracker into her mouth.

"Not really." Kate's eyes glisten. "Selfishly, I'm glad you're back. I still don't understand why you'd even attempt it with your MedID number."

"We want our kids to be safe. It's that simple."

"You guys are everything to me. And now you're back. And well-protected."

Sebastian reaches over and rubs Kate's back. "She's been worried about all of you. Not sleeping, not eating."

"Well she got what she wanted," Lily says.

Kate stares into the depths of her glass.

"Sebastian," Cole says, "you've bitten your tongue this whole time. Even before we left. You think we were fools for trying?"

"Fools? No." He pauses, clearly considering his words. "But you knew the odds were against you. I don't understand giving up the life you've built here when the MedID numbers are clear. And, in the big picture, if everyone runs away, the terrorists win. The government, the country, needs our support. Without it, we might as well quit right now."

Cole shakes his head. "Maybe. But millions of people are suffering because of genetic classism. Companies don't hire people with subpar DNA. Unemployed people can't afford homes. Can't afford to feed their families. Desperation kicks in. And either they go looting or they join some organization with an antigovernment bent that promises to feed and clothe them. Why would those people fight on behalf of a government that's taken their lives from them?"

Sebastian runs his hands over the day-old stubble covering his cheeks. "I get it, I understand. But we need to fight to restore the country. The cities. We could build again. Then we might actually gain some ground. We might not have to live in places like this."

"Part of the reason I love my job is that I remind people about the beautiful parts of this country," says Kate. "We can't just leave it all behind."

"Beauty is a luxury," Lily says. "The walls of this house and this district are the only things between us and the war. Put aside politics, right and wrong. For us, for our kids, the decision was simple."

The scent of roast chicken suffuses the room and reminds Lily she should see to the food. She steps away to check on the various dishes and then returns, avoiding her sister's gaze.

"Listen." Cole looks pointedly at Kate and Sebastian. "We can talk around and around this for hours. So let's agree to disagree. We're family. I'm sure we all consider that to be the most important thing."

Slowly, everyone nods.

"To family." Kate holds up her glass and they toast.

A sudden kick to the ribs jolts Lily. She feels the spot, presses gently against it. It's as though the baby is telling them to shut up. Kate reaches over and Lily positions her hand over the action. They wait. Finally another kick.

"This is what we should talk about," says Kate. "This is what's right about the world."

"I'll drink to that." Cole refills the wineglasses.

Footsteps make them all turn in the direction of the hall. Ian's sneakers look three sizes too big for his short, lean body. A smile appears as soon as he sees his aunt.

"Hey Aunt Katie."

She wraps an arm around his shoulders. "How's the studying?"

"Math test tomorrow."

They both make a disgusted face.

"Want me to quiz you?" Kate says.

"Yeah." Ian goes to a glass jar on the counter filled with cookies. His hands are full as the pair disappears down the hall.

Lily watches them go. The past few years have brought so much sadness to all of them. But now they have Kate's wedding to look forward to, and soon, a new baby to celebrate. They deserve to let go of fear and embrace some happiness.

Chapter 9

Boston

TAYLOR HENSLEY SENSES the commotion of the press five stories below in front of their apartment building. More questions, judgment, humiliation await her. They've been relentless since her father accepted the vice presidential nomination, and it's only gotten worse since she stepped over the threshold of Patriot's Church. She should be used to it. Thanks to her family name they've been on her since she came out of the womb.

In soft lamplight, she lies next to her daughter, Sienna, on the five-year-old's bed. For the millionth time she studies her daughter's smooth skin and long eyelashes. Her nose curves up at the tip and the slope makes Taylor want to run a finger along it. Their nighttime routine gives Sienna structure, but Taylor needs it as much as her daughter does.

"Time for happy dreams," Sienna says.

"Bad thoughts out." She touches the tip of her index finger to Sienna's ear and makes a *shhh* noise as though letting air out. Taylor would like someone to expel her own bad thoughts. Though it was five years ago, when she closes her eyes she can still summon the moment the bomb went off. The heat. The blinding flames. The searing splinters of glass and metal that landed in her cheek and neck. And Mason. *Mason.* He should be here right now, beside them.

She continues, "Now let's put in fairies and princesses." With each new item she gently presses her finger against Sienna's ear, as though physically stuffing her head full of lovely thoughts. "Sunshine, cupcakes, friends. What else?"

"Macaroni and cheese and sparkles and Mommy."

"Can't fit all that in one ear. Let's seal this one shut." Taylor clucks her tongue to mimic a door, touches Sienna's other ear. "Mac 'n' cheese, sparkles, Mommy." Another cluck and the ritual ends.

" 'Night, my girl." She kisses her daughter. "I love you."

Sienna's eyelids close easily. Taylor switches on a mermaid night-light at the foot of the bed and closes the door behind her.

When the babysitter arrives, Taylor is ready. She steals out through a window in the back of the building, descending the rusted fire escape to her waiting bike. As she cruises down the darkened alleyway, the warm night air is like fingers through her cropped hair. The courier bag slung over her back is heavy, packed tight with her tools, including aerosol paint cans and various nozzles.

Hardly any cars are on the road as she winds through the grid of city streets, crosses over the Boston line. She pedals rapidly, her imagination infused by the sheer freedom of movement. She visualizes her canvas. Wind pulls tears from her eyes. So senseless, the Liberty Party bombing. Every bombing. It's impossible not to think of Mason, as though her husband dies again with each new attack. And her hate for her father grows. If she's honest, the guilt that's lived inside her for so many years grows stronger. After all, she went along with her father's MedID plan. Blindly. Willingly. Stupidly.

Only a few blocks left. She passes abandoned buildings that once held life and promise. It depresses her to no end. Growing up a Hensley, she always felt that Boston—and the country—owned a piece of her, not the other way around. Perhaps that's why she chose the city as her canvas. They're unalterably entwined, a marriage of polish and grit. Generations of Hensley senators and their New England families had carved a life for Taylor and taken the guesswork out of her future. Piano, tennis, ski team, private schools, Harvard. After graduating, she had everything she'd ever wanted, replete with a high-profile corporate marketing career at the MedFuture corporation.

The Back Bay neighborhood is quiet. The only people here are those that live on these streets. A few of them nod to Taylor, used to her presence. Some actually change direction when she passes in an attempt to see what her destination is tonight.

The air is burnt. Taylor rubs her nose, slows the bike and hops off. Twisted metal, chunks of cement, and shattered glass litter the pavement. The twenty-foot cavity in the Liberty Party headquarters gapes at her. She'd volunteered here when she was a kid, later contributed to their marketing efforts. Her whole life was entangled with the party.

The streetlights shed just enough illumination for her to work. She ducks under the yellow police tape and hoists the bag from her shoulder. Methodically, she spreads the paint cans on a patch of charred grass. From inside the bag she pulls a respirator and fastens it over her nose and mouth.

After a few unsuccessful throws, she loops a rope over an iron rod in the facade overhead. From the rod, charred ribbons of the American flag wave in the mild breeze. With a harness tightened around her waist and powerful suction cups attached to her feet, she begins to climb. Her feet wedge into divots in the brick, using architectural details that protrude just enough to get her footing. Finally in place above the hole, she starts with the black paint, a thick nozzle for the hard lines of a mouth, nose, and eyes. Her father's face is indelibly etched in her memory, though she sees darkness in his eyes that doesn't come across to the public.

Eight years ago, when Taylor's father brought her on board at MedFuture, she believed everything he said about the biochip program. Convinced it would strengthen the country and help end the War at Home, she wanted to be a part of it. So did Mason, whom she met and worked with there. They married. Savored their time together. Got pregnant. All while they built the backbone of the MedID to ensure its success.

She maneuvers easily, her muscles taut, her focus clear. Her father's signature mane explodes up the front of the building in white flames. Scarlet letters *TBA* drip from the black hole of his mouth. *Take Back America.*

After the MedID went nationwide, people discovered inequities in the system. They realized how chained they were by their DNA. There were riots, marches. Attacks multiplied. Then one day a few of those opposed to the MedID stormed the heart of the device—MedFuture Corporation—and martyred themselves. They took seventy-nine lives. Including Mason's. Taylor, five months pregnant, had walked away from everything that day, including her father. Were it not for him and his grandiose ideas, Mason would be alive.

By the time she slips off her harness and repacks her bag, her body is shaking from six hours of flexed muscles. She stands back and takes a last look. Of all the graffiti she's written, this is her favorite. As she rides away, a forty-foot ghoulish likeness of vice presidential candidate Richard Hensley appears to laugh at the destruction, the lives lost. When she passes the black Cadillac SUV parked a block away, she knows she's been caught. But she just doesn't care.

Chapter 10

Concord, Massachusetts

In his home gym, Reverend Charles Mitchell runs at a swift pace on the treadmill, formulating his next sermon. With his hair tied at the nape of his neck, a light sweat coats his fit body, shaped by a strict exercise regimen. People always guess he's younger than his forty-five years. Hannah cycles next to him, wearing the E-Trans Glasses he gave her as a gift last Christmas. He wonders what locale she's chosen to cycle in today. He glances at her long legs, the way her face has thinned in the past year or so. As if sensing him, she flips the glasses up, looks over and smiles.

"Hot out today," she says.

"Yes, it's thick out there," he says. "Unusual this time of year."

"I don't mind." Her eyes wander, staring at nothing.

"Me either. Where are you, Hannah Jane?"

"Back home, New Orleans. I'm starting to forget what it looked like."

"Hmm. This weather takes me back, too."

"To Alabama?"

He nods. "Summer days were like walking through water."

By now she's heard his story countless times. The foster families he lived with. The evangelicals who spoke in tongues and preached creationism. When he was old enough, he chose what to believe, lead by the Holy Spirit. As soon as he was old enough, he left, built his own house, constructed his own family, and now serves a Father he will unite with one day.

Hannah's mouth sags into a pout. "Charles, will I see Joe, Jr. and Mary again someday?"

"If it's God's will." It's the easy answer, he knows. After Hannah's father died in the Planes, her mother killed herself. Hannah was shipped up to him as a future bride as promised by her father. The other two kids were sucked into the foster care system. He couldn't take them—it's not possible to care for all the orphans of this war.

"You said you'd help me find them." Her feet stop pedaling.

"Of course. Soon as this mission is over, I can focus on that."

She nods, wipes at her eyes.

"Excuse me, Reverend." Henry enters and slides a thin electronic panel into a holder on the treadmill. "Militia applications are in."

"Excellent." Another thought crosses Charles's mind. "And I need you to bring me Huan Chao."

"Right away." Henry leaves.

Hannah pulls back on her glasses, retreats once again into her New Orleans ride. Without breaking stride, Charles taps on the screen to play applicant videos that are prescreened by his top BASIA officers. Despite the size of his organization, he insists on viewing each applicant that makes it to the final tier. A visceral process occurs when he watches these individuals tell their stories, make a plea to serve. After all, these men and women may give their lives in the quest to reach the final Day of Judgment.

Most videos he dismisses quickly, reviewing only a few applications in their entirety. One is a man who appears fit, ex-military, a born-again Christian bent on change. A candidate ripe for picking. After seminary school, Charles obtained a master's degree in psychology, concentrating on the social aspects of influence, conformity, and obedience, as well as personality traits and how to read individuals. Invaluable knowledge when choosing his soldiers.

When he sacrificed his first militia in the Planes, he put the world on alert. In a dream, God had spoken to him, told him the MedID was the Mark of the Beast. The war had just begun and the world was spinning chaotically in the hands of evil men in the form of government officials. Other than the one-off crazies and militias hiding in the woods, it appeared Charles was the only one preparing for Armageddon. He'd taken that as a sign from God that it was his charge to lead. A decade later his revitalized Christian militia is fifty thousand strong. His reach ripples to the smallest towns and the remaining city dwellers on both coasts. Soon the MedID will be abolished. Charles has painstakingly planned His Holy War, and there will be no missteps on their path to salvation.

Of the thirty candidates, Charles chooses eight. Pleased with the latest crop, he shuts off the monitor as Henry enters with Huan Chao, BASIA's chief technologist. The slim Chinese man stands just over five feet but wields a hundred times his weight in knowledge. Formerly a CIA system administrator with high-level security clearance, Huan trained in the CIA's secret school for technology specialists. Five years later he left the Company, disillusioned with the blatant disregard for civilian privacy in exchange for a supposedly safer world. He disappeared from his former life, taking with him an unrivaled cyber arsenal. Now safe in the folds of Patriot's Church and BASIA, he serves God with a clean conscience.

"Huan, my friend." Charles grins as he hops off the treadmill. He shakes Huan's hand. "Give me good news."

"We're on schedule, Reverend," Huan says. Thick spikes of black stick out from his scalp, defying gravity. "And I've found the candidates that will round out my team."

"Go on."

Huan describes two men and a woman whose technological knowledge would be an asset for their upcoming mission: an MIT graduate and current professor in the Media Lab, a self-taught young man with an impressive résumé that includes "cross-site scripting, botnets, and phishing," and a seemingly benign housewife who has made a nice living selling crimeware to fellow hackers. Charles is well-read in technology, but in this regard he defers to Huan, trusts him implicitly. Still, finding the right people is the easy part.

"Vulnerabilities?" Charles asks.

"Both MIT professor and housewife have families. Their children have health issues and they're dealing with aging parents. The woman and the self-taught kid have put themselves at risk with their cyber activities. With threat of exposure, plus pay and supplemental medical services, they should acquiesce."

"Tell me more about the kid."

"More of a risk on our part. He's seventeen, a senior in high school. Nothing to lose. He's a loner, lives with his mother and stepfather. But he's brilliant. Kid hacked the U.S. Department of Education when he was twelve." Huan's eyebrows rise in excitement. "Twelve. Imagine what he's learned in the past five years. Actually, I don't have to imagine. He's mastered numerous tools. Zero-day. TOR. Fuzzing . . ."

Charles stops listening. "You said he has nothing to lose?"

Huan bobs his head. "He's pretty comfortable right now. His stepfather is the owner of Hudson's Funeral Homes."

"A hacker and a mint under one roof? Huan, you've done well."

"The only issue I can see is that he never leaves the house. On rare occasion he goes skateboarding."

"Let's think on it. In the meantime, well done. Do what you need to do to secure the professor and the housewife."

As Huan leaves, Charles returns to the treadmill. Sensing him, the machine moves under his feet. He barely notices that he breaks into a sprint, his thoughts caught up in how to approach this reclusive teenage hacker. It's useful that he's still living under his stepfather's roof. That funeral chain is a multi-million-dollar business. God is good.

"Want some lunch?" Hannah asks, not looking up from her screen.

He'd almost forgotten she was there. His eyes wander across the room and land on Hannah. Beautiful, sweet Hannah.

Chapter 11

Boston

RICHARD HENSLEY SITS on a vinyl bed in the examining room of his general practitioner. For twenty-five years Dr. Wendall has kept him healthy and, more importantly, kept him *appearing* healthy to the public and administration. It's more important than ever, now that he's running for vice president.

There's a knock on the door and Richard's aide, Carter, peeks his head in. "Sir, we need to leave in ten minutes for the National Tourism office."

The doctor cocks his head. "You just got here, Richard."

"I'm a specimen, Doc." Richard places his hand over his heart. He waves Carter away and the door closes. Retrieving his phone from the bed, he opens the MedID app. Dr. Wendall touches a tablet to his phone, transferring information instantaneously. "It's all there. I have my father's genes. Just try and kill me before the age of ninety."

The doctor traces a finger over the screen of his tablet, scrutinizing the data. "Apparently you exercise daily. Maintain a low-fat diet. Indulge in a glass of wine on occasion. And have no physical complaints." He looks up with one eyebrow raised. "Yes, clearly this is evidence of a superior being. Now, hold out a finger please and we'll talk in the nonfiction realm." He retrieves a fist-sized electronic device and guides Richard's finger into it. A needle pokes him, claiming a drop of blood. The doctor slips the device off and observes the screen.

"Your O2 level is low. Total cholesterol is 206. That's on the high side. Your liver enzymes are also elevated. You should cut back on red meat, dairy, and on that, quote, occasional glass of wine." He shakes his head. "You haven't been taking your medications."

"I know I don't seem the type, but I believe in a more holistic approach."

"At your age, your genes need to be supported by meds and a healthy lifestyle."

"I've been on the road with the campaign the past couple months. I hardly know what city I'm in each morning, let alone remember to take my meds."

"Senator, you're a smart man and that's a sorry excuse. If you don't take your medication you'll have a very short-lived term as vice president."

"Understood." Richard hates revealing his daily habits, resents having his life boiled down to statistics. It's amazing what a drop of blood can betray. He recognizes the irony of his role in the MedID. But despite his own genetic weaknesses, his job is to strengthen the U.S. He didn't anticipate the country spiraling as it has, but eventually disease and deformities will be a thing of the past. Future generations will be thankful. And these idiots claiming to fight this so-called Armageddon will be delivered unto their own destiny. A flash of Taylor comes to him, knowing that she's defected to their side. Heat climbs from his neck to his face. He stands from the bed and retrieves his undershirt from a nearby chair.

"I haven't done your physical exam yet," Dr. Wendall says.

"It's all there." He gestures to the tablet. "It's for them, not for me."

The doctor rises to his feet, eye-to-eye with him. "All due respect, you're not twenty-five anymore. Why don't you let me do a proper workup?"

"You know why."

"This is about your life. No one has to know."

"Oh what a tangled web I've woven." He slips on his pants. "Our system has worked for the past ten years. Let's not mess with it."

"As you wish. But at least take your pills." Dr. Wendall opens a cabinet, pulls out his MRS. He scans the false information from the app. "Hold out your forearm, please."

The MRS flashes a red light over the MedID site. In less than a second Richard's medical record is updated. "You're good to go for another year."

"Thanks, Sam." He shakes the doctor's hand. "Things go as planned, you'll be the physician to the vice president when I see you next."

Dr. Wendall sets his scanner down, the expression on his face suddenly serious. "I saw Taylor on the news. I'm sorry."

Richard frowns. "She's marching to her own beat."

"It's a dangerous beat."

"Like all kids, she does things for shock value. But I'll admit, she got me this time."

"I hope for your sake it's temporary." Dr. Wendall opens the door. "Best of luck with the race. And be safe."

"Thanks, Sam. Hey, don't forget to vote."

When the doctor leaves, Richard finishes knotting a navy blue tie and gathers his things. In the hall, he finds Carter, voicing notes into his smartwatch. His aide's cheeks are darkened by day-old stubble and he needs a haircut, but his clothes are pressed and fresh.

"Sir, we're five minutes late to the meeting. If we shoot down Storrow and up Charles Street to Beacon, we can get there in ten."

"You worry too much." Richard strides past him into the corridor. Two statuesque men in tailored suits appear and walk next to them, their earpieces well-hidden but their roles obvious.

"We're meeting with Kate Manning," Carter calls from behind. "Director of National Tourism's Northeast Division."

"I know Kate. Hard to forget a lovely girl like that."

"The setup will be on the State House steps at the top of Beacon Hill." Carter's shoes click madly against the tiles. "It'll be a quick run-through of the event schedule and evacuation plan. Forecast says seventies and sun. We should get a good crowd."

"It's a waste of time having me there just to stand mute, next to Gardiner," Richard says. "Obviously they want to see the presidential candidate. I can think of better uses of my day."

"Your presence is essential to the event, sir." Carter finally catches up. "I'm sure that's President Clark's reasoning. New England and the Hensley name go hand in hand."

Blinding sun hits them as they exit the medical office and make their way to the black town car where a driver awaits. On their way to the meeting, Carter phones ahead and speaks to Kate Manning, while Richard uses his phone to catch up on the latest polls. Turns out their numbers are up. Richard's never felt healthier.

Chapter 12

Safe District 149

Lily hasn't felt the baby move in hours. Cole is on an overnight shift at Mass General and it's just after midnight. She sits in front of the computer with her shirt pulled up, her hand on her bare belly.

In a group chat for pregnant women, she waits for her turn to speak. The other mothers-to-be are annoying. They're discussing how they chose sex, eye and hair color. Asking about the options of gene therapy in utero. At one point she typed: *Doesn't anyone enjoy the element of surprise? Isn't the process more amazing when you don't know what this little life will hold?* But no one responded to her post.

She pushes on her belly, hoping to make her daughter move. The past few hours she's tried all the tricks: drank coffee, walked up stairs, took a bath. The only outcome is a kind of crampy feeling in her abdomen. When she was pregnant with Ian, he'd never stopped moving. From what she's read, in the thirty-seventh week it can be typical for fetal movement to slow since the space inside is now so limited. But she hasn't felt so much as an elbow. Something's not right.

Finally an icon appears on her screen, asking if she'd like to speak anonymously or on camera. Lily makes her choice and a new window appears. She sees dark circles under her blue eyes, her hair tied in a messy bun.

The moderator, a perky blond avatar, introduces Lily by her first name only.

"Hi," Lily says. "My baby hasn't moved in about six hours. I'm not really sure what to do. And I don't want to overreact but—"

Something wet gushes from between her legs. In the dimly lit room Lily can't see clearly. Excusing herself from the group, she sprints to the bathroom. She flicks on the light and looks down to find a steady stream of blood running down her thighs. *Oh God oh God oh God.* She grips the sink to steady herself. Taking a deep breath, she rushes to find her phone and calls 911.

THE AMBULANCE HAD been swift, a neighbor had taken Ian, and Kate met her at Mass General. In the triage section of Labor and Delivery, Lily lies with electronic sensors hooked up to her belly. Occasionally a stabbing pain strikes her abdomen, taking the wind out of her. Downstairs, Cole is still on his shift, attending to victims of a lone gunman. They'll page him when it's time.

In a private room, Lily's OB examines her. The hospital johnny is like a tent on her bulbous body. She stares at her sister, gorgeous in subtle makeup and a stunning blue dress.

"Why do you look like this before dawn?" Lily says.

"This is not my first emergency, believe it or not." Kate kicks off her heels and stands in bare feet. "What if this is the real thing? Her birth day?"

"And you thought that was the appropriate outfit?"

"Ha. No. I'm sure Cole will be here for the big event. I have my own not-as-big event. You know, the James Gardiner, Richard Hensley, tourism thing. Starts at noon and I can't be late. I figured I might as well dress as though I'm leaving straight from here."

A swift cramp grips Lily and she groans.

"You okay?" Kate leans closer.

Lily can only nod.

"All right." The doctor pushes back with her rolling stool and tells Lily to relax her legs. "The membranes of the amniotic sac have ruptured, which was part of the gush of fluid you felt. The placenta is separating from the uterine wall and there's a tear, but the bleeding has stopped for now." She stands and goes to a monitor, pointing to spikes in the readout. "These points here. This is your baby's heart rate. And this is her heart rate during your contraction. See the difference? The dip? That's when she's losing oxygen. We need to induce you right away. If the bleeding starts again we'll need to do an emergency C-section."

"Is the baby okay?" Lily asks.

"She is," says the obstetrician. "But if induction doesn't take, and bleeding starts again, we'll get you into the OR. Both of you are safer in that situation."

"I'll text Cole," says Kate.

Lily lies back and stares at the tile ceiling as the nursing staff readies her for transport to the labor room. Tears stream from the corners of her eyes, past her temples, wetting her hair. Kate kisses the top of her head, whispers that Cole is on his way. Lily clutches her belly with both hands. *Please be okay.* Pain grips her again and she closes her eyes. They still haven't chosen a name. She imagines what this baby might look like in her arms and repeats their list like a meditation. Daisy. Talia. Sadie. Esme. Gala.

Chapter 13

Memorial Day, Boston

TEN MINUTES TO go until Kate's introduction speech. She stands at the podium on the Boston State House steps that lead down to Beacon Street, a narrow road that's been blocked off to traffic. Across the street is the Boston Common, a sprawling park created for the commoners of the city two centuries ago. National Tourism spent a year and a hefty budget to restore the neglected land. For years no one tended the lawns or gardens since it was no longer safe to lounge or picnic in a public place. Kate plans to change all that, and the first step is reminding people how good it feels to enjoy fresh air and outdoor activities together, as a community. Lush oaks and maples provide shade to the thousands who stand in anticipation on the freshly cut grass that runs several city blocks long. A respectable turnout. They've come from all over New England to see the candidates and to celebrate the ruined but much-loved Boston. Everyone is here to resurrect it, to honor it.

Kate left Lily two hours ago in the labor room with Cole. She checks her phone. No text, no news. This is a career-making moment as she prepares to host the future President of the United States, yet all she can do is chew her cuticles and smile nervously. Lily had looked so pale and scared. What if she loses the baby? She swallows hard. What if *she* loses Lily?

The phone vibrates. Her heart drops when she sees it's not from Lily or Cole. Instead, it's a message informing her Richard Hensley will arrive a few minutes late. Mentally she goes over the agenda and adjusts by five minutes, texts her team the update. After she introduces Gardiner and Hensley, Gardiner speaks for ten minutes. Hensley tags on to the end for a quick address. Then restaurants will open booths, and at one o'clock the band will take the stage.

The hope—the plan—is to create a sense of yesteryear. The snipers on the rooftops and strategically placed in buildings have orders to remain unseen. Every entrance to the Common contains a full body scan for weapons, and the newly installed electronic fence around the perimeter forces the crowd to proper entrances. Police and Secret Service, along with the National Guard, are a major presence. It's striking a delicate balance to ensure safety without using overt measures that will cast a shadow on the event.

Luckily, it's a cloudless, seventy-eight-degree day. It's heartening to see so many families here, mulling around within the protective layers of security. Teams of reporters and camera operators are capturing the event, waiting for a glimpse of the candidates. Kids play on the jungle gym and splash in the shallow Frog Pond.

For one sun-splashed moment Kate soaks it all in. The happy chaos, people simply enjoying one another in the heart of the city. She wishes Lily were here to see this. If Kate didn't know better she'd think it was 2015. There should be more days like this.

PRESIDENTIAL CANDIDATE JAMES Gardiner's speech is predictably charming, engaging and bipartisan. Behind him, with a winning smile, stands vice presidential candidate Richard Hensley, the country's most famous senator. Kate has caught him looking at her breasts on the few occasions they've met. The world would be a different place without him in it, without his precious MedID. Still, she admits that the MedID has the potential to help their country. If only Lily and Cole saw it that way.

A text startles her. Subtly, she checks her phone and sees the photo ID for Sebastian: *Sorry I'm late! Mtg ran long. Be there in 5. xo.*

Three minutes remain in Gardiner's speech. Out of the corner of her eye Kate sees movement. From the crowd in the street and behind, in the Common, people randomly begin jumping up and down. One on the left. One in the back. One on the right. The front. The middle. They're all wearing masks. She squints to make out details. The masks are all different. Wait, she recognizes them. They're masks of past Presidents. There must be forty-eight of them. James Gardiner, who is rarely caught off guard, stumbles on his words.

Secret Service and uniformed police speak into the e-COM bands on their wrists, debating a plan of action. Kate watches several of them move toward the performers. But they're going upstream, struggling against the thousands of onlookers who also turn to see the action, equally curious. Please don't let them pull guns, she thinks. It'll all go to hell in a hot second.

As if hearing her thoughts, the men and women guarding the candidates unlatch their weapons and move in closer to Gardiner and Hensley, crowding around them. From somewhere in the Common music begins to play. The volume is turned up until it competes with the speech. The masked performers continue to jump, adding dance moves. Kate wonders if this is a planned protest of some kind. Gardiner stops speaking. Sweat forms on his brow and his mouth twitches between smile and frown. He looks at her. She shrugs, shakes her head. Damn it. She watches the reaction from the crowd. Everyone is mesmerized.

The words are clear now. It's the national anthem with a hip-hop beat. The performers are getting close, moving up the slope of the Boston Common. Clapping along with the music, the crowd makes way for them, creating a path to the State House steps. They think it's all part of today's event, she realizes. They're wearing long-sleeved T-shirts with an American flag on the chest and carry what look like a child's magic wand in varying colors. They toss the sparkling props skillfully into the air.

The crowd has become a blockade for law enforcement. Police officers shout at them but no one seems to notice. Farther away in the Common, Secret Service moves in on a few of the masked people. Kate overhears an e-COM exchange. "Closing in on three of them. They're carrying something. Unclear if it's a weapon. I have a clear shot." The Secret Service and police surrounding the podium grip their holstered guns.

As the performers near the end of the song—"And the star-spangled banner in triumph shall wave"—they cross Beacon Street and begin to ascend the State House steps. They're too close now. The Secret Service agents who flank Gardiner and Hensley grab the candidates' arms, readying for evacuation. All the other officers pull their weapons.

"O'er the land of the free and the home of the brave!" The audience erupts in applause. A text buzzes Kate. It's Sebastian. *Here now. Only 5k people stand btw us. Coming!* She begins to text him back, her fingers working furiously.

A shot pierces the air. Screams. More shots. Kate drops her phone, searches the crowd. Several hundred feet away in the Common people scramble and sprint toward the exits.

"Sebastian," she whispers.

The masked performers charge up the steps. Everyone with a gun aims at them. Secret Service walls off the candidates and rushes them toward the State House entrance. Kate takes a step in their direction. Shots ring in her ear. A wet mist lands on her arm. Then more—on her dress, in her hair. *What's happening?* The performers aim their wands, pumping one end as a clear aerosol sprays out the other end. She glances up the stairs, finds the senators and their guards just as three performers pump the wands, sending a mist over the group. Richard Hensley ducks, pulls an agent on top of him to block the liquid. Officers shoot the attackers, who hesitate but don't fall. They must be wearing ballistics skins. Finally, someone shoots all three of them in the head and they collapse.

But it's too late. The agents grip their throats, crumble onto the stairs. Kate watches James Gardiner pressing his hands to his chest. Wheezing sounds all around make her heart pound. Her nose begins to run and she wipes it with the back of her hand. The last few masked performers empty their wands and walk away.

The scream of thousands is piercing. People run, push, crash against one another. Kate's legs give way and her body slams into the cement stairs. In her vision, a blur of sandals, flip-flops, sneakers, dress shoes. A sharp pain in her stomach seizes her and she vomits violently. With great effort she opens her eyes. There are no clear shapes, only a haze of colors. She lies splayed across the sharp edges of the steps, unable to move her arms and legs. The drumming of soles finally stops. She blinks, focuses. Everyone left on the stairs is like her, fallen, unmoving.

Help! In her head her voice is thunderous. Her eyes close and with the darkness comes quiet. Her throat burns. She opens her mouth wide to take in air, but there's only a desperate rasping sound. *Is that me? Help! Sebastian* . . . She opens her eyes and gazes past the bodies to the park. Everyone is running. Lying a couple feet away, her phone vibrates with a text. She strains to grab it but it's just out of reach. With her final ounce of energy she lifts her head and squints to see clearly. She can't read the words, but there's a picture of a beautiful baby girl.

Chapter 14

FROM THE FAR end of the Common, Sebastian slams against panicked bodies, fighting his way to the State House and Kate. There must've been an attempted assassination for Secret Service and the police to pull their weapons, let alone shoot into a crowd of families. Even news crews are fleeing.

Up ahead, the flow of people parts to avoid something on the ground. In seconds he's there. On a stretch of grass lie four dead or dying agents and officers. Their bodies are rigid, faces strained, weapons drawn but discarded. He studies the men and women: vomit, hands on throats, mouths gaping. Across from them, three bodies are unmoving, faces hidden by masks now ruined by bullets. Beside them lies what looks like a child's magic wand. *My God.* His attention snaps back to the State House steps. From here he can see several bodies collapsed around the podium. Right where Kate's supposed to be.

He breaks into a full run, pushing through anyone in his path. He touches his smartwatch. "Call Renner!"

After a brief pause, Renner's face appears on the tiny screen.

"Send backup to the State House," Sebastian shouts. "There's been a chemical attack!"

"BPD just called it in. We're mobilizing—"

"Alert Mass General, all area hospitals."

"How many casualties?"

"I don't know." Sebastian squints at the State House stairs. "Twenty? Thirty? But the crowd is jammed at the exits, physical contact on all sides. There's mass exposure here."

"I'm locating you." Renner looks away from the camera. "Okay. You're almost at Beacon. Too close. Stop right there."

"Not a chance."

"Whatever they used is probably still in the air. You're no good to us dead. I'll be there in five minutes."

Finally, the grounds are clear, the crowd now at the opposite end of the Common. Sunlight gleams off the gold dome of the State House. At the top of the hill, Sebastian steps into the street. It's eerily quiet. What was Kate wearing this morning? Her blue summer dress. He moves slowly, studying the discarded magic wands. Black and navy suited bodies litter the pavement, all wearing the telltale earpieces of the Secret Service. Some weapons are drawn, but many are untouched in holsters. These people had no idea what hit them.

Kate. Reaching the bottom of the stairs, he scans the podium area where she should have been standing. The steps are thick with legs and arms, twisted faces, bodily fluids. His eyes tear and his nose runs. *Shit.* He rips off his suit coat and throws it on the ground along with his tie. Unbuttoning his shirt, he fastens it around the back of his head so that it covers his nose and mouth. Sweat soaks through his T-shirt and drips down his brow. Focus. Blue dress.

There—maybe twenty stairs up, to the right of the podium. The wind lifts her blond hair. Carefully, he steps over hands and thighs and heads. Some of the wounded are still moving, still breathing. There's still hope. A chance.

Finally, Kate. His hand covers his mouth, pain hits his chest. He falls to his knees. There's no question, she's gone. "No! Goddammit no!" His voice sounds like a stranger's. It takes everything he has not to touch her. Crossing his arms, he buries his tight fists against his body. Whatever toxin this is has ruined her, turned her body into a contaminated weapon. She looks nothing like his Kate. His tears splash onto her gray and unmoving face. Her mouth is stretched wide by some unknowable pain.

He rocks back and forth. The shirt over his face is suddenly suffocating, claustrophobic. Standing, he pivots and almost slips on vomit. When he looks down, he sees her phone. Without thinking, he picks it up and types in her code. First he sees the image of Lily's new baby girl. He shakes his head, blinks it away and swipes to find their last communication. He sees a text she never sent to him: *Protestor flash mob ruining my day. Love y*

He drops the phone and leans over, hands on his knees. It's hard to tell if he can't take a full breath because of Kate or because of whatever shit they sprayed in the air. Closing his eyes, his heart throbs. Sirens scream as they surround Beacon Hill from all sides, swallowing his cries.

A PERIMETER SURROUNDING the State House is cordoned off, as dozens of emergency personnel in Hazmat suits and gas masks set up a decontamination area and attend to casualties. Vehicles—fire, medical, police, FBI, along with Homeland Security and the CDC—are parked along the narrow streets, leaving barely enough room for ambulances to pass.

In the decontamination area, a man in a Hazmat suit cuts off Sebastian's clothes and disposes of them, inspects his body for sarin exposure and wipes him down with a neutralizing solution. The man directs him to bend at the waist. When he does, the person wets Sebastian's hair and washes it, careful to avoid spilling water on his body.

Renner walks into the tented area just as Sebastian is handed a pair of scrubs. His partner wears a gas mask and a Hazmat suit.

"What do we know?" Sebastian asks, pulling on the scrubs.

"I saw . . ." Renner stumbles on his words. "I'm so sorry about Kate."

He nods. "What do we know?"

"Well, you know by now they used sarin." Renner slides the bulky mask off his face. "The wand devices are thin tubes that were rigged into an aerosol spray so it would vaporize quickly. Hard to execute. Hard to trace."

He goes on, saying something about James Gardiner being the primary target, with Richard Hensley a secondary target. The words meld, it seems like a foreign language. With effort Sebastian refocuses on the conversation.

"Hensley got lucky," Renner says.

"He's alive?"

"Yeah. Wait till you see the footage. As soon as they sprayed the devices, Hensley ducked behind a Secret Service agent and used him as a shield."

"Classic."

"They just took him to Mass General. Word is he'll be fine."

"What else?"

"The event was publicized nationally. Everyone knew Gardiner would be here. Could be BASIA, the Sons of the Revolution, Army of God. The wands have prints but we don't expect to find anything. It's doubtful they're in the MedID system. We've pulled all video, including news footage, but the masks are going to make this a challenge. Maybe we'll get lucky and someone will ID one of the three bodies. Someone may still claim credit."

"You hear from your informant today?"

Renner shakes his head. "I sent a message."

A sudden wave of nausea hits him as he grips the edge of the gurney. A vision of Kate, the sound of her laugh. He breathes through it.

"You've gotta get checked out. Chances are you were exposed to sarin vapor. It could still be in the air."

Sebastian slides his feet into disposable slippers. There's so much to do. So many angles to consider. Hell, it's possible one of the terrorists is in a hospital bed next to Richard Hensley.

"First we need to canvass medical facilities for anyone with signs of exposure," he says.

Renner shakes his head. "A group like this will have underground resources."

"Probably. But we can't rule anything out."

The door to the tented area opens and someone in a Hazmat suit and gas mask joins them. "Agent Diaz, I'm Dr. Karen Riley. I'm with the emergency response unit from Mass General. I'd like to do a few routine tests to gauge your level of exposure."

Renner shuffles out of the way. From her medical kit, Dr. Riley takes out several instruments. Sebastian sits on a gurney and she moves a penlight back and forth in front of his eyes, takes his pulse and listens with a stethoscope to his heart and lungs. After a few other cursory tests, she takes out a pill and a bottle of water.

"Take this," Dr. Riley says. "Diazepam. It'll lower the risk of convulsions and relax your muscles, reduce any anxiety you might have."

He does as he's told, swallowing the pill and gulping down the entire water bottle.

"You need an IV drip right away." She takes an IV kit from her bag. "Atropine sulfate will increase oxygen to your blood. You'll feel better almost immediately."

"I need to work," he says.

The petite doctor connects a capped needle to the IV tubing. "You need to lie down. You're sweating profusely and your pulse is rapid. You won't be working at all if you don't get treated for this."

"Go," Renner says as he heads for the door. "I'll call you with updates."

"Shit," he mutters. Lying down amidst all the chaos feels unnatural. But he does as he's told, watches as the doctor hooks the bag to a stand and deftly guides the needle into his arm.

"Let's go." Dr. Riley slips a gas mask over his head, motions to two medical attendants, also in Hazmat suits. They wheel the gurney out of the tent as she explains, "Sarin exposure lasts two to eighteen hours. You shouldn't have to be in the hospital for more than a day."

Back outside, the nightmare is glaringly real. His stomach turns. As they wheel the gurney through the scene, he can't help himself. He looks one last time. Kate's hair still dances on the wind. He's not close enough to see the pain in her face, but the memory will never leave him. Next to Kate, someone in a Hazmat suit bags and labels her personal belongings. He or she places a number by her body: 4.

The ambulance is parked to the side of the State House, at the edge of the mayhem. Dr. Riley gives instructions to the EMTs as they lift him on board. One of the EMTs takes Sebastian's arm and uses an MRS to scan his MedID.

"You're gonna be fine, Agent Diaz," Dr. Riley says. "I'll check on you back at the hospital."

The ambulance doors close and the siren wails as they speed down the hill. Sebastian shivers as sweat from his torso soaks the thin shirt he was given. He closes his eyes but there's no rest, no calm that awaits him. *Fine, she'd said. No, Dr. Riley, fine is something I'll never be again.*

Chapter 15

"WHY HASN'T KATE called?" Lily demands as Cole enters her hospital room. "What aren't you telling me?"

The past few hours, Mass General has had a hushed, yet hurried air. Nurses and doctors run in and out of her room with barely a word, their eyes only connecting with machines and charts. The hospital shut down all outside communications. Clearly, they're trying to keep patients calm. Cole stares out the window, unblinking. His lips part and then pinch together. After more than a decade of war, she understands.

"There was an attack," she says.

After a moment he comes over, sits next to her on the bed. He takes her hand in his. "There was an assassination attempt on Gardiner and Hensley. At the State House."

A heaviness comes over her. But she savors the moment that remains, the peacefulness of ignorance. Finally, she nods. "Say it. I need you to say it."

Red tinges his eyes. "There was a group of terrorists. I'm

not exactly sure of the details but they released sarin into the crowd."

"Oh my God." Her mouth goes dry. "But there are survivors, aren't there?"

"Yes, but—"

"Is she in the ER? She's being treated?"

"No, Lily." Cole tightens his hold on her hand. "Kate's dead."

Every muscle in her body releases as she sinks deeper into the mattress. The pain in her abdomen is pushing through the drugs. If she begs, maybe they'll give her another epidural to numb it. To numb everything. She stares at the ceiling but the tears don't come. As Kate was dying, she had been so mad that Kate hadn't called to check in. Can she really be gone?

The door opens and a stout nurse with a wide grin wheels in Talia, who is sealed into a bacteria-free, heated box.

"I thought she needed a break from the NICU," the nurse says as she parks the incubator at Lily's side. "She's eating, crying, and she's very alert. Look at those eyes. Perfect, isn't she?"

"Perfect," Lily whispers.

The nurse must sense the emotion in the room. "I'll be back. Ring if you need anything."

Thin pink arms break free of the tightly wrapped hospital blanket as the baby stretches and pumps her fists. Cole moves around the bed to see their daughter, pure and uncomplicated. Lily wants desperately to hold her and nestle her close, brush her fingers along Talia's fine black hair that stands on end.

"I'm so sorry, Lil," Cole says.

Lily reaches inside the plastic box, rests a hand on the baby's belly. "Talia Kate Fitzgerald."

Cole repeats her name, his voice soft. He kisses the top of Lily's head. Warm tears roll down her cheeks, down her neck. The thought of life without Kate is unimaginable. *How could we have brought another child into this world? What have we done?*

June, 2032

Chapter 16

It's madness in front of Mass General. Wearing sunglasses and a baseball hat, Taylor Hensley keeps her head down as she weaves through the horde of reporters and cameramen. Over the past several hours, video of the State House attack has played nonstop on seemingly every screen. Each time Sienna sees it she yells, "Grandpa!" The terrorists' wands make her think it's a game. She giggles, delighted at the grown-ups playing as if they're kids. But all Taylor sees is her father using a Secret Service agent as his shield. Maybe now everyone will see him for who he really is. Still, he lies incapacitated in a hospital bed, and the medical staff won't update her over the phone. And maybe this is the end for him. So she came.

As she's about to cross the hospital threshold, they spot her. "Taylor Hensley! Are you here to reconcile with your father? Is it true you're now a member of Patriot's Church? Taylor!"

The glass doors shut behind her and the verbal assault ends. She navigates security and follows a stream of people to the designated treatment area for victims of the attack. But at the security kiosk, when she gives her father's name, she's directed to elevators and a special unit on the twentieth floor. She rides up alongside an armed guard.

At the entrance to the locked unit, she holds up her forearm to a wall scanner. It processes the chip and brings up her credentials. A buzzer sounds, the doors open. She passes through a decontamination vestibule that sprays something overhead, coating her clothes and skin with a faint film. After another set of double doors, she's in the unit. Medical personnel attend to several patients in a large open room. The faces in these beds look familiar. She studies them. Yes, the news footage. Many of them were on the State House steps. Secret Service. Public servants. Media personalities. Most are unconscious with tubes down their throat or noses.

"Can I help you?" A stout nurse stands at Taylor's side.

"I'm here to see Richard Hensley." She pulls the hat and sunglasses from her head. "I'm his daughter."

"This way." The nurse leads her down a long corridor. "He's stable. That's good because the first twenty-four hours are the most important. He's lost some muscle control, but that should come back relatively soon. An hour ago he woke up and spoke to Dr. Wendall. Given everything he's been through, it's quite a miraculous recovery."

Miraculous, indeed. *Please let him be asleep.* By habit her fingertips stroke her cheek, lingering on the scars left by the fragments from the MedFuture explosion. A constant reminder of Mason, of all that she lost. She remembers the eyes of the young intern who had bent over her face for hours picking out the tiny bits of debris. Flecks of amber in pools of green. With the mask over his nose and mouth, she'd only seen his eyes. He'd gotten out almost all the glass, but every now and then a little piece will work itself out.

Up ahead, two broad-shouldered Secret Service agents stand on either side of a glass door. Beyond them she can see her father, gray and unmoving, in a bed. The men give her a cursory glance as she brushes past them with the nurse.

The room is alive with intermittent beeps, the hum of monitors, a controlled flow of circulating air. Taylor hates hospitals. She'd spent too much time in one watching her mother die. She stares at her father, slack-jawed, a tube in his nose and an IV hooked into his arm. The nurse checks monitors and fluids.

"So he could wake up any time now?"

"Yes." The nurse gives her a wry smile.

Taylor knows the look. The rift between she and her father is widely known, though they've never confirmed it. The press has speculated about it ever since the MedFuture attack. The public knows the Hensley family history almost as well as they themselves know it.

"The doctor will be in soon." The nurse leaves, the doors shutting behind her.

Suddenly, it's harder to breathe, as though she's been sealed into an enormous pouch with her father. If this were one of her graffiti pieces, it would be a bubble and her father would fill almost all of the space. Her face would be pressed against the surface, her nose exaggerated as she searches for a hole to slip through.

From a distance, she studies him. On his ring finger is the wedding band he's never taken off, though it's been fifteen years since Taylor's mother died. The deep creases in his forehead and cheeks are relaxed, making him look younger. This was the face she trusted and loved most of her life. She remembers when they used to go to Castle Island for hot dogs and ice cream at Sullivan's. Families would carry in charcoal grills and lie on blankets under the trees. The air smelled of barbecue and the ocean. Sienna shares those kinds of uncomplicated times with him now. Taylor has allowed it and hopes she made the right decision. She wonders if an hour here and there can have too much influence. Maybe.

An hour later he hasn't moved, hasn't made a sound. His private physician, Dr. Wendall, comes in to speak with her. Apparently her father was fairly lucid when he woke up. From early tests, the doctor believes he hit his head on the State House steps and has a concussion. They're monitoring him to rule out a stroke, but the MRI shows no evidence of brain damage. From the nerve gas, he has respiratory issues that will fade and headaches that will subside. The doctor expects a full recovery.

She thanks him and he leaves. So, her father's not at Death's door. This is almost a vacation for him. Good PR. They'll probably throw him a parade after this. She slips back on the baseball hat and steps toward the door.

"Taylor?" His voice is a raspy whisper.

So close. She turns to face him. "They say you're going to be okay."

"Lucky."

"That's one word for it."

"What word—" His breath is labored as he continues. "—would you choose?"

"There are just so many."

His eyes close. She forces the memory of Sullivan's into her mind once again. Be nice, she tells herself. "Sienna wanted me to tell you she hopes you're feeling better."

A grin spreads across his dry, cracked lips. "Sienna."

She inches closer, considers talking about the swimming lessons Sienna's taking and how she's learning to read. But Taylor can't be bothered with small talk. He points to a cup of water and she holds it for him to drink. Several awkward minutes pass as he appears to awaken more fully, taking deeper breaths. Finally he speaks again.

"You've been busy." The lines in his face deepen, his eyes fix on her.

"Single mothers are generally busy."

"The Liberty headquarters piece was inspired." His words are slow but his brain is not.

"Thank you." So, it was his SUV that night. She has a fleeting moment of satisfaction.

"Does your new *friend* like it?"

"Excuse me?"

"Reverend Mitchell."

"Don't you have better things to do? Aren't there more pressing matters of state than my social calendar?"

"Not when your friends try to assassinate me."

Every muscle in her tenses. "The Reverend and Patriot's Church had nothing to do with the attack! They have a strong belief in God, and last I checked, that's one freedom we have left. And yes, we're at war. But BASIA isn't out killing innocent people."

"Aren't they?"

"Are you really going to point fingers?" At his bedside now, she enjoys looking down at him. "You flicked that first domino with powerful force and you've done nothing to stop it."

"Why would I?"

"Why *wouldn't* you?" She runs her fingers over the pockmarks on her cheek and neck. "How can you look at me and not want to stop it?"

He closes his eyes. When he opens them again, there's renewed energy in his voice.

"I'm not responsible for the actions of terrorists. I didn't blow up MedFuture. I didn't scar your beautiful face, and I didn't kill Mason. Any more than you did."

"Goddamn you." Her hands curl into fists.

"No one twisted your arm to join the party and to take the job at MedFuture. If you're feeling guilt about Mason, you should ask yourself why. No one's innocent, Taylor."

An old ache inside her stirs. She should walk away, but she can't help herself. "I was young. I went along. If it wasn't for you, the MedID wouldn't be law. The terrorists wouldn't have had a reason to bomb MedFuture. Your grand idea. You damned us all."

"If you want to go down that road, you wouldn't have Sienna if it wasn't for the MedID."

"Don't try and take credit for anything as good and innocent as Sienna."

"You're always so dramatic."

"Go to hell."

"Taylor." His tone is a snarl, a warning. "You're aligning yourself with dangerous people. Don't make yourself a party to the machine that killed Mason."

"Reverend Mitchell and his church did not kill Mason."

"I'm speaking simply as us against them. They—the terrorists and this war they've started—they killed Mason. I didn't. This government didn't."

Above his bed is an oil painting of Beacon Hill, familiar brownstones stretching up narrow slopes with cars crammed bumper-to-bumper. She stares at it and silently counts to ten.

"Do you remember what it was like before?" she says. "People held jobs for years. Went on vacations. Saw doctors. Went to school. Saved money in a bank and bought a house."

"They were delusional." Her father struggles to prop himself up on his pillows. "I'm glad your mother isn't here to see this world."

"I'm glad she's not here to see what you've done."

"I'm helping to cure cancer, Taylor. I'd imagine your mother would support my efforts."

"You can't really believe that." A laugh bubbles up in her. "You're not a doctor or a scientist. Don't take credit for their efforts."

"The MedID helps everyone. Gene editing and preventive medicine are conquering diseases. None of it would happen without the device."

"You twist reality so easily." She shakes her head. "You changed everything. There's no one more dangerous than you."

Taylor spins around and reaches for the door handle.

"Let me give Sienna a clean MedID," he says. "I'll arrange one for each of you. You'll be free to do what you want."

In the reflection from the glass he is two-dimensional and without color, less than a man. "You've arranged enough."

"You and Sienna could have the world, you know. You could live in a Safe District. Travel. Come November you may have a President for a father."

It takes a few seconds for her to process the statement. He's right, of course. This tragedy has left a void to be filled, and already the news is hailing him a survivor, a hero. It's a foregone conclusion that he'll become the Liberty Party's presidential candidate.

"Ten feet from this room people are dying from yesterday's attack." She turns back to face him. "But you only care if it affects your campaign."

"This isn't about me. It's about this country. If they'd killed us both yesterday, another party member would step in to run for office. Leaders rise to the occasion."

"Unless they're ducking."

His cheeks flush and he gives a small shake of his head. "Well, my dear, if you don't like it here, in a country where I might be President, you can always leave."

"This is my country," Taylor says as she opens the door. "I'll be sure to exercise my right to vote."

The door shuts behind her with a satisfying click.

Chapter 17

MID-AFTERNOON SUN SLICES through Sebastian's bedroom. A ray runs from the foot of the bed to the pillow, onto his face. He stirs and slowly blinks awake.

The first thing he sees is Kate's pillow. A few strands of blond hair stand out from the gray pillowcase. It's all that's left, pieces of her. Not the whole. Not Kate. He reaches for them and runs his fingers the length of the shafts, wraps them around his index finger until his fingertip turns blue.

A muffled, intermittent vibration. He sits up, forgets the hair, which falls back onto the bed. Foraging through a mound of clothes on the floor, he pulls his cell from a pants pocket. For the briefest moment he wonders if this wasn't all just a dream.

"Kate?" he says into the phone.

There's a pause. "Sorry, man. It's Renner."

His words are blocked, a jagged rock lodged in his throat.

"You okay, Sebastian?"

"Yeah." He sits back on the bed and strokes the prickly black scruff on his face.

"Take the week off. I've got it covered."

"There's not a net wide enough to cover this shit."

"Washington sent us twenty agents as backup. We'll find out who's behind this."

"Any news from your informant?" asks Sebastian.

"We met." An audible sigh. "But again, Mitchell is claiming to be surprised by the attack. I gotta tell you, I'm not convinced BASIA was behind this one."

"The one thing we know is that Mitchell is highly organized and virtually untraceable."

"He's never done a chemical attack," says Renner.

"Not that we know of."

"This was done with technology our lab hasn't seen before," Renner explains. "They studied one of the wands and found a miniature heating device that vaporized the sarin. It was a near-perfect execution. Maybe there's a rogue team of scientists out there, I don't know."

"It was Mitchell," Sebastian insists. "It's been a decade since the Planes. He was due to deliver a big one."

Renner ignores him. "Hey, you need anything?"

"You gonna make me a casserole?"

"Fuck you."

"Thanks, man." He paces. Nothing feels right. Not the air in these rooms, not the clothes he's wearing. He needs to do something. He needs to be of use. "I'm ready to go in."

"Go where?"

"BASIA. Mitchell's church."

"Now?" Renner asks.

"Now is the best time. A big event is like recruitment for new terrorists."

"Things have changed. Don't you think you're too close to this?"

"Name someone you know that hasn't lost a family member in this war."

Silence.

"It's personal for all of us. Yeah, it happened for me this week. But this week, next week, what's the difference? I'd say we're all pretty damn passionate about the topic, wouldn't you?"

"I'll go." Renner's voice sounds unsure.

"You heard Satterwhite. You're my handler. Plus you've got your dog and your informant depending on you."

There's a loud exhale in Sebastian's ear. "You been studying the legend?"

"I've reviewed it. Need to go deeper. Develop more details while the techs create an online history that fits with the alias."

"You gonna shave your head?"

"Thinking about a beard instead."

"I hear DARPA has developed some cool new surveillance toys."

"Let's set up a meeting. Start playing."

"Hey, I spoke to my informant about being a witness and helping you on the inside."

"And?"

"Just need another conversation or two. Need to make some reassurances. Supplying intel is one thing. Introducing you increases the potential to be caught."

"Absolutely." His mind wanders. "You wanna meet at the range later?"

"Let's do it."

He hangs up and glances around his Seaport condo, imagining

everything in boxes, walls bare. He can still smell Kate here. Her towel hangs in the bathroom, her clothes next to his in the closet. Her almond milk sits in the fridge, and the pint of chocolate fudge brownie she craved awaits her in the freezer. At the front door, her shoes are still parked neatly next to his. He'd never even told her he was going undercover, he just couldn't find the words. Now that she's gone, there's nothing left for him here. This mission is the only path that makes sense.

Hunger hits him, and he realizes he hasn't eaten since yesterday. Just one more thing. He opens the screen on his smartdesk, his fingers flying over the keys. An address autopopulates. He doesn't recognize it—must be one of Kate's. The window opens, revealing her work email. It's automatically set with her user name and password.

The inbox is brimming. He clicks through, sees that most of the emails in the past week are about the State House event. Several are from someone named Carter Benson from the office of Richard Hensley. One is an edited version of Kate's speech, another provides the final schedule of the event. Sebastian checks the addresses in the recipient line and forwards the message to himself so he can cross-check the individuals in the FBI database.

Chapter 18

Jonathan Hudson's last class ends and he closes the school application on his desktop. The room is dark, except for the glow of sun that outlines the drawn blinds. He rubs his stinging eyes. Though he'd logged into school, he spent most of his time in a separate window, exploring the Department of Defense intranet. It took him a few days, but he was able to crack it, create a back door and input a Trojan. Pretty goddamned cool. There are plenty of people in the world willing to pay for that kind of access.

His talent is his shield. With it, he's invincible. It's better than any high. Time to celebrate and bust out to the abandoned estate down the street—the empty pool is prime to catch some air with his new board.

He slips on his sneakers, grabs a pockmarked helmet from under a mound of clothes, and opens the bedroom door. Standing there with a hand poised to knock is his stepfather.

"Hey," Steven says.

"Hey." Jonathan takes a step back. *The fuck does he want?*

Steven peers into the room. "Smells a little ripe in there. You ever open a window?"

Jonathan stares at him.

"Looks like you're heading out." Steven nods to the helmet.

"Thinking about it."

"I'll make you a deal."

The last deal involved enough cash to buy crimeware for a year. And though he and his stepdad spend most of their time avoiding each other, Jonathan listens.

"With all the State House victims we're getting, I'm short-handed in the morgue and the viewing rooms. Help me out and I'll tell your teacher you're out the rest of the week. And I'll throw in a new gadget of your choice."

"Why?"

"Like it or not, Jonathan, one day you'll inherit Hudson's. Or at least your mother will. You think she'll be able to manage it? She can barely manage to get out of bed."

He wants to punch Steven's smug face. He knows his mom is using again, he's seen the signs. "Shut up about her."

"Well, you're more vocal than usual." Steven sighs. "Regardless, this is a multi-million-dollar business. You don't need to go to college. You just need the university of Hudson's."

The strap of the helmet in Jonathan's hand feels like a lifeline. His grip tightens.

"Let's not bullshit anymore." Steven's tone is serious. "I love your mother, despite the fact she insists on wearing that robe twenty-four/seven and sleeps for hours on end. Let's try to be civil. For business' sake. For your mother's sake."

Jonathan nods his head to the side, swinging the bangs out of his eyes. "Okay. Fine."

"Good." Steven rubs his hands together. "You won't be needing that helmet. Unless you're worried about slipping on body fluid and cracking your skull. Could happen, I suppose."

Tossing the helmet onto the bed, he follows Steven downstairs to the morgue. A few more inches and he'll be able to look his stepfather in the eye. Funeral homes creep him out, and here he is, living in one. Inheriting death. The darkness of this place is sucking the life out of his mother. She's an artist, a painter. It's her sanity, and it's obvious when she's not doing it. So while she is off tripping, Steven's dealing with the business and no one is paying attention to him. They'd be pretty shocked to know how he spends his time.

"After the CDC had their way with them, we received sixteen deceased from the State House." Steven opens the door to the basement and they descend the stairs. "Most from sarin. A few are victims of the stampede. We'll handle six of them here and I sent the others to our Brookline and Cambridge branches."

"Are they contagious?"

"Not anymore. They're well past the eighteen hour exposure mark."

The smell makes Jonathan's stomach wrench. He covers his mouth and nose with his hand. It's like a rotten soup of shit and mold mixed with antiseptic and formaldehyde. He breathes through his mouth. This is only the third time he's been down here. He's seen wakes, looked at the dead posed on those pillows, like they're having the best sleep of their lives. He used to hide on the stairs outside the viewing rooms and watch people. Some walked in crying and left with dry eyes. Some the opposite. Some never cried at all. When he was a kid, he had nightmares about zombies attacking him in his room. He made his mother put a lock on his door.

Steven flips on the overhead light, illuminating the large

basement-turned-state-of-the-art-morgue. He strides along a wall with several refrigerated compartments, yanking on handles as he passes. Naked bodies roll out one by one.

"Et, voilà." Steven does a flourish with his hand. "They'll all be cremated but the families chose to have wakes. They're almost ready. All but one have been cleaned and embalmed. A little makeup, some clay, their best clothes, and they'll be ready for their bon voyage."

"It's not a fucking party."

"Oh! I like this side of you, Jonathan. You need an edge in this business."

He can't take his eyes off the body nearest to him, a guy who looks only a few years older than he is. He does look asleep, kind of. The corpse is a bluish-white. And the fingertips aren't right. They're slightly deflated. Flat.

"You're like the Grim Reaper," he says.

"I didn't kill them." His stepfather opens a closet and pulls out a pair of blue scrubs. "I'm the middleman. I give dignity back to these people. We're all identified by our looks. Our style. Our hair. It helps families to see their loved ones as they remembered them."

"Huh." With his mouth closed, Jonathan plays with his tongue piercing.

"Most people don't want to work with the dead." Steven strips off his pants and pulls the scrubs over his boxers and T-shirt. "But I grew up with this. I don't have to get my hands dirty anymore. There's enough money to keep me in embalming fluid for a century. But preparing a body reminds me what Hudson's is about." He walks to the other side of the room and turns on a computer. "Beyond that, it's a business. And lucky for us, death is a sure thing."

"So what am I doing here?"

"Yes. Let's start small." He motions to a counter along the far wall. There are neat stacks of clothing and shoes, among other items. "The admin side. We itemize all personal belongings and bag it for the family. As you do each one, you'll use the MRS—the Medical Record Scanner—to scan in the MedID and start the Death Certificate process."

"Fascinating."

"Respect the process." Steven stands at the first body, a woman who looks to be in her mid-thirties. "First, we scan in the MedIDs and the government deactivates the record. Just press that button there as you wave the scanner over the MedID. You'll hear a beep."

Jonathan takes the MRS and does as he's told. It works.

"Once that's in the database, you're prompted to answer some questions. Cause of death, time, etcetera. I'll help you with that. That's all there is to it. Then match up the deceased with the personal items. It's alphabetical by last name."

The next couple hours pass quickly. Steven's technical assistant helps to prepare the bodies: dressing them, applying makeup, and fixing imperfections with clay.

Scanning and matching items is easy. Jonathan recognizes one of the faces from the news. It's Kate Manning, the person who organized that political rally, tourism thing at the State House. Fucking Richard Hensley was there. Prick. Whoever did this, good for them. Jonathan scans in the next guy's MedID. He's young, twenty-four. Jonathan glances back at his stepfather and the assistant, who are engrossed in their work. He reaches over and swipes open the guy's phone, checks out his pictures. Preppy kid. Wears ties. He scrolls through the images and pauses. There are mad photos of this kid freestyling on a board. Huh. Maybe there was hope for this one.

Chapter 19

ON THE DAY of Richard's hospital release, Carter coordinates with Secret Service to ensure there are no details left to chance. Despite Richard's protests, he is zipped into a body bag with hidden breathing holes and placed on a gurney, which is ushered through the Mass General corridors and into an elevator. It's as though he's on some bizarre amusement ride. In the darkness, he strains to recognize anything through the pin-sized holes. Jostling, sounds of men grunting, and finally the gurney settles and locks into place. Doors slam shut and the ambulance siren wails.

"We're twelve minutes out, sir," Carter says as he unzips the body bag. Flanking him on either side are his Secret Service agents, dressed in EMT uniforms.

Richard blinks against the bright light. "This is all a bit dramatic."

"Not compared to what happened at the State House," Carter says.

"Can I sit up?"

"Afraid not, sir."

Being forced to lie in this submissive position, under the noses of men who work for him, is unacceptable. He'll have a word with Carter later. He's been meaning to talk to him about the State House attack. The event was loud and there was a lot going on, but he could have sworn he heard something in his earpiece just before the terrorists started spraying.

With few cars on the road—and the assistance of the siren—the ambulance flies through the city. In no time they pull into the driveway of his Chestnut Hill estate. The wrought-iron gates close behind them as they round a curved driveway and park at the entrance. Finally, he's allowed to shed the body bag and exit the ambulance. Ah, his magnificent stone-and-shingle Victorian, circa 1900. Home at last. If only Norah were here to greet him. As he stretches his stiff legs, he fills his lungs. The fresh air tinged with the scents of pine and roses is better than any drug the hospital could offer.

The moment passes and it's as though he goes from crawling to sprinting. Carter shuttles him into his office for a call from President Clark, as the agents wait outside, guarding the room. Richard twists open a bottle of water and lowers himself into the soft leather chair behind his desk. A thin panel of glass slides up out of his desk. The presidential seal appears on the monitor as the White House operator connects the call.

President Clark's face appears. "Good morning."

"Good morning, Mr. President. To what do I owe the honor?"

"Don't be humble, Richard. You're a hero. A survivor. You can relate to the citizens of this country on their level now. You've been witness to the war, as they have."

"I might have survived, but I'm no hero."

"Let's not mince words."

In the hospital, Richard read a steady stream of articles and blogs written by people eager to label him: hero, survivor, coward, pawn. No need to bring up the latter two.

"Our country needs a hero right now," President Clark says. "And I'll level with you. Our party has both suffered and received a great amount of attention in the days since the attack. People are asking how we could let the attack happen. How a chemical attack on that scale could take place after we've spent years and millions combing the country for stockpiles of them. Well, to ease their hearts and minds, we'll give them a hero. You're the uncontested presidential candidate for the Liberty Party. Are you ready?"

Under his desk, he twists the platinum band around his ring finger. "I've been ready, sir."

"Very good. I'll make the necessary calls. Plan to address the party and the nation to accept the candidacy in two days."

"Yes, sir."

"You should know that we've pulled the State House footage from every video outlet. It's too damaging to the American psyche. And no one needs to see you take a nosedive again and again."

"Sir, I—"

"One final note. Of course your campaign team will be your own, appointed by you. I know Kendra is the obvious choice for campaign manager. But I want to put in a good word for Carter. That talented, dedicated man has spent twelve years entrenched in our world and he's the future of the Liberty Party. We know him. We trust him."

"I couldn't agree more, Mr. President. I think he'll make a fine deputy campaign manager."

"Excellent. Build up your strength, Richard. This is ours to win."

The screen goes black.

"Congratulations, sir," Carter says.

Richard had forgotten he was standing there. Heat rises from his chest to his neck, his face and ears. He reaches for the closest thing—a glass paperweight—and pitches it through a window. Glass splinters fly in every direction.

"Sir!" Carter steps back, his arms shielding his face.

The Secret Service agents charge through the door with guns aimed. Richard waves them off and after a brief hesitation they leave. He stands behind his desk, grips the edge. "Time for a little come to Jesus."

"I don't know that saying, sir."

"At the State House, you said something in my earpiece. It was just before those assholes sprayed at us."

Carter holds up his hands. "I said a lot of things. There was a lot going on."

"I remember, Carter."

"I'm sorry but I have no idea what you're getting at."

"'Duck.'"

"Excuse me?"

"Duck. You said, very clearly, 'Duck, Senator.'"

Recognition comes over Carter's face. "Of course I said 'duck.' I heard the shots fired down on the Common. And the performers were spraying something into the crowd."

"But you said it *before* they sprayed." He steps around his desk and slowly approaches his aide. "How did you know?"

"You hit your head, sir." Carter backs up, nearly against the wall. "And you did have some effects from the sarin. You're remembering wrong. If you think for one instant that I knew anything about this . . ."

Richard takes his time. He returns to the front of his desk and leans against it. The rush of adrenaline has left him a little weak, but Carter doesn't need to know that. He studies this man who rarely leaves his side. Dark eyebrows overhang light eyes, and his hair has thinned in the past year, though it's subtle since he keeps it closely cropped. Richard wonders at his ethnic background, has never thought to ask.

"Maybe you should lie down." Carter dares a step closer. "Concussions can cause confusion. They say it happens all the time after these events. If you need someone to talk to, I can find you someone who specializes—"

"I need to know what's going on. I need honesty from my staff."

"Sir, you're going to be the next President of the United States. You have a loyal staff and a loyal base. What happened to James Gardiner was horrific. But we all know the agenda of those terrorists. They want to keep the U.S. shackled by fear. And they want this government scrambling. You can disarm them, sir. You're the only one who can."

Carter is making perfect sense. Richard feels foolish for even thinking he somehow had insight into the attack. He must be misremembering. Gesturing with his hand, he beckons Carter closer, within arm's reach. Richard rests a hand on his shoulder and says, "Guess that knock on the head got me a little harder than I'd thought."

A lopsided grin skews Carter's features. "We have a lot of work to do."

"We do indeed. Call the team. Tell them it'll be a working dinner."

"Yes, sir."

"And Carter?"

Carter pauses mid-step. "Yes?"

"It appears we're all in agreement that you should fill the role of deputy campaign manager."

"It would be an honor."

"Congratulations."

Carter closes the door behind him. Richard's head is pounding as he sits in a stiff armchair. That day on the State House steps is a blur, the aftermath of which he's blacked out entirely. It's absolutely possible Carter said to duck as the wands were being pointed. *That* does *make the most sense.* He closes his eyes, summons the memory.

Gardiner was speaking, but Richard wasn't listening to the speech. All bullshit, predictable rhetoric. He'd looked past his running mate to admire Kate Manning, noticed her look of concern, her furious texting. Out in the audience he saw people wearing masks, jumping and singing. More entertaining than Gardiner, he remembers thinking. But then shots were fired. Suddenly several masked people rushed the stairs, as his agents dragged him in the other direction. The terrorists were pumping aerosol out of those asinine magic wands. *Duck, Senator.*

Yes. Of course, that's what happened. He's been sounding like one of those paranoid conspiracy theorists. Best to concentrate on the future. He's got a campaign to win.

Chapter 20

COLE HAS BEEN to the Newton branch of Hudson's Funeral Homes far too many times. Inside the property's Safe Wall, Lily leans heavily on him as he helps her out of the car. After a few days she still has pain from her C-section, but the support she needs isn't physical. In some ways it's a relief that Talia is still in the hospital's NICU for another few days. He isn't sure Lily's up to fulfilling the demands of a newborn. Not today anyway.

Wordlessly they walk up the stone steps and through the massive white doors, into the funeral home vestibule. The space is wide and welcoming with wood floors and darkly upholstered armchairs. A faint floral scent hangs in the air. Wearing a navy suit, Steven Hudson enters the room. He gives a small bow of acknowledgment.

"Welcome, Dr. Fitzgerald, Mrs. Fitzgerald," he says. "I'm sorry for your loss."

"Thank you," they say in unison.

Cole met the funeral home magnate when he'd made Kate's funeral arrangements. He's a quirky man. Everything about him is manicured, his nails buffed, his suit perfectly pressed. Hudson shakes his head occasionally and his hand goes to his hair, as though it's getting in his eyes. But that's impossible, since it's clearly sprayed into place. There's something a little off about him. Probably just working in this business. It'd make anyone a bit odd.

"You're a little early," Hudson says. "Which is good. You can take some time alone in the room with Kate."

At the mention of her sister's name, Lily squeezes Cole's arm. She says, "I'd like a moment alone with her."

"Of course." Hudson directs her to a set of French doors with opaque curtains.

Noiselessly, she crosses on the plush carpet and closes the doors behind her. An antique grandfather clock announces there's another thirty minutes before the wake begins. Cole imagines Lily behind those doors, and Kate. Impulsive, passionate Kate.

Shuffling over to the window, he glances out onto the freshly cut lawn. It's been just a few weeks since they returned from London, and everything has changed. New home, new routine, new baby. New loss. This is the very reason they left. He sniffs, rubs his nose. At least Lily can have some closure with Kate, instead of mourning from so far away.

Meanwhile, poor Kate's lying in there with a nearly pristine MedID. An 86. If they could swap it for Lily's they'd be on the next plane out. Kate would want Lily to have her MedID, if it meant she could be safe. The randomness of it all pains him. The floor creaks, reminding him that the funeral director is still standing across the room. Hudson is where all the madness ends. Cole's eyes unfocus through the glass pane as he considers this. The MedIDs are buried along with the dead.

But what if they weren't?

The thought jolts him. He suddenly craves fresh air.

"I'll be right outside if she needs me," he says, glancing back at Hudson.

Through the doors, he breathes easier in the open space. He trots down the steps and hastens along the edge of the drive. Ideas dart and connect, though he's not sure what he's working out. Kate. MedIDs. Funeral homes. There's no way around the MedID. Luck and DNA are the keys to living, it's that simple. And DNA is black and white. Unalterable, factual details that set each of us on a particular path. Details that separate families. Details that kill hope.

There must be at least twenty minutes left before people start arriving. He tosses his jacket in the front seat of his car, loosens his tie and rolls his head around his neck. Running is his release, one of the few things left in his control. Obviously, he can't run here in his suit. But despite the stiffness of his dress shoes, he can walk at a quick pace.

Striding around the lengthy drive, he takes in the ancient maples and oaks that create a canopy overhead. He pumps his left hand, the muscles in his arm flexing. The MedID feels like a part of his body, no different from an organ. So, if facts on the MedID can't be changed, what can be? Personal information on biochips can't be modified. Names, social security numbers, DNA, birthdates—those are hardwired and encrypted. Many have tried and failed to alter the data. Those same people now serve life sentences for treason. From their mistakes, it's clear the only way to change a person's MedID is to get a new one. His soles clack rhythmically against the asphalt. At the side of the house he finds a stone path and alters his course.

The ideas push through, unrelenting. Only infants are issued new MedIDs. People with clean DNA, and nothing glaring on the medical record, are both in the minority and hold sacred their biological status. Perhaps the key is someone who no longer needs or wants their MedID. Someone, say, dead.

He stops, bends, hands on his knees. Looking around, he's come full circle, back to the front of the building. At the driveway entrance several feet away is a tasteful Hudson's Funeral Homes sign. *Holy shit.* A national funeral chain. The government forgets about MedIDs once they hit this place. Unwanted treasure. A solid, weighty pit lands in his stomach. It's dangerous. Maybe deadly. And it's undoubtedly a treasonous idea.

The Hudson's front doors open and Cole bolts upright. His heart leaps to his throat as though he's been caught. Steven Hudson peeks his head around and spots him.

"Sorry to interrupt, Dr. Fitzgerald," he says. "But you're needed inside."

"Right, thank you." Cole retrieves his jacket from the car and heads back into the building. A low wail fills the air like some appropriate music for the occasion. Behind the French doors he finds Lily on her knees at the casket. Kate lies on a silk pillow, with rosy cheeks and waves of hair. Lily's last sibling, her last family member. Her cries penetrate him and he envelops her. They rock back and forth. After a few minutes he hears people shuffling into the vestibule. Mercifully, no one intrudes.

Having Talia should bring them solace during this time. Instead, he feels irresponsible. Audacious. Another innocent child brought into this war. The impetus to leave has never been greater. It's a problem he needs to solve.

IN THE RECEPTION area, Jonathan Hudson does as promised, helping his stepdad during the wake. The collar on his shirt chafes his neck; the tie feels like a noose. But it's an easy enough job; be quiet, polite and patient. There's a crush of people waiting to go inside the viewing room, but the family is inside, requesting a few more minutes of privacy. So he people-watches.

Most adults wear the requisite black. A few kids poke around, bored. They don't belong at funerals. Depressing shit. As he scans the room, a flash of red catches his eye. A rope of strawberry blond, a grass-green dress.

Suddenly, the French doors to the viewing room open and Steven ushers in the mourners. The seats fill, the standing room grows crowded. And the doors close.

"Hey." The voice is a smooth rasp.

His head jerks around to see the girl in the green dress. *Holy shit, she's beautiful.* Must be around his age, seventeen or eighteen. He can't remember the last time he was this close to a girl. He musters, "Hey."

"You work here?"

"Kind of."

"You just like hanging out in funeral homes?" One side of her lips curves up.

"That'd be fucked up."

They both laugh. She puts her hand over her mouth to quiet herself. He follows the path of freckles up her arm, onto her neck. There are so many it's like her skin color instead of individual dots.

"I live here," he says finally. "This is my stepfather's business."

"Wow. So you're used to all this." She gestures to the closed doors of the wake.

"Not really."

They both look around the room.

"I'm Hannah." She extends her hand and he shakes it.

"Jonathan." Her hand is cool, while his is sweaty. Damn. He lets go. "You friends with the woman in there?"

She shakes her head. "Just here for support. My friend knew her."

"Sucks."

"Yeah."

"You going in?"

"I can't deal with open caskets." Her eyes scan the floor. "Guess I'm not much support."

"They'll be in there awhile." He checks the grandfather clock. "Maybe an hour."

"Hmm." She rocks on her feet.

What to do? He wants to keep her here. He's never seen anything like the color of her hair, gold and red. "You like, uh, you like video games?" Idiot. His tongue isn't cooperating.

She shrugs. "More than funerals."

"Follow me."

Loosening his tie, he leads her through the living area, up the stairs, and into his room. Conversation flows, weaves through common ground: food, school, music. Gesturing with his hand, Jonathan prompts the video game. His room is transformed into a futuristic world, their avatars fighting against aliens that explode to bits, drip down the walls. He's never had a girl in his room. He steals glimpses of her, watches her alternately smile and frown as she concentrates on the game. She's easy to be with. He knows he's awkward, but she doesn't seem to notice. Suddenly his phone vibrates, startling him. It's Steven.

"Sorry," he says. His hand swipes the air to shut off the game. Lights on again, he notices dirty clothes on the floor and he kicks them under the bed. "They're wrapping up downstairs."

"That was fun." When she smiles, he sees for the first time the slightest space between her front teeth. "I didn't expect to have fun today."

"Me either."

She touches her smartphone, waits as she locates him. "Found you. Just sent my info."

"Cool." He nods, speechless. Dumb.

"See you soon, Jonathan." She breezes by, shoots him a smile and elbows him on her way out.

By the time he gets back down to the visitation rooms, people are filing out. Steven asks him where the hell he's been. Whatever, it was worth the lecture. As he cleans up after the service, images of her take his mind off his work. Her hair. Her smile. The rest of the day her name is on the tip of his tongue. Hannah.

Chapter 21

KATE'S FUNERAL IS terribly, predictably, sad. Upon seeing Sebastian, Lily hugs him fiercely, but the energy quickly drains from her and he and Cole practically carry her to her seat. Throughout the service there are heartfelt exchanges, clasped hands. But Sebastian doesn't feel Kate here, not at the funeral home, not at the cemetery. She's only in the home they share. Shared. In their bed, in the nook where they had breakfast each morning, the places they settled into at night. In those rooms he grieves, violently at times. To be there without her is torture. And so he won't be. Ever again.

It takes amazingly little to physically wrap up his life: three days, five rolls of packing tape, twenty-seven boxes, ten garbage bags, help from Renner, a van, a storage unit, and a lock. Ten of the boxes are Kate's, plus her clothes, which he and Lily decide to donate. He'll store the rest of her boxes until Lily's ready to see them. He tells Cole and Lily he's going away for a while. They know better than to ask details.

There's something therapeutic about packing and locking up all of his belongings for an indeterminate amount of time. When all paperwork on his covert mission is approved, he locks his valuables in storage, puts a hold on utilities, and places in a safe deposit box the key and a microchip containing personal information in the event of his death. Surprisingly mundane, but necessary. Within the week he is living in a furnished apartment in Milton. His address is known only to Renner and the one tech assigned to their team. Sebastian's new alias is William Anderson. Though he prefers Will.

THE BOSTON FBI branch is uncharacteristically noisy with several agents sent up from Washington, and all efforts are dedicated to the State House attack. Sebastian walks through the halls feeling oddly removed from the action. Some colleagues don't recognize him with his newly grown beard, his longer, wavy hair. He scratches his chin—it feels like someone else's—as he searches for the right office. Finally he spots it.

Waiting for him inside is a creative technologist from the Defense Advanced Research Projects Agency in Arlington. If there is any fun to being a spook, it's in the devices created by DARPA. They spend an hour in the windowless room, as the bald man who resembles a teenage Dalai Lama instructs Sebastian how to use the cutting edge inventions that will enable and enhance his mission. When the meeting wraps, his briefcase contains microchips, a ventilated plastic box with several remote-controllable Mecynorrhina torquata beetles, and .50-caliber bullets that can alter course mid-flight. Among other things.

After, he wanders over to Renner's office. There's no sign of him. Sebastian texts. A return message reads: *Carter Benson, Hensley's asst. Rm 3.* He hurries to the Interrogation area, eager to see what his partner is up to.

Inside the observation room, Sebastian activates the video wall and a live feed of the interview appears. He watches the action, happening just down the hall. Renner sits across from a twenty-something man with dark features, wearing a suit and tie. The Bureau's reached the end of a long list of interviewees connected to the State House attack. Their questions are growing stale and their initial theories are losing momentum.

"It wasn't easy getting on your schedule, Mr. Benson," Renner says.

"I apologize," Benson says. "Senator Hensley's campaign has us traveling nonstop."

"Well, I won't take much of your time." Renner wears a poker face. "The Bureau is thorough in every attack, but even more so when it involves the assassination of a presidential candidate."

"Of course." Benson folds his hands and nods earnestly. "Happy to help, if I can."

Renner brushes a hand over the table, cueing a glass monitor to rise. On it is Benson's file, which he instantly shares with Sebastian. Scanning through it on his handheld, Sebastian sees it's an interesting read. This guy's connection to Kate appears to be a simple administrative task they shared when scheduling the event.

"You were lucky," Renner says.

"Excuse me?" Benson cocks his head.

"You walked away from the attack unscathed," Renner clarifies. "I'd call that lucky."

"It was horrible." Benson straightens. "I may not have been affected by the gas, but I'll never forget what I saw. I don't call that lucky."

"As someone so integral to the campaign, I'm surprised you weren't up on the steps with Richard Hensley."

"At the time, I was his personal aide. I got him coffee. Made calls on his behalf. Arranged meetings. Aides aren't considered integral at these events."

"You have a new title now, correct?"

"I was promoted to deputy campaign manager."

"Congratulations." Renner waves a hand over the screen and it tilts in his direction. He studies it. "You've worked in some capacity for the Liberty Party for over a decade. White House intern. Personal aide to President Clark, then chief aide to Hensley. Sounds like a successful career track."

"I like what I do. Right time, right place, I suppose."

"Don't be modest." Renner's tone has an edge of sarcasm. "Exeter, Yale. I'm guessing it was a bit more calculated than mere chance."

Benson leans in. "I'm happy to answer any questions. Are there any?"

"Kate Manning," Renner says. "From the National Tourism office."

At the mention of her name, Sebastian tenses.

"Kate Manning," Benson repeats, his eyes searching the ceiling briefly. "Yes. Kate. I was in touch with her to coordinate the event schedule."

No response from Renner.

"I was sorry to hear she was one of the victims. I met her only once at a run-through of the event."

"There was a last minute change in schedule." Renner holds up a printout of an email from Benson to Kate. "You requested they start five minutes late."

Benson sighs. "Mr. Hensley runs perpetually late. It's my job to keep him on time, but he moves at his own pace. That morning he couldn't decide what suit to wear."

Renner cocks his head at him.

"What? You don't believe me?"

"They delayed an event involving thousands of people and the presidential candidate because Hensley couldn't decide between beige and navy?"

"Essentially. Welcome to my world."

That's easy enough to check when they interview Hensley. Once again Renner swipes a finger across the screen and reviews Benson's file. "You were arrested at a protest in 'eighteen."

"I was a juvenile," Benson says. "That's no longer relevant."

"Let's say for the hell of it that it is relevant."

"I got involved with the wrong kids." Benson shakes his head. "Doesn't everyone have a story like this?"

"Not everyone."

"We staged a protest against the MedID. I fell in with a group of kids who were strongly against it when it came out. I'm sure you remember the debates that went on." He waits for a reaction, doesn't get one. "Anyway, someone brought some firecrackers. People got in the way. We got arrested."

"You've changed your political views?" Renner prods. "Your boss is essentially responsible for the MedID law."

Benson shifts in his chair. "Kids do a lot of stupid shit. And then they grow up. Now. Is there anything else?"

"Just one last thing." Renner glances at the screen. "Your mother was an elementary school principal?"

Benson's eyes widen slightly. "I don't discuss this. Clearly you already know the answers to your questions."

"Must be hard to carry that around all these years," Renner says. "Your mother, a self-proclaimed martyr. Murderer of children."

"I'm not her."

"Were you surprised when you found out?" Renner asks. "No one would ever have imagined she'd sacrifice kids for her own agenda. According to interviews at the time, she was beloved by her fellow educators, neighbors. A regular pillar of society."

Benson pushes his chair out, stands.

"You would've been eight at the time," Renner adds. "Second grade? She kept you home that day. Guess her devotion only went so far. It seems you've ended up paying your mother's penance working for the government she hated."

"The shame is hers." Benson's tone is calm. "I have my own views, and my own life to live. So unless you have any other questions, I need to get back to work."

"Send the candidate our regards," Renner says. "Thanks for your time."

"Don't forget to vote." Benson's dark eyes stray to the camera nestled in the ceiling. Finally he turns and leaves.

A minute later Renner joins Sebastian in the observation room. They're both quiet, processing everything.

"It's hard to know what to make of him," Renner begins.

"So," Sebastian says. "He was ashamed of his mother. Did a one-eighty and joined the Liberty Party. Simple psychology?"

"Maybe. Probably."

"He's not off the list yet."

"No. Is it worth monitoring him?"

"At least his calls. All that travel, he's pretty protected in Hensley's bubble."

Renner's eyes glaze as he pulls at the tight curl at the nape of his neck.

"Wanna see what DARPA brought?" Sebastian asks.

That wakes him up. Like school boys, they open the DARPA briefcase and examine the contents and discuss possible scenarios for using the new tools. It's a welcome, if brief, distraction.

Chapter 22

THE SAFE WALL gates to the Hudson estate swing open, allowing in a grey SUV. Jonathan squints against the chrome and glass that gleam in the midday sun. On his way out of the house he'd passed his mother. She barely noticed him, her eyes black, her face pale. No doubt she'll crash all day, coming down from her high. And Steven won't know he's gone until hours from now when he emerges from the morgue.

Hopping into the backseat, he greets the driver, who then closes the privacy window. As they leave the estate, his breath catches. He's only ever ridden with his mother or stepfather, and those times have been for special—or tragic—occasions. Since the war started, parents let kids have social lives online but that's about it. He rolls down the window; the fresh air warms his skin. Hannah's invitation is like a door to freedom.

They're on the Mass Pike, heading west. Her family is having some kind of party today and she insisted on sending a car for him. It's not like he could have ridden his skateboard down the highway. Unease creeps in; he's not often plunged into new situations. Since the day he met Hannah, they've spoken every day. They video chat and play online games, talk about movies or random things, like where they'd travel if they could go anywhere in the world. Their voices run together in a nonstop stream. When she gets tired, she plays with her hair and her voice grows singsongy. They talk until the light changes, the shadows moving across the room.

A half hour later the car pulls off the highway and onto a dirt road overgrown with a lush canopy of trees. The dirt turns to pavement, ending with a wrought-iron gate that opens into a circular driveway. An enormous white mansion looms. The word that comes to his mind is geometric. Angles pointing this way and that with a lot of glass. Cool. And a little intimidating. He brushes his shaggy hair out of his eyes and runs his palms over his jeans. *Shit. Hope the party's casual.*

An attendant opens the door and escorts him into the foyer and down a long hallway. Inside it's cold, spotless. White and marble. Everything echoes. He second-guesses himself. Maybe he shouldn't have come. Or at least gotten high before coming.

In the living room, glass doors open onto a stone patio. Classical music plays softly under a din of voices. The party is in full swing, with a crowd of people spilling from the deck onto the pristine grass. His mouth is dry. Maybe this was a bad idea. With his feet fixed at the door, he notices that everyone looks to be his age or younger. He searches for Hannah, to no avail. The crowd is a mass of white and khaki and he senses eyes on him. On his jeans and T-shirt. Sweat pools under his arms and a trickle runs down his back as he stares straight ahead and moves directly toward his salvation. The bar.

"D'you have beer?" he asks the bartender.

"You have ID?"

Jonathan looks around. When he confirms no one can hear him, he leans in closer. "No, but I have a twenty."

The bartender, a man seemingly round as he is tall, flashes a grin. "Reverend Mitchell pays me well enough, thanks. So. Coke? Lemonade?"

Reverend Mitchell. The guy who leads that megachurch? The one conspiracy theorists claim was behind the Planes? No way. Hannah's too normal to have a father like that. Jonathan takes his lemonade to a corner of the deck. The other kids have already forgotten him, returned to their conversations. As he stands with his back against the railing, someone slides next to him.

"You came." Wide smile, freckles, a mass of red hair.

They clink their glasses. "Cheers."

"It's good to see you in person."

His face grows hot. "Nice house."

She glances back. "It's a bit much. All I need is a kitchen and a bedroom and I'm good."

"Is your father really *the* Reverend Charles Mitchell?"

"My adoptive father. Yes."

Rumors about the Reverend are well-known. "They say he doesn't believe in MedIDs."

She turns her forearm over to reveal a tiny scar, evidence of an extracted biochip.

"Now it makes sense."

"What?"

Shit. He hadn't meant to say that out loud. "Sorry. I just wanted to know more about you. So I did a search, a pretty thorough search. But there was nothing. Like you don't exist."

"It's okay." She gestures to the other partygoers. "We're all off the proverbial grid here."

"They go to your father's church?"

"They're my sisters and brothers."

"How is that possible?"

"We're all orphans. Most of us lost our parents in the war. Charles has so much to give and he doesn't hold back. Part of his mission is to care for those of us who've given the most for our country. Our parents."

"That's . . . amazing." Or weird. It's certainly a different image from the one painted by the media.

"Let me introduce you." She takes his hand and leads him across the deck.

Her touch distracts him, thrills him. But it's fleeting. In seconds he sees the face he recognizes from countless articles. The man is a few inches taller than Jonathan, and wears a suit jacket and a button-down shirt opened at the collar.

"Charles, there's someone I want you to meet." Hannah releases Jonathan's hand. "This is Jonathan Hudson."

They shake hands. The Reverend's grip is firm and his eyes are intense. Jonathan wants to look away but forces himself to hold his gaze.

"Nice to meet you, Reverend Mitchell."

"I've heard a lot about you, Jonathan."

Hannah blushes, stifles a grin.

He's at a loss for what to say. "Your house is beautiful."

"Would you like a tour?" Reverend Mitchell asks.

"Oh. Sure."

"I'll join you in just a minute," Hannah says, excusing herself to the restroom.

"Walk with me." The Reverend heads toward the house. "And don't be alarmed. Henry is like my shadow."

They are trailed by a statuesque, silent man in a suit. Jonathan swallows. What the hell? He reminds himself it's just Hannah's house. And her father. Strange as that is.

The house is vast, and during the tour there are hallways the Reverend doesn't mention, and doors he doesn't open. Finally, Hannah finds them as they're heading into an office that resembles a vault. In fact, he's pretty sure it is a vault, with a thick door and locking devices. Henry waits outside as Hannah and Jonathan sit on a leather couch across from Reverend Mitchell.

"So, Jonathan," he says. "I hear you know your way around a computer."

There's a pit in his stomach. He confided in Hannah. Trusted her with some of his secrets. As if reading his thoughts, she gently places her hand on his arm.

"I just told him you might be able to help him. He's hopeless with anything technical."

"You might say I never touch the stuff." The Reverend grins.

Weird that someone with this kind of house and his reputation doesn't know how to work a computer. He glances at Hannah then back to Reverend Mitchell. "Uh, sure. What do you need help with?"

"I'm told our network needs updating. Something to do with the cloud." He waves his hand. "We're working to create a private communications channel that will bring the members of Patriot's Church closer together. As you may know, our flock is spread out nationally."

"Sounds simple enough."

"If you say so. It's not my forte so I must defer these matters to the experts."

"Right. Sure."

Reverend Mitchell's face grows serious. "I pay well, Jonathan. But in exchange I ask for complete confidentiality. My lawyer will draw up a contract."

"Oh. Okay." He's not sure exactly what he's just agreed to. He's never had to sign anything before. But his cyber business isn't exactly legal. Sounds like this would be. Helping them create an encrypted chat for their church should be cake.

"Good." The Reverend stands, shoulders back, chest broad. "I look forward to working with you. Now, let's get back to the party."

Once again Reverend Mitchell leads with Henry trailing behind the three of them. On their way, Jonathan's curiosity gets the better of him. "Hannah was telling me that she and everyone here are your adopted children?"

"There are two great gifts in this world, Jonathan. Life and death. When people die in the name of freedom, die for our future, it's our duty to protect the lives they created. When I realized that children were being orphaned in the name of our cause, I had to step in. I can't let these precious souls be handed over to a government system rife with corruption."

"And you legally adopt them?"

"What's 'legal' these days? We care for our own."

It seems extreme to take in so many kids. Like a little cult he's growing here in this big compound. But whatever. If Reverend Mitchell has the money, it's generous of him to give them a home. Jonathan wonders what happened to Hannah's family.

Back outside, the Reverend pats him on the back. "I'll send a car for you tomorrow morning at nine and you can get started."

"Thank you, sir."

"I'm glad you came, Jonathan. I think you'll like the Mitchell family."

The Reverend and Henry disappear into the crowd. Hannah loops her arm in his.

"I'm glad you came, too."

"You're full of surprises."

"No more for today. Come on. Let me introduce you."

Somehow, in just a few hours, everything has changed. He's out in the world, separate from his parents. He has a real job. And he has Hannah, whatever it is between them. The darkened room that awaits him at home seems so far away. The rest of the afternoon he spends with her siblings, making small talk. When she's not at his side, he watches her through the crowd. He feels slightly off-balance in this world, this place. But being with her eclipses all of it.

Chapter 23

TAYLOR HENSLEY'S AT it again, strapped to the side of a building in Boston's Financial District. She wields her paint cans and dangles perilously. Sebastian's not one for heights, he's glad they can watch from the ground. It's after midnight on a warm June evening as he and Renner sit with the engine off in an old—but stunningly fast—Honda Accord. The Bureau has a host of these cars that aren't flashy on the outside but are outfitted on the inside with the latest technology. The car's 360-degree surveillance cameras reveal quiet streets and only the occasional passing vehicle. Parked a block away in the shadows, Sebastian strokes his beard while contemplating Taylor. There's no doubt she'll be integral to his mission, once he's inside Patriot's Church. Politically, he needs to keep her safe. So he'll get to know her habits, her daily routine. Tonight, Renner offered to keep him company.

"You get any more info from Kate's email?" he asks.

"Everyone's clean," Renner says. "I checked her colleagues at National Tourism. Nothing."

They stare down the street, but it's hard to make out Taylor, illuminated only by a headlamp she wears. Sebastian taps on the Smart Shield and live video from their camera appears before them. He gestures with his fingers and in seconds they have a grainy but close-up image of Taylor on her perch.

Renner's phone vibrates. He pulls a burner out of his coat pocket. "Hey."

Sebastian recognizes the familiar soft tone Renner uses with his informant. As though it's a family member.

"You sure the weather's gonna be sunny this weekend?" Renner closes his eyes. "Okay. Keep on it. Maybe the forecast will change. How about that other thing we talked about?"

The code is their own, but his partner's face shows his disappointment. There's more back-and-forth and finally the call is wrapping up.

"Not yet," Renner says. "Hey, there's a piece of art you should see. I'll leave it for you. And let me know your decision about the trip. Right. 'Bye." He shuts off the phone.

"Let me guess," Sebastian says. "Mitchell wasn't involved in the State House."

"Apparently not."

"Maybe he doesn't want to claim it." He considers it from Mitchell's perspective. "Chemical warfare, presidential candidate assassination. Maybe it's too high profile."

"The Planes were high profile."

"He didn't claim that one either."

They sit silently for a few minutes and watch Taylor. Sebastian circles back to the conversation. "Sounds like your CI isn't ready to cooperate when I'm inside."

"Unclear. Needs more time."

"More time. Shit." He leans in closer to the video, watching Taylor work.

"What's up with the artwork you mentioned?"

"My CI has siblings that might be alive. Maybe in foster care. I pulled a favor and got renderings on what they'd look like now, ten years later." Renner tugs the curl at the nape of his neck. "Needle in a haystack."

As they watch the paint dry, literally, Sebastian spins this new intel around in his mind. It's just not possible. If Mitchell wasn't behind the State House, that means there's another highly organized enemy that's not even on their radar. He rolls his head around, his neck cracking. It's sunrise when Taylor finally peels off her harness and packs up her equipment. He examines the unmistakable image of her father's face peering out from behind a medieval shield. The shield is a distorted Secret Service agent, bent and twisted to fit inside the protective armor.

Chapter 24

Los Angeles, California

RICHARD INHALES THE moment. A hundred thousand voices—delegates, media, attendees—bounce off the cavernous ceilings of the Los Angeles Convention Center on the evening of the second election primary for the Liberty Party. All this pomp and circumstance, the waste of party money for what is a foregone conclusion. There were never any other legitimate contenders, and his opponent in this race is an afterthought. She doesn't know how to play the game. Doesn't cater enough to her constituents. But she was their best option.

Since he accepted the nomination, Richard has felt propelled forward by a force he can only describe as fate. His team spends hours pouring over daily polls and honing strategies. But all of their calculations and predictions won't change what he already knows. The White House is his. It was always his.

Beside him backstage, his campaign manager Kendra coaches him on the event. The keyhole neckline of her conservative dress draws his eye. He's not sure if she ignores him or doesn't notice, either way, he always enjoys being close to her.

"Next is the moment of silence for James Gardiner," she says. "Let them see you feel the weight of his sacrifice."

"Yes, yes. I've been doing this for a while, my dear."

"Many of your delegates are sixty-fives and forty-eights. Their kids, too. The speech will show your compassion, acknowledge that you're their President, too."

"That's precisely the reason I'm pushing the new health agenda. It's for the under seventy-fives." Richard ticks off the items on his fingers. "Federal ban on smoking, mandatory fetal testing, checking waistbands after age forty, limiting television—"

"You're right," she interrupts. "Those things will change the way we live. But today we want to excite, not make them dwell too much about one detail or another."

Richard waves a hand in the air, indicating that she can move on to the next subject.

"Governor Glickman will walk on stage with you and take a seat after greeting the crowd."

"He's a child," Richard mumbles.

"He's a child the party loves. And he'll go along quietly. Both good things."

"True enough."

"Okay, that's it." Kendra checks her smartwatch. "Three minutes."

Carter appears and hands Richard a bottle of water. As he drinks, people talk at him: an aide, his speechwriter, a senator. None of it registers. He's busy conjuring Norah. Imagining her walking hand in hand with him on stage. The audience would fall in love with her instantly.

Finally, it's time. With a triumphant smile and an arm raised in greeting, he strides onto the stage to the sound of massive applause. A step behind, his vice presidential running mate, David Glickman, waves both arms. The energy in the room is unlike anything Richard's ever felt and it makes him gasp. It's a full minute before they settle down and he takes his place behind the podium.

"It's good to see you, too." Laughter. "I am honored and humbled to be your presidential candidate." Cheers. He gestures to the young governor. "And of course, I'm excited and thankful to have David Glickman as my partner, your next vice president." Slowly, the din quiets.

"However." Richard thinks again of Norah. His eyes glisten. "It saddens me beyond words that we've been brought together in the wake of a national tragedy. We will never forget James Gardiner and the inspiring, distinguished life he lost in the name of this great country. Please, let's share a moment of silence in his name."

Richard closes his eyes and focuses on the next part of his speech. After what feels like enough time, he returns his gaze to the crowd.

"And just as we can never forget James Gardiner and the other souls lost in Boston, we can never forget that we are a country at war." He grips the podium. "Our nation is in shock at the constant loss of life. Horrified by the viciousness of our enemy, these terrorists who make our streets unsafe and pretend to be good neighbors. But as I stand here today, I promise you we will spare no resource to expose and capture them." A burst of applause.

"As Commander-in-Chief, I will greet each day with renewed energy and determination to win the War at Home. I will work ceaselessly with the Department of Defense and Homeland Security to strengthen our military. In time, the United States will be home to the healthiest, most resilient citizenry on the planet. With the MedID as our tool, you will be well-cared for. Your health and your safety. You will be free to live your lives. To work your jobs. To go to school. To care for your children." Shouts of yes echo off the walls. "The MedID was instrumental in facilitating emergency care for the victims of our recent tragedy. With the MedID, the incredible medical community, and with God's blessing, we will be healed. No more disease. No more evil. Health and happiness will be our just desserts."

Thunderous approval. "I want to take a minute and speak to the Independents. Those of you who do not have MedIDs. We share this beautiful country, its resources, its government. And I want you to be safe, too. I've spoken to folks in Atlanta and Dallas, in Minneapolis and Seattle, and in small towns and cities across this country. I understand your concerns and your fears. And let me be clear. Everyone in the United States is free. Free to travel, to work, to own property, to earn money. Free, in fact, to run for President. But let's be honest. No one wants a president with a fifty-eight." Laughter. "My number is on public record—I'm proud to say I'm an eighty-two."

Cheers. He moves on to highlight the party platform: education, unemployment, and international relations. After fifteen minutes he is ready for the finish.

"When I'm in the White House, we'll work together to get a handle on this war that's been brought to our doorstep. Together, we'll build a healthier nation. Doctor visits will be a rare occurrence. No one will need to file for unemployment. We will once again be the strongest country in this world because we will bring this war to an end. We will come together. And all will be well. That's what I want you to remember when you vote for me come November. All will be well."

Chapter 25

Newton, Massachusetts

It's midnight when Jonathan returns home from his first day of working for Reverend Mitchell. Hannah had ridden along with him in the car on the way to BASIA headquarters. It was crazy. They blindfolded him. Said the location was top secret. It's pretty paranoid behavior if the Reverend hasn't done anything wrong. But Jonathan pushes that aside, happy to be employed, happy for the distraction. He spent the day working with their chief technologist on tedious server clean-up and upgrading their software. All in all, not a bad first day.

Meanwhile, if his mom is sober, she'll be pissed that he's home so late. This morning he'd told her and Steven he was starting a new job. They'd fired questions at him: where was he going, what was he doing, why did he need money? Steven told him he already had a job—at the morgue. His mother argued that he should be able to work remotely. Jonathan made up a story about working for an IT company that helps people in their own homes. Finally they'd agreed to let him try the new job. A test run.

As he trots up the front steps, he hears his mother through the door. *Shit.* He fumbles for the key. She's screaming. Not crying, not shouting. Screaming at the top of her lungs as though she's being bludgeoned.

Following her voice, he drops his backpack and sprints to the kitchen. On his way he passes smears of bright colors along the walls: red, yellow, green, orange, blue. The rainbow goes from the baseboards to the wainscoting.

At the kitchen doorway he stops abruptly. Perched atop the island is his mother. Naked and covered in paint, she's holding a large knife pointed at Steven, who stands on the other side of the room. Jonathan opens his mouth but has no idea what to say. He can't look at her. Wants to help her. Desperately, he scans the floor for a shirt, a towel, something to cover her. Nothing. "Mom?"

"Your mother has stepped out," Steven says in a calm, even voice.

Jonathan moves closer to her. "Mom, it's me."

"She's been like this for a couple hours."

Together, they wait. Finally his mom's dilated eyes focus on him. Tears stream down her face and she begins muttering unintelligibly. She sinks down on the countertop, hugs her knees, rocks back and forth. She holds the knife, pressed against her leg, no longer pointing at Steven. Now it's a danger to her.

"I thought you changed the lock on the morgue door," he says to Steven.

"I did. Twice. Where there's a will."

Moving slowly, Jonathan hops up on the kitchen counter,

across from her. It's going to be a long night. "Why can't she just get high?"

"That doesn't take her far enough away," Steven says. "Doesn't make her feel invincible."

"She didn't used to be like this."

"Not exactly, no. But it's always something isn't it? When she takes on a new vice, she becomes consumed by it. Relationships, food, painting. She's all or nothing. It's in her genes."

Jonathan watches the curved spine of his mother, coated in green and yellow like a lizard. It turns his stomach. This is his fault. Years ago she'd caught him smoking weed and before long they smoked together. He provided the pot that initially had the effect of calming her. It helped her moods, made her happier. But then one day he'd read about dipping bud into embalming fluid and decided to try it. After a few minutes of a kick-ass high, he'd grown angry and ended up tearing his room apart. He was so out of his mind he couldn't hide it from his mother. When he'd confessed what he'd done, she hadn't punished him. Instead, she'd had him show her how to do it. It only took one time for her to be hooked.

"Don't blame yourself."

His head snaps in Steven's direction. How does he know?

"Sarah told me you get her the pot. But you don't make her smoke it, you don't make her dip it. She makes her own decisions."

The knife clangs to the tiled floor. His mother's body sags as she sobs quietly.

"We need to put a stop to this." Steven crouches to the floor and quickly retrieves the knife. "This little secret of ours won't hold for much longer when she chooses to get high during a wake or when we're meeting clients."

"This is more important than the fucking funeral home."

"Agreed."

"What are you talking about?" He watches as Steven moves slowly toward his mother. When he reaches her, she crawls readily into his arms like a child. He kisses her cheek, comes away with a smear of blue on his face.

"Rehab, Jonathan." Steven's voice is raspy with emotion. "She needs to be checked into a rehabilitation facility."

"She won't go."

"She won't have a choice."

"You'd have her committed?"

"She's a danger to all of us."

It's a hard point to argue. "When?"

Steven shrugs. "Now?"

When the ambulance arrives, the two of them wrap her in her bathrobe and guide her to it. Jonathan stands in the driveway and watches as his mother and stepfather are driven away. The warm summer night is like a blanket, and suddenly he craves his bed. They did the right thing, he knows. She needed to get out of that house, just like he did. When death is everywhere, how can they live? Maybe he should try out Patriot's Church. See what it's all about. There must be something to it if Hannah goes. Maybe his mom will even come with him.

July, 2032

Chapter 26

A WHITE ELECTRIC company van with a silver lightning bolt on the side pulls to the curb on Central Avenue in Milton. Sebastian glances at the dirt yards, unused bikes, and discarded furniture scattered throughout. Abandoned cars without tires. Few people live in the Boston suburb since the mass exodus to rural New England. Even on a warm day it looks cold.

Carrying old, dented toolboxes, he and Renner step out of the van. They wear matching black T-shirts with a fake company logo, baseball hats, and sunglasses. It's midday Wednesday. With Taylor Hensley at work and her daughter at preschool, the apartment will be empty. Inside the entryway the paint is peeling and there are holes along the baseboard. The darkened tint of their sunglasses fades into clear lenses.

"Nice place." Renner points to mouse droppings.

"She obviously isn't tapping into her trust fund," Sebastian says. "The senator must be anxious to move them into a Safe District."

At the top of the third flight of stairs they find the right door.

In seconds Sebastian opens the locks and they're in. On the other side of the door, Taylor's home is another world from the building in which it's housed. Walls have been taken down to create a large, open room. One wall is clearly a child's canvas, part chalkboard, part paint splatter and crude yet pretty paintings. But the rest of it comes from Taylor's hand. In the far corner, a small kitchen is painted red and in cartoonish letters on the cabinets is the word *eat.* To their right is a comfortable space with a cozy couch, beanbag chairs, and a shag carpet. The wall is painted burnt orange with Taylor's signature graffiti writing in black with a daily reminder to: "relax, enjoy, cuddle, love, escape."

"Don't get any ideas," Renner whispers.

"Don't flatter yourself." A red signal in Sebastian's smartglasses indicates existing surveillance sensors.

"Got it," Renner mumbles.

They both swivel around, catching more red signals. TV monitor. Refrigerator. Toy robot. Another one across the room, nestled into the frame of a large historical map of Paris. He motions for Renner to follow him into a bathroom. Closing the door behind them, Renner flips on the light and the fan, for noise. A quick sweep reveals no devices.

"Abort?" Renner asks.

"No way." Sebastian removes his glasses, rubs the bridge of his nose.

"They've seen us."

"And we've seen them, so to speak. They don't know who we are."

"What if it's Mitchell? You're about to enter his militia. They could run you through facial recognition and make a match."

The bathroom is too small to pace. Sebastian catches a glimpse in the mirror and for a tenth of a second doesn't recognize himself. His dark hair has grown longer, wavy, and his face is partially hidden behind a neatly trimmed beard. The premature gray streaks serve him well in this disguise, turning his thirty-five years into a believable forty.

"I don't think it's Mitchell," Sebastian says.

"Why not?" Renner asks. "He could have surveillance on his entire congregation."

Sebastian shakes his head. "He's egomaniacal and supremely confident. Once you've passed through the threshold of Patriot's Church you're in his world. He doesn't need to spy on someone like Taylor Hensley."

"Unless he's trying to get to the senator."

"Maybe the surveillance is Richard Hensley's." The bathroom has grown warm. They stand about three feet apart with their backs against opposite surfaces. "Either way, we need to place our sensors and get out."

They move silently. Continuing the facade that they're electricians, they study wiring and circuitry while strategically placing the microchip sensors in the digital board of Taylor's microwave, into the overhead lighting fixture in her bedroom and a game console in the living room. Now they'll observe her every move, along with whoever else has a vested interest in her. After surreptitiously slipping a sensor onto Taylor's bedside table tamp, he notices a picture on her dresser. In it, she has long blond hair, a wide smile like her father. And she's on the arm of Sienna's father, Mason Jenner.

Finished, they lock the door behind them. Back in the van, Renner pulls out and they head back to the city. Sebastian stares out the window. Taylor's FBI file is thin, the info mostly about her father and the MedFuture bombing. Of course, he understands her anger after losing her husband. But why would she turn to Mitchell?

THE REST OF the week, Sebastian hones and memorizes his alias. Will Anderson's walk, his dry sense of humor, family details, and career history. When he's alone, he talks out loud, practicing a lazy tongue that allows a Boston accent to creep in. He's traded in the button-down shirts and suits for T-shirts and jeans. At least he'll be comfortable. Yesterday his MedID was removed and it's being stored in an FBI safe box. His new MedID was then injected, giving him a 69. The tech had applied a salve over the injection site that made the wound disappear in minutes. He's ready.

He texts Renner. Despite the encryption on Renner's end and Sebastian's disposable cell, they communicate in code. He wanders around the stark apartment in a T-shirt and boxers.

Sebastian: *I'm hungry for take-out.* (Ready to go in.)

Renner: *Great. Will get you the Thai menu.* (I'll alert the tech and have him add your alias near the top of the BASIA applicant list.)

Sebastian walks into his bedroom and sits on the bed. All these years, analyzing and watching Charles Mitchell and his militia. He can't wait to get inside, to expose this fanatic responsible for so much chaos, so much blood. And for taking Kate's life. The ache of missing her is ever-present. From a drawer in the bedside table he pulls out a black velvet ring box. Stiff, it opens with a creak. Her engagement ring. He takes it out and watches the light play off the surface of the diamond.

Renner: *You're all set. Menu on its way.*

Sebastian: *Thanks.*

Renner: *Unless you want a casserole?*

Sebastian laughs out loud. *Sounds damn good actually.*

Renner: *I'll be watching for your order.* (I'll be tracking you.)

Sebastian tosses the phone on the bed and replaces the ring in the box, settling it back into the drawer. The pillow is cold on his neck as he lies down. Above, on the dropped ceiling tiles, someone left plastic stars that glow. He switches off the light and stares at them.

Sleep is swift and takes him just as he's thinking of Kate, just as he's saying one more time, *I'm sorry for being late.* Always his last thought of the day. A flash of blue ripples through his unconscious, the fabric of her dress. When he awakens in the morning, he knows that he dreamt of her death once more. It's exhausting to start every day so angry.

Chapter 27

The Fourth of July is a predictably busy overnight shift at Mass General. Cole oversees his staff as an endless flow of casualties are treated, scanned, and discharged. In a rare lull, he retreats into his office for a coffee break. He pulls out a notepad and pencil from a desk drawer.

Since Kate's funeral he's been consumed by the MedID issue, studying it from every angle. Steven Hudson and his funeral chain intrigues him. Countless buried MedIDs that could provide a future for anyone without a clean number. Cole has chosen not to bring up the topic with Lily. She's fragile, clinging to Ian and Talia as though they might be taken from her. Years ago, when she was a survivor in a school bombing, it seemed to make her stronger. Then her parents were killed in an attack. That they went together was some solace, and perhaps even some strange relief without her constant worry about them several states away. But Kate's death has sucked her into a dark place. And telling her now about his treasonous idea would be akin to cruelty. *Treason*, punishable by life in prison or death. Being taken from his family in the midst of war is inconceivable. Still, there must be a way around the system.

In the quiet of his office, he puts pencil to paper. The soft scratch of his writing is oddly comforting. Nearby he keeps a lighter in case he needs to quickly dispose of the evidence. He makes a list of qualifications for MedID donors.

- *The donor would need to be unemployed and not due any pensions/benefits/insurance. The MedID triggers these payments and it would alert the government if checks aren't cashed, funds are unclaimed.*
- *Physical description needs to be a close match. Create a database that matches donors/recipients by age and appearance.*
- *The donor is ideally without family. Immediate or extended.*
- *Could recipients of clean MedIDs offer fees to the donor's family? Attractive to families in financial need. Riskier but possible.*

A knock at the door startles him. He turns the notepad over. "Come in."

Nurse Huberty leans in. "A car accident's arriving in five. Multiple vehicles."

"Let's go."

Gurneys burst through the double doors and the struggle for life is on. Wails and screams. So much blood. A metallic taste is on the tip of Cole's tongue. He dispatches patients to beds, assigns residents and interns as the voice-activated data populates a floor plan on the smartwall at the nurses' station.

He steps in alongside Dr. Riley, who's intubating a seven-year-old girl suffering from internal injuries. According to the EMTs, she'd been traveling in the car that caused the accident, sitting in the backseat with her older brother. No one will ever really know what happened, not that it matters. Her parents and brother are dead.

The girl's outcome is inevitable. Still, they fight for her despite her injuries and vital signs. For the better part of an hour they work on her, but finally the moment comes.

"Time of death, seven-eighteen P.M." he says. His latex gloves snap when he peels them off, dropping them to the floor. An entire family wiped out. He closes his eyes against the beauty of the little girl. Senseless.

"She reminds me of someone," Riley says quietly. "I can't think who."

He opens his eyes and takes in the girl's long brown hair, her pale skin. Gently, he lifts one of her eyelids to reveal blue eyes. "Did you scan her?"

"Yes. Typical pediatric record. Tonsils out. Stitches in her hairline. Nothing else."

"Genetic predispositions?"

Riley shakes her head. "Clean. Lucky girl." Her tone is ironic.

Lucky. Someone should be lucky today. My God. This is strangely a perfect moment and he can hardly breathe.

"What a waste," Dr. Riley says.

"Maybe it doesn't have to be."

"Excuse me?"

Two nurses shut down machines and begin cleaning up. Protocol states that within the next hour this child will be scanned and transferred to the hospital morgue. The next of kin—presuming there are any—will be called—and she will be transported to a funeral home. There isn't much time.

"Stay with her," Cole says.

"What?" Riley exchanges glances with the nurses. "I should check the board."

"In a minute."

"Dr. Fitzgerald, this girl is dead. There are a line of patients—"

"I'm aware. I'll check on the residents. Stay with her, please. I'll be back."

Riley presses her lips into a thin line. For the past month, since he caught her refusing to update MedIDs, their relationship has lacked any pleasantries. She'd relented, but she cooperates grudgingly and barely acknowledges him. Perhaps he can change her mind about him.

Pulling the curtain closed, he moves through the ER and scans the beds, but his focus isn't here. Back in his office, he shuts the door. His heart is pounding. He's thought this through countless times now. Considered the consequences. It's the right thing to do and it's time to act. He adds to the list on his notepad:

- *Children (infant—age 18). They aren't due monetary payouts, which is a positive. Either orphans or MedIDs donated by parents.*

He waves a hand over his desk, prompting his monitor to rise. Verbally, he scans medical records, filters a search by date, age, gender. And there she is. Tess Connelly. The patient Dr. Riley had refused to scan a month ago. Brown hair. Blue eyes. Just a year older than this girl.

Despite weeks of insomnia, he couldn't be more alert. He tears the page from his notebook and hurriedly makes his way back to the curtained area. If he's right, his young colleague will be eager to join in this effort. If he's wrong, she may expose him, cost him his career. Maybe even his freedom.

He slips through the opening to find Riley alone with the girl. Quietly he says, "Walk with me."

Furrowing her brow, she does as she's told. For such a slight person, she takes up a lot of space. Not one to hold her tongue, he couldn't have been more wrong about her being mousy. Through the maze of hospital corridors, he leads her to a rarely used exit. He presses his finger against the security screen and it opens. They are alone in a darkened alleyway between hospital buildings.

Riley crosses her arms. "I did nothing wrong in there."

He shakes his head. "We all tried our best."

"Then what are we doing out here?"

"Have you done her scan yet?"

A bitter smirk creeps onto her lips. "This again?"

"I assume your politics haven't changed?"

"You can't fire me for having an opinion. Since you gave me the ultimatum, I've done the scans. I'm here every day, I sleep here, I can't even get away when I'm unconscious. I'm an asset to this hospital, but more importantly, I'm an asset to the patients. I'm here for them." She steps closer. "This is all I have left."

He takes a deep breath. "If you were President, what would you do about the MedIDs?"

"What?"

"Humor me."

She searches the ground and finally meets his gaze. "I'd make them obsolete. And if that wasn't an option, I'd reverse the number system. Anyone under a seventy-five would get priority treatment. They'd be entitled to full-time employment to ensure they'd receive income necessary to pay for any care above and beyond what is covered by government-funded health care."

It's the answer he'd hoped for. "Do you remember your patient, Tess Connelly? The little girl whose mother begged you not to scan?"

"Yes. Why?"

"I'm showing this to you and you alone. Do you understand?"

"Yes."

He pulls the wrinkled notebook paper from his pocket and hands it to her. As she reads, he studies her. It's impossible to know what's going through her mind. When she finishes, she looks up. "What is this?"

"The beginning." He shrugs. "It is what we make it." He explains how the idea emerged, to swap MedIDs from the deceased to the living. The outline of a rough plan is sketched aloud, and as he talks, she nods along. By the time he finishes, her entire face has softened.

"You've gone along with—and enforced—the system," she says. "What's changed?"

There's no need to go into Kate's death or their denied emigration. Not yet. He shifts on his feet. "My wife and I just had a baby girl. She's pure. Perfect. But someone in the government disagrees. One point separates her from the lucky ones. So despite all our parental efforts, she's damned by her DNA. Controlled by it. As we all are, by design of the MedID law. So for that and many other reasons, I want to level the playing fields. And since we can't get rid of MedIDs, let's use them to our advantage."

"Sounds like a revolution, Dr. Fitzgerald."

It's not a label he'd considered. "I suppose it is. But it's not as simple as just helping people get out of the country. We need to build a network of people who'll be held together by more than political or religious beliefs. Citizens who want to stay in the U.S., who believe that freedom and family is the most important asset in a society, and that government has no place in private matters. Those people, the ones who receive donor MedIDs, will *appear to be* the healthiest out there. Somehow, we need to covertly find doctors willing to care for them under our own code of ethics, without proper scans. Then, personal data will only show standard care issues, nothing more. Years from now our group will outnumber the true clean MedIDs. And in time we'll make the rules."

"You dream big." Riley smiles.

"I have a new baby. Maybe it's the sleep deprivation."

"I'm in." Her voice is hushed, her tone excited. "This is everything I believe. Each time I do a scan I hear the words 'Do no harm' and my stomach burns. How can I help?"

A rush of relief lets him breathe easier. "I'm sure you understand how dangerous this is. There's no turning back once we do this. Treason is treason."

"I suppose people that commit treason think they have a just cause," Riley says.

He nods. "For now it's just you and me. We'll start a database of potential MedID recipients. We need to build our network slowly and very carefully. And we need a core team."

"You have anyone in mind?"

"Yes." Details rush at him, a flurry of images that he needs to sort through to make this a fluid process. "Have you been to Hudson's Funeral Homes?"

"Hasn't everyone?"

"Steven Hudson. His funeral chain is national. There could be unlimited possibilities."

"Why would he want to help us?" she asks.

"Leave that to me," he says. "I think there are a few ways to approach him."

"Is there a Plan B?"

"There's barely a plan." A nervous laugh escapes him. "Let's concentrate on today. Your patient, Tess Connelly. She's a perfect match for the little girl down the hall. Would her parents be interested? And desperate enough to keep this quiet?"

"The mother pleaded with me not to scan her." Riley nods. "I think it's safe to reach out."

"They'll need to get here stat."

"What's the process? Today, I mean."

"We do what we always do. Make calls to next of kin. Tell the family, if there's anyone to tell. Call the funeral home. And do the scan. But this time we'll remove the donor's MedID and Tess Connelly's MedID and reimplant them into the other's arms."

"But what about postmortem skin damage?" she asks. "The MedID retrieval site on the forearm will be obvious. It'll raise suspicion."

"We use Dexyne," he says. "It's a new topical enzyme just approved for market use."

"I've heard of that. When applied within forty-eight hours after death, it induces healing in the skin."

"Made for morticians," he adds. "Steven Hudson must love it."

"So Tess Connelly will effectively be in the system as deceased."

"And Tess will become . . ."

"Emma Gifford was her name," Riley says. "But how will she travel with her parents when they don't have the same last name?"

"Emma Gifford is an orphan. The Connellys will petition for adoption. They'll need to stay in the States while the process is happening and then move once it goes through. Adoptions have been fast-tracked since the war started. Too many orphans."

"We don't come across clean chips every day. So many people need them."

"Millions." It's overwhelming, so he tries to focus on the details that are right in front of him. Otherwise he might never begin. "I'm working on it. In the meantime, we have one."

"Thanks for this. For including me." Riley holds out her hand and he shakes it.

"I'll clear a room. You call the Connellys." Having a partner gives solidity to it, especially since she sounds even more convinced than he is. They head back inside.

The incessant cycling of patients continues throughout the night. There is so much noise and action throughout the ER that no one notices when Emma Gifford is scanned out and discharged. She clings to a much-loved pink teddy bear and wears long-sleeved pajamas, despite the humid July night. With a final wave to her doctors, Emma walks past the automatic glass doors hand in hand with her soon-to-be adoptive parents, the Connelly's.

Back in his office, Cole sits again at his desk, his body aching from hours on his feet. He stretches his arms in an attempt to free familiar knots that pull at his shoulder blades. Remembering the page of notes in his pocket, he pulls open his desk drawer and retrieves an ornate cigarette lighter a patient had once given him. Over his metal trashcan he flicks it open and a small blue flame licks the single piece of paper. Within seconds it turns black, curls into itself, and finally disintegrates into ash.

"And so it begins," he says aloud.

Chapter 28

NEVER ONE FOR religion, Sebastian sits in the pews at Patriot's Church and listens to Reverend Mitchell's sermons with a mix of bewilderment and disgust. The blatant manipulation of his congregation is breathtaking. Men and women alike appear completely drawn in by this heretic. Will Anderson does as they do. He listens and nods. Kneels when he's told to. Reads along in the Bible. But he also studies those few allowed into Mitchell's inner sanctum. The bodyguard, a long line of children who follow him out each service, and several others dressed in navy who are placed strategically throughout the nave.

The pews and extended seating must hold fifteen hundred, with probably another thousand in the standing room and balcony sections. It's a shame; Mitchell bastardized Trinity Church. Sebastian remembers the National Historic Landmark well from childhood, an impressive stone facade, enormous tower with a clay roof. The centerpiece of the Back Bay. When everyone fled the city for rural areas, the real estate market crumbled. Mitchell purchased the church. He must've bought off the Historical Society because he distorted the Romanesque style, melded it with a modern, twenty-first-century megachurch aesthetic. Each service, a children's choir belts out something that sounds like pop music about Jesus. Kids do cartwheels down the aisles. People of every age and race clap along with the beat.

No one's taken particular note of a tall, broadly built man in his late thirties with a beard who mostly wears polo shirts and khakis. A few weeks in now, Will Anderson is friendly, talks to anyone who sits next to him, and doesn't hold back his enthusiasm during the service. A welcome member to the flock.

Getting close to Mitchell has been impossible, but he can't rush it. Renner's informant still won't commit to being a cooperating witness and working with Sebastian inside. Last week at coffee hour he met Taylor Hensley. It was brief, but even in two minutes of conversation, he can tell she's warm and outgoing. Two things the press never mentions. The tiny divots in her cheek had drawn his eye, and she seemed to shy away when she caught him looking at them. She's stunning, despite the marks. She cuts her hair so short, tries to look severe, but instead the focus is on her face. He had a hard time looking away.

Thanks to the Bureau tech assigned to his case, Will Anderson's BASIA application has been bumped up the list. Just yesterday he received a piece of mail that said nothing more than date, time, and address. One thing they've learned from the informant is that militia applicants are screened and must give personal testimony explaining his or her interest in serving BASIA.

Last night, Sebastian ran the speech backward and forward until it felt natural. Unable to sleep, around three A.M. he'd gotten out of bed and had tea on the couch. It's something he used to do with Kate when they both had insomnia. He'd talked to her as if she was there, allowing the steam from the hot drink to warm his face like her breath might have.

He arrives promptly at the Patriot's Church offices wearing a brown suit and a plain blue tie. Inside the main entryway, he follows signs to the Testimony Room. It's a long corridor that feels particularly empty without the usual flow of people on church service days. A few more turns and he's there. He doesn't recognize the men and women who wait outside the room. No one makes small talk.

Intel on Patriot's Church dates back to when it opened in 2020. Bureau analysts estimate that a hundred people from around the country give testimony weekly with the hope of joining the militia. The NSA has intercepted several video transmissions from applicants, but they've provided no proof of conspiracy, only belief in the church and antigovernment sentiment. It's unclear how many are accepted, but Sebastian calculated that if Mitchell accepted ten people per week over ten years, he'd have over five thousand new recruits. Far too many unidentified enemies of the state. Today, it's crucial that he be chosen as one of them.

The door opens and a lean man in a dark suit calls a name. Sebastian hoped *Anderson* was a shoo-in for first, but evidently they're not going alphabetically. A woman with the last name of Foreman leaves with the man. Exactly fifteen minutes later another applicant is called. Sebastian checks his smartwatch and it's clear there's a schedule being followed. People shift in their seats, exchanging glances. The door opens.

"Will Anderson."

Adrenaline courses through him. He stands and follows the man, who is several inches shorter. Sebastian stares at flecks of dandruff on his navy blue shoulders.

"Right in here, please." The man leads him into a windowless room with four white walls, one of which contains a one-way mirror. In the center of the room there's a table with two seats, one on either side.

"Mike Michaels," the man says. They shake hands. "Please, have a seat."

"Will Anderson." Sebastian sits down, facing the mirror.

"You have three minutes to testify," Michaels says in a bored tone as he takes the adjacent seat. "Tell me about yourself. What brought you here. And why you'd make a loyal and contributing member of BASIA."

"I grew going to St. Paul's Episcopal in Baltimore. It was like a second home to me. When the war started, I got my MedID along with everyone else. At the time I didn't think much about being a seventy-two. I went to school, got good grades, got married, worked in finance. But then a doctor visit exposed a weakness in my DNA sequencing. I have alpha-1 antitrypsin deficiency. Basically, I'm missing an enzyme in my lungs and liver and I'm prone to respiratory infections. Employers equate this to meaning I'll miss more days of work. There's no cure, no treatment. I was laid off and now I can only get contract work. With the war, the unemployment rate, I'm lucky if I work six months out of the year. Then my wife . . ." He shoves a hand in his pocket. Inside is Kate's engagement ring. He touches the smooth edges of the platinum band, the jagged edges of the diamond. "She died before our first anniversary."

"I'm sorry for your loss."

This guy must hear countless stories, he thinks, have stock responses at the ready. "So. I can hardly work. I lost my wife. I've got nothing." Sebastian brushes his nose with the back of his hand. "Nothing but God. And anger. I have a lot of fucking anger."

Almost imperceptibly, Michaels nods, his eyes narrow.

Sebastian balls his fists. "I keep asking myself . . . why and how did everything change? I want some accountability. And every time I think about it, I get the same answer."

"What's that?"

"Our government is a danger to its people."

"May I ask how your wife died?"

His chest aches as he envisions Kate. "She was a lieutenant in the army based in Southern California. During the L.A. Riots of 'twenty-four she was out fighting with her squad, but they were outnumbered. No helicopters were sent in. No backup troops. They let them burn."

A low buzz sounds and Mike Michaels pulls out his phone. He consults the screen a moment and regards Sebastian once again. "Sorry. So, your wife died, you can't work, you have a strong hate for the government, you've returned to the church, and this has led you here today."

"I suppose I could have said it more succinctly."

"Not at all." Michaels taps his smartwatch. "I just have a strict schedule to keep. Want to be sure I have all the details."

"Can I add one last thing?"

"Please."

"I read the Bible every day, have for years now." Bring it home. "And one passage stays with me. I believe it's what led me to BASIA. Inspired me to fill out the application."

"Do tell."

He closes his eyes as he recites one of Mitchell's favorite psalms. " 'Put on the full armor of God, so that you will be able to stand firm against the schemes of the devil. For our struggle is not against flesh and blood, but against the rulers, against the powers, against the world forces of this darkness, against the spiritual forces of wickedness in the heavenly places.'"

"Ephesians 6:11-12." Michaels nods. "Well said."

Another buzz. Sebastian watches as Michaels consults his device.

"Congratulations." Michaels's voice has an edge of annoyance. "Welcome to BASIA."

His knees are week. No need to feign surprise. "Wow, thank you. I was expecting a longer process—"

"It's an unusual honor to be informed immediately at this stage, but you were fortunate to have Reverend Mitchell himself observing today. He was evidently moved by your testimony."

"That's the best news I've had in years."

"Yes, I'm sure. All right, Mr. Anderson, we'll be in touch."

They both stand and Sebastian shakes Michael's hand vigorously. When he leaves the building and steps into the bright daylight his nerves disappear. He is this much closer to nailing Mitchell. The door is open to him now.

Chapter 29

All eight pounds, two ounces, of Talia radiate heat onto Lily's chest. Finished breast-feeding, the seven-week-old infant is fast asleep, a thin flannel blanket tucked around the edges of her tiny body. The two of them could lie here on the living room sofa for hours, and sometimes do.

Loud thumping disrupts the peace as Ian bounds down the hallway dressed in his soccer uniform. Last year, students were offered a specific DNA test that would reveal academic and physical predispositions. Ian's results surprised her and Cole. They'd never noticed much physical inclination in him. But high quantities of the gene ACTN 3 indicated he'd be an excellent athlete. With a little encouragement, Ian chose soccer. In the past several months he's hardly left the field.

"Is Dad here?"

"He'll be home for dinner."

"Can you take me?"

Moving is a feat, her limbs heavy as though filled with concrete. She wishes the games were in-district. Instead, the districts compete against one another, which requires traveling. Last year she spoke to the State Soccer League and brought up the idea of avatar-based games. The technology is available but the majority of players still prefer human contact.

"Mom? The game is in, like, an hour."

"What district are you playing today?"

"Eighty-six."

She hasn't left District 149 since Kate's funeral. For the first time in her life, fear has taken over. It was a stupid thing to do, but she'd sought out the news footage of the State House attack. She couldn't help herself. Now, it's all she sees when she closes her eyes. For her family, she goes through the motions, keeps up the facade of normalcy. But everything's an effort.

Ian bounces a soccer ball off his knee. Her eyes run over the newly defined muscles above his knee, sculpted calf muscles. Thick bangs hang in his eyes.

"You need a haircut," she says.

"I need to get to the field."

The game is only a half hour away. She can do this. The roads are patrolled and there are no obvious targets between the two districts. Still, there's the occasional drive-by shooting or the terrorists turn their cars into suicide missiles aimed randomly at oncoming traffic. It's impossible to guess what they want, what they think they're achieving with the madness. The prescription patch of anti-anxiety medication is on the side table, and she sticks it onto her arm, just below her shoulder. It should kick in any minute. Ian wears a torso ballistics skin, hidden beneath his team jersey and shorts. Lily quickly changes into hers, and zips Talia into her protective footy pajamas, woven with the specialized thread that repels bullets. With a handgun hidden in the diaper bag, Lily moves on shaky legs, carrying Talia in her car seat. In minutes they're belted into their autonomous SUV, windows up and locked despite the gorgeous seventy-five-degree day. As she powers the car, she announces the address, prompting a map graphic on the windshield. Seated behind the steering wheel, she is still merely a passenger. And the car begins to drive, expertly executing the course.

"I can't breathe in here," Ian says as he attempts to put down his window.

"I'll put on the AC."

"We need fresh air, Mom."

"We need to be safe."

"Breathing oxygen is safe."

"Right. Keep breathing." She reaches a hand back and playfully pinches his leg.

At the District 149 gate, the guard waves her through. In the rearview she watches as the twenty-foot doors close behind them. She swallows. Everything out here looks gray, in contrast to the once vibrant neighborhood. Overgrown lawns. No kids play in yards. Only a few cars are on the road. After a while she concentrates only on the asphalt ahead. The familiar yellow lines. Before long they're driving up Beacon Street, nearing District 86.

A block ahead, Lily spots a metallic gray Land Rover. It's Cole's—she recognizes the MD plates. Without thinking, she presses her foot on the gas to catch up. The car jerks forward into manual drive.

"Mom!" Ian shouts.

All at once she sees the yellow light turn red. She slams on the brakes. A horn blares as a truck flashes in front of them.

"Sorry, sorry. Are you all right?" Heart racing, she instinctively reaches behind for Ian, but he brushes her away.

"I'm fine. Jeez, Mom. You're all worried about us being safe and you almost get us in an accident."

She twists her body to check on Talia, whose car seat is directly behind the driver's seat. Amazingly, she's still asleep. The light is green again but Cole's car is out of sight. Once again she commands the car to drive autonomously. What's Cole doing? It's not like he does house calls, and his shift at the hospital goes until 5:00 P.M. It's the middle of the afternoon.

In five minutes they're safely inside District 86. Ian bounds onto the field, and as the game begins, he deftly maneuvers the ball around his opponents. It's remarkable to watch. He's such a different kid here. His smile is easier, his shoulders are back, and there's a confidence she's never seen in him. A wave of guilt comes over her. She's spent the past ten years hiding him away from the world. No wonder they didn't know he had this ability—how could she have seen it inside the walls of their home? And what else isn't she seeing?

WHAT R U doing? A text from Lily. Strange that she's texting him now, in the middle of his shift. Cole debates whether to respond. In his parked car, he glances through the windshield at the entrance of Hudson's Funeral Home. A procession of cars and limousines is leaving the parking lot. He glances back at the text message. Best not to lie outright. But now is not the time to tell her he's in the midst of committing treason. *Treason.* He shakes it off and slides the phone into his jacket pocket.

It's a relief to enter a funeral home without the need to mourn. Instead, his mind is racing. This meeting with Steven Hudson could be the linchpin to their project. Cole might not make the deal today—he knows his proposal would change this man's life. But he's done his homework on Hudson and his funeral homes. There's nothing to suggest that Hudson's politics support the MedID or the Liberty Party, in fact there's evidence to the contrary. He's donated to parties and causes that support civil liberties. Hudson stays out of the public eye except for his ghastly commercials. And, like Cole, with a wife, a child, and a successful business, he has everything to lose. On paper this isn't an easy sell. Hopefully, the man's values run deeper than the image he projects on TV.

Inside the foyer, he does as Steven Hudson instructed, continuing down the hall to the main office. Behind a walnut desk, Hudson sits with three computer screens in front of him.

"Steven, hi." He pauses in the doorway. "Cole Fitzgerald."

"Yes, of course." Hudson stands and extends his hand. "Always good to have a doctor in the house. Though it's a bit late for my clients."

Cole grips his hand. "Three computers. I can hardly handle all I have to do on one."

"One's for business, one's for personal business, and one's purely for pleasure. I never mix the three. Even electronically." He flashes a grin, but it disappears within seconds as he waves a hand, prompting the monitors to disappear into the desktop. "So. You were cryptic on the phone. What can I do for you?"

"Do you mind?" Cole nods to the open door.

"By all means."

Not prone to perspiration, he's surprised to feel wetness under his armpits. He closes the door but freezes in place, a gnawing in his gut. He can't tell if it means he's doing the right or the wrong thing. The room could be bugged . . . but there's no reason it should be. Finally, he turns around and takes a seat.

"We've met a few times," Cole begins, "though I can't imagine how many faces you see in your line of work."

"You do look familiar," Hudson says, squinting his eyes.

"Unfortunately, I was here a few weeks ago for my sister-in-law, Kate Manning. After the State House attack."

A slow nod. "Yes, yes. Of course I remember."

There's an awkward pause as Hudson stares expectantly at him.

"Look, obviously we don't know each other. And we certainly don't know each other's politics."

Hudson eases back into his chair and appears to relax. His face lights up. "Are you running? Is that it? Looking for my support?"

"No, no, nothing like that."

"Oh. Disappointing. You should consider it. You have a sort of JFK, Jr. quality about you."

"I'm not running. Listen, you're an astute businessman. You took your father's business and created a successful national chain. It's impressive. I imagine you reap a multitude of benefits from this long and nasty war we've got going on."

The skin on Hudson's face slides south. "I never wish for death, Dr. Fitzgerald, but it is a fact of life."

"I'm not disparaging you." He shakes his head. "That wasn't my intention."

There's a knock on the door that makes Cole flinch. It opens and a woman in a summer dress comes in carrying an iced tea. Her black hair is tied in a messy bun at the nape of her neck, and her face lights up at the sight of Hudson. But when she notices Cole, her mouth and eyes grow wide.

"I didn't know you had an appointment," she says.

"Sarah, this is Dr. Fitzgerald. Dr. Fitzgerald, this is my wife, Sarah Hudson." He takes the tea from his wife. "Thank you, honey. Keeping me hydrated and awake for years now."

"Nice to meet you," Cole says.

"Would you like some tea?" she asks.

He notices that her fingernails are tinged with purple, yellow, and green. "No, thank you. You a painter?"

"Getting back into it." Her eyes dart to the floor.

"She paints beautifully," Hudson says. "Abstracts. Which is refreshing because everything in this house is so damned literal."

"I'll let you get back," she says. "Nice to meet you, Doctor."

When she closes the door behind her, Hudson says, "On the phone you said something about an opportunity?"

"Your first wife." The moment he mentions her, Hudson's body straightens, his lips press together. "Your son and daughter. I can't imagine what you went through. At the time, I remember reading countless articles. About the victims, and the terrorists, the planning involved. Fifty planes taken down at exactly the same time, mid-flight. The war was so young, and we were raw . . . processing everything. That event destroyed our collective freedom, it paralyzed all of us."

"Is there something I can help you with, Dr. Fitzgerald?" Hudson's voice is tired.

"Why were they on the plane?"

"Excuse me?"

"Their flight was heading to Paris. Why were they going there?"

For a long moment Hudson stares at him. Then without a word he pulls a bottle of scotch and two glasses out of a bottom drawer in his desk. He holds an empty glass up in offering.

"No, thank you."

"More for me, then." Hudson pours liberally and takes a good swig. "I cannot wait to see the point of all this."

"Paris."

"They'd just begun the lottery. As you know, they issued MedIDs according to birth date, starting January first. Kelly—my wife—she wanted us to get out before that happened. She had dual citizenship, so our kids did as well. Sam and Georgia." At the mention of their names he finishes his drink. He recovers and flashes his teeth. "I have good hair and teeth but the rest of my genetics are crap. Kelly worried about me being allowed entry into France. We knew what would happen at the borders once the scanners were in place."

"But you weren't on the plane."

"It takes time to tie up one's life. My business, the house. Since I was near the end in the lottery with my November birth date, it made sense for me to follow."

"And all these years later, how do you feel about MedIDs?"

"Is this a therapy session?" Hudson cocks his head. "Should I be lying on a couch?"

"It's not a therapy session. It's a business opportunity."

"Well, that clears it right up."

"I realize this is not your average business discussion, but if you'd allow me a little leeway—"

Hudson's eyes roam over Cole's torso. "Anyone else listening in here?"

"What? No."

"You'll excuse me if I don't take your word for it."

"Okay." Cole sets his powered-off phone on the desk.

"It's quite easy to hide devices these days. Let's have a look."

Fair enough. No reason this man should trust him. Cole unbuttons his shirt and demonstrates that he carries no other electronics.

"Pants, too, please," Hudson says.

"Jesus." But he does as he's asked. It's humiliating, but finally Hudson nods and Cole pulls his pants back on and buttons his shirt.

"Let me see your shoes."

Cole hands them over. Hudson studies them and after a moment stands and places them in the hallway, closing the door again. Finally they sit across from one another again, their eyes locking.

"You were saying?"

"After everything you've been through, how do you feel about MedIDs?"

"It's all gone to hell, hasn't it? The government hasn't made any strides in the war. Under the guise of protecting us, the MedID has limited us. Labeled us. And ruined hope in this country."

"And what about all the emigrants?"

"I don't know why they bother. Unless they have a clean MedID or a hell of a résumé, what's the point?"

"What if you could help them?"

"With what? My wit and charm?"

"Sure. Let's say your wit and charm would get them across borders."

"This is a strange conversation, Doctor. Sure. Why not."

"Let's say you could help in a slightly more risky but nonetheless beneficial and perhaps profitable way."

"Go on."

Once he says the words, there's no going back. Just the act of initiating this conversation endangers Lily, Ian, Talia. He swallows, fills his lungs. Finally, he explains his idea, beginning on a local level and expanding to eventually become a national movement. Hudson's eyes narrow while he listens.

"Why do you need me?" Hudson asks. "You have access to deceased patients at the hospital."

"Of course. But you have broader access, I only have Mass General. Plus, the funeral home is the last in the scan process. You file the death certificate, triggering any insurance or pension payments due the deceased. Unless it's a child, in which case that only matters if the parent has taken out an insurance policy. Which is unlikely."

"So you need Hudson's national reach."

"We won't be successful if we don't have a partner in this."

"You mentioned that this could be lucrative."

"That's something we can discuss. Donor recipients may pay to receive their MedIDs. But I'm not in this for the money."

"No?"

"No."

"Again, more for me." Hudson pours himself another drink.

"Does that mean you'll consider it?" He leans forward slightly in his chair.

Hudson sips his scotch and examines the amber liquid. Finally he sets down the glass. "I'm sure it hasn't slipped your mind that this is treason?"

"Not for a minute."

"What's in it for you? What's worth risking your family, your career, your future?"

"The MedID was supposed to help put an end to the war. To root out terrorists while strengthening citizens. But the violence hasn't stopped. People are angry, whether they want civil liberties restored or a theocracy or the end to government, period. They're desperate and unpredictable and we can't go outside without wondering if we'll make it home that night. For ten years I've gone along. Done as I was told. I scanned MedIDs and didn't allow myself to think about the consequences. But what I write on those records has lifelong, rippling effects. It changes lives, families. It's not what I signed up for. I've been perpetuating a system that I don't believe in. It's gone too far."

"What's to keep us from getting caught?"

"The administration's focused on the presidential race and the war. They're short on manpower and funds, so eventually they might catch on to a MedID black market, but for now we're under the radar. As for staff, we'll need to vet them carefully. Our donors will all be deceased and their families will either be none the wiser or else they'll be active participants. And the MedID recipients aren't interested in exposing us. They're interested in their futures."

Hudson sighs, stares at the closed office door. Finally he looks back at Cole.

"I live in black and white, Dr. Fitzgerald. Life and death. These MedID numbers—like them or not—are black and white. They are, quite literally, who we are. So you can fight the MedID. You can fight the government—whoever's in office—Hensley will be the victor this year, no doubt. But families around this country count on Hudson's to bring them peace in this time of war. I won't gamble my family and my responsibilities in the name of some idyllic yesteryear. As I recall, it wasn't so idyllic."

He doesn't disagree. But he wants to get Hudson to see the future, not the past, or the present. There's only one argument left. "Your family. What if you needed to get them out? There's your wife. And you have a stepson, is that right?"

"It won't come to that," Hudson says. "Whatever our fate, it's right here. It just matters that we're together."

"But don't you want the option? If we're partners, we can arrange it." It's his Hail Mary. "A new one for you would ensure you can travel anywhere with your family."

"How do you know my number?" Steven's nervous tic kicks in and he shakes his head, his hand brushing his stiffly sprayed hair back as though it's getting in his eyes.

"You've been a patient at Mass General. It was easy enough." Cole envisions the ocean horizon line from the terminal in London, remembers acutely the devastation of being turned away. "We all deserve options."

Hudson sinks back into his chair. His voice carries the unmistakable tone of defeat. "We're comfortable, Dr. Fitzgerald. It's not a perfect life but it's what we have."

Silence. Clearly there's nothing left to say. Anxiety replaces Cole's adrenaline. Has he just ruined his family's future? Gambled their safety on this man, all for nothing?

"You certainly don't owe me anything." Cole runs his hands over his pants, wiping away sweat. "But I'd like to ask that you forget we ever had this meeting."

"Consider it forgotten." Hudson stands and extends a hand. "Good luck."

"To us all." They shake hands.

Crestfallen, Cole returns to his car. He sits with his hands on the wheel, staring out the windshield. Another line of cars has parked. Mourners dressed in black exit cars and swarm the entrance of Hudson's. It had been the perfect plan, all the pieces would have fit just so. He can't tell his partner Karen Riley just yet. He needs to have a backup plan. He remembers the text from Lily. *What r u doing?* I don't know, he thinks. I just don't know.

Chapter 30

VICTORY WILL BE ours. Though he knows it's the truth, Charles would never speak it aloud. *Pride goeth before a fall.* Sitting in BASIA Headquarters Command Center, his chest swells as he watches the security cameras. A stream of men and women funnel into the warehouse, faithful souls, eager to fight in this Holy War. They will help him rebuild and unite the country under God, as it was intended from the beginning. Militia applicants doubled in the past couple weeks since the State House attack. It also brought in additional donations from followers, which will propel their mission to the next level.

"Five minutes, sir." Henry's voice startles him.

Charles traces his thumb along his tattooed palm. "Systems ready?"

"Yes, sir. Encrypted video feeds to twenty-three states tonight."

"Fantastic." He whirls his chair around to face his bodyguard. "How's the family?"

"Fine, thank you."

Henry's been with him for the better part of ten years. Every

Christmas and Thanksgiving, Henry extends an invitation to join his family. Charles finally accepted last year, attending their Christmas day festivities. But it was too much. The intimacy of being in their home, of watching Henry bend and bow to his children's and his wife's every request, is not how Charles wants to see this man who protects him. Better to maintain distance, though there's nothing he doesn't know about Henry. One gives up privacy when one protects Charles Mitchell.

"Ava's well?" Charles asks.

A blush comes over Henry's fair features. "She's pregnant, actually. Sixteen weeks."

"Congratulations! That's wonderful news."

"Thank you."

"You going to have the testing done?"

"No, sir."

"Good man. A child is a child."

"We're excited. Maybe we'll break our streak of girls on this one."

Don't count on it. Two X chromosomes say otherwise, information courtesy of the OB/GYN on Charles's payroll. In fact, Henry's fourth daughter will have cystic fibrosis. Just like his second daughter, though the six-year-old is a lovely girl and there's hope a cure is on the horizon. Charles himself has donated to the cause. He feels for Henry, knows it must be terrible to watch his child suffer. So he does what he can to ease the man's pain. He provides complete coverage and access to private medical care for his family. He's happy to do it.

Charles stands and straightens his perfectly tailored black suit as Henry holds the door open, adding, "Hannah and the other children are waiting for you by the stage. There are just over seven hundred seated in-house, and the medical staff is in place."

"Excellent." Charles pats him on the arm as he passes. "Let's go greet our new recruits."

SEBASTIAN LEFT ALL of his devices at home. No reason to take a risk now. This is Mitchell's world, and at BASIA HQ no electronics are allowed, enforced by detection systems at the entrance. Nervous energy courses through him and he shifts on the cold metal seat, one of hundreds lined up to face a stage. The space is an old airplane hangar. In the back, one corner is marked Area A, with a curtain around it, and another is marked Area B, with another curtain. It strikes him that men and women of all ages and sizes are here. No doubt they cover a range of talents Mitchell will attempt to harness for his next mission.

The buzz of conversation ceases, everyone stands. Reverend Mitchell strides across the stage to the podium. Following, and taking seats behind him, are a group of children and teens. Sebastian studies them. There are twelve here today, though rumor is he's collected many more who were orphaned in the war.

"Welcome," Reverend Mitchell says, lifting his arms in the air. "You're here tonight because you sought out the truth. The truth that we are one nation under God, and our God put us on this earth to be free. It's a divine mandate to realize this freedom that is being denied you by your very own government. Together we will change our future and the future of our families. It's our duty. If we don't change it, no one else will."

Mitchell's right about one thing; Sebastian is here for the truth. The soldiers remain standing with their arms at their sides for ten minutes as Mitchell expounds the value of their commitment and the impact it will have on not just America, but the world.

"The State House attack was brilliant." Mitchell's voice is clear and strong. "Whoever was behind it thought of everything. The choreography, the weapon of choice, delivery method, down to the last ten seconds. It was devastating. Wish I'd thought of it myself."

Laughter erupts. Mitchell grins proudly. And though Sebastian's stomach turns and bile rises to his throat, he forces a laugh. Assuming he's telling the truth, Renner's informant was right. Goddammit. Then who?

"But we will learn from it," Mitchell continues. "Over the next few months, we'll gather information. Organize. And then execute our plan. Each of you has the potential for massive impact. Don't underestimate yourself. I certainly don't. You will touch lives. And they will never see you coming. Look around."

Feet shuffle, bodies turn. To Sebastian's left stands a woman in her fifties, plain but athletic. On his right is a man in his twenties wearing a suit and tie, the air of a financial institution.

"You are neighbors," Mitchell says. "Classmates. Coworkers. Friends. The fabric of society. Nothing about you is insidious. Obvious. You aren't depressed or psychotic. You're every man. Every woman. And you are key to BASIA's mission. Have confidence in yourself. The impact of one can be great. One can change everything."

The Reverend extends an arm toward the back of the room. "Behind you on the left is Area A. There, you'll form an orderly line and have your MedIDs scanned by our medical technicians. After that, on the right is Area B, where you'll have your MedID removed by one of our physicians. For those of you in other states, the room setup is the same."

Murmuring spreads throughout the crowd. Sebastian runs his fingertips over his forearm. Thankfully the spot has healed since the insertion of Will Anderson's chip. This comes as no surprise since the Bureau rarely arrests a terrorist who wears a MedID. Mitchell invites questions from the new recruits. *What if I don't want to get my MedID out? What if someone notices? What if I die and my family needs my pension?*

Without exception, Mitchell explains, BASIA troops are expected to get their biochips extracted. The MedID has brought Armageddon, after all. They are free people and thereby free to remove this evil harness. He tells them that the government has no right to withhold funds from a family even if a MedID has been deactivated.

"Unless he is a terrorist!" someone shouts.

"There are no terrorists here," Mitchell counters.

"What do you do with all of them?" Sebastian asks. "Our MedIDs."

"They're held in a safe place. If a soldier leaves BASIA for any reason and requests that his or her MedID be returned, we'll oblige. From this day forward you will have access to the medical staff at any of our bases and coverage for you and your families. Our doctors do the initial MedID scan to create a record and access your medical history. But they won't update it or do any functional scanning that the government requires. And in the unfortunate event of death, each of you will sign a document to specify what will happen with your MedID. We can destroy it, give it to your family, or bury it with you."

That cache of biochips would be priceless. If Mitchell's truly been collecting them since the MedID law was instituted, it could be the key to making the case for the Planes. This means that somewhere, Mitchell has hidden the MedIDs for each of the fifty suicide pilots. Sadistic trophies. It's the first inkling of hope he's felt in weeks. The room grows quiet. There appear to be no more questions.

"Be here fully," Mitchell announces, "mind and body, or don't be here at all. Our mission is to fight for the liberty that's been taken from us. Accept these terms and you'll be forever welcomed in the house of God. When we win the war, the opportunities will be endless. Each of you is an integral member in our secret forces. One enormous, harmonious family." His face brightens. "No discord here, brothers and sisters. Unlike in some families."

More laughter. Sebastian smiles. A fucking comedian.

"If you're ready to join BASIA, please proceed to lines A and B and you'll be given your orders from there. God bless America." Mitchell presses his right hand to his heart and then extends his arm, palm open with the famous cross tattoo. The soldiers mimic the action. With his bodyguard leading the way, he exits the stage followed by the line of orphaned kids. As the door closes behind them, the communal adrenaline fuels instant conversations between the soldiers.

Sebastian introduces his alias, Will Anderson, to as many people as he can. He takes his time getting to Area A, where a long line awaits. As he makes small talk, he watches the exit, counting people who've decided to leave. Looks like a couple dozen have made the choice to keep their MedIDs, and just maybe made them rethink their priorities.

When the process is finished, he boards a bus along with thirty or so other soldiers. They weren't allowed to drive tonight, escorted to the secret location in a vehicle with blacked-out windows. On the journey back into Boston, a mother of three sits next to him. She lost her husband several years ago, talks about retribution for her children. She goes on and on. He wants to shout at her, to ask her why she'd want to orphan her children. Instead he nods along. He stops listening and concentrates on the stash of MedIDs. Renner's informant must know about them. It's time to make some promises to their one and only potential witness.

Chapter 31

It's early Sunday morning as Huan Chao walks a few paces ahead of Jonathan, through the echoing halls of BASIA HQ. Mitchell's chief technologist has been a decent boss so far, though he only speaks when he has something important to say. The past few weeks he's given Jonathan surprisingly simple projects. Doesn't matter. He's getting paid *and* he gets to see Hannah.

"In here." Huan stops at a door and holds his hand over a security screen. It opens to reveal a large room filled with monitors but no people. Jonathan hops onto a chair with wheels and spins it around. Huan makes sweeping gestures that bring the machines to life. A hum fills the air. Focusing on one monitor, he motions with his fingers as the electronic sensors follow along and find the page he's searching for. He rotates the screen to face Jonathan, who leans in for a closer look. It's a file on him. Information about his mother. Steven. His father. Facts, history.

"What's this?"

"This is public knowledge. There are no secrets these days."

"Sure there are."

"Indeed." Huan's grin is lopsided and somewhat creepy.

"I don't understand."

"The past few weeks have been a trial period. It's time to discuss your role here. We know you're a gifted hacker."

Jonathan's leg bounces rapidly. He wants to bolt.

"You were only a child when you hacked the Department of Education site."

"That file's sealed. I was a juvenile."

"You're still a juvenile."

"For less than a year."

"In any event, performing system upgrades and troubleshooting is well below your skill level. But we had to ease you in. Do you like working for Reverend Mitchell?"

"Yeah." He shrugs. "It's been cool."

"And at the same time, your crimeware business is booming. You've been busy. I was impressed with your DoS attack in June."

His jaw drops. No one knows. No one knew. Are they going to turn him in?

"Credit where credit is due." Huan glances at the screen with his family's data. "That power outage you caused cost the state a small fortune."

"What do you want?"

"Cooperation."

"Are you threatening me?"

Huan grimaces. "Just the opposite. I'm presenting an opportunity."

Bullshit. He nods.

"Good." Huan touches the screen and the Hudson family file disappears. "I need three things. Your time, as much as it takes to complete the task within our deadline. Your talent. Hold nothing back and we will support you in any way you require. And your MedID."

"Why?"

"Make that four things. No questions."

In just minutes the ground beneath him has shifted. What just happened? He watches Huan's mouth but the words are fuzzy. It's like that paranoid feeling he gets sometimes when he's high. But this time it's for real.

Chapter 32

If she was to paint him, Taylor would add peacock feathers fanned out behind him, and his hands would be exaggerated, bigger than his head perhaps, his tattooed palm in the foreground. It's hard not to stare at Reverend Mitchell, seated across from her at his desk. His white teeth gleam, his skin is so smooth it makes her question his age. Thirty-five? Forty-five? He looks her in the eye and his voice is warm, drawing her in. After a month of church services, he'd pulled her aside, singled her out. She's sure it's because of her bloodline, but it doesn't bother her. He listens like no one has listened to her in a long time.

"Have you seen your father since your hospital visit?" Reverend Mitchell asks.

"No. And I don't plan to."

"It'll be hard not to see him everywhere, now that he's in the race."

"I try not to follow the news. It's too depressing."

"Yes. I've had many sleepless nights considering our role in this war. But we saw it coming and it's here now. It's God's will."

God's will. She researched the Reverend, knows the rumors. But she's here to see for herself why he has countless followers nationwide. In all likelihood, he's a victim of the press and politics, much like she's been her whole life. Otherwise, why wouldn't the FBI march in here and arrest him? She doesn't believe he's the man they make him out to be. Though she's never embraced God to this point, who is she to say it's not Armageddon? It certainly looks like it when she steps out her front door. The one line she's drawn here is that she won't introduce Sienna to this world until she explores it further. Obviously, her own crossing the threshold of Patriot's Church was as much metaphorical as it was literal. But why shouldn't she try religion? In the past, the only faith she ever followed was politics. She needs to know what else is out there.

"Do you feel at all responsible?" Reverend Mitchell asks. "I mean, your father's responsible for sparking the flame. He brought the Mark of the Beast. That must weigh on you."

Warmth spreads in her chest. Her voice is louder than she intends, echoing off the high office ceiling. "I don't feel anything but anger toward my father, and I won't take responsibility for his actions."

"Still, you must carry some guilt at having a hand early on. As I recall, you were marketing the MedID. Putting a shine on it. Hiding its true nature."

"When I worked at MedFuture, I believed the MedID was the greatest health-care tool ever invented. I never imagined how it would spiral. We've all been betrayed."

"True." His eyes are intense. "I'm sure you know, having you in my congregation is quite the spectacle. I need to be sure what side you're on."

"I'm on my own side. I'm sorry about the press, they're relentless. But I've chosen to be here. I need to see if this is a better path for us. My daughter deserves a safe world to grow up in, and I'll do anything I can to make that happen."

"I understand. As long as you're a member of Patriot's Church, I will personally offer you and your daughter safety. We have our own schools. Our own doctors. And there's no need for her—or you—to be in harm's way."

"Thank you." They're just words, but they sound so reassuring. It's as though he could put an arm around her and envelop her in armor. "Now. What can I do? How can I help you?"

"We should work together." Reverend Mitchell leans on his desk. "Your graffiti is well known. God gave you a special gift. Let's use it to spread His word and our mission."

Of course that's what he wants. She hesitates. *Maybe I owe it to the country, like a penance for being involved with the MedID.* "Okay. I can use about any structure or surface as a canvas. Are you thinking of Boston proper? Or around New England?"

"Patriot's Church is a brand like any other." His words resound like a sermon. "We need to reach the younger generation. They're the first to be genetically altered. The first to experience the loss of siblings because of DNA testing. A holocaust in vitro is being sanctioned by our government, and the victims are the brothers and sisters of these children."

That's extreme. Her imagination quickly paints pregnant bellies and a land of infant angels. And who is she to judge? She'd opted out of the testing when she was pregnant. The temptation had kept her up nights. To help her child before she took a breath could have been an unfathomable gift. But it also felt like playing God.

"Let's take a walk," he says.

With Henry trailing them, they travel through an extension of the church that looks more corporate than rectory. With her courier bag strapped around her, she attempts to keep up with the Reverend's long strides. They didn't discuss payment, so she assumes she's donating her time. It would be funny if she used this as a tax write-off. The government would love that, and it would give her father a heart attack. She grins to herself.

"As you spread the word of our mission," he says, "you should keep in mind the men and women who are BASIA. That will guide you in reaching new recruits."

"BASIA." Her tongue brushes the roof of her mouth. "Your militia."

"Yes. I want you to meet some of our soldiers. Most of them come to us after facing death, after an attack, a betrayal of some kind. They're seeking safety. Hope. When tragedy strikes, people remember God. And that's when they find us."

Over the years, BASIA has been in the news, though charges have never been brought against them. Public accusations run from corporate attacks to the Planes, and recently, the State House. She has to ask.

"Your militia," she says. "What do they do, exactly?"

"Our methods are quite progressive." His chin juts out proudly. "We find cyber strategies to be highly effective. So, under this roof, we wage a silent war. Codes are our weapon."

What he says makes sense. Since the War at Home began, cyber attacks have rendered banks nearly obsolete. The stock markets are hacked monthly, turning the few remaining investors on their heads. And highly classified government secrets were being revealed weekly, until government programmers changed the way they encrypted their system. Perhaps BASIA does function in the nonviolent realm.

At the end of the hall, Henry opens a plain white door on which *Private* is stenciled. Inside, the room is dark and empty except for a few chairs.

"Activate BASIA headquarters communications," Reverend Mitchell orders.

A smartwall fills with video feed of a room with twenty or so men and women who stand at attention. They appear physically fit. Maybe three or four are over the age of fifty. Some of the men sport buzz-cuts, and she wonders how many have served in the U.S. military. Her eyes linger on a face, a man she met a week or so ago. She thinks his name is Will.

"Good morning everyone," the Reverend says. "I want you to meet Taylor. She's going to help spread our message. Take a few minutes to get to know one another. Then get back to work."

She whispers, "They're training?"

"This Holy War will be won partially on a virtual battlefield. If you can succeed strategically, then the game is yours."

"One-to-one chat commence," Henry commands.

A soldier's face fills the screen, and Reverend Mitchell encourages her to ask questions, anything that would help her understand their mission and to strategize for the Patriot's Church brand. Perhaps just a taste of their passion, their goals, their lives, will help her to begin to shape this "brand" he wants to create. Without any time to prepare, she'll have to wing it.

As Will Anderson, Sebastian sits at his desk and listens to Taylor's voice. She is making her way virtually around the room, speaking to soldiers. From the surveillance data he's collected it appears she lives a quiet, ordinary life. She doesn't drink alcohol. Doesn't smoke. Has no health issues. She pays her bills and is likely living off the life insurance from her husband's death. She lives bare bones in a sketchy neighborhood when she could be living in a Safe District, courtesy of her father. She has no contact outside her daughter and babysitter; her close friends have all relocated, emigrated, or died in the past few years. Seeking out Patriot's Church might signal her desperation at creating a community that doesn't include her father, who she clearly blames for her husband Mason's death. As a graffiti artist, she is occasionally commissioned, which supplements her income. Her work is decidedly antigovernment, which must be of concern to her father and the party that wants him elected. That alone puts her at great risk, though from whom it's hard to say. Last week Sebastian listened to a call on Taylor's cell in which Mitchell asked her to meet him. Nothing notably suspect. Mitchell didn't even call from an encrypted line.

Eventually, a window appears on his screen, inviting him to video chat with her.

"Hi," she says. "It's Will, right?"

"Right," Sebastian answers. "Taylor. Looks like you're getting the grand tour."

She nods. "I'm helping Reverend Mitchell spread his mission. He thinks seeing behind-the-scenes might inspire my writing."

"What are you writing?"

"Graffiti."

Purposely, he waits a beat as though he's working out a problem in his head. "Of course. I didn't put it together until right now. You're Taylor Hensley. As in Richard Hensley."

At the mention of his name, her lips press together. "I don't want to talk about my family."

"So that's a yes."

"Yes. But—"

"Don't worry, I'm not going to vote for your father." He grins.

"Well that's a relief."

"The guy's a regular hero. That State House footage when he pulls the agent on top of him?" He shakes his head. "That video disappeared pretty quickly. Lucky for him people have short memories. He's a shoo-in for President."

"Please," she says. "Change of subject."

"You have to admit, it's *interesting* that the daughter of one of the most renowned senators—who happens to be an enemy of Patriot's Church and BASIA—has joined Patriot's Church. Wouldn't you agree that's interesting?"

She takes a moment, her eyes wandering. When she finally returns to the conversation, there's no trace of anger in her voice. "I don't agree with my father or his politics. Not that it's any of your business. But don't assume I'm anything like him."

"Okay," he says. "Got it. I'm sorry."

"That's okay." She leans in closer. "You're passionate about your beliefs. And you're here to defend them."

"Yes. As are you."

"Yes."

"Reverend Mitchell already has a million followers, doesn't he?" he asks.

She smiles. The pockmarks in her face turn into dimples when her cheeks rise. The effect softens her whole face. "Doesn't matter. Everyone always wants more, don't they?"

"Except minimalists."

The tension between them dissipates. "Your hand. Is that a training wound? Carpal tunnel?"

He laughs, holding up his bandaged right palm. "A new tattoo, actually."

"The cross?"

"Yup." It's a necessity to fit in here. Thank God for laser removal.

"So. What does the Reverend have you working on?"

"Video games." He creates a separate window for her to see a 3D game with several avatars in various forms: soldiers, supermodels, elves. Together they're rebuilding a world that's been destroyed. "Believe it or not, this is my assignment today."

"Who are you?"

"The supermodel."

She snort-laughs. "Nice legs."

"Seriously, though, we're able to use the game for Virtual Field Communication."

"What's that?"

"Using these avatars, BASIA soldiers can converse in the field. We can manage money, communicate directives, plan training exercises. Using an encrypted chat, we can interact no matter where we are. Right now I'm chatting with our team in Oregon and Minnesota."

"Chatting sounds like you should be drinking tea and eating scones."

"You should use that in your marketing. Come chat! Eat scones!"

More laughter. It penetrates the air, slices through the quiet.

"So if these people are so far away, have they ever been here, to headquarters?" she asks.

He tells her that most have never met Reverend Mitchell in person. Still, they're devoted and they meet faithfully. The Reverend's weekly sermon streams live to their local Patriot's Church. On occasion a believer makes a pilgrimage to Boston. Some faint in his presence. Others have reported feeling a sense of calm come over them at his touch.

"Do you have that same feeling when you're with the Reverend?" she asks.

"Only one person has ever given me a sense of calm." The words are out before he remembers that he is not Sebastian Diaz.

"And who was that?"

Shit. He sniffs. "My wife. She died. It was a long time ago."

"I'm sorry." Taylor looks off camera.

"So, does all this help figure out what you should paint?"

"It will."

"I've seen some of your graffiti."

"It's not for everyone."

"That's art, isn't it? I, personally, love graffiti."

"I should let you get back to work. Nice to see you again, Will."

"See you later."

She leaves him with a warm grin, then appears on the soldier's screen beside him. Sebastian knows he's in now. A memorable exchange. From here, via Taylor, he can build a bridge to Mitchell.

August, 2032

Chapter 33

WITHIN THE MORGUE'S thick walls, Steven savors the silence. Here, there is no chaos, no discourse, no interruptions as he works on a body. If he's honest, the reason he's down here is to escape Sarah in what has become a more and more frequent "state." Rehab didn't take. She had returned home, a breath of fresh air, back to her lovely, fiery self for a couple of weeks. She even started painting again. But then one night Jonathan didn't come home and there was a bombing downtown. The next thing he knew, the lock he'd installed on the cabinet containing embalming fluid had been cracked open with a hammer. He'd found Sarah in the middle of the afternoon lying naked on the front lawn talking to her dead mother.

He tilts his head, shifting his perspective on the woman that lies before him on the table. It's taken eight hours to recreate her face. It's a work of art. Her head went through a windshield and still her husband insists on an open casket. People are crazy. He slides her into a refrigerated chamber, removes his latex gloves and switches off the lights, closing the door behind him.

On the first floor landing, he checks his watch. It's just past 8:00 P.M. and the house is dark.

"Sarah?" It's quiet. This time of night she's usually painting or preparing dinner. He wanders from room to room, then heads up to the second floor. A faint light shines from the third floor and he hurries up the next flight of stairs. At the top, the bathroom light is on, illuminating Sarah splayed on the floor.

"Oh God." He drops to his knees on the cold tile, feels her neck for a pulse. *No, no, no.* "House, call 911." Hands trembling, he opens Sarah's mouth to check her airway, then begins CPR. An operator takes the information as Steven stares at his wife. Lips blue, skin gray, chest still. Going through the motions helps him to stay focused until the EMTs arrive. Leaning heavily against the nearest wall, he holds his breath as they work. From three floors down a door slams and a voice echoes up the stairwell.

"Mom?"

Jonathan. The kid is going to blame himself. Footsteps pound the stairs and Steven stands in an attempt to block the view of the bathroom.

"What happened?" Annoyed, brushing hair out of his eyes, Jonathan strains to see over his shoulder. "Where's Mom?"

"The EMTs are working on her. I'm sorry, Jonathan. I think she's gone."

"What?"

"Gone." A flash of anger makes his voice louder than he intends. He gestures with his hand in the air. "Heaven. Angels. All that."

"Jesus Christ!" Jonathan pushes past him into the bathroom. "What happened?"

"The body's only meant to take so much."

"Oh my God." Jonathan repeats this over and over. He alternates between standing and bending over at the waist, hands on his knees.

Minutes tick by without words or tears as they watch the EMTs. At some point it occurs to Steven that they've stopped working on his wife and are packing up their equipment.

"That's it, then?" Steven says.

"I'm sorry, Mr. Hudson," says one of the EMTs. "We were unable to revive your wife. They'll be able to give you more answers when they do an autopsy. I'm very sorry."

Though he's seen it coming for months, he can't believe she's dead. He knows he should cry but he can't. A pang travels throughout his body and settles in his gut. It's a familiar, reoccurring dream. Never in his life did he think he'd be twice a widower.

Uttering something that sounds like a growl, Jonathan punches a wall. He flies down the stairs into his room and slams the door. Seconds later, angry, jarring music fills the air.

Steven asks the EMTs for a few moments alone with his wife. They disappear quietly down the stairs. Sinking down next to her, he strokes her cheek, her arm, touches her fingers. She's still warm. His thoughts rotate automatically through the process of death. Scan, wash, embalm, dress, makeup. Scan. He turns her forearm slightly to see the MedID just under her pale skin. Her 83 is a prize MedID number. A true tragedy that her addictive trait overshadowed everything she could have been. Such a waste. Someone could get out with an 83. Someone could have a good life with that number. It would be a waste to bury his beautiful Sarah with her good fortune. He closes his eyes against the sting of tears and holds her gently one last time.

THE HOUSE'S COOLING system works overtime against the oppressive heat. Still, Cole is warm. He pushes off the cotton sheet, all of their bedding in a bunch at the footboard. Ian is long asleep but Talia is up for her usual midnight feeding. Cole reads on his tablet as Lily feeds the baby in a rocking chair that creaks with each motion. The sound is distracting. He's been reading the same page for five minutes.

"What are you reading?" she asks.

"Nothing really." He sets down the device. "I'm tired of hearing about Hensley."

"People love a hero."

"He's far from a hero. Funny how that State House footage disappeared so quickly after the attack."

A doorbell sounds from his phone.

Lily's brow furrows. "You expecting someone?"

"No." He answers the call.

"Dr. Fitzgerald." It's the guard from the District 149 gate. "You have a visitor named Steven Hudson. He checks out. And he's clean, no weapons."

Strange. Why would he be here? It's been over a week since their meeting. Since then, Cole and Karen Riley have brainstormed options and performed just one MedID swap. The idea hasn't fully taken shape and is moving so slowly, he fears it may just disappear altogether. Because of that, he still hasn't mentioned it to Lily. She's still grieving Kate and she has enough on her plate just caring for the kids. If and when Project Swap becomes real, he'll tell her.

"Sir?" the guard says. "Do you want me to allow him entry?"

"Yes, thanks."

He feels Lily's eyes on him. From a heap of clothes on the floor, he grabs a T-shirt and a pair of jeans. Excuses run through his mind.

"Who is it?" Concern creases her face.

"It's just . . . the server's down at the hospital. They sent an intern to have me look over an urgent case for the morning."

"Can't it wait?"

"Apparently not. Being chief has its responsibilities, Lil." He kisses her on the head on his way out, adding, "It might take a while. Don't wait up."

Maybe Hudson's changed his mind. Then again, he could be here with a threat to expose the MedID project. Cole closes the front door and steps out into the thick air. Headlights brighten the pavement as a sleek Mercedes rounds the block and pulls up to the curb. A haggard-looking Steven Hudson gets out. His hair is wild, his button-down shirt wrinkled.

"This is a surprise," Cole says, shaking his hand.

"Yes, sorry." Hudson's eyes are tinged with red. "I'm not completely thinking things through tonight, but I wanted to talk in person."

"It's midnight."

"Life and death. Two things that know no time."

"True enough." Cole leads the way to the patio where they sit in adjacent deck chairs. Mercifully, the air stirs with a slight breeze. "I have to say, after our meeting I thought the conversation was over."

"As did I." Hudson's hand goes to his hair, his fingers lingering on the uncombed spikes. "But life has yanked the proverbial carpet once again and I've had to reevaluate."

"How do I know you're not here to entrap me?"

"You don't. But you know they did a full body scan on me at

the gate. Other than my manicured hands, I don't have any weapons on me."

"You could be recording this."

Abruptly, Hudson stands and raises his shirt, then drops his pants.

"Okay, okay."

Hudson tucks in his shirt, sits back down. "You did your homework on me. So I brushed up on you."

"What do you mean?"

"You're squeaky clean, Dr. Fitzgerald." Hudson cocks his head. "My sources found only one offense in your past. You smoked pot in your teenage years, when it was illegal, that is. Otherwise you appear to follow the rules."

"Appear is the key word here. That should benefit me in this endeavor." The excitement is back, a feeling in Cole's gut about this man. "Tell me why you're here."

Hudson hesitates and then leans in. "My wife died tonight."

"Oh, God." Not what he was expecting. The energy rushes out of Cole. "I'm so sorry."

The confident, jovial look Hudson often wears is gone. His face sags. "She was only forty. Beautiful, just . . . breathtaking sometimes. But lost. She walked around like she was missing a limb and she filled the emptiness with whatever she could get her hands on. Painting. Her children. Me, for a while." Absently, his hand fluffs his hair. "Her last vice filled her a bit too completely, I'm afraid."

"I don't know what to say." As many times as he's said the requisite words and consoled families at the hospital, each time is as raw, as unfair, as agonizing as the first.

"As she was dying I had this, this, moment of clarity, I suppose." Hudson's eyebrows rise, wrinkling his forehead. "I think I'm in shock, but if something good can come of this, she'd want that. I want it."

"I'm not sure I'm following."

"Sarah's MedID number is eighty-three. Was eighty-three. Would have been higher if it wasn't for her addictive genes. Luckily we wouldn't be passing on her actual DNA with the chip."

"Look, Steven, we don't know each other. But when I approached you, you had solid reasons for not doing this. This is clearly an emotional time—"

"Life is an emotional time, Doctor. And I know the emotions associated with mourning and loss more than most. Two weeks ago things seemed black and white for me. The reason I turned you down was my family. But losing Sarah changes everything. I'm left with a stepkid and a business. The kid and I have our differences but I'm all he's got now. I need to make sure he has a future. There are two sides to this war and I don't like either one of them. Perhaps it's time for the rest of us to have a say."

The words are familiar, they could be Cole's own. Inaction may be just as dangerous. Relative safety for a lifetime of limited, chaotic existence is no life. Still he needs to know what he's getting into. "You could lose everything."

"I'm aware."

The words hang in the air. Crickets chirp from the shadows, wind rustles leaves. Cole grabs them two beers and for a while they sit in silence, listening to the night. Finally, they move on to the business at hand, talking things around until words shape plans and calls to action.

The starlit sky is replaced by swatches of pink and orange.

When he realizes Lily will be getting up with Talia any minute, he shakes Hudson's hand and walks him to his car, one foot in front of the other, as people do in life, despite the shit life hurls at them. As much as Hudson's acquiescence is a victory, it's bittersweet. It will be a constant reminder that everything can be lost in an instant.

Chapter 34

SEBASTIAN IS ONLY allowed to watch the interrogation. It's 3:00 A.M. as he sits in the observation room, lights off, live video feeding into the smartwall across from him. Several hours ago agents in western Massachusetts captured one of the terrorists in the State House attack. The man had been identified by facial recognition from video at the scene. He'd been holed up alone in a cabin without electricity or running water. They transported him immediately to the Bureau's Boston office, and thus far he hasn't lawyered up. SAC Satterwhite agreed for Sebastian to be here on the condition that he remains unseen while Renner runs the interview.

In Kate's memory, he wears a simple black tie. He should be in there with Renner. Though if he were within arm's reach of the suspect, he couldn't guarantee self-restraint. Security performed a full body scan and confirmed that the man has no embedded electronic devices to allow his conspirators to track his movements. So far all they know is he's from Springfield, is twenty-two, and didn't graduate high school. His name is Michael O'Brien. And he killed Kate.

"There were forty-eight of you that day," Renner says. He sits across from the suspect, who is handcuffed to the table. "Eventually we'll find more of you."

Dirty blond hair hangs over O'Brien's eyes, which avoid the cameras. He's been given water but no food since they picked him up that afternoon after several tips and a chance speeding ticket.

"Looks like you escaped without any nasty side effects," Renner says. "Did the pyridostigimine bromide and atropine they give you take the edge off?"

O'Brien smirks.

Renner nods, matches his smirk. "Good for you. Unfortunately, for three of your fellow performers the antidotes didn't have the same effect." Upon his voice prompt, the adjacent wall fills with images of the three terrorists they found dead from sarin exposure. O'Brien stares at the table, refuses to look at the gruesome images. "Did you know that one of your associates accidentally killed his entire family? Yeah. The idiot left a vial of sarin at home. Little brother found it. Neighbors found them days later."

"People die," O'Brien says, meeting his eye. "This is war."

"Spoken like a true soldier. But of what army?"

O'Brien sniffs, almost a laugh.

"Did I say something funny?"

"This isn't going anywhere, man."

"You assassinated a presidential candidate, murdered twenty-three, and injured over a thousand. I assure you, Mr. O'Brien, this is going somewhere."

Too on edge to sit, Sebastian stands, crosses his arms, feels the tightness in his back. Renner's doing fine in there, but if they could do it together the two of them would crack this shitbag. Suddenly the door opens and Satterwhite enters the observation room. He holds up a hand in greeting. They regard the wall as Renner continues.

"What's the name of your organization?"

O'Brien's eyes flicker to the camera.

"BASIA? Sons of the Revolution?

O'Brien snickers. Sebastian balls his fists.

"Your parents bring you up in Patriot's Church?" Renner asks, taking a different approach. "Teach you all about Jesus and Armageddon?"

"You'd be surprised how my parents brought me up," O'Brien counters.

"There it is," Satterwhite whispers.

"Enlighten me." Renner reclines in his chair.

"Fuck you."

"You were following orders, we know that. But unless you tell us who plotted the attack, yours will be the public face of blame. No judge or jury will hold back a sentence of death—or life in a windowless cell. If you don't work with us, that's fine. We'll find the others, it's just a matter of time. Someone'll want a deal. It's a shame, though. Your family might get pulled into the fray." Renner strokes a hand in the air and new images fill the wall. "Your mother, Margie, dad Ronald. It would be a shame for your brothers and sisters to go down with you."

"They had nothing to do with this." A flash of anger as O'Brien sits up straighter.

"Families are broken apart every day. As you said, this is war. And when you're an enemy of the state, the world tends to be unkind to the families of terrorists."

O'Brien forgets his hands are cuffed, yanks them up as though he might lunge at Renner. He winces in pain.

Consulting his tablet, Renner adds, "I see that your mother is awaiting production of her 3D liver transplant. It should be finished any time now. Gosh, it would be a shame if something went wrong."

"That's bullshit, man."

"The world just isn't fair."

Silence. O'Brien sighs, shakes his head. "What kind of deal are you talking about?"

"Work with us, we'll work with you."

A tense minute passes. The suspect says, "You don't understand what you're asking."

"Then help me to understand."

O'Brien studies his filthy fingers. Finally he looks at Renner. "Are you ready to die?"

"Every day."

"That's good. You should be ready to die."

"Is that a threat?"

"Not from me."

"So, you'll work with us?"

A thoughtful nod. "Put it in writing. I want a lawyer, I want immunity and safe passage for my family to another country, with new identities, new MedIDs. They don't know I was part of this. You protect them or I'm out."

"All right." Renner cocks his head. "Anything else?"

"They'll find me. And I'm ready to die. But if you fuck this up, they'll kill my family. They'll kill you."

"It's in my job description. Must be willing to die. But we'll ensure your family's safety."

The suspect's eyes drift away. "Okay. And right now I want a pizza with everything on it. And a Coke."

Three hours later, with a contract in hand, Renner and Satterwhite sit across from O'Brien, who now appears more comfortable with his hands free in his lap. An empty pizza box and a can of Coke litter the table. Seated at his side is a public defender, Lydia Bessudo, a brunette thirty-something with a streak of gray running down the part in her hair. The district attorney himself is here, bloated and weary-eyed but seizing the high-profile moment. Everyone takes turns signing the agreement. In the observation room, Sebastian alternates between sitting and standing. He drank too much coffee and it swirls in his otherwise empty stomach. This moment has played out in his imagination a million times since Kate died. After Mitchell's praise of whoever was behind the State House attack, he can't help but have doubts.

The district attorney sets aside the paperwork and Renner produces a tablet from his briefcase, props it up and slides his fingers on the surface of the monitor. "This is the recording device and this meeting will be on official record." After reading O'Brien his Miranda rights, Renner calls out the names of all attendees, the date, the reason they are gathered. "Where do you want to start Mr. O'Brien?"

"I went to Exeter," O'Brien says. "Before they shut it down, I lived on campus. I wasn't a jock. Not much for English lit. But I got involved in some prowar student rallies. Followed some girl to a meeting one night and it changed my life."

"How so?" Renner asks.

"The meeting wasn't like the others. The message was different. The guy leading it was a junior councilman from New Hampshire. Name was Ramsey. At that point we'd all just gotten MedIDs, we were new to the system. I didn't really understand the potential of the biochip. I mean, the amount of control over citizens is extraordinary. But these idiots crying foul at their diminished civil liberties aren't seeing the big picture."

"Which is?"

"Eventually, everyone in this country will be healthy. Strong. No more chromosomal defects. No more obesity. No heart disease. There's no need for physical suffering anymore, once weaknesses are phased out. It's only a matter of time."

"A pure race."

"Yes." O'Brien leans his elbows on the table. "Ramsey said that the war has to go on. The government needs supporters who are for the war, not against it. By that point in time everyone in the room had lost someone to an attack. About six months before, my older brother died in a bombing at a concert in New York." Veins in his neck bulge, his face reddens. "These terrorists attack indiscriminately. They whine about their right to bear arms and their right to privacy. How they can't see a doctor for a year because of the health-care system. That they have a disabled kid because they didn't do the prenatal screening. So the fuck what."

A progovernment rant from a terrorist? An extremist on our side? Sebastian struggles to process the information.

Nonplussed, Renner continues. "So you joined this prowar group?"

"It was small then, and they were just starting to recruit. Thirty of us from Exeter joined up. But we're going on our eighth year. We must have a base of around ten thousand now."

"Let me get this straight," Renner says. "You're prowar, progovernment. And yet you assassinated a presidential candidate."

"Objection, move to strike from the record," Lydia Bessudo says. "There's no evidence that proves my client was the actual assassin. He was involved in the attack, which is all we're willing to state at this juncture."

"I'll rephrase," Renner says. "O'Brien, if you're a supporter of this war and the U.S. government, why were you involved in an attack to assassinate a presidential candidate?"

"I'm a soldier, sir," O'Brien says. "I just follow commands."

"Who's your commander?"

"Listen, I just do as I'm told."

Renner and Satterwhite exchange glances.

"You expect us to believe that you're blindly following orders?" Renner asks.

"I believe in the cause. I trust that the orders given to me are for the greater good."

"It sounds as if you were a founding member of a ten-thousand-soldier army," Satterwhite says. "If you expect us to hold up our end of the deal, you can't withhold details. Especially details such as the identity of your commanding officer."

No one speaks. O'Brien chews his lip, sips the dregs of his Coke, glances at his lawyer.

"You ready to continue?" Renner says.

"You're about to step in it, sirs," O'Brien says.

"I can't wait to hear this," Satterwhite mutters.

"My commanding officer is your commanding officer," O'Brien says.

"Clarify," Renner says.

"If I'm progovernment, doesn't it stand to reason that my commanding officer is the Commander-in-Chief of this country?"

"Objection!" Lydia leans in to her client to whisper something, but he waves her away.

"Are you . . ." Satterwhite sputters, his forehead wrinkled. "Are you implicating the President of the United States?"

"Implicating?" O'Brien makes a sour face. "I'm stating a fact. In the United States there is one Commander-in-Chief. And he is the only one I answer to."

"I strongly suggest you watch yourself," Satterwhite says. "Enough of this bullshit. You don't expect us to believe that the President of the United States has been issuing direct orders to your group to carry out terrorist activities?"

"Direct orders? No, sir. We don't meet with our commander. Not in person anyway. We have a handler who is given direct orders and relays them."

"I object to this line of questioning." Lydia slams her palm on the table.

"A 'handler '?" Renner repeats.

"He coordinates everything, ensures the details are in place. For the State House he put together the schedule. Arranged the costumes. Shipped us the chemicals."

Renner's eyes dart to the camera. Sebastian stands stock-still. *What the hell is going on?*

"We need a name," Renner says.

"All I got is one. Name, that is." O'Brien sits back in his chair. "Dash."

"Dash?" Satterwhite says.

"That's it," O'Brien says.

"How does he make contact, or vice versa?" Renner asks.

"He dead-drops instructions and burners. Occasionally, I get a piece of mail that I memorize and then burn. Look, I don't know who he is. Where he is. I just do what he tells me."

"Not anymore," Renner says.

Sebastian finds he's been holding his breath. Dash. Prowar. Progovernment. Under President Clark's command? Guy's got to be full of shit. It's impossible to gauge if there's any truth in his story. Sebastian shakes it off, runs his hands over his face. He'd had high hopes for tonight. Instead, he wasted hours staring at a man responsible for changing his life, unable to face him, and unable to avenge Kate's death.

Chapter 35

The autonomous rental car transports Steven and Jonathan three hours northwest of Boston. Steven thought it best not to bring the Mercedes, lest his license plate—HUDSONS—give away their identity. Reclined in his seat, Jonathan has slept most of the way. They're heading to one of many communities of outliers who eschew both society and technology while preaching nonviolence. This particular "town" he learned about from a client whose daughter moved here a few years ago. The people grow their own food, build their own homes, and rely on one another for all things. It's like a hippie commune. Or the Amish. Steven wonders if they have toilet paper and other trivial, yet civilized luxuries.

It's after dusk as the car steers down a long dirt road through the New Hampshire woods. The handgun stashed under his seat unnerves him, but he thought it best to bring it along. Despite their nonviolent beliefs, there could be survivalists among them that don't look kindly on strangers. Beside him, Jonathan stirs.

"'Morning, sunshine."

"You look ridiculous," Jonathan says.

Steven glances at himself in the rearview mirror. For the occasion, he borrowed from his mortician's arsenal and is wearing a strategically placed mole, glasses, and streaks of gray in his hair. With his advertisements everywhere, he can't take the chance someone will recognize him.

"Are you gonna tell me what we're doing here?" Jonathan asks. "Is someone dead?"

"Always."

"What's this for?" Jonathan holds a medical supply kit from the morgue.

"We're diversifying."

"You gonna kill someone?"

Steven coughs. "Let's hope it won't come to that."

The members of Project Swap, as they're calling the MedID effort, are eager but cautious. The MedID database is growing at a rate impossible to keep up with, on the recipient side, of course. Each of them—Cole, Karen, and Steven—already knew a handful of potential recipients. But the donor side is impossible to predict, and considerably slower to fill. While they all brainstorm how best to find donors, this is Steven's first foray into Project Swap's underground outreach. Donating Sarah's MedID had gone flawlessly, thanks to Karen, who connected them with a former patient desperate to shed her medical history. Something about the transaction helped Steven sleep better at night, as though he'd finally put Sarah to rest. Or maybe it was the opposite—giving her a second chance at life. At any rate, in an effort to find more donors, he had the idea to seek out those who might need money more than MedIDs.

Finally they pull into a clearing with a smattering of housing structures, built of wood with a roughness that brings colonial times to mind. Torchlight illuminates an area in the center with several long wooden tables. Adults are eating while children wander and play. Everyone turns and freezes in the headlights.

"This a family reunion?" Jonathan asks.

"There's that wit. But this isn't the time." He takes the Medical Record Scanner out of the kit. "We're here to run the MRS on these people. If they'll let us."

"Why?"

"Do you know your MedID number?" Steven asks.

"Yeah."

"As I recall, it's impressive."

"Eighty-six."

"Yes. You should live to be a hundred and ten."

"Why the fuck would I want to do that?"

"Why indeed." Frankly, he's just trying to keep his stepson alive long enough to see thirty. He wants him to wake up. To understand what life is like outside the wrought-iron gates of their estate. Since Sarah died, Jonathan disappears even more, gone for hours at a time to this new job of his. Steven works so much he can't keep tabs on him, and there has to be a level of trust between them. He hasn't pressed him for information, for fear of pushing him away. Perhaps if he gives the boy just enough freedom, he'll want to stay. Now that Jonathan is his sole responsibility, Steven has decided to try something drastic. Hopefully this plan works and Jonathan will start to understand the bigger picture.

"We're here to find clean MedIDs," he explains. "If we find anyone seventy-five or over, we can make an offer."

"What kind of offer?"

"Just follow my lead." He feels for the gun under his seat and retrieves it, tucking it into the back of his pants. Jonathan gapes. "At this point you listen. Ask questions later."

The humid night, and his nerves, make Steven sweat. He should have changed out of his suit, dressed casually. Jonathan is wearing ripped jeans and a T-shirt, a better fit for the circumstances. The slam of the car doors is jarringly loud in the silence. In the flickering light, children look up and people stop eating. A few men stand from the table, their puffed out chests and furrowed brows causing Steven to stop several feet away.

"'Evening!" Steven holds up a hand in greeting and hopes they can't see it shaking.

"What's your business here?" One of the men leaves his table, approaches while keeping a hand tucked behind his back. He wears army fatigues and waves of dark hair brush his shoulders, blending in with a beard that could use a trim. He stops about ten feet away.

"I'm sorry to interrupt your dinner," Steven says. "My name is Brandon Goodby and I've come to your community today with an opportunity."

"We don't need anything," the man says.

"We all need something."

"You've come to the wrong place. Move on."

"Please. I'm not selling anything. I'm not here to convert you or to disrupt your lives."

"Then what?" a middle-aged woman asks as she stands, hands on her hips.

He shifts on his feet, the metal against his back nudging him. He's sure the man he's speaking to is carrying a gun. Maybe they all are. Gravel crunches behind him. Jonathan. He shouldn't have brought him. This is a dangerous, poorly-thought-through idea.

Suddenly, he wants to turn and run. Instead he takes a deep breath and swallows. Make the offer and get out.

"Do any of you have clean MedIDs?"

"Fuck you, suit," calls a teenage boy. Kids around him laugh.

"What're you after?" asks the man in army fatigues.

"Fair trade," Steven says. "Clean MedIDs are a commodity. And I'm buying."

Murmuring from the crowd.

"Why do you want clean chips?" Army Fatigues steps closer. "You from the government? The FBI?"

"No. Not even close." Trying his best to look confident and relaxed, shoulders back, he approaches the man. "Listen, this isn't about me. This is about you. About all of you."

"As I'm sure you already know, we don't use MedIDs here. Some of us have them, some don't. Either way, it's not part of our life."

"Precisely. You don't need them. So I'm here to ask if any of you would be willing to part with any clean chips you might have."

"In exchange for what?"

"Five thousand dollars."

Army Fatigues laughs, then turns to the rest of the pack, who laugh along. "You want a spotless medical history for your own? For five thousand dollars?"

"Not my own, per se."

"This has been entertaining, but you need to go."

"I understand the choice you've made to live here. It's like one sane pocket of society while the rest of it has gone mad." The laughter stops. All eyes are on him. "You have your own doctors, teachers, carpenters, gardeners. You communicate face-to-face instead of multitasking with machines. And you're not doing anything illegal. It's quite brilliant, actually."

"But?"

"A lot of people can't get out. They're trapped, afraid to leave the only place they've known. And they have no hope because they're stuck with subpar DNA. Remember when people used to get organ donations, before the 3D printers? This would be just like that. What if you could donate a priceless organ to someone who would die otherwise?"

The night noises grow suddenly loud in the quiet. An owl, crickets, wind in the leaves.

"But someone would have our identity," the woman from earlier says softly.

"Your name," Steven says. "A DNA number that isn't really theirs. And if you truly have left the world in which all of that means something, do you really care?"

"For five thousand dollars?" Army Fatigues asks.

"Per MedID. Buys a lot in this economy," he counters. "Clothes. Supplies. Medicine."

The man looks up to the night sky. Steven chews the inside of his cheek. Finally Army Fatigues says, loudly enough for everyone to hear, "Everyone here is free to make his or her own decisions. But we've built our society on several rules. One of which involves material things and finances. Anything of personal value goes to the improvement and maintenance of our buildings, along with supplies for sustenance and anything else deemed necessary by majority vote."

Steven matches the man's volume, glances over his shoulder at the others. "So, ridding yourselves of your MedIDs would not only be a selfless act to help another in need, but it would also enable you to live here, longer and more comfortably."

A ripple of whispers spreads throughout the group. The children have gone back to playing, while the adults have abandoned their dinners.

"I got rid of my chip years ago," Army Fatigues says. "My wife, too. Kids never had them. But feel free to talk to the others." He steps aside, clearing the way for Steven and Jonathan.

The next two hours pass quickly. Jonathan trails wordlessly behind as Steven makes his way down the line of donors. As he preps and cleans the MedID Extractor, Jonathan reads from a tablet, asking each person a litany of questions that ultimately decides whether someone is a candidate. An ideal donor has no relatives, no pension, and no debts. As though, other than the MedID, he or she doesn't exist. Out of the hundred or so that live here, around thirty don't have MedIDs, and out of the remaining people there are twenty-three clean chips. Better than he anticipated. Eighteen of them are willing to part with theirs. Together they've earned ninety thousand dollars. Good thing, since he only brought a hundred thousand, an investment that will be repaid once recipient matches are found. When the equipment is packed up and almost everyone has gone inside for the night, Steven hands Army Fatigues a duffel bag, heavy with cash. They shake hands.

"Good luck," the man says.

"And to you," Steven says. "Though it doesn't seem like you need it. I have to tell you, I didn't know what to expect coming here. But it looks like you've figured it out. How to live like there's no war. No crumbling society. It's tempting to join you."

"The door is always open."

"Thank you. Maybe when our lives get less complicated."

"They are what you make them."

Indeed. The images of the night stay with him on the ride

home. Happy families, dining and playing under the moonlight, as natural as the forest that surrounds them. The car is quiet most of the way home, until finally Jonathan asks, "Why are you doing this?"

"Change of pace. Helping people live rather than burying them."

"Is it the money? Are you making money on this?"

The words sting. After everything they've been through, the boy still thinks he cares for no one and nothing. "I'm tired, Jonathan. Tired of losing. You should understand that. And if there's a way to give us a better future, I need to do something about it."

This shuts him up, but the air is like a wall between them. Exhaustion settles into Steven's bones and he craves his bed, where he can drift off to sleep, shutting out reality for at least a few hours. Perhaps dream of living under the stars.

Chapter 36

SEBASTIAN HAS SUCCESSFULLY secured his alias, Will Anderson, a place within Mitchell's world. He's an active member of Patriot's Church and is quickly becoming a friend to Taylor Hensley. They've had several easy conversations and trust between them is growing. She's an easy subject to study, finished with pretending and pretenses, after a childhood and early adulthood filled with both. As far as he can tell, she has no criminal agenda and there are no ugly truths lying just below the surface. Sitting across from her isn't difficult. She's beautiful. But just the thought sends a pang of guilt through him, as though Kate is in the room.

After the evening service, the congregation funnels out into a large conference room for coffee hour. Rubbing his eyes, he activates the camera in his smart lenses that live-feeds to a tech at the Bureau. He scans the crowd, allowing the facial recognition software to hone in on anyone of interest, anyone that might be of use in this operation. Sebastian watches as Mitchell seeks Taylor out in the crowd. Before long they're in a corner of the room talking, with Henry standing as a barrier. This "singling out" of Taylor by Mitchell has been going on since he arrived. Clearly Mitchell's after her bloodline, eager to see how he might use her.

Although she's vehemently opposed to her father and the government, Taylor doesn't seem to have any concerns or reservations about Mitchell and the rumor that he was behind the Planes, along with other attacks. Whenever Sebastian tries to lead the subject in that direction, she shrugs it away, saying only that after a while in life you have to go with your gut. He understands. Unfortunately, her gut has led her down a dangerous path.

He checks his watch. In an hour he's meeting with Renner. Taylor asked him for a ride home tonight after blowing a tire on her bike. Rather than intruding on their conversation, he waves to her. She sees him, nods. In ten minutes they're in his beaten-up Honda Civic cruising through Boston's South End, past endless abandoned brick town houses on their way to Milton. Their windows are open and Taylor swims her hand through the rushing air.

"The Reverend had you cornered tonight," he says.

"He does like to talk," she says.

"Did he share any earth-shattering revelations or gardening tips?"

"We were swapping recipes." He can hear the smile in her voice.

"Can you imagine the Reverend in a kitchen?"

"He does have a personal chef," she says. "But he's pretty normal, you know. Down-to-earth."

He glances at her. "Down-to-earth?"

She laughs. "I just mean he's interested in normal things. Home life. Education. Things we all care about."

"This is what you two talk about?"

"Yes."

Of course. The closer he is to her, the closer he is to Richard Hensley. Invite a lonely woman to dinner, ask about her child. Suck her in, emotionally. So far the surveillance hasn't revealed anything interesting or out of the ordinary either on Taylor or anyone in contact with her. She rarely uses her computer and isn't tech savvy. Without noticing, she opened a virus that allows him to monitor her usage and correspondence. Listening to the banality of her phone conversations puts Sebastian nearly to sleep, but the more time that passes, the more he's reassured that she's naive to any game her father or Mitchell may be playing. Sometimes he feels less alone when he's observing her. Momentarily, he'll lose himself in her world. A grin will unconsciously form on his lips when she plays with Sienna, or when she's singing to herself as though no one in the world can hear. He's come to know the way her body moves, her habits, her comforts. They're intimacies he's only known with Kate. So he reminds himself that he's doing this to avenge Kate, not to find her replacement.

"Does Reverend Mitchell ask you about your father?" he asks.

Taylor's hand stops moving outside the window. "You know I don't discuss him."

They drive through a row of green lights as he considers what to say next. Time is wasting with this silence.

"He's been hard to avoid, though," she says finally. "Now that he's running, he's everywhere. I can't walk outside my house without seeing his face or hearing his voice. And if he wins . . ."

"*If* he wins?"

"He'll be one of the most powerful men in the world. How can I avoid him if he's the President of the United States?"

"If Reverend Mitchell has a say in the future of our country, there may be some *restructuring*. Regardless of who wins the race."

"What do you mean?"

"I don't know his plan. But he's organized the massive training of thousands. He has followers and soldiers in every state."

"I thought BASIA used only cyber warfare."

"That's part of it." He considers his words carefully. "But we also do weapons training. Study how to engage enemies in different situations."

"What kind of situations?"

"They're vague. We're not given details. Not yet."

Recently, Mitchell had one of his techs create a fake chat room run by Patriot's Church. It's meant to be easily infiltrated, to mislead any agencies listening in. Renner has identified the stream and alerted the Bureau. The messages are code, though it may take weeks to crack..

"What do you think it all means?" she asks.

He pulls the car alongside the curb in front of her apartment building. "I just follow orders. Try not to second-guess my commanding officer. I believe in the cause, you know? Reverend Mitchell is a brilliant strategist—look at the Planes. He's—"

"Wait a minute." She unbuckles her seat belt and turns to face him. "There's no proof he had anything to do with that."

"Name one other person who has that kind of power, who's not in government? Someone who has the leadership, the organization, the mind? Thousands of militia groups out there wish they had a tenth of BASIA's strength and reach. There is no one else."

She shakes her head. "If there were proof, he'd have been arrested by now."

"There's no proof because everyone who would have testified died. Anyone who's changed their mind and left the church would think twice about giving him up. I'm sure he's quite thorough in covering his tracks. He can't lead a movement if he's imprisoned."

Her gaze wanders out the windshield to a news van that's stationed outside her apartment. "I know that we have to fight to change things. But, I'm sorry, Will. I don't believe Reverend Mitchell's responsible for murdering all those people. He's clearly powerful enough to incite a massive countrywide movement without the need to massacre people."

"We're at war, Taylor. This is Armageddon."

Avoiding eye contact, she gathers her bag and reaches for the door handle. He puts a hand on her arm. The warmth of her tanned skin surprises him. They both freeze. When she finally looks at him, he can't think what to say next.

"Thanks for the ride." Her voice is a soft rasp. She gets out and shuts the door.

He pops the trunk and goes to help her, but she's two steps ahead of him, already holding her bike.

"I'm sorry," he says.

"For what?"

"I don't know." He shuts the trunk. "I didn't mean to upset you."

"It's war, like you said. It's upsetting."

"The Reverend has a vision." He has to sell her on his loyalty to Mitchell. "We're there because we like his version of the world. We have to trust him on the journey there."

"You drank the Kool-Aid, didn't you?"

"Could've sworn I saw you filling your glass, too."

She smiles as she starts to walk away. "You want to come over for dinner tomorrow?"

"That'd be great." Finally, he's in. There's no room for error, he'll only get one shot.

The news van doors are thrown open and two men with video equipment jump out and rush toward Taylor. More gracefully than Sebastian would think possible, she waves and flips them off. The skirt she wears sways at the back of her knees. As she disappears into the building, the news crew heads in his direction. Quickly, he hops into the car and drives a few blocks away, until he's sure they didn't follow him. He parks under a broken streetlamp. On a handheld device from DARPA he launches the encoded surveillance app with live feed from Taylor's apartment. She puts her daughter to bed and organizes her graffiti gear. Using the Silent Talk app, Sebastian sends an encoded message to Renner, who tracks him via locator chip. In minutes they're parked down the street from Taylor's apartment in Renner's Bureau-issued black SUV, the windows tinted beyond legal limits.

TAYLOR REPLACES THE ruined bike tire and straps on her helmet and her messenger bag. She locks the door behind her, securing the sitter and Sienna. Balancing her bike, she navigates three flights of stairs and leaves through the back door, into the alley.

Outside, the air is still, peaceful. Her muscles burn as she pumps her legs through the darkened streets. Tonight she's scouting locations to find a good canvas for the church piece. She steers left then right, no clear destination.

Focused on the road ahead, she replays her conversation with Will. Talking about Mitchell had made her tense. And Will's hand on her skin was disarming. There's been no one since Mason. The moment he'd taken his hand away she craved it. Unfortunately, his touch was eclipsed by his words. Her stomach is still in knots. Of course she knows the rumors about Reverend Mitchell. But Will appears to have no doubt. In fact, he seems all for it.

She pedals faster. Does she care if the Reverend orchestrated the Planes? Regardless, millions have suffered and died as a result of her father's MedID law. Her early contribution to MedFuture eats at her, though it also fuels her. She thinks of the aborted babies. The would-be parents so distraught they commit suicide upon discovery they can only produce babies deemed less than perfect. Not to mention those under–75s, denied work, unable to feed and clothe their families. Her father has affected millions. Yes, it feels right to be standing on the other side.

A flash of headlights behind her prompts her to take the next right. After a block, she scans the buildings, sees she's just on the edge of Boston proper. On the deserted road, the headlights follow. Coincidence? Her father? She glances behind; the glare is blinding. She turns onto a street with abandoned warehouses. Spotting a potential canvas, she slows to a stop. A screech of wheels makes her jerk her head around.

Two cars swing around the block, neck-and-neck, speeding toward her. For the briefest moment she can't move, but then she whips the bike right, down a narrow alley. In seconds a loud scraping sound—metal against concrete—follows her. *Go go go. Shit shit shit.*

Air rushes off her body, siphoned away by the cars. They're close. She spots an opportunity twenty feet ahead. In a split second she steers her bike into a slight indentation in the alley, what used to be the back entrance to a restaurant. Her heart pounds in her ears.

A Cadillac sedan cruises past her. The driver slams on the

brakes just as a black SUV hits them at full force from behind. The SUV lands directly in front of her. She's backed up against the wall, her legs still poised over the bike. No escape. The driver's tinted window is close enough to touch. She holds her breath and glares directly at a face she can't see.

The Cadillac's tires spin in place until burnt rubber stings her eyes and nose. Both cars inch forward as the SUV pushes the Cadillac. The tail of the SUV passes her, giving her an exit. In seconds she's flying back down the alley, riding for her life. Her legs are numb and she's all but forgotten the reason she was here in the first place.

Sienna. What if someone came to the house after she left? Taylor pushes harder, faster. Within a few turns buildings are familiar again, a convenience store she frequents, a late night pizza place. In her mind, a flash of the SUV and the Cadillac. Neither car looked familiar and she couldn't see either driver. She didn't even see the plates.

Finally. She takes the stairs two at a time and rushes in, past the babysitter and into Sienna's room. Taylor climbs into the bed and curls against her daughter's small, warm body. Muscles shaking, mind spinning, she clings to this little person she loves more than anything in the world.

Richard recognizes the number that appears on his phone, but he can scarcely believe it. Except for the light emanating from the phone, his bedroom is pitch-black. He switches on the bedside light and unlocks the screen with his index finger.

"Is everything all right?" he asks.

"You're sick," Taylor says. "You've gone too far this time."

"Calm down. What are you talking about?"

"Watching me paint is one thing." Ragged breaths interrupt her words. "I'm used to my privacy being invaded. But when you come after me—for what? For supporting Mitchell? You want me dead because I'm not supporting your candidacy?"

"Hold on a minute—"

"You want Sienna to grow up without a mother?"

"I don't know what you're talking about, Taylor."

"Bullshit."

"Whatever you may think of my motives, I don't want you dead."

There's a brief pause. "Well, maybe your campaign or the party does. Maybe they're trying to do you a favor."

"Please, tell me what happened?" He throws off the covers and gets out of bed, his feet sinking into the carpet as he paces. It's impossible not to be angry with her, for shutting him out, for blaming him for all of her problems. But the sound in her voice is desperate. "Taylor?"

"I was out riding tonight and I heard cars behind me." Her voice quavers.

He closes his eyes, his mind creating images to match her story. She was in a dangerous part of the city, late at night, alone. A car chase, probably nothing more to it. She's being paranoid. When she finishes, he opens his eyes. He isn't going to win her back tonight.

"Sounds like you were in the wrong place at the wrong time," he says.

"They were after me. When I turned, they turned. It was obvious."

"What's obvious is that South Bay is a rough area. Somehow you ended up in the middle of someone's business. Drugs, probably. Could be anything."

"I'm not an idiot. I know those Cadillacs are owned by the Liberty Party."

"It's an American made car. Of course we have Cadillacs. Thousands of them are sold each year. Are you going to interrogate everyone with a Cadillac?"

"So you're denying it."

"Denying what?"

"Did you have me followed, or not?"

"In the past I've been guilty of, let's say, having a keen interest in your whereabouts. But I had nothing to do with this. It sounds like an unfortunate coincidence that you're overthinking."

"Excuse me?"

"It's understandable. You're feeling vulnerable and a little paranoid, thanks to the good Reverend Mitchell."

"I'm hanging up."

"The more he makes me out to be the one with twisted ideals, the more you'll run in his direction. He's a bright man."

"You almost had me killed tonight."

"I didn't. But you believe what you want to believe. You're consistent, at least."

"As are you."

"I didn't kill Mason, Taylor. And I didn't try to kill you."

"Just because you don't do the physical act yourself doesn't mean you're not responsible."

"If I killed everyone who isn't voting for me, I think someone would catch on."

"Stay away from us. No more visiting hours with Sienna."

"Taylor—"

She disconnects the call. Amazing. She accused, tried, and sentenced him, without an ounce of evidence. If Mason had survived, her life would be so different. Instead she'll never stop blaming him, as though he ordered the MedFuture bombing himself.

At his desk in the corner of the bedroom, Richard powers up his computer. He launches an application and four windows appear. In seconds live video streams: Taylor's living room, Sienna's bedroom, the view from the handlebars of Taylor's bike, now stored inside the entryway, and a perspective from the top of the building doorway, monitoring visitors.

In the dim glow of Sienna's nightlight he can see her shape under the covers, her many dolls and stuffed animals taking up at least half of the bed. Just knowing she's sleeping peacefully and safely makes him smile.

In the living room, Taylor stares at the main wall, plainly painted with homey words. She's wearing a mask over her nose and mouth and she's holding a spray paint can. Music must be playing. Her head is bouncing in time with something. Suddenly she attacks the wall, rages against it with her paint. She begins to define a form that he can't quite see. Probably going to be him on a crucifix, though that's not very child appropriate.

He rewinds footage from the bike cam. There's only one quick shot of a Cadillac speeding past her, pursued by a dark SUV. The images are too blurred to make out license plates. He shakes his head and crawls back into bed, though sleep won't come easily now. Tomorrow he'll need to inquire about the Cadillac with his staff.

Chapter 37

IN THE TEMPERATURE-CONTROLLED vault in Reverend Mitchell's basement, Jonathan performs the monotonous task of logging in MedIDs extracted from thousands of BASIA militants across the country. Of course, his own MedID is now among the biochips housed here. It pisses him off that it wasn't his decision. Pisses him off that they're bribing him. That someone is using his talents for their own agenda. But he can't risk Steven's safety. And he sure as shit doesn't want to go to prison. Now when he wanders the BASIA HQ or halls of the residence, he remembers the rumors, all the unsubstantiated news reports about the Reverend. He has to shake off the thoughts, though. Because whatever the bastard is up to, he's now part of it.

He scans and stores, scans and stores. Repeats. At least tomorrow will be more interesting when he goes back to BASIA HQ to work on something they call Operation Darkness Falls. From what he can tell, they want him to cause another power outage. Though he feels trapped working for Mitchell and Huan Chao, he's oddly relieved to have the distraction. Lately, without warning, flashes of his mom hit him through the day. Memories, her voice. It's been just three weeks since she died. Somehow he's kept going. He hasn't cried or done anything that resembles appropriate mourning, the kind he sees at the funeral home. Sometimes he catches himself thinking she'll still be there when he goes home.

"You hungry?" He jumps at the sound of Hannah's voice.

"Hey!" Wandering from the monitor, he meets her in the doorway. She smells like this flower his mother used to keep in a vase. He can't remember the name. The past few weeks, they talk or message every day. She's not what he assumed girls were like. She's interesting. Gets his jokes. Laughs like a lunatic. Every time they hang up or leave one another, he still has things he wants to say. "You shouldn't be down here."

"It's my house." She plays with a strand of hair, fallen free of its bun. "Want a snack?"

"Sure. Give me a few minutes." He concentrates on his task, occasionally glancing at the curves of her body, the way her shorts end a thread before it's inappropriate. She waits patiently, wandering the tight quarters, gliding a hand over the many containers.

"If my daddy could see all this." Her voice is quiet, as though she's talking to herself.

"What would he think?"

"I suppose he'd think everything's going according to plan."

"Whose plan?"

"God's."

"Hannah?"

"Um hmm?"

"Can I ask how your parents died?"

Sliding down the wall across from him, she sighs, closes her eyes like she's gone into a meditative state. "He was a pilot. Flew one of the Planes."

"The planes?"

"*The* Planes." She nods. "Mama couldn't take it. Had to join him. She went, peaceful enough, in the garage. Car running all night while we were asleep."

"Jesus Christ." He drops the scanner, fumbles to pick it up. His thoughts run to Steven, of his family that was killed on one of the fifty hijacked planes. Saliva fills his mouth and he fights the urge to hurl.

"Jesus Christ, indeed," she whispers.

"Did you know? I mean, the last time you saw him. Did you know your father was about to . . ."

Hannah stares at the ceiling. "He kissed me on the head that morning, hugged me tight, like always. Then he said, 'Hannah Jane, you take care of this family. God is coming soon and you need to be ready.' It didn't mean anything to me until after."

"You must've been shocked."

"Life is one long string of shocks, isn't it?"

"I guess."

"I never imagined I'd live in a mansion one day. Have so many brothers and sisters to take the place of the two I lost."

"What happened to them?"

"After my parents died, Charles sent for me. Child services took Joe, Jr. and Mary. My brother and sister."

He can't keep up with the details, they don't string together right. "What did your parents have to do with Reverend Mitchell?"

"They were loyal to the church. My father was a minister at our local Patriot's Church in Louisville."

"Are you saying that Reverend Mitchell and Patriot's Church were behind the Planes?"

"I didn't say that."

She's not denying it either. "Why didn't the Reverend take your brother and sister, too?"

Hannah turns her head and subtly wipes away a tear. "The plan was only for me to go."

"What plan?"

Avoiding his eyes, she says, "I found out after he died that my daddy promised me to Charles. Said I'd marry him when I came of age."

"What?" His face grows warm. "That's not legal. That's like slavery."

"It's no different from an arranged marriage."

"But, the Reverend's like a father to you."

"It's hard to explain. He's been kind to me. Generous. But I'm not fighting in the war. This is my duty."

"How does that serve God's cause? It sounds like you're living in a history book."

"In a way it is. Charles says Armageddon is the final chapter."

"So if it's the end, what's the point of marrying?"

"I don't know all the answers, Jonathan." She stands and places a hand gently on his arm. A smile spreads across her face. "I do know my stomach's growling, though."

He tenses at her touch but refocuses on the screen, finishes the final MedID entry. When she pulls her hand away the sensation of her skin lingers.

Their conversation sits like a stone in him. He can't shake it. They wander the hallways, create ice cream sundaes in the kitchen and eat them on the terrace. In the distance, fireflies put on a show over the darkened lawn. Jonathan's eyes float from one spark to the next. Hannah's voice is a constant stream but he's not even sure he's heard anything she's said in the last half hour. He glances over, watching as she absently rakes her hands through her hair.

"Beautiful night." Reverend Mitchell appears. He stands in the space between their chairs.

"I finished downstairs," Jonathan says, standing. "Did you need me to do something else?"

With a wave of the hand, the Reverend dismisses him. "It's late. You're welcome to stay the night here, or my driver can take you home."

"I should go." He gathers their plates from the table.

"Good night, Jonathan." Hannah's voice is quiet now, muted. Not the Hannah of a few minutes ago.

"'Night." Dishes in hand, he hurries into the kitchen and deposits them in the sink. He practically runs to the front door to find the driver. During the ride home, the Reverend dominates his thoughts, along with Hannah. And the Planes. His gut burns and he balls his fists until his nails leave indents in his palm. An arranged marriage for a ten-year-old girl. Her father must've been sick. And how could Reverend Mitchell marry a girl he raised as his daughter? When Jonathan finally peels down his covers and climbs into bed, his head is throbbing. It's impossible to sleep, and impossible to think of anything else.

Chapter 38

SEBASTIAN KICKS THE toe of his shoe against the black tar surface. It's Tuesday, his regular meeting time with Renner in Kenmore Square, on the roof of the old Boston University bookstore. The ninety-year-old red, white, and blue Citgo sign looms overhead, though it no longer illuminates the Boston skyline. He waits in windless summer night, squinting through the haze of clouds in an attempt to see stars. The roof door clangs open and Renner steps out, carrying two Dunkin' Donuts cups.

"Cream, no sugar." Renner hands a cup to him.

"Thanks. Any update on your CI?"

"Negative. But we did scan the footage from your lenses at the BASIA meeting. We ran facial recognition and came up with a few people that'd be easy to lean on. But they're not close enough to Mitchell. You know the Reverend's main bodyguard?"

"Henry."

"Right. Henry Keener. He's clean. But he's in the right position."

"He doesn't leave Mitchell's side."

"Except to go home. To his pregnant wife and three daughters."

"Hmm. I don't know. Guy's loyal to a fault."

"We need to test him, then. Apply a little pressure. See his reaction."

"We can't risk it. If he tips off Mitchell, the operation's over."

"Think about it."

"Okay. You got news on the Caddy plate?"

"Belongs to the Liberty Party."

The news settles. The night they basically saved Taylor's life, the Cadillac had lost them after several minutes racing around the city. "Shit. You sure?"

Renner nods. "There should be record of who signed it out. But we need a court order to gain access."

"Taylor's bad press for him. But Hensley doesn't want his daughter dead. So who in the party would target her?" From a call she made to the senator that night, Taylor believes her father was involved. It doesn't ring true, though, regardless of their history. If anything, Hensley's protective of her.

"Your phone on?"

"No."

Renner strolls to the edge of the roof. "I got a contact in Transportation says we should be looking closer to home."

"What does that mean?"

"Maybe the Bureau. Someone in the administration."

His thoughts are tangled, trying to make sense of this. As he steps next to Renner, an ambulance siren pierces the air. "Why would anyone go after the presidential candidate's daughter? Satterwhite gave us a direct order to protect her. Anything happens to her, it's our jobs."

"I'm telling you, we put in a court order for the plate, we're gonna be shut down."

"We don't have any choice. Someone's gone rogue. Someone inside. Shit, I thought Mitchell was the enemy." And he is. Mitchell's next mission is ramping up, the date and details yet to be revealed. The BASIA soldiers are studying martial arts, firearms, and cyber warfare. Once a week several of them, Sebastian included, practice driving at high speeds on closed courses constructed to approximate a grid of city streets. It's not comforting.

"So, Satterwhite called me into his office this morning." Renner shuffles his feet. "Talked about the suicide bomber on that transit bus in Houston yesterday. He wants our focus to be on counterterrorism in the future, not the past."

"What the hell does that mean?"

"He pulled me from the State House attack. Said they have enough resources on it."

The image of their State House suspect surfaces in his mind. "What about O'Brien? He's still in custody. He gave us Dash, we have leads to follow—"

"O'Brien's dead."

"What?"

"Somehow he got a razor blade. They found him this morning."

"Goddammit!" With a sudden burst of energy, Sebastian throws his cup across the roof, coffee splattering across the tarred surface.

"They're checking the security tapes to find out who might've slipped it to him." Renner shakes his head. "And Satterwhite's full of it. No one else is investigating the State House."

"The past predicts the future. Satterwhite can go screw. It doesn't end here."

The words settle in the air, fill the space between them. Renner looks back at the Citgo sign. "I remember going to night games at Fenway as a kid. The whole drive in from Framingham I'd be watching for this sign. I knew as soon as I'd see it that we'd arrived. The Sox were just around the corner."

"Sounds like a beautiful childhood," he says. "So. We don't let this go, right? You in, Renner?"

Just the slightest pause from his partner. "Yeah, I'm in."

"Far as I'm concerned, we just got a little further in this investigation."

"How do you figure?"

"Our only State House witness died under our watch," he says. "Let's assume it wasn't a suicide. Now the Bureau's ordered us *not* to investigate one of the most important attacks in the history of this country, in which a presidential candidate was killed. Not to mention, the one name they don't want us looking into."

"Right, Dash," Renner says. "We find their identity, maybe we find out who's behind the State House."

"The three aren't tied, necessarily."

"You realize we'll be suspended if Satterwhite finds out?"

"Depending what we find out, that may be the least of our worries."

"Touché." Renner holds up his coffee in a mock toast. "You're missing your coffee right about now, aren't you?"

"Maybe." They stand in silence, gazing at the tops of brownstones. There's an answer they just haven't thought of yet. Maybe it's in the encrypted files that Mitchell is having him send to their soldiers around the country, codes that mean nothing to him but take shape on the other end of the protected chat. "Have you had any luck deciphering the BASIA chat?"

"We're close." Renner heads toward the exit. "Techs think they can crack it in the next twenty-four hours."

"Good. We need a break."

"I don't have a good feeling about any of this."

"Me either."

The door slams shut. One last time, he looks skyward in another vain attempt to see stars. He slips a hand in his pocket and fingers Kate's ring. The cool platinum and rough diamond edge always anchors him, a solid reminder that everything he says and does is an attempt to gain justice for her. It won't bring her back, but it might give him some peace. It's the best he can hope for.

Chapter 39

IT'S JUST AFTER midnight as Cole sits across from Karen and Steven at Steven's kitchen table. They drink beer and take turns lobbing ideas and debating issues. In the few weeks since they started Project Swap, they haven't gained much traction. For his part, Cole's been discreetly researching his Harvard Medical School network, searching for signs of government mistrust. He bought a separate device to use when contacting colleagues, and tosses burners after only a few uses. But getting people to talk about their fears, their real beliefs, is near impossible. He doesn't want to come on too strong. The best way to unearth honestly is often at the bottom of a wine bottle in a dim bar. And even those meetings hold no guarantees.

Steven's had some luck with technology/government outliers needing money more than MedIDs. And from a list of patients she's treated, Karen created a database of potential donors and recipients based in New England. At this point they're mired in logistics and contemplating process. After working a twelve-hour shift at the hospital, Cole wishes he had more to contribute. But he's been around and around these problems and the danger involved. He's afraid their movement may end before it begins.

"How about an orphanage?" Karen offers. "No inheritance, no familial issues."

"Are you suggesting we kill children to save other children?" Steven asks, arching an eyebrow.

"I'm saying that if anything ever happens at an orphanage—a bomb, a natural disaster—it would be a horrific stroke of luck for our purposes." Karen runs her fingers over her beer bottle, making streaks in the condensation. "The demand for clean MedIDs for children is overwhelming."

"Maybe Steven's on to something," Cole says. "Boston's lost half its citizens to the countryside in the past ten years. People who left the IT and financial sectors are getting their hands dirty now. Sharing crops, raising animals. And those areas are always in greater need. They have maybe one or two doctors in their communities and the people barely have enough money to get by."

Karen takes a thoughtful sip of beer and adds, "And they're off the grid."

"The risk is encountering violence," Steven says. "Last week I backed out of a camp with my hands held high. Felt like I was in a movie."

"What else could we offer?" Cole asks. "If they don't want or need money, and they've moved away from technology, what else could sway them?"

The room falls silent. Cole takes a swig of beer and stares at a picture of Steven's family, stuck to the refrigerator by a magnet. He thinks of Ian and Talia. The more he considers the risk he's taking, the less he wants to include Lily. Putting them both at risk is unfair, irresponsible. The least he can do is protect her from a charge of treason.

"I know where you can get clean MedIDs." From the hallway shadows, Steven's stepson, Jonathan, emerges.

All heads swivel in his direction. He's a handsome kid, in need of a haircut. His pale skin contrasts with his black outfit of jeans and a T-shirt. *Holy shit. How much has he heard?*

"When did you get in?" Steven says.

Jonathan ignores him, shuffles to the refrigerator. He grabs a beer and hops up on the kitchen counter. Between sips, his mouth opens and closes as he plays with a tongue piercing.

"Jonathan, meet Doctors Fitzgerald and Riley. Doctors, this is my stepson, Jonathan."

"What's up," the boy says.

"Isn't there somewhere you'd rather be?" Steven asks.

"Nope. I'm pretty sure I should be right here."

This kid could undo them all. But the carrot he's dangling can't simply be left there. Finally Cole says, "I'll bite. What was that you were saying, Jonathan? About knowing where to find MedIDs?"

"I know where there's a stash." His head jerks, tossing the hair out of his eyes. "About ten thousand, give or take."

Cole narrows his eyes at the kid, trying to get a read on him. Smudges of purple underline his dark eyes. Two facial piercings, though piercings don't make him untrustworthy. Still, Steven's told him the kid is troubled. Into God knows what. And he's probably doubly lost since his mother died. Too unstable to get pulled into their project.

"Where does one get ten thousand MedIDs?" Karen asks.

"Let's just say they're up for grabs." Jonathan shrugs. "No one's using them. They've sort of been given up."

With a loud sigh, Steven stands and strolls to the refrigerator. "What are you into, Jonathan?"

"Do you want them or not?"

Bottles clang together as Steven retrieves another round. The room is silent with unasked questions. Everyone waits, sips his or her drink.

"I imagine there's a price to this generosity of spirit," Steven says.

Jonathan drums his fingers on the granite countertop. "What are ten thousand lives worth?"

"There it is," Steven says. "Your mother would be proud."

"Fuck off." Jonathan hops off the counter and begins to make his way out of the kitchen, down the hall. "If you have another offer, by all means."

When his footsteps have ascended the stairs and a door slams, there is a collective exhale from the group.

"What just happened here?" Karen says.

"Was that a legitimate offer?" Cole asks.

"I wouldn't know." Steven takes a long drink. "But I have a confession to make. You know my . . . let's call them, community outreach excursions? Well. I've been taking him with me, looking for MedIDs."

"What the hell?" Cole grips the tabletop. "That could jeopardize everything! You can't make unilateral decisions like this."

"Cole's right," Karen says. "Teenagers are unpredictable and self-centered. No offense to Jonathan."

"You're right." Steven holds his hands up in surrender. "I'm sorry. I should have asked. But he's been with me for ten years and this is his home. I'm all he has left since his mother died. I need him to see that he has options in life, and that he can make a difference. He's old enough to help and young enough to still need some direction. I believe we can trust him."

"Dammit, Steven, that was reckless." Cole shakes his head. "I haven't even told my wife! You yourself have said Jonathan isn't stable. And somehow he has access to ten thousand MedIDs?"

"Why didn't he tell you this when you were out combing for MedIDs?" Karen asks.

"I don't know." Steven's face sags. "Would have saved a lot of time, though. I imagine he was gauging if he could trust me. But his offer means that he's willing to put himself on the line. Wherever he's getting these MedIDs, there's a risk. Probably a great risk."

"And are you willing to risk him?" Cole asks.

"He's almost eighteen and certainly seems willing. He's already put himself in precarious situations. Illegal, illicit dealings, who knows. I'd rather have him on our side. To know how he's spending his days."

"Where could he have access to that many MedIDs?" Cole searches out the darkened window for an answer. "Hospitals. Funeral homes. The government. Another group like us."

"Doubtful. All of that," Karen says.

"The kid's handy with a computer," Steven says. "Maybe he stumbled on a stash electronically. Maybe he's found an online source."

"Suppose it's true. For the moment, let's ignore how he's getting them." Cole stands and paces around the kitchen. "Ten thousand chips is our equivalent of venture capital. We could hit the ground running and our network would grow exponentially."

"Let's at least talk to him," Karen says.

Cole looks pointedly at Steven. "We're all adults here. We know what's at stake. But can we expect a teenager to grasp the consequences we're facing? What if he can't keep his mouth shut?"

"If there's one skill he's honed, it's keeping his mouth shut. But I should talk to him alone. Regardless of our history, he doesn't really want to hurt me."

A full moon illuminates the pathway for Cole when he leaves. Jonathan's offer sits uneasy in his gut. As he navigates the back roads to District 149, their conversation plays in his head. He tries to imagine where this kid could get his hands on that many chips. It can't be legal and is likely dangerous. But there's an element of darkness they all need to get used to. Quickly.

Chapter 40

WITH THE TOUCH of a finger, Steven moves two million dollars from his business account into his Swiss bank account. Next he moves the same amount into an account in the Cayman Islands. The access codes are in his personal vault, hidden behind a false wall in the morgue. And for ultimate security, he's requested an in-person retinal scan in order for any money to be removed or transferred. He looks forward to visiting both places.

Also in his vault, one floor below where he sits in his home office, is his cash reserve. That is strictly for emergencies should Project Swap's actions trigger any suspicions. Moving the bulk of his money offshore helps to settle his nerves.

The slam of the front door pulls his attention from the screen. Jonathan. After what happened at the Project Swap meeting, he needs to talk to him. The pad of footsteps through the house leads Steven into the kitchen, where he finds Jonathan's head buried in the refrigerator.

"I'm afraid it's been a while since I've done food shopping," he says. "You might be able to pull together a condiment sandwich."

"We still have some frozen meals." Jonathan opens the freezer and pulls out a container of lasagna, one of many graciously delivered after the funeral.

Sarah would have gone crazy to see Jonathan's hair like this. It's like a tic, the way he tosses his head to get the brown mop out of his eyes. As Steven considers what to say, he takes a bottle of red wine from the rack and uncorks it.

"So." He eyes the boy. "Ten thousand MedIDs?"

"Um hmm." Jonathan watches the food in the microwave.

"Imagine my surprise."

The boy shrugs.

"What are you up to?"

"None of your business."

"Isn't it? Your actions effect this family. What's left of it. Regardless of how you might feel, I am your family."

"Whatever. If you want them, let me know. If not, I'll move on."

"'Move on'? Do you understand the consequences you'll face if you're caught?"

Jonathan's face contorts in anger. "You're a hypocrite! You're in the market for them. You're out bartering for clean MedIDs. What if you get caught? What happens to me? What happens to your little empire of death here?"

"Fair enough." He retrieves two wineglasses from the cabinet. He pours generously into one and hands the other with a lesser amount to Jonathan. "Sit."

At the kitchen island, they sit on bar stools. Jonathan is tentative with his wine, while Steven takes a few rather large gulps. He's never had a "real" conversation with his stepson. Man-to-man, with the potential to shift the ground beneath them.

"If I'm going to be honest with you, I want the same in return," Steven says.

"Fine."

Because context is everything, he starts at the beginning. He talks about losing his first wife, his son and daughter, the day the Planes Fell. How he threw himself into his work, then met Sarah. About how politics never mattered to him until he watched lives spiral because of the MedID law and the war. Sarah had felt trapped, unable or unwilling to go beyond their front door, the only way out was to get high. When she died, she took his complacency and left him with a need, a drive to change things. Not by joining the fanatics, and not by giving in to the government. A new movement. About family. About helping people to live the lives they want to live, wherever they want to live them. Jonathan's face softens. For the first time in their history it feels like he's actually listening.

"What do you want with all the MedIDs?" Jonathan asks.

"If they're clean, we'll find matches—people looking to swap out their less than stellar MedIDs—and we'll transfer the new MedID to that person."

"So you can only use MedIDs that are over seventy-five?"

"Yes."

"What if you get a seventy-five with a shit medical history?"

"Doesn't matter. Someone might have post-traumatic stress disorder, depression, what-have-you, but they could live to be a hundred because of low cholesterol and strong genes. The MedID number is the potential for wellness."

"Why did you bring me? To the camps?"

"You've lived with me since you were eight, and still I don't know what side you're on."

"I'm on my own side."

"You've been out a lot lately. You brought that girl over, the redheaded one. Shannon?"

"Hannah."

"Right. And now you're offering up black market MedIDs. I think it's your turn for some honesty."

Jonathan rotates his wineglass, swirling the burgundy liquid. "You know my job?"

"I know you have one. You've been rather vague about it."

"It's . . . it's, uh, this antigovernment group."

Steven's heart beats faster. "What group?"

Shifting in his seat, Jonathan's eyes meet his. "BASIA."

The word penetrates him, sends a chill through his bones. Without thought, Steven throws his glass across the room. Glass shatters. Pink streaks mar the walls in an abstract piece of art. Looks like a piece Sarah might have done.

"How could you?" he shouts. "Don't you know? Haven't you heard the rumors?"

Jonathan stands, takes a few steps backward. "I didn't join BASIA. I just took a job. They needed a tech and Hannah—"

"Hannah?"

A flood of red colors the boy's cheeks. "She had nothing to do with this."

"What is your job exactly?"

"I log in MedIDs to their storage vault."

"That's it?"

"And. Shit. And they have me hacking."

"Hacking what?"

"Power grids."

"Power grids! Of course! Your specialty. But they knew that, didn't they?"

Jonathan rubs his hands over his face. "Apparently."

"Mitchell killed my family, Jonathan."

"How did he get away with it?"

"Because all of the witnesses and low-level conspirators died in the Planes! Because Mitchell's somehow convinced millions of people that Armageddon is here and if you're not with him, you're condemned to hell. Because he provides what looks like a safe haven for anyone who's lost family in this war. He's a psychopath."

"I just thought it was a job," Jonathan mumbles.

"It's just a job. He's just a reverend. And Hannah's just a girl."

They sit motionless. Steven's mind is frayed, his body shaky. Anything he planned to say went out the door with this admission.

After a minute Jonathan says, "The MedIDs. The ones I have access to."

"Whose are they?"

"Everyone in BASIA." He rolls up the left sleeve of his shirt and points to a minuscule scar revealing that his MedID has been removed.

"He makes you take them out."

"I have access to all of them."

"How?"

"Don't worry about it."

"I won't put you in danger. Just get out. Leave that psychopath while you still can."

"But what if you're caught with your little side business?"

"There's a plan in place. If the situation becomes dangerous, we leave. You and I. Investors are ready to snap up Hudson's. We'd need forty-eight hours to get out."

"You've thought of everything."

"I hope so. Let me ask you something. What changed? Why are you suddenly willing to steal from Charles Mitchell?"

Jonathan takes the bottle of wine and refills his glass. "I learned something about him that I don't like."

"Only one thing?"

But the boy looks quite sad and doesn't offer more, so Steven leaves it alone.

Chapter 41

"TELL ME THE schedule again?" Richard says. His campaign team is piled into a stretch suburban cruising west on the Massachusetts Turnpike.

"First, the orphanage in Waltham," Carter says, consulting his phone. "Then at one there's the League of Women's Voters lunch. And tonight it's the National Institute of Health dinner."

"Stay on point," Kendra interjects. "No going off-script."

"Yes, yes," Richard says. "Where's David today?" His vice presidential running mate, David Glickman, is a bit off-beat, but he has a following and solidifies them as a team.

"He's at a rally in Wisconsin," Carter answers.

Skimming her tablet, Kendra reports, "Your response to the Houston bombing bumped up your polls in Texas. You came off very strong and reassuring."

"Easy to say the right things. Harder to execute them."

A low intermittent hum announces an incoming call. Carter checks his jacket pockets and pulls out two phones. He answers one. "Richard Hensley's line. Yes, of course." He passes it to Richard. "It's the President. They're connecting you."

Richard straightens. He puts the phone to his ear and hears a click.

"Richard," President Clark says.

"Hello, Mr. President."

"Great interview last night."

"Thank you, sir. I—"

"Listen, Richard, I'm a family man. But when I took the oath of this office, the citizens of this country became my extended family. It's not just my wife and kids anymore."

"Of course."

"I'm going to be frank here. Your daughter could cost you the election."

"Taylor?"

"As you know, her new affiliation with Patriot's Church is well-known. Any day now every news analyst and media outlet will have the headline 'Hensley in Bed with Enemy Number One.' Regardless of the truth behind your relationship, the public sees black and white. The only question they'll care about will be: how is it that the President of the United States has a daughter who is a member of this country's number one terrorist organization?"

"I can't control her actions, Mr. President."

"She's made herself an enemy of the state. You can't have anything to do with her."

"Actually, we're not on speaking terms."

There's a beep on the line and suddenly he hears his own voice:

"Sounds like you were in the wrong place at the wrong time,"

"They were after me. When I turned, they turned. It was obvious."

"What's obvious is that South Bay is a rough area. Somehow you ended up in the middle of someone's business. Drugs, probably. Could be anything."

"I'm not an idiot. I know those Cadillacs are owned by the Liberty Party."

Stunned, his mouth parts to form some kind of a response, but nothing comes. It's a recording from the night Taylor called to accuse him of trying to kill her. They're monitoring his communications. He supposes he shouldn't be shocked.

"Recognize that?" President Clark says.

"She's my daughter, sir."

"A minute ago you lied about your relationship with a known enemy."

Kendra is staring at him, her fingers paused midair over her phone. Dammit. He's been faithful to the Liberty Party for thirty years. Why would they doubt him now? Finally he says, "I forgot she called."

"Of course. Still, it's a concern. Imagine if this gets out."

"Yes. It wouldn't look good."

"If you want to repair your relationship with her in eight years, by all means. But today, you need to look at her as though she's an ordinary citizen who poses a threat. And we can't have one citizen derailing our efforts. We won't let it happen, Richard."

"I understand." But does he? What does "we won't let it happen" mean, exactly?

"I'm glad we're on the same page. What would a race be without hiccups along the way?" There's a trace of a gloating in the President's voice.

"Mr. President, if you don't mind me asking, is there a chance Taylor was right about the Cadillac following her?"

"Excuse me?"

"The party's efforts to keep the campaign on track have been comprehensive, understandably. I'd like to know, was the Cadillac that followed Taylor a Liberty car?"

"I wouldn't know, Senator. Of course our intelligence agencies use their resources in the interests of this government and its citizens. But to the best of my knowledge, we're not mowing down constituents in alleys."

"Of course not. My apologies."

"Do well, be well, Richard."

"Yes sir."

Heat radiates from Richard's ear as he pulls the phone from it. Kendra's eyebrows are arched in anticipation. Carter hasn't looked up once from his phone.

"What the hell was that?" Kendra asks.

"I need to cut off Taylor completely. It's too damaging to the campaign."

"We know that," she says. "What's changed?"

"She called me. They heard the conversation."

Kendra blows air out her lips, shakes her head.

"Carter, get me the sign-out database for Liberty Party campaign cars," he orders. "I need the log for last week."

He may not be able to speak with Taylor, but perhaps he can still protect her and Sienna.

Chapter 42

Blood is spattered on Cole's scrubs, on sheets and the floor. One of the last standing arenas in the city, the Boston Pavilion, had a sold-out concert tonight. Because venues are a high-risk target for anyone trying to make a point, shows are rare. But with high security and extra precautions, on occasion some people take the chance. It's a shame so many did tonight.

As he studies the smartwall display of ER bed assignments, Cole voice-activates the system. Names on the monitor change or move from one area to another. He never fails to note patients' MedID numbers. The sheer number of people without clean numbers is overwhelming. Can Project Swap even make a dent? Is this venture worth risking everything? He wonders if another group is out there somewhere, attempting the same thing. They could pool their resources. At night, he can't sleep. He wanders into the nursery and watches the soothing rise and fall of Talia's back in her crib. Four months have passed and she's just weeks from having her own MedID implanted.

It's four in the morning. All but one of the thirty-two survivors have been dispatched to recovery rooms or the O.R. Karen joins him for the last victim of the shooting who suffered only a minor wound. Behind the curtain, the patient is asleep. Cole scans the chart: Sean Cushing, MedID number 78, aged forty. No genetic markers of particular concern. No history of significant illness. Karen lifts the johnny for him to inspect where a bullet grazed the right leg.

"Lucky guy," he says. "Another centimeter and the bullet would've done some damage." He tips the tablet with the patient's record so that Karen can see it.

"But look at that." She gestures to deep purple bruising up and down his legs, inconsistent with his wound.

"Maybe he fell in the chaos. There must've been a stampede to get out of there."

"Maybe." Her brown eyes narrow as she scrutinizes his chart. "That's strange."

"His CBC?" He glances at the numbers. "He's anemic. Makes sense. He's lost a fair amount of blood."

"But his platelet count. Is his blood clotting?"

"Hmm." Cole gently peels back the blood-saturated gauze covering the wound. It gapes open, a rivulet of blood pooling on the paper beneath him. "Thrombocytopenia maybe. Let's run a test."

Sean Cushing stirs, groans as his eyes flutter open.

"Mr. Cushing, I'm Dr. Fitzgerald, and this is Dr. Riley." He moves to the head of the bed.

"Hi," Cushing says. "Look, I'm fine. Can I get some pain meds and get scanned? I've been here like eight hours."

"It's not on your medical record," Karen says. "But are you on blood thinners?"

"A bullet just ripped into me," Cushing says. "I'm pretty sure that's why I'm bleeding. How about you sew me up and we call this a day?"

"So that's a no," Cole says. "Do you have a history of bleeding?"

"What? No." Cushing tries to sit up in bed, grimaces, lies back down.

"Do you work with any specific chemicals or metals?" Karen asks.

"No." His tone is somewhere between bored and sarcastic. "And no, I don't have fevers or kidney trouble."

Cole and Karen exchange looks. He says, "So you've been through this line of questioning before?"

"Can I just get some stitches and blow?"

The wound sealant should have worked, yet he's still bleeding. Cole scans the history. Clean MedID. Annual physicals indicating normal lab results. Something's missing. He could have leukemia, a bacterial infection, or a complication with his liver. Maybe these are new symptoms. Or maybe he's lying.

"Dr. Riley will stitch you up," he says.

Karen pulls up a stool and positions herself at eye level with the wound. She sprays the area with a topical anesthetic, but pricks the skin before it takes full effect. Cushing groans.

"Help me understand something," Cole says. "You have a spotless medical history. Clean DNA. There's bruising that might be explained by tonight's incident. Or not. Is there anything you can add? Something that's not on your chip?"

"I'm a private person, Doc."

"It's interesting." Cole traces his finger over the screen. "You have no record of any prescriptions in the past five years. Looks like you're an exceptionally healthy individual."

Cushing taps his temple with his index finger. "Health is a state of mind."

"And if we ran more tests? Would the results show that you're as well as your MedID file reads?"

"Why are you busting balls? Do you really care about my personal well-being?"

Positioning the syringe, Karen injects pill-sized sponges that will seek out and adhere to the source of the bleeding, stanching it. Cushing winces. The room is quiet with unease as they wait. Finally the bleeding stops. From behind the curtain, Cole produces a wheelchair.

"You look pale," he says. "Let's get you some fresh air."

"I just wanna go home, man."

"We'll scan you out as soon as you take a quick detour." Cole nods to his phone on the side table. "Leave it."

Karen wheels Cushing through the ER, passing several colleagues who are too exhausted at this hour to take notice. Cole leads them to an exit in back of the building. The night air is ripe as they stop by overflowing garbage bins.

"Between the trash and the piss smell, I can tell you're trying to impress me," Cushing says.

"We don't know each other," Cole says.

"Though I'm clearly at a deficit."

"I'm not out to prove that you have sepsis or leukemia or are in liver failure. What I really want to know is, how did you get a clean MedID?"

Cushing sniffs. "Luck?"

"Maybe. Or maybe you know how to manipulate the system."

"This is bullshit." Cushing tries to stand but he's weak and settles back into the chair. "Take me back. Scan me out."

Always direct, Karen says, "Maybe you know someone who cleans MedIDs as a hobby?"

"Oh, I get it. You're progovernment, rah-rah-who-needs-civil-liberties assholes. You gonna call the Feds? Based on a hunch?"

Subtly, Karen nods to Cole.

"Like I said, we don't know each other," Cole says. "Maybe we're after the same thing."

This disarms Cushing, who is momentarily speechless. "Then what do you want?"

"What if I could get you the treatment you need. For whatever disease or infection you have. Off the record. Privately. At no cost."

"Why would you do that?"

"I want to know how you have a clean MedID."

Cushing looks back and forth between them, glances at the building. "You recording this? There cameras out here?"

"It's just us. This isn't a planned meeting. It's a chance meeting."

"How do I know you're not full of shit?"

"You don't. But then again, I don't know that I can trust you either."

"Trust me with what?"

"You first."

Everyone waits. Finally, Cushing speaks, almost whispering. "I used to work for the MedFuture Corporation. Started there maybe ten, twelve years ago now. Right before the biochip went public."

"What did you do for them?" Cole asks.

"I was a programmer. Software design and management."

"So you know your way around a MedID chip?"

"You could say that. I learned how to program and finesse the codes. Then I moved up and taught the newbies."

"But isn't the basic information on the chips hardwired? Unalterable?"

"Nothing's perfect."

"So you know how to adjust the encrypted information? Change numbers? Erase medical history?"

Cushing's eyes dart to Karen.

"Neither of us has any interest in exposing what you share," Cole says.

Firmly, quietly, she adds, "I don't believe in the system. Never have."

"Huh." Cushing takes a minute. "And I get what? Private health care?"

Cole nods. "Tell us more."

"All right. Look, the system isn't perfect. With millions of citizens, the government doesn't have the capacity to track inconsistencies. They rely on people like you to do that for them. Let's say you input all of your theories about my leg, my platelet count, whatever else, into my MedID file. You scan it and it goes into the massive cloud at the Federal MedID Database. But no one actually looks at it unless they're tracking me individually, have me flagged. They don't have a dedicated staff tracking everyone in the U.S. population with a MedID. It's too overwhelming."

"So there are holes in the system," Cole says. "But I still don't understand how you get a clean MedID number with a clean history when, clearly, you don't have either."

Cushing takes a deep breath. "I wipe it. Rewrite it. Resend the clean file to the Fed Database. And no one's the wiser. It's not a foolproof system, not yet."

"So you know how to decode the encrypted information?" Karen asks.

Placing a finger to his lips, Cushing says, "Shhh. The government doesn't care about one man. So what if I'm changing my own information? It allows me to work in this shitty economy. It allows me to travel or move anywhere I want to. Having an eighty-three is like being a celebrity. I can be anything I want to be. The minute the system realizes I'm a sixty-two, my life ends. I can't even get a date. Women think they'll be widowed by retirement age, and that's not a selling point. With the war and election going on, the Feds don't have time to worry about those of us that don't pose a threat to national security."

"You ever do pro-bono work, Mr. Cushing?" Cole asks.

Cushing's features lift with curiosity and, perhaps, amusement. "For a good cause, sure."

"Let's schedule a follow-up appointment for that leg," Karen says. "Off the record. Maybe a home visit. Is the contact information on your chart accurate?"

"It is."

"We'll be in touch, then," Cole says.

They discharge Cushing and return to the ER pit, finish up their shift. They need to vet him—if he checks out, and Steven agrees, they'll ask him to join Project Swap. The solution seems so obvious now. They can have good intentions and Harvard medical degrees, but if they don't have a key player with technological insight, they simply won't be able to change the system, much less save lives.

IN THE QUIET of Safe District 149, in the middle of the night, Lily wanders through her darkened house. Cole is, supposedly, working the overnight shift. Since Kate died, he's gone all the time. And when he is home, he's distracted, distant. A few times he told her he had to cover a shift, but she called the hospital and he wasn't there. She even tried to geolocate him, but his phone was off. Her imagination stirs, thoughts make her stomach burn. Could he be having an affair? Despite being with the kids all day, she's never felt so alone.

And angry. At first she didn't recognize the feeling—knots in her back, tension headaches, irrational feelings, and irritability. It's been building for years, she knows. She's angry at the terrorists, at Sebastian for not saving her sister, at Kate for being so goddamned career-driven. And now Cole. Poor Ian is keeping his distance. The other day after going through a box of Kate's clothes, she began to wail. Scream, really. She hadn't known Ian was standing only feet away, had crept up on her. He'd rushed away without a word. She's scaring her son. She's scaring herself.

In Cole's office, the lamp illuminates when it senses her. Maybe there are answers here. She voice-commands his computer on but it doesn't work. She tries again. He turned off her access! *Dammit.* What is he hiding? The room is orderly, as always. For the first time in their marriage, she rifles through his things, searching for evidence of betrayal. An empty notebook on the desktop, framed family photos. Old medical books, pens and paper clips. Her knee knocks into something under the desk. It's a small paper shredder that empties into a trashcan, filled to the top with white strips no larger than a quarter inch.

Sinking to the floor, she dumps the tangle of paper. An hour passes as she sifts through it, sweats over these puzzle pieces. It's useless. The white shade on the office window begins to glow with morning light. From down the hall Talia stirs with her groggy morning cry. Exhaustion, so complete, makes her wonder for a moment what would happen if she didn't go to Talia. If instead she curled up right here and slept.

Her glazed eyes stray from the shreds. Again she focuses on the notepad on the desk. She bolts to standing and finds a pencil. With a light touch, she shades the top sheet of paper. There's indentation, Cole's writing. She stares at it.

P.S. to date:
Sarah Hudson 83—Hazel Berman
Lucia Simpson 80—Rayna Stillman
Mark Hammond 79—Derrick Degas
Beatrice McGinnis 86—

The list is long, probably fifty names. She guesses the numbers are MedIDs, but why are two names next to one number? He has electronic files for all his patients. Why handwrite and then shred it? None of it makes any sense.

Talia's cry is louder now, impatient, angry. It's exactly how Lily feels.

September, 2032

Chapter 43

Jonathan has been patient. He's waited for the right time to talk to Hannah alone, away from Reverend Mitchell. Even now her driver sits outside the Hudson's gate, probably reporting on every step she takes. Since Huan Chao made it clear to him that he *will* carry out his new assignment—or face consequences—Jonathan can't help but wonder what Hannah knows.

They lie on Jonathan's carpeted floor listening to a DJ spin in a club halfway around the world, the video feed lighting up an adjacent wall so it feels like they're part of the crowd. His hands drum to the beat but he barely hears the song. Being with her demands all of his senses.

Without warning, Hannah explodes into giggles. He props himself up on his elbows.

"What's so funny?"

"I gave it a try, but this is so not me. Look how serious they all are!" She points to the clubbers.

Hundreds of bodies move in unison, arms akimbo, hair tossed

wildly. True enough, there's not one smile on the faces that fill the wall.

"It's dancing. Dancing! Shouldn't they look happy?"

"So what music do you like?" he asks. "What makes you dance?"

She grins, taps her temple with her finger. "I only dance mentally."

It's his turn to laugh. They face each other, the smiles slipping away. Jonathan replaces the pounding music with a playlist of acoustic artists. The energy in the room mellows. And in the quiet, he decides to ask the one question that's been plaguing him.

"Did you know?"

"Know what?"

"Did the Reverend send you that day? To the funeral?"

Her lips part then pinch. He watches her neck as she swallows.

"You weren't friends with someone at that funeral, were you? He sent you to find me. To bring me back."

"Yes." She avoids his gaze.

"Did he tell you why?"

She shakes her head. "I run his errands. Send messages. Meet people. He never tells me why, never involves me in BASIA's mission. It's probably better that way."

"Guess it helps you sleep at night." The edge in his voice is stronger than he intended.

"I don't sleep." She turns away. "I'm sorry, Jonathan."

"You don't even know what you're sorry for."

"So much."

"Do you know what he's capable of?"

"Of course I know." She jerks around to face him. "It's why I'm here! I'm proof of what he's capable of. Collateral damage in the war of Armageddon."

"And his future bride."

She stands, ties her rope of hair into a bun as she goes to the window and stares out.

"You okay?" he asks.

"No." It's a whisper. "I miss my parents. I miss the farmhouse I grew up in. How simple everything was. I miss my sister and brother."

Her back shakes as though she's hiccupping. He realizes she's crying.

"Hey." Shit. He doesn't have a tissue and he has no idea what to say. Slowly, he ambles over to her.

"Sorry." With the back of her hand, she wipes her cheeks.

"Where are your brother and sister?"

"I don't know. Charles is trying to find them for me."

Bullshit. A man that powerful could find anyone. "Want me to try?"

"How?"

He waggles his fingers at her. "Magic."

This seems to calm her, and she eagerly sits back down with him on the carpet. He changes the smartwall, gesturing, turning it into his own private search engine. Hannah shares all the details she can remember. Joe, Jr. and Mary, how old they must be now, hair and eye colors, though with ten years since she's seen them, she doubts her memory.

As the minutes tick by, he considers telling her about his plan to steal the MedIDs for Project Swap. They could all get out of here and start a new life. He steals glances at her. There's a tiny white scar on her cheek and her earlobes are double-pierced with no earrings. He has a constant urge to touch her.

An hour later he still has no solid leads on her siblings. He rubs his eyes. "I'll find them. Everyone has an e-trail. Tomorrow I'll check the national education database. It'll just take a few more hours."

"Thank you." Hannah moves closer and kisses his cheek.

Without thinking, he turns and presses his lips against hers. She leans into him, slides a hand down his arm. He takes her hand in his. The feeling is electric. Suddenly she pulls away.

"I'm sorry," he says.

"No." Hannah looks at her lap. "Don't be. You make me feel normal."

"You are normal."

"I'm many things, but normal isn't one of them."

"Why do you think that?"

"Well. My parents martyred themselves. I've lost my brother and sister. I was given—like a cow or something—to Charles. I live in that big mansion like I'm privileged, but none of it's mine. I don't know who I am anymore. If I was set free in the world tomorrow, I wouldn't know where to start. I don't know the first thing about normal, Jonathan."

"If you had a way out of the Reverend's world, would you take it?"

"I can't even imagine that."

"There's always a way out."

She stands abruptly. "It's late. I should go."

Maybe it's better this way. He'll tell her after he figures out how to steal the chips. It's after midnight when he sneaks her out of the house. Thankfully, Steven's asleep. It would be disastrous for their paths to cross now that Steven knows her connection to BASIA.

Down the lamplit driveway they walk to the gate and the waiting car. He grabs her hand and squeezes it.

"There's always a way," he says.

Hannah slips into the backseat and the car pulls away. He watches until the taillights disappear. It's a tangled mess he's in, but he'll work it out. He'll do everything he can to hang onto her.

Chapter 44

FLOODLIGHTS ILLUMINATE THE training field behind BASIA HQ. Standing amid his regiment, Sebastian's breath vaporizes in the unseasonably brisk air. Recently, night drills have become routine. There's a new urgency in the tasks they're given, reiteration of significant psalms, a push to hone skills, whether it's hand-to-hand combat or—Sebastian's specific talent—sharpshooting. They're watching each and every soldier, and he needs to be among the best.

Summoning his fury over Kate and his frustration over the web of politics he has yet to untangle, he pushes his body harder. Running through tires, climbing ropes, hurdling obstacles. After three months he still hasn't penetrated Mitchell's inner sanctum or attained clarity on their mission. Only one thing is obvious: that the attack will include thousands of soldiers from different BASIA regiments throughout the country. Several days coming up—Election Day, Thanksgiving, Christmas, New Years Eve/Day—could provide a meaningful platform for Mitchell. Initially, Sebastian hoped Taylor would be his way in, but she's provided no insight into her father, much less Mitchell. The only thing she's given him is a boatload of guilt, for enjoying her company. Coffees have led to dinners and late night conversations. The relationship is platonic, but the pull is there. At times she reminds him of Kate. Her fierce independence and her hope that she can change the world. Maybe that's why he keeps going back, aside from his assignment.

Hours pass, the stars fade and the sky turns gray-blue as the soldiers file into buses with blackened windows. Sebastian sits next to a man he's watched in the field. The guy's a talker. They begin the trip back to Boston. Sebastian's body sinks into the faded seat, his energy spent. He stares out the window at the orange leaves that glow in the morning light. Earlier in the week, Renner called him to download information on the encrypted emails that Mitchell's been having him send to anonymous I.P. addresses. Some appear to be directions, one reads like a cookie recipe, a few are psalms. The messages are with analysts, who are working to trace the addresses, crack the codes, and attempt to piece together a clear picture.

As the bus bounces over potholes, his body jostles against the man next to him. The talker is forty-something, medium build, thinning hair, who looks like he was in finance in another life. They've met before, and though Sebastian's weary, this is no time for sleep.

"It's Joe, right?" He extends his hand.

"Yup. Joe Shonkoff." The man's grip is firm. "Will Anderson?"

"Good memory. You working tomorrow?"

"You mean today? Yeah."

"Right. It'll be a long one."

Joe sighs. "They're all long."

"Amen." Joe gives him a long look, so long in fact Sebastian has a hard time not looking away. "What's up?"

"You got a family?"

"No. You?"

"I do." Joe gazes out the window. "They know what it's all about. They know what we have to do."

"Right." Sebastian nods. "I just figure, why bother when I have one foot out the door?"

"That's one way to look at it."

"You been with BASIA long?"

"Long enough." Joe glances at the soldiers sitting across the aisle from them, in the seat behind and in front of them. Most of the men and women are sleeping or staring off.

"Things are getting intense the past few weeks."

Glancing at him sideways, Joe says, "Life and death are intense. Gotta be ready."

"I've been ready. Before BASIA, I worked alone. Tried to change things. But I realized a team has greater impact. One man can't change the system."

Joe snorts, smirks.

"You disagree?"

"Depends on the man." Joe lowers his voice. "One man can change the course of history."

A familiar twist in his gut. There's something here. He has to prod gently. "I guess if he has the right plan, sure."

"A Plan. Determination. And action."

"You got a plan?"

The man chews on the inside of his cheek. "Look, I don't know you."

"Hey." Sebastian raises his hands, palms out, revealing his

cross tattoo. He looks around them and whispers. "We're all in it for the cause. And in the end, we all act alone."

"That's the truth."

He looks straight ahead, acts disinterested and waits.

"That State House attack was awesome," Joe says. "You see that son of a bitch Hensley use that agent as a shield? Shit. Now they want him to lead this country. I can't see it. I just can't see it happening."

"You going to vote against him?"

Joe cracks his knuckles as he scans the bus, checking to see if he has an audience. His lips curl and he leans closer. "I just have a feeling, that's all."

"Hensley's going to lose. That's your gut feeling?"

"Hensley won't be alive long enough to lose."

There it is. Lead him to it. "You know he lives a few miles from Boston?"

"You seen his mansion?"

"Driven by it."

"Yeah, me, too." A full-blown smile erupts onto Joe's face, revealing a large space between his front teeth. "He thinks he's safe behind those iron gates, all those Secret Service agents. Fact is, he's just a man. He'll die like any other."

"Not soon enough," Sebastian says. "When he's in office, he'll be untouchable."

Joe's face grows serious. "Have faith, Anderson. It only takes seconds to kill a man."

"You looking to get in the history books?"

"I don't need fame. Just some justice."

It's not an admission, but it's enough for Sebastian.

As a BASIA soldier, Will Anderson should have no idea where Reverend Mitchell lives. Of course, Sebastian has known for the better part of ten years where his sprawling estate lies in the hills west of Boston. It's daybreak when he reaches the gates that secure the property. He rings the buzzer and stares into a camera. A woman asks for his name.

"Private Will Anderson. I have urgent information for Reverend Mitchell."

The gate opens and he cruises down the driveway that leads to the behemoth, angular mansion. Not the home of a humble servant of God. Outside the entrance, Henry greets him with a gun aimed at Sebastian's chest. In Henry's other hand is a scanner.

"Turn around slowly," Henry says.

Sebastian does as he's told. Holding his arms away from his body, he's swept for audio or video sensors, or explosives, though his surveillance lenses won't be detected. After a rotation, Henry regards the machine then slips it into his jacket pocket. "Follow me."

The soles of their shoes echo down the marble-tiled hall. When they reach a set of double doors, Henry knocks. Voices seep from under the door. Sebastian strains to hear. The conversation is a continuous murmur with different tones, no discernible words. Then suddenly it's quiet.

"Come in," Mitchell calls.

Henry opens the door to reveal Mitchell standing in front of a glass desk, dressed and not a hair out of place. There's no one else in the room. It must have been a video conference.

"Sir, Private Will Anderson," Sebastian says, clasping his hands behind his back.

"I know who you are."

"I apologize about the time."

The Reverend cocks his head. "Tell me, Private, how is it you know where I live?"

"I—" Sebastian blushes, caught. But he's ready. "Before I joined up, I was sort of a Reverend Mitchell, Patriot's Church hobbyist, if you will. I was dedicated to the cause but I wasn't involved yet. I learned all I could before I came forward. And, I'm sorry, sir. One night I followed you from the church to your home."

"You were spying on me?"

"I'm sorry, sir."

Mitchell grins. "It's impressive, actually. My men are sharp, they have keen eyes. They always catch on if someone's tailing us."

"Not always, sir."

Silence. And then Mitchell laughs. Relief washes over him; he was just starting to sweat. Henry stands silently at the door as Mitchell invites Sebastian to join him in a seat by the window. Sunlight warms the room and causes Sebastian to squint at Mitchell, illuminated in bright yellow across from him.

"I don't like surprise guests, Private. What's so urgent?"

"I have information that may impact BASIA's impending mission."

"Go on."

"This morning on the ride back into the city, I sat next to a man." He tells the story, omitting the name of the potential rogue soldier. It's hard to say what Mitchell will do with this information, or with Sebastian, for that matter. Though it's a risk, he had to use this, needed to get closer. Best case, this will prove his allegiance to Mitchell, make him more valuable. Worst case, he'll be killed. He studies the Reverend's face as he sits with the news.

Finally, Mitchell says, "And you brought this to me because . . . ?"

"As I said, I was concerned that it might jeopardize BASIA's mission."

"Which you have insight into?"

"No sir. But this man may attempt a presidential assassination. If he does, it could come out that he has ties to BASIA. A rogue soldier could be dangerous."

Mitchell stands, moving closer to the window. He stares out at his grounds.

"Maybe I shouldn't have come." Sebastian rises.

"Are you a believer, Will?"

"Excuse me, sir?"

Mitchell lifts his hands in the air, palms skyward. "'Put on the full armor of God, so that you will be able to stand firm against the schemes of the devil.'" In the tone of his weekly sermons, his voice reverberates off the walls.

"'For our struggle is not against flesh and blood, but against the rulers, against the powers,'" Sebastian continues the Ephesians psalm. "'Against the world forces of this darkness, against the spiritual forces of wickedness in the heavenly places.'"

Mitchell turns back around, a broad smile lifting his face. "You belong here, Private Anderson. You came here this morning because you feel in your soul that BASIA is threatened by one of our own."

"Yes, sir."

"Tell me the name of this soldier."

"Joe Shonkoff."

"Joe Shonkoff." Mitchell closes his eyes. They snap open a few seconds later. "Henry, give him the file."

Henry goes to an old-fashioned file cabinet and rifles through it, eventually pulling out a manila folder. He hands it to Sebastian.

"Your intuition brought you here, Anderson," Mitchell says. "I wonder where it will take you now."

It's a test. He won't say it, won't direct him to make the hit. Mitchell walks over and shakes his hand. His grip is firm. Almost painful.

"Thank you, sir."

"Thank *you*, private."

Henry escorts him out. As the heavy doors shut behind him, Sebastian sucks in the crisp air as though he's being resuscitated. He's got Mitchell's attention, perhaps the first inklings of trust. Finally, some traction. Back in his car, he flips through Joe Shonkoff's file. He needs to speak to Renner, who was watching the meeting live via his lenses. This task needs to be executed perfectly, no room for error. For Will Anderson to be accepted fully by the Reverend, Joe Shonkoff must die.

Chapter 45

"THERE'S A PROBLEM." In her white coat and scrubs, Dr. Karen Riley rushes into Cole's office, shutting the door behind her. She's breathless as she hands him a tablet and a writing pad.

"What's wrong?"

"We took all the precautions." Her voice is low.

The note she scrawled reads: *On paper the match was solid. I checked it twice.* He stares at the screen. It's a day-old article on the suicide of Jack Gardiner, son of assassinated presidential candidate James Gardiner. On the pad he writes: *?*

The scrape of her pencil is frantic. *Yesterday we donated Jack Gardiner's MedID. A perfect match. A common name.*

"Christ!" he whispers, hand over his mouth.

They've only just finished vetting the former MedFuture technician, Sean Cushing. Cole will offer to treat Cushing's medical condition, lupus, and if he accepts the opportunity and does indeed wipe MedIDs for Project Swap, it will change everything. But in case it doesn't work out with him, they hadn't wanted to stop their progress. Dammit, they've been too eager.

Karen sinks into the chair across from him. He writes: *This is not okay.*

She takes the pad: *He fit the profile. Orphan, no living relatives. He was seventeen, no pension fund. He's never worked.*

He writes: *Inheritance. Must be tied up.*

What do we do?

Where's recipient?

Winchester. His parent's house.

JG's suicide is on every site, everyone's talking about him. He leans in, whispers. "Fix it, Karen. Fix it before it's too late."

She nods and runs out. Taking the notepad, he rips the pages off and sends them through the shredder under his desk. Then he closes his eyes and wonders if this is the one misstep that will undo them all.

BY TEN IN the morning Richard Hensley has already been up for five hours. The campaign trail is arduous—even when one knows the end result is a sure thing. Each day he begins with one hour of exercise, followed by two cups of coffee and a briefing by Kendra on updates from the fund-raising manager and communications department. He then reviews national and international news. Thus far she's been successful in reining in his focus and ensured that Taylor is off his radar. Still, at night in the glow of a monitor, he reads tabloid stories on his daughter's involvement with BASIA. She's going to get herself killed. Thankfully, his doctor prescribed good pills, or he'd never sleep.

Today promises another relentless agenda with calls, handshakes, debate prep, plus myriad issues and decisions to be made. At campaign headquarters, he sits alone in his office, running through a speech he'll make in a few hours at a senior center.

Carter flings open the door. "Sir, take a look at this." He thrusts an e-sheet into Richard's hands. It's a news article.

"Jack Gardiner." Richard hands back the device. "Suicide, yes, I know all about it. Terrible waste. We've sent flowers, haven't we?"

"That's just it. I can't seem to find anyone to send flowers to."

Suddenly Richard remembers. "Of course. He was an orphan. Well who's arranging the funeral?"

"Far as I can tell, no one. I can't even figure out which funeral home he's at."

"Well then." Richard slaps his hand on his desk. "See to it."

"Excuse me?"

"Let's get Jack a proper burial. Track him down, Carter. We can't have the son of the former presidential candidate missing. It's bad enough he's dead. Christ, one of the best things about the MedID is that we can track people. It should take one phone call to the hospital where he died to figure this out."

"Yes, sir."

The thought of James Gardiner's son reminds him of Taylor. "What did you find on the Liberty car database?"

Carter's mouth hangs open in question.

"The night Taylor was followed?" he prompts.

"Right, sorry." Carter shakes his head. "There were two cars signed out on the night of the eighteenth. One was to a couple volunteers who took a road trip to the Berkshires to do some campaigning. We have the hotel and gas receipts, so we know they went."

"And the other?"

"It was me." He holds up both hands in defeat. "You caught me. In my off hours I like to get involved in the occasional car chase, hit-and-run scene."

"I told her it was an absurd accusation. The girl has a vivid imagination."

Carter smiles and starts back toward the door.

"What were you doing?"

"Sorry?"

"With the car. On the eighteenth."

"Kendra and I had a meeting with the editor to go over the script and footage for the latest promo. I dropped her at home. Brought the car back in the morning."

"Thanks for humoring me." Another dead end. It was probably that psychopath Reverend.

Richard watches through the glass walls of his office as Carter leaves, navigates past the staffers and volunteers. It's a shame about the Gardiner family. On a positive note, arranging the funeral of James Gardiner's son will gain him favor in the eyes of mothers everywhere. Perhaps he can weave Jack and the subject of mental illness into his intro at the debate tonight.

NERVES GNAW AT Cole's stomach. The remains of Jack Gardiner are in a ceramic blue urn, fine gray ash with a few hard bits of bone that didn't quite disintegrate completely. His MedID is fifty miles away in Winchester, Massachusetts, where Cole and Karen stand at the front door of a white colonial, circa 1850. Green shutters on the windows are badly in need of a coat of paint and the yard is wildly overgrown. Inside is the recipient of Jack Gardiner's MedID, Quinn Feeney. Karen called his parents and Quinn several times to try to explain the situation. They've been uncooperative, unwilling to hear her out. Karen carries Quinn Feeney's original MedID, wiped clean courtesy of Sean, to be exchanged for the one in his arm. Everything is at stake.

"They're home." Cole nods to a curtain on the second floor that moved.

"They must think I'm the Grim Reaper," she says. "First I give Quinn a new chance at life, now they think I'm here to take it back."

"We're still giving him a clean MedID." He rings the bell a third time. "He can't really believe he can walk around as Jack Gardiner, can he?"

From behind the garage an engine revs. They turn just as a motorcycle appears and the driver, wearing a black helmet, guns it out of the driveway and down the street. Cole and Karen race to her Mini Cooper. She reverses out of the driveway and floors it in the direction he went, banking a left that leads into some hills through a nature preserve.

The houses thin, then disappear. They pass a runner, a few cyclists. Cole scans the woods, lowers his window. "That's it. Listen."

"What?"

"The engine. We're close."

Cool wind whips through the car as they round a corner and, yes—there he is. Karen shifts gears and the distance between them closes.

"Steady." Cole braces himself with one hand on the dashboard. "Don't lose him."

The road becomes gravel, it turns this way and that. Quinn Feeney can't go as fast on this terrain with his bike. They're gaining on him. Finally his motorcycle is directly in front of them, almost too close. "What's he doing?" she shouts. "Why doesn't he just stop?"

"Maybe he didn't understand your messages. Let's ask him."

Karen's eyes dart to Cole. But her hands follow her glance, and the steering wheel turns. She tries to correct but the car spins, fishtails. It catches the rear wheel of the motorcycle. The woods are a blur. She screams and lets go of the wheel. Cole sees the tree an instant before he's jolted by the impact, metal against tree. The motion stops. The engine sighs. Silence.

"You okay?" he asks.

Lifting her head from the air bag, blood pours from her nose and she wipes it with the back of her hand. "I'm sorry."

"It's okay." He looks out the shattered passenger window. "Do you have any internal pain?"

"No. You have a cut on your head. You'll need stitches."

He doesn't feel any pain, his body is shaking but numb as he releases his seat belt. "Shit. Where's Quinn?"

Karen shoves her shoulder against her door. "It won't open."

Cole helps her crawl out his side and they struggle to their feet. A skid line mars the pavement and they follow it to the ledge of an embankment, overlooking scattered gravel and shredded grass several feet below.

"Oh, God." She covers her mouth.

The motorcycle is on its side, pinning the driver beneath it. One wheel is suspended, spinning. The helmet, still on Quinn Feeney's head, looks unnaturally twisted to one side.

"Shit." Cole repeats it under his breath as he descends the embankment with Karen a few feet behind.

Kneeling at the man's side, Cole flips open the plastic face shield on the helmet. Blank eyes stare out. Despite the obvious, he attempts to find a pulse in Quinn Feeney's carotid artery.

"Goddamn it," Karen says. "If he'd have just stopped for one minute to hear us out! This didn't have to happen. It would've been fine." Tears pour down her face, mixing with dirt and blood. She wipes her cheek with the sleeve of her jacket.

Cole gets to his feet, glances in both directions. If anyone drives down this road, they'll be found out. There isn't time to consider consequences. He reaches into his coat pocket and pulls out the MedID kit.

"What are you doing?"

"What we came here to do." He pulls up the sleeve of Feeney's left arm and deftly applies the retractor, removing Jack Gardiner's MedID. Karen is silent as he takes the injector with Quinn Feeney's cleaned MedID and places it back into the dead man's forearm. He retrieves the postmortem salve and wipes it over the tiny wound. In minutes it will be undetectable.

"I'm sorry." Sitting cross-legged like a child, Karen repeatedly touches each finger on her right hand to her thumb. "I've put all of us at risk."

Already, stiffness is setting into Cole's back and neck from the crash. He offers her a hand and she takes it, standing slowly, ignoring the dust and grass that cling to her.

"We're all responsible," he says. "Time to clean it up."

They work quickly. In twenty minutes Karen's car is clean of anything that could be traced back to her: plates, registration, vehicle identification number. *Do no harm* runs on an endless cycle in Cole's mind despite trying to refocus his thoughts. They call Steven for help, but there's no answer. There's only one other option.

An hour later Lily pulls the Land Rover onto the side of the road. She doesn't get out. Through the open window, her eyes wander over Cole's disheveled, bloodied body and then Karen's equally wounded one. He goes to the back of the car and lifts the rear gate. As he requested, Lily brought five gallons of gasoline and lighter fluid. He can't believe he's gotten her into this.

"Thank you, Lil."

"What have you done?" She gestures to Karen. "Who is this?"

"Later."

In the rearview mirror, their eyes meet. She shakes her head and mumbles something he can't decipher. This isn't the time. He has to get this done.

The fire ignites and spreads in blue flames. Within seconds an explosion rocks the car. Cole's skin tightens from the heat, his breath catches. Karen's car is blackened, fumes making her cough. Now it's time to deal with Quinn Feeney and his motorcycle. Cole motions to Karen to stay where she is while he slides back down the embankment. He stares at Feeney's face, commits it to memory.

The stench of gasoline stings his eyes. When the bike and man are drenched in it, he adds lighter fluid and then takes a few steps back. He lights a match, flicks it strategically onto the engine. He's halfway up the hill when a second explosion knocks him down, into dusty earth.

Lily doesn't look at Cole when he gets into the front passenger seat and Karen takes a seat in the back.

"The kids at home?" he asks.

"You'd rather I brought them?" Lily turns the car around and presses down on the gas. "You want them to see their father destroying—what? Evidence? What have you done? What's down that embankment?"

He glances at Karen.

"You want your kids to meet your girlfriend, Cole?"

"She's not my girlfriend—"

"I know you're not picking up extra shifts. When I call the hospital, no one's seen you for hours. You don't answer my calls. My texts. Stop lying about everything, goddammit."

"Okay. I'm sorry, I'm so sorry." He puts a hand on her arm, but she wrenches it away. The whole point of Project Swap is family. If he loses Lily and the kids, this has all been for nothing. So he starts at the very beginning and tells her, and doesn't skip a detail. All this time he's spent supposedly protecting her, and now he's plunged her into the middle of it. Do no harm, indeed.

Chapter 46

"'It is God who arms me with strength,'" Charles quotes from Psalms 18:32. "He teaches my hands to make war, So that my arms can bend a bow of bronze. You have also given me the shield of Your salvation; Your right hand has held me up, Your gentleness has made me great. You enlarged my path under me, So my feet did not slip. *Will* not slip, gentlemen."

At BASIA HQ, Charles sits at the head of a table in an empty conference room as Henry stands guard outside. On the smartwall opposite Charles, twelve separate, encrypted video feeds display the faces of BASIA's board of directors. It's taken twenty years to assemble them: an engineer, a congressman, a military specialist, a businessman, and a billionaire, among others. They're his advisors, his eyes and ears. No one suspects them. They've gone to great lengths to conceal their relationship to Charles and this movement. He grips the edge of the table.

"At last, Operation Darkness Falls is within sight," he says.

"How are the soldiers?" the congressman asks. "They'll be ready in six weeks?"

"Everything's on schedule," he says.

"Have they been briefed?" the former U.S. army general asks.

"No need, yet." He shakes his head. "They're doing drills, sharpening their weaponry skills, and studying blueprints they've been provided. Without labels, of course."

"Is Dash prepared?" the congressman asks.

"Absolutely," he says. "He's integral. But in case he's captured or killed, we're equipped to keep moving without him."

"Tell us about your progress on the power grids," the congressman asks. "I want to make sure my generator's ready."

Laughter.

"Darkness will indeed fall and keep our soldiers safe during their mission," Charles says. "Each and every venue hosting an election event will be rendered powerless at the stroke of midnight. At that time, our shooters will take out both existing and newly elected government officials."

"Let's discuss the citizens attending those events," the congressman adds.

"No harm will come to them," he explains. "We only want them out of our way. BASIA soldiers have specific targets and will do everything they can to ensure there is no—in the words of our current administration—collateral damage. When the power is cut, people will funnel outside. If and when they hear shots, they'll run from the site. But they won't learn the truth until hours later. In complete darkness, video won't record the moves of our soldiers. Obviously, citizens will be less traumatized without being exposed to those images. The lights will go out. They'll wander home. And then, with the sunrise, will come illumination. We want them to feel safe, back in their homes. And that's when we'll address them. We'll explain—briefly—what's happened. They'll see that we took great care not to harm them. And they will listen. They'll see that our reach is far, our power great with the hand of God that guides us."

Heads nod in unison. They know Charles is working to keep citizens safe.

Without skipping a beat, the businessman says, "Let's discuss budget. I reviewed the numbers and in another two weeks we'll be in the red."

"Supporting our militia is costly, Rob." Money is a detail that should never get in the way of their goal. "We have close to a million soldiers. That's travel costs for operations, weapons, and medical needs. But we always have new sources of support. I'm planning to tap them today, as a matter of fact."

"Is weather an issue?" the engineer interjects.

"Won't matter. Our troops will get there with enough time to get settled and acquainted with their targets. Let it rain."

"Security's going to be tighter than in previous years," the billionaire says, alluding to the Gardiner assassination.

"We're ready." Charles makes eye contact with his associates. "We have schedules, blueprints, guest lists, and soldiers on the inside of every one of the venues. BASIA is tight. Disciplined. Dedicated. They will systematically attack and render the U.S. government speechless. Literally." There are nods and grins all around. He relaxes.

"And if you're caught or killed," the congressman says. "What then?"

"If and when I can no longer be a part of this, you'll be in place, ready to step in. You're as ready as I am. God willing, together we'll guide this country back to greatness on a foundation built of Christianity and patriotism. So with or without me, if you carry through on our promise, the masses will be appeased."

Each board member discusses his or her plan for the country post-Election Day: financial ramifications, handling of media coverage, political fallout, security issues, international relations. Charles listens, pleased with his colleagues' thoroughness. This kind of revolution happens once in a lifetime. When it's deemed safe, the board members will divulge their identities and wield their collective power to assure the citizens there is strength in the new government. He has waited years for this. There isn't room for error.

"One final point," the billionaire says. "The MedID. Yes, we'll phase it out and ultimately destroy the system. But as we've discussed before, I strongly advise the board to consider utilizing it initially. We need to know how the masses are responding. We'll explain that we're eliminating the system but that it will take time. That allows us to continue monitoring the existing infrastructure to see where we're at in the first year."

"It's the Mark of the Beast." Charles leans his arms on the table. He flexes his tattooed hand. "It's everything we're fighting against."

"It's temporary," the billionaire argues. "It's business. And we won't use the information against our citizens. It's merely a device to monitor our success. The feedback is crucial in a new government. The data will tell us what we can or should be doing differently."

Silence from the group. He desperately wants to bend his neck to crack it but refuses to show his tension.

Finally, the businessman says, "I'll agree to it. We'll use it as our own tool. But the MedID number hierarchy won't exist anymore. We'll promise citizens that it ends the day we take power. They'll almost forget they're wearing them."

The group votes. They are unanimous, except for Charles. But he must trust his advisors.

"God is great," he says. "We'll have our final meeting three days before the mission. Then we won't speak until after the event. I'll be in touch."

Pressing his hand to his heart, Charles extends his open palm. They return the gesture, though their palms have no ink to give away their BASIA affiliation. The lines disconnect, screens go black. He presses a button on his watch. Instantly Henry enters.

"Yes, sir?"

"I need you to deliver some messages."

There is money to be made. His connections have supplied ample documentation on the financial situations of both Steven Hudson and Richard Hensley. Jonathan and Taylor are Charles's best investments in years. Within an hour Henry regurgitates his assignment, the names and addresses of his targets, and alternative executions should the originals fail. Charles considers the word "fail." It's simply not an option. When lives hang in the balance, people make the right decision.

Chapter 47

DRESSED IN A black suit, Richard takes in the beauty of the White Mountains, the colored leaves appearing to hit their peak of glory this very moment. An intimate crowd has gathered at a national park in memoriam of Jack Gardiner, who took his own life a couple weeks ago. Born in New Hampshire, it seems an appropriate place to release his ashes. There was a delay in finding the son of the assassinated presidential candidate, but Carter had come through, thanks to the MedID tracking system.

"Be sure to hold the urn away from you," Carter says, miming the act with his arms outstretched. "Winds up here change on a dime. The audience is seated to the west. You'll need an east wind."

Richard glances around, nods solemnly when he makes eye contact with anyone. Off to the side, at a respectable distance—if there is such a thing—throngs of reporters and cameramen await an opportune moment. Sadly, this service feels like any other venue to him. Now that they're near the end of the campaign trail, the sheer number of performances is like an endurance test. He's sweeping the polls. It used to be more fun when it felt like a legitimate race.

The moment arrives. He summons thoughts of Taylor and Sienna, imagines these could just as easily be their ashes. The speech is heartfelt, the words crafting him as a fellow parent and a friend to his former running mate. The crowd is tearful when, at the end of his speech, Richard steps a few feet away and releases Gardiner's ashes. The easterly wind carries them swiftly toward majestic Mount Washington.

Within the hour, Richard, Kendra, and Carter are in the Town Car, cruising back toward Boston. He warms his hands on a travel mug filled with hot chocolate, courtesy of a local coffee shop. His eyes fall upon a grayish spot on the thigh of his pants. Ashes. Furiously, he pats at it until it's undetectable. A wave of nausea. Though he's got the stomach for politics, he can't deal with blood or any bodily fluids. He clears his throat as he glances at his team. Kendra is working to finalize their schedule, while Carter confirms their dinner with party donors this evening. It would be a luxury to have a home-cooked dinner. His phone vibrates with a text but the number is blocked. There's a grainy image. He squints to make out the details.

A video plays. Taylor and Sienna are eating lunch at home, in their kitchen. He grins, warmth spreading in his chest. But something's not right. This is one of his cameras, the ones he had placed. Someone has intercepted his feeds and is watching his daughter and granddaughter!

He types: *Who is this?*

The response: *We have a shared interest, as you can see.*

What is this about?

Money.

It must be those goddamned terrorists. Is this a live feed, or are Taylor and Sienna tied up somewhere? His mouth fills with saliva, he thinks he might vomit. Despite their history, the thought of Taylor dying or being hurt in any way is unbearable. Everything he's done since the day she was born has been to protect her, and now Sienna. How dare that Reverend bastard do this! One call to the FBI and they'll be on this. Well, maybe, maybe not. President Clark warned him that Taylor won't cost the party the presidency. His head pounds. Screw it. He'll handle this himself.

Richard types: *Who are you?*

Friends of Taylor's.

BASIA? Charles Mitchell?

No response.

Richard asks: *Are they okay?*

For now.

There's only one question remaining. *How much?*

How much are they worth?

"Mother fuckers," he says aloud.

"Is everything all right?" Kendra asks.

He waves her off. Finally he types: *How do I know they'll be safe?*

This is a simple agreement. You deliver. We deliver.

What's your price?

Five million.

Five million! He closes his eyes, desperately considering his resources. His Cape house, the Nantucket estate. But the market has bottomed out, no one's buying, especially not vacation properties. The only liquid cash he has is tied to the campaign. There's Taylor's trust fund, probably untouched, but legally untouchable by him.

He types: *That'll take time.*

There's not much of that left, is there Mr. President?

Meaning what?

Money's due before election. Or the deal's off.

Richard can't catch his breath. *How do I get in touch with you?*

You don't. And if Taylor discovers this exchange, forget the money.

The text conversation self-destructs. He attempts to find it but it's gone. My God, Taylor has no idea what her *friends* are doing. What happens if he can't get the money? But that's out of the question. He must. He simply must.

Chapter 48

IN HIS OFFICE, Steven Hudson rests his head against his chair, his eyes following the gray cloud of smoke from his cigar. These quiet moments are few and far between. But keeping busy keeps him sane. Project Swap is a welcome distraction so that he's not dwelling on Sarah all the time.

Just this morning their team officially welcomed a new partner. Though he's rather anemic-looking, Sean Cushing is an ex-MedFuture software programmer whose experience and knowledge changes everything. They no longer need to match recipients and donors. Cushing will clean MedIDs and assign new numbers that are 75-plus, pure and simple. Soon, he'll train others to do the same. Cushing has assured them that with the sheer volume of the MedID system, it would take the government years to catch on to inconsistencies and revisions. And by then they'd need to track millions of citizens.

Steven can't wait to tell Jonathan. With the new system, he won't need to steal the BASIA MedIDs. Unfortunately, he hasn't been able to reach his stepson since he left for work two days ago.

He's not answering his phone, not returning texts. Steven's impulse is to call the police, but obviously he can't do that. Instead he checks his watch incessantly, his imagination running, leaving him with a dark, sinking sensation. He texts again: *Come home. Big news.*

The doorbell rings. He stubs out the cigar in an ashtray and makes his way to the funeral home entrance. Bright sunlight silhouettes the visitor. Steven is struck by the man's height and broad shoulders.

"Hello," he says. "Do you have an appointment?"

The man shakes his head. "Steven Hudson?"

"Yes. And you are?"

"Henry."

"Henry . . . ?"

"Is there somewhere we can talk?"

The man takes a step forward and Steven steps back in response. Henry is wearing a crisp suit and has a spiky military haircut. Behind him, a gray SUV with tinted windows is parked. *Jesus.* Steven's mouth is suddenly dry, his heart races. My God, he's from the government. We've been caught. Backup plans aren't in place. Blood drains from him, the floorboards sucking his energy through the soles of his shoes.

"Mr. Hudson?"

"Yes, of course." Steven waves him into the foyer. Working to steady his breathing, he leads the stranger into his office and immediately regrets the cigar, the scent detectable before they're even in the room. He sits at his desk, the hulking man sitting across from him. "So, Henry. What brings you here?"

Henry reaches into his jacket pocket. Steven stiffens. A weapon? Under his desk, in a makeshift holster fastened to the underside of the drawer, is a handgun. Subtly, he feels for and finds it.

Instead of a gun, Henry pulls out an electronic device detector. Taking the finger-sized machine, he holds the device out in the center of the room to sweep for bugs. Within seconds it releases a single beep. He tucks it back into his pocket. "One can never be too safe."

"Safe from what, exactly?"

"We have a mutual interest," Henry says.

"I'm guessing you don't mean reading, or tennis?"

"Jonathan Hudson is your stepson, correct?"

Steven blinks. "What is this?"

"You've had many losses, Mr. Hudson. Your first wife. A son and daughter. A second wife." Henry feigns empathy, his face contorting unnaturally. "All you have left is Jonathan."

Still touching the gun, Steven's hands begin to tremble. "What do you want?"

"Let's discuss your stepson."

"You're with BASIA."

"He's become quite an asset to the organization."

"Why do you care about one boy out of the thousands you must have at your disposal?"

"Jonathan is a very special, very valuable young man."

Valuable. Of course. Why didn't he see this coming? "How much do you want?"

Henry grins. "It's so difficult to put a price on a loved one."

You motherfucker! Steven wants to shout. His legs flex as though he might jump over his desk and lunge at the man. But if he does, or if he pulls out his gun, what then? "Where is he? Is he all right?"

"Of course. We all want Jonathan well. And highly functioning."

"What does that mean?"

"Never mind." Henry stands. "Three million, cash. Untraceable bills. Seems such a small amount to pay for a life, don't you think?"

Sadistic asshole. He moves his hand away from the gun. If they can get through this, get Jonathan back, they'll leave. Shut Hudson's. Disappear.

"I don't have three million in cash lying around. I need time."

"You'll see Jonathan when we see the money." From a pants pocket, he takes out a phone and tosses it to Steven. "I'll be checking in. Oh, and I'm sure you've already guessed this, but if any of this leaks out, there won't be a Jonathan left to barter for. Understand?"

The hulking man turns and disappears down the hall. Steven hears the door shut, followed by an engine revving. Finally, the noise fades. His fists ball, nails digging into his palms. He closes his eyes and envisions his family, all of them, past and present. Ten deep breaths later he opens his eyes and begins logging into his bank accounts.

RIGHT NOW JONATHAN wants his board. To ride the half-pipe a few blocks from home, feel the rush when he flies over the edge and catches air. Things are so intense here, he needs a break.

Until recently, he'd worked alone or with Huan Chao. But tonight at BASIA HQ he's being treated like a soldier. They've split up the soldiers by expertise. A sharpshooting team is in the Ballistics Quad. Another group grunts and sweats through physical drills in the field. A third group spars one-on-one, refining defensive and offensive skills. Jonathan's team sits alongside one another at long tables working on individual screens. Mitchell's cyber warriors. Jonathan can't help an occasional peek at another screen, but it's hard to tell exactly what they're working on. He wonders if Huan Chao and the Reverend have files on their families, too, if they've been threatened into doing this. But something must be different about him, since the Reverend has him on such a tight leash. The past few nights he's even been coerced into staying overnight at the Mitchell mansion. Steven must be worried, probably calling him every hour. Meanwhile, Jonathan is honing his exit plan. He knows when the MedID Vault is unattended and has excuses lined up if he's caught. The only complication is Hannah. He's hardly had a minute alone with her since they kissed. He's ready to tell her, to ask her to disappear with him. She can't possibly want to stay and be forced into marriage.

Every day, he works on his sole assignment, focusing on the power grid infrastructure across the country with the aim of gaining control of the grids in every state capital and major city. Via TOR, he's anonymously established numerous botnets to use them for DoS attacks, allowing him to shut down power in these areas. Huan Chao and the Reverend have yet to tell him why he's doing this. Still, he has to admit, it's pretty cool. But when he's not refining his tools, he's plotting the mission he calls the Great MedID Heist.

At midnight the soldiers are dismissed. They break ranks and head to the parking lot and the buses that will take them back into the city. Jonathan feels in his pants pockets for his phone but remembers that he lost it. Maybe left it at home. He needs to call Steven, who must be panicking. It's late, but maybe Henry can take him to a corner store for a disposable.

In the gray SUV, he hops in the front passenger side, with

Reverend Mitchell in the back. Henry steers them down the long gravel drive off militia property and onto the road.

"Hey, Henry," Jonathan says. "Can we swing by a convenience store?"

"What do you need?"

"A phone. Just a disposable. I can't seem to find mine."

"It's late."

"I'll just be two minutes."

"The Reverend's tired. He doesn't like detours."

Jonathan glances back to where the Reverend sits. It can't hurt to ask, so he repeats his question directly to the man in charge.

"Let's just head back," Reverend Mitchell says. "Do you need to use my phone?"

"That's okay."

The route to the Reverend's home is familiar now. Jonathan checks street signs as they pass and calculates that he could walk home from here. It may take a while, but he could do it.

The men are silent for the rest of the ride. Jonathan's imagination kicks in. Is there a reason they don't want him to have a phone? He's tired of all the drama. Time to move on. He's not for government, he's certainly not for BASIA. He's for family, whatever's left of it.

Chapter 49

THE NEEDLE SINKS in. Almost immediately Joe Shonkoff stops struggling against Sebastian's grip. In the quiet of early nightfall, between abandoned buildings, he and Renner settle the limp body onto a blue tarp in Renner's trunk. Thick dingy fog coats the roadways that Renner navigates on their way to a Bureau-owned condo on the other side of town.

Charles Mitchell's message to Sebastian—as Will—had been clear; get rid of the soldier who was threatening to go rogue. Monitoring Shonkoff showed him to be a creature of habit. Daily, he rides his bike to a strip of fading businesses just outside Boston. A former investment banker, he was crushed in the Crash of '26 and now works as an accountant for a few retailers that pay him minimum wage. Shonkoff is dangerous and certainly treasonous. Funny, they're both eager to restore freedom to the country, both willing to fight. Both willing to die. Maybe they're not so different.

Carrying the bulky roll of tarp up three flights of stairs is tough to navigate, but Sebastian's adrenaline gives him a burst of strength. In silence, he and Renner arrange things, posing

Shonkoff's body on the living room carpet in a manner to suggest he fell naturally but violently. His arms and legs are splayed, shirt untucked, hair mussed. From his briefcase, Sebastian takes the makeup and applies it expertly. Meanwhile, Renner destroys the sparsely furnished room, knocking over chairs and lamps, breaking a vase. Together they create blood spatter to match the story Sebastian will tell. Then it's time for pictures.

Close-ups of the wound in Shonkoff's head, the room from every angle. When that's finished, they place a single chair in the center of the living room and tie him securely to it. Then they wait for the tranquilizer to wear off.

"I have something for you," Renner says. From his breast pocket he pulls out his phone and touches the screen. He aims it at one of the walls and a message is projected. The left side shows one of the codes Sebastian sent on behalf of BASIA. The right side of the screen displays a number 110232.

"A date?" Sebastian suggests.

"Could also be a coordinate. Or a digital key."

"What does the tech think?"

"The date theory makes the most sense. It's Election Day."

They both stare at it.

"Anything else?" Sebastian asks.

"If this is a date, it makes sense for the other codes to include coordinates. Locations. But we haven't confirmed it yet."

"What's taking them so long?"

"We're working against Huan Chao," Renner says. "He trained alongside some of our very own. These are complex codes. We read them wrong, we may be looking at losses on par with the Planes."

"Are we ready to alert Satterwhite? The candidates?"

Renner shakes his head. "We can't without concrete evidence. But we could tell them there's chatter and advise them to double up on security for the candidates. As soon as we confirm the codes we'll move."

"It's four weeks away." Nervous energy prompts Sebastian to stand and pace.

"I've been doing some digging on the name Michael O'Brien gave us. I think Dash is a nickname."

Sebastian repeats the word. "Someone who runs?"

"Specifically, someone who runs or ran a race like the hundred meter dash."

"Well that narrows it down. To every high school and college team in the U.S."

"Maybe. Or maybe it was a serious athlete. Broke some records. Came close to making the Olympics." Renner types into his phone and hands it to Sebastian. "Recognize this guy?"

It's not possible. He reads and rereads the words, scans the face of Carter Benson, Richard Hensley's deputy campaign manager, and before that aide to President Clark. Several pictures show Benson running, headlines predicting his future as an Olympian. The last image is of him on his knees at his final competition, clearly a loss. "Are you serious?"

"It's just a theory."

"Have you shared it with anyone?"

"Not yet."

"Good." He hands the phone back to Renner. "We need more proof than a hunch about a nickname."

"Someone at his level isn't acting alone. He's a middleman."

From outside comes a sound like a glass bottle hitting the pavement. Sebastian glances out the window. Renner's accusation is dizzying. It could mean the State House attack originated from the Office of the President, that Benson coordinated all logistics—which they know he had access to—and then had a team of homegrown terrorists kill James Gardiner. Why would Clark or Hensley want to kill Gardiner? He wheels around. "Jesus Christ, Renner. This is a crazy fucking theory."

"Sometimes crazy happens."

The air is thick, the ceiling close. Has he been working on behalf of Kate's killer this whole time? "Satterwhite gave you a direct order to stop this investigation. You need to watch your step."

"If there's truth to this, I want a piece of these assholes," Renner says. "All these years in the service . . ."

Neither one of them talks much after that. Finally, their hostage stirs. Renner goes into the kitchen and returns with a glass. He tosses water on Shonkoffs face and the man immediately coughs and sputters awake. Lost, wild-eyed, he struggles against the handcuffs. He glances at the "blood spatter," quickly inspects his body.

"You!" Shonkoff shouts at Sebastian. "I should have known."

"It's the beard," Renner says. "Makes him look like a trustworthy teddy bear."

"Don't worry, Joe," Sebastian says. "You get to call the shots today."

"I'm going to the Reverend," Shonkoff growls.

Sebastian cues the recording he has of Shonkoff on the bus, implying he intends to kill Richard Hensley before he gets to the White House. When the audio ends, Shonkoff spits in his direction.

"You have three options." Sebastian wanders in a circle around him. "One. Become a cooperating witness. Work inside BASIA with me. We guarantee time served and witness protection for you and your family. Don't forget your beautiful wife and son."

"Fuck you."

"Two. Testify when the time comes, in exchange for a lesser sentence and witness protection for your family."

"Fuck you."

"Three. Be fully prosecuted for conspiracy and intent to assassinate the vice presidential candidate Richard Hensley."

"Fuck—"

Renner backhands him across the face.

Real blood mixes with the fake blood already caked on his face. The night passes with no progress, only proof that Shonkoff is indeed ready to die and give up his life for his beliefs. The only time he flinches is when they threaten his wife and son. But it's not enough.

Just before daybreak a Bureau paddy wagon arrives and several men haul Shonkoff away. As an admitted enemy of the state, he'll be put in solitary confinement until they can figure out how to use him. Maybe, Sebastian thinks, his earlier thoughts were wrong, and Shonkoff and he are on very different sides after all. Wouldn't it be ironic if Shonkoff is the patriot and he is the real terrorist?

Chapter 50

At Project Swap HQ, Cole holds the woman's forearm and scans her cleaned MedID into the system. Her eyes are wet as she thanks him, then disappears through the back door. At 2A.M., Cole checks the appointment notes, handwritten into a log that will be burned at the end of the night. Despite a full day at the hospital, he's reinvigorated by the faces of those who pass through their humble headquarters. The building is in disrepair—a property bought by Hudson's Funeral Homes, Inc.—but no one cares about the peeling paint or smell of mildew. Priorities are elsewhere. Here the "patients" don't speak, don't exchange names or stories with one another. They come in one door, out another, and are given very specific directions on how to depart the neighborhood so that no one notices a pattern.

The Jack Gardiner escapade had been a disaster, but they learned their lesson, and there's been no news on the burned remains of a motorcycle accident. Surprisingly, they've heard nothing from the family of the man who'd been unwilling to give up Gardiner's MedID. Perhaps the man's parents hope he made it out of the country, is sunning himself in the Mediterranean.

"Next," Sean Cushing calls out from a procedure room.

In two other rooms, associates of Sean's reprogram more chips. Evidently, MedFuture Corporation made a few enemies among its employees. In an adjacent room another Project Swap volunteer extracts MedIDs for those who simply want them out. Now that MedIDs can simply be "wiped" and rescanned, the list of those willing to take their chances has grown dramatically. Less than a week into this new process, Karen can't keep up with prioritizing her database of who has urgent employment needs, who's trying to leave the country, who might be trying to buy a home or start a business. All things contingent on health.

In the dim light of the hallway, Cole checks his phone. No messages. Lily isn't speaking to him and she barely looks at him. Since the day he called her to the crash site and explained everything, she's shut him out. At home he pleads with her, apologizes over and over again, but she walks away. God, he misses her. But she knows he's endangering their family. And she's right. It's amazing how with children, the house can be so lively and loud, yet so lonely. Their voices are woven throughout Ian's and Talia's, but they never actually connect.

"Cole." Steven blows in through the front door. Behind him a sheet of water slicks the pavement, pulls at the trees. He's winded, his hair wet and dripping, his suit drenched.

"What's wrong?"

"I waited as long as I could. I tried to get the money. I didn't want to worry you and Karen."

"What are you talking about?"

"They have Jonathan."

"Who has Jonathan?"

"Mitchell. BASIA." In a hushed voice, Steven explains Jonathan's confession, how he's working for Reverend Mitchell's BASIA and plans to steal the MedIDs for Project Swap.

"But we have Sean now," Cole says. "There's no need for donors."

"Jonathan's been gone for days." Steven's voice catches and he coughs. "I keep calling but they must have taken his phone. The last time I saw him we still needed donors."

Cole remembers the kid's smugness that night, offering up ten thousand MedIDs. "What can I do?"

"They gave me an ultimatum. Three million dollars for his safety." Steven paces. "Since

Mitchell's henchman paid me a visit, I've spent every minute trying to put the money together. I didn't want to involve you. I didn't want to endanger the operation."

"So you don't have the money?"

"Not on me."

It's surprising that Steven can't simply produce the funds, given the success of Hudson's. Something in his face must show his doubt, because Steven adds, "I've just bought two new funeral homes. Our savings are in Swiss and offshore accounts. The money's tied up."

"Untie it."

"It's impossible." Steven leans against the wall. "Most of the money has to be withdrawn in person. A safeguard I set up, thinking I wouldn't need to tap into it until retirement. Most of my other money is tied up in overhead. I have several thousand liquid, but not millions. Cole, they'll kill him if he tries to steal those MedIDs."

What would he do if Ian or Talia were taken hostage? A pang settles in his gut. And he knows. "I'll go."

"Where?"

"To Patriot's Church. No one knows me there. I'll see if I can find him during the service. If he's valuable, maybe the Reverend is keeping him close."

"They're probably holding him somewhere else." Steven shakes his head, runs his hand through his hair. "The church is their public facade. Who knows what other properties they have? He could be anywhere."

"While you figure out your finances, I'll just take a look around."

"You have a family."

"Jonathan put himself at risk because of us." Cole gestures to their surroundings. "I owe it to him."

They stand in silence as MedID patients quietly pass by them in the hallway. All these people. No one is changed, but everyone has a chance now. He places a hand on Steven's shoulder. Trying to find Jonathan is the right thing to do.

Chapter 51

AT BASIA HQ, Charles stares out from behind his podium at his loyal troops. Thousands stand before him, and thousands more watch him via streamed video. He touches his hand to his chest, then reaches it out to them, palm open. In unison, they do the same.

"It's God who arms you with strength," he proclaims. "And with it, we will strike down the evil that infests our society. Finally, our great country will serve Him, under his laws, with the Great Book as our guide. And God will thank all of us by opening his eternal kingdom to you and your families. But before that, you'll enjoy the riches of his love here on earth."

"Amen," they say in unison.

"Thy will be done," he says. "Dismissed."

The soldiers salute and the monitors turn to black as the men and women in the room funnel through the aisles, on their way out. He gives a subtle nod to Henry, who walks purposefully through the crowd to retrieve Will Anderson.

In the Command Center control room, Charles waits. An

e-map of the U.S. spans an entire wall. Opposite, security monitors with live feeds display different angles of BASIA HQ. Several touch keypads are embedded into a table the length of the room. He pushes buttons on one of them, causing a small red light in each of the fifty states to illuminate. His chest swells, tears sting his eyes. It's hard to believe the moment is almost here. "Thy will be done," he whispers.

There's a knock on the door. He presses a button and the red lights disappear from the screen. "Come in."

Will Anderson trails Henry inside. He's not much to look at, but he has balls. Shave the scruffy beard, cut that hair, and he'll be a force within the organization.

"Leave us," Charles commands. Henry closes the door behind him. Anderson waits at attention as he walks a circle around him, stopping to look him in the eye. "You have something for me?"

"Yes, sir." From inside his jacket he produces a phone. He unlocks it, finds what he's looking for and hands it to Charles.

In vivid color, photographs show a murdered Joe Shonkoff. The graphic nature prompts the sharp pain in Charles's temple and he rubs it with his free hand. "When were these taken?"

"Last night."

"Where?"

"Quincy. But he's in the northwest corner of the state now."

"This is a serious offense, Anderson."

A sharp inhale, his brow twitches slightly.

"Was this your first time?"

"No."

Anderson appears humble and honest. He's committed a necessary evil in the interest of BASIA's mission. There's nothing questionable in his history, either online or MedID. And evidently he's ready. More than willing.

"Pictures can be created," Charles says.

"I brought proof. May I, sir?"

At Charles's nod, Anderson reaches into his jacket pocket and pulls out a small plastic bag. Inside are two bloody teeth.

"While I appreciate your effort, it is possible to survive without teeth."

"I burned the remains."

Despite their research, it's always possible that someone has infiltrated BASIA and has an agenda to shut them down. He leans in close to Anderson and whispers, "Are you setting me up, Anderson?"

"No, sir." He stares ahead, unflinching. "I have nothing to gain but my salvation and the honor of serving BASIA in the name of God."

Charles drags the moment out. Finally he pats him—hard—on the back. "Well done, Anderson. You've demonstrated your commitment to BASIA. Proven you're able to act alone. And you deliver results."

"Thank you, sir. I did what was necessary."

"Indeed. Shonkoff might have spoiled our mission. Everything we've worked for."

"I'm here to serve, sir."

"Aren't we all." Charles closes his eyes, gives a moment of thanks for this dedicated soldier. Then he continues, "For your bravery and exceptional service, I hereby promote you to Sergeant."

"Thank you, sir."

Anderson nods as relief and, Charles thinks, gratitude soften his face. Perhaps this one can lead without being sacrificed.

"With your new rank comes a higher level of clearance," he explains. "More personalized assignments as our mission nears."

"I'm ready, sir."

Charles wanders to the window and takes in the brilliant autumn leaves. "Thanks to the State House attack, we learned a lot from the government. They made some mistakes, some missteps. But then again, they're not used to pulling off chemical attacks."

"Excuse me?"

"You remember the sarin attack?"

"Of course."

Spinning back around, he returns to where Anderson stands. "They removed a presidential candidate that wouldn't do what he was told. Gardiner had plans to phase out the MedID program. President Clark and his administration couldn't let that happen. All their precious systems would explode! Their reins on society would slip away. It's amazing, really. People turn to God in times of war. Killing their own promotes our cause and increases our membership."

"You're saying President Clark had James Gardiner assassinated?" Anderson's brow furrows.

"Don't look so shocked. A government that enslaves its people is capable of anything."

"I'm sorry. It's just, I thought it was our accomplishment."

"Our efforts will make that look like child's play."

"Can I ask, sir." Anderson shifts on his feet. "How do you know it was President Clark? Tell me if I'm overstepping, but—"

"You are." Too curious for his own good. "BASIA is everywhere. Our resources are vast. That's all you need to know."

"Yes, sir."

"That's all for now, Sergeant Anderson."

"Thank you, Reverend Mitchell. And thank you for this opportunity."

"Make Him proud."

Anderson salutes.

"Dismissed."

When Anderson leaves, Henry enters. "The car's ready."

"What the status on our two investments?"

Henry's lips pinch together. "No word from Hudson or Hensley, sir."

"Dammit." Unwelcome news. His board will be asking for an update on funds any day now. "Make our presence felt, Henry. Send reminders to the senator and the undertaker. Time is of the essence."

JONATHAN LIES IN bed, waiting for the right time. Reverend Mitchell must think he's an idiot. For five days he's only been allowed off the compound for cyber training at BASIA HQ. The Reverend tells him that with the long hours he's putting in, he might as well stay. When Jonathan tries to argue, Henry tells him they can't spare a driver to transport him. There's no way for him to contact Steven. And Henry blatantly ignores his requests to buy a new phone.

Poor Steven probably thinks he's dead. After what his stepfather has been through—at the hands of Charles Mitchell—his imagination must be getting the best of him. Jonathan's chest is heavy at the thought. No matter what's happened between them in the past, Steven is his family. Enough already. Tonight is the night.

At 3 A.M. the mansion is quiet, the only sound a whisper of heat through the vents. He wears sweatpants and a T-shirt so if he's caught he can just say he's grabbing something to eat. In socks, he pads along the darkened hallways until he reaches the basement stairs. In seconds he's there, inside the MedID Vault, the door triggering the overhead lights. He works fast. Taking one of the heavy metal briefcases, he logs into the computer and accesses the MedID database. Methodically, silently, he pulls clean MedIDs from a temperature-controlled safe and places them one by one in the briefcase in individual slots. As he places the last one in the case he notices his hands are shaking.

"You're up late."

His hands fly up, his whole body jumps. "Hannah, what the hell!"

"Seriously. What the hell?"

"I'm just working." Breathe. Without skipping a beat, he reverses the direction of his actions. He takes MedIDs back out of the case, logs them into the system and places them into the storage vault. He feels her watching him. If he tells her, maybe she'll go with him.

"Why are you doing this in the middle of the night?"

"Couldn't sleep." He avoids her gaze. "Nothing better to do, might as well work."

"You've been staying here a lot lately."

"Uh huh."

"Charles has taken to you. He doesn't usually have soldiers in the house."

"I'm not a soldier."

"I know you don't want to be. But you're a cyber soldier."

Her hand on his arm makes his body tense. She presses against him, her chest to his back as her arms slide around his waist. His breath catches. Being with her makes him believe it's possible to be happy, that maybe the future doesn't have to be so grim. After tonight he may never see her again. She wants out, he knows it. He needs to make her see the possibilities. He reverses direction, once again placing the clean MedIDs in the case.

"What are you doing?" She moves away from him, the warmth from her body still clinging to him.

"Remember I told you there's always a way out?" he asks.

"Stealing from Charles is not a way out."

"I'm not stealing. These are banned at BASIA. Everyone in the militia gave them up." He places the final chip in the case and shuts it. They lock eyes and he can tell she's scared. "These clean MedIDs can help people. They can save lives."

"We don't believe in MedIDs."

"No. But right now this is the system. And people need them. To get jobs. To move. To get special medical treatment."

"We take care of our own. Those people should come to the church."

"Hannah. Not everyone believes this is Armageddon."

"Do you?"

Jonathan secures the lock and picks up the case. "I believed in my mother. I believe in my stepfather. I believe in you."

She stares at him a minute. Her eyes fill. "That's not what I asked."

"Well that's my answer. At the end of the day, I only believe in people. My family. My friends. I don't care about getting back at the government. I don't care about getting vengeance for a God I don't know exists."

"Are you leaving?"

He swallows. "Come with me."

Tears tumble onto her cheeks. "I can't."

"Won't."

"It's complicated, Jonathan. He takes care of me."

"You can take care of yourself."

Hannah leans against the door frame, her head bowed so that her hair partially hides her face. "Things are going to change," she says. "Just wait. Wait a little longer."

"I can't. We've got to go now."

"You're so good, Jonathan." She takes a few steps backward, into the hallway. "I'm sorry. Forgive me." She pulls a lever on the wall. Piercing sirens burst throughout the house.

For a moment he can only stare at her. How could she do this? Why not just let him go? She brushes the wet off her cheeks as he runs past her, briefcase in hand, down the hall and up the stairs. Heart thumping, breath short. With each stride he works out his path. Get to the kitchen. Out the sliding glass door. Across the lawn. Through the field.

"Stop right there."

In the reflection of the kitchen's sliding glass door he sees Henry with his gun raised. Jonathan does as he's told. In just his T-shirt, sweatpants, and socks, he feels naked. *Goddammit, Hannah.* Does she understand she might have gotten him killed? He lowers the briefcase to the ground and turns to face Henry.

"How disappointing." Reverend Mitchell enters from the darkened hallway. He wears a robe and slippers. "I had high hopes for you, Jonathan."

"I just want out. I have some stuff going on at home."

"Stuff that involves my MedIDs?"

"All due respect, Reverend, they're not yours."

"And they're not yours."

He can't argue that.

"You're stealing from our soldiers. And you're stealing from my home. What were you planning to do with the biochips?"

There's no way he's going to tell Reverend Mitchell about Steven's Project Swap. Just lie. "I need money. Clean MedIDs are like gold."

A long silence fills the room. The Reverend takes a stool at the kitchen counter and studies him. Finally he says, "Money and MedIDs should be the least of your worries, Jonathan."

"I'm done, sir. I just want out."

"I wish it were that easy."

"It is." Jonathan's stomach aches with nerves. "I'm just one guy. You have thousands."

"After the mission, you may go."

"No. Listen, I don't want any part of it."

"Sleep on it. You may change your mind." The Reverend gestures to Henry, who takes the briefcase and continues aiming the gun at Jonathan.

Without another word, Henry escorts him back to the basement, this time to a cell-like room. When the door locks behind him, Jonathan falls onto the bed, exhausted, his muscles tight and throbbing as though he ran a marathon. He stares at the ceiling. Steven is probably calling and texting him every hour. And Hannah.

He was so stupid, trusting her. Believing she might actually choose him over the Reverend. He's out of ideas now, out of a plan. Mitchell's residence is off the grid, so how would anyone even find him? It's like he's buried alive.

October, 2032

Chapter 52

AS NIGHT BURNS into morning, Sebastian rides his bike aimlessly through the outskirts of Boston. Faces, theories, and memories have kept sleep at bay lately. He's numb. Confused. And the rush of the air, the sheer speed he can reach on the empty streets, is invigorating.

Last night Renner didn't show at their meeting place. Despite numerous attempts, Sebastian hasn't been able to reach him. It's unlike Renner. He needs to brainstorm with his partner. Get his take on things.

They need to dig deeper into Mitchell's accusation that the government orchestrated the State House attack and Gardiner's assassination. And Kate's murder. But is it just an accusation? It's in-line with Renner's theory that ties the nickname Dash to Carter Benson, then to President Clark, along with Richard Hensley. But it goes against Sebastian's gut that Mitchell is behind everything. It's dizzying.

Suddenly, he realizes where he's going. Two lefts, a right. Past streetlights and buildings. He can't get there fast enough. Before he knows it, he sees the apartment building, hoists the bike over his shoulder and runs through the front door, up the three flights of stairs. He unstraps his helmet and knocks. The door opens.

"Will?" Taylor wears a T-shirt and boxers, her hair messy from sleep.

"I'm sorry."

"For what?"

"I don't know."

"Come in."

Behind the closed door, he sets his bike against the wall, tosses his helmet over it. Then he cups her face in his hands and takes her in. Her furrowed brow softens. Everything that's been building in him comes out now and he can hardly control himself. He peels off his sweat-soaked shirt and realizes he's wearing his skins. She doesn't seem to care or think twice. She peels the skins off him, runs her hands over his bare chest. Thoughts dissipate, he is right here, fully in the moment. She leads him into her bedroom. Light leaks in through the shades, the air smells of citrus. Her touch unravels him, makes him want her, need her more. They slam against the wall, moving blindly, falling onto the bed. Their eyes connect and she smiles, full and happy, as he's never seen her before. And he wishes more than anything it could last.

A FEW HOURS later Sebastian and Taylor sit together in a pew at Patriot's Church. He hasn't heard a word of Mitchell's sermon. All he can think about is Renner. What if Renner told Satterwhite his hunch about Dash being in the government? Sweat coats his palms and he rubs them against his pant legs, pressing the one with the tattoo harder, as though he might be able to rub it off. He needs to find his partner.

Mitchell says the blessing and the congregation stands, moving through the aisles toward the exits. Sebastian and Taylor are propelled along with the crowd into the main hall.

"Want some coffee?" She slips her arm through his and nods at the line forming in front of large coffee urns. Her touch still surprises him, though they've been together for hours now.

There's nothing to be learned here in Mitchell's public facade. "Let's go to a café. There's a great one in District 19."

"Perfect." Taylor checks her watch. "Sienna's with her sitter for another couple hours."

"Sebastian?" From somewhere in the crowd a man is calling his name. His real name. There must be other Sebastians in the room, though. "Sebastian." The tone is insistent, the voice familiar. He looks over Taylor's shoulder. *Shit. Oh shit.* He scans the room for the closest exit, but there are so many people there's not a clear path. What the hell is Cole doing here?

"Is something wrong?" she asks.

"No, just thirsty."

"Sebastian." Cole is at his side, searching his face. "What are you doing here?"

Calm. Cool. Breathe. He won't let his cover be blown. It's been four months since he'd visited Cole and Lily and told them he had an assignment and wouldn't be able to see them until it was completed.

"Sorry, you've got the wrong guy," Sebastian says, working to keep his face emotionless. He takes Taylor's hand and pulls her in the opposite direction.

"Lily would love to see you."

Lily. The name lands in his stomach and takes root. He turns back around. "Look, my name is Will. Will Anderson." He stares intently into Cole's eyes. Please understand. You know who I am. You know what I do.

"Oh, sorry." There's desperation in Cole's voice and his eyes are ringed with a badge of exhaustion. He raises a hand in apology. "They say everyone has a doppelganger out there. Sorry to have bothered you."

"No problem."

"But maybe you—or your friend—can help me with a church member I'm looking for," Cole says, indicating Taylor.

"Who's that?" Sebastian asks.

"Jonathan Hudson. Young kid. Mop of hair. A couple facial piercings."

"Hudson," Taylor repeats. "Doesn't ring a bell."

Sebastian shakes his head. "Sorry we can't help."

"Well," Cole says. "Again, sorry to bother you." He pivots and disappears into the crowd.

"He seemed pretty convinced he knew you," Taylor says.

"It's probably the beard. Half my face is hidden, after all. Now how about that coffee?"

Together they wend their way out the front doors of Patriot's Church. Their chatter streams along, with her doing most of the talking. What the hell was Cole doing at Patriot's Church? And who's the kid? Sebastian needs to keep Cole as far away from BASIA as possible.

At the café in District 19 they sit outside wearing parkas, enjoying the sunny, crisp air. As though it's a normal day, in a normal world. Sipping lattes and holding hands are luxuries now. Still, Sebastian sips his drink, trades smiles with Taylor, and mentally squashes the spikes of memory and emotion that are attempting to break through.

It's late in the afternoon now, as Cole focuses on Sebastian's car, several feet ahead. It was disorienting, shocking even, to see him at Patriot's Church. It was so natural to approach him, it hadn't even occurred to him why he might be there. Last summer when Sebastian had told them that he was going away on assignment, Cole had assumed it meant he was relocating. But there he was, holding the hand of that blond woman. She looked familiar but he couldn't place her. Has Sebastian moved on from Kate so easily? Either way, maybe now there's a different inroad to find Jonathan and get him out of BASIA. Cole can't let this go—the only reason Jonathan's in danger is because of Project Swap.

After dropping off the woman, Sebastian parks on a side street off Commonwealth Avenue. Cole pulls into an adjacent alley. He follows Sebastian on foot, leaving a block between them. Tracks in the slush lead to the back door of the old BU Bookstore. The door is ajar. He slides through and it takes a few seconds for his eyes adjust to the darkness. Except for heavy footsteps leading upstairs, the building is completely silent. Four floors up there's no sign of Sebastian. An emergency fire exit leads to the roof.

Cole opens the door. The air is weighted by a heavy mist.

"What are you doing here?" Sebastian's voice comes from directly behind him.

Cole spins around and they're face-to-face. "I could ask you the same thing."

"I'm an FBI agent. Doing my job. And you almost blew my cover today." Sebastian's voice is tinged with anger and his eyes are intense. A side of him Cole's never seen.

"I'm sorry. Really. I was thrown off, seeing you there."

"What the hell are you doing? Why are you following me?"

"It didn't start out that way," he says. "But now that I know you're inside Patriot's Church, I was hoping you could help me."

"I'm in neck deep, Cole." Sebastian wanders away for a moment, then returns. "You have about three minutes and then you need to get out of here. I have a meeting."

"Steven Hudson—Jonathan's father—has been threatened," he explains. "Reverend Mitchell is extorting money for Jonathan's return."

"Far as I've seen, everyone's there of his or her own will."

"He didn't join the church or BASIA. He took a job with the Reverend."

"Doing what?"

"Not sure exactly. But he's a hacker. Talented but reckless, apparently. Kid's already been arrested. I'm guessing Mitchell is utilizing his talents."

"Sounds feasible."

Can he tell him about Project Swap? It's impossible to explain without implicating himself. But Sebastian was almost a member of his family. There has to be a degree of trust. "The last time we saw Jonathan, he had a plan to steal clean MedIDs that Mitchell's been collecting from the soldiers."

"What?" Sebastian steps closer. "Why?"

"Let's leave it at that."

"It's helpful to have the bigger picture."

"I can't. Not yet."

"Jesus, Cole. Okay. I'll look into it, see what I can find out. But I'm in a bit of a shit storm myself."

"I appreciate it."

"You need to go now."

"Don't you clandestine types meet under the cover of night usually?"

Sebastian grins. "Usually. But I just got a message and my handler wants to meet at dusk. So here I am."

A creak makes them turn and the door to the roof slams shut. A loud click sounds—the lock? Sebastian draws his gun and he runs toward the door. Cole follows. Attached with putty of some kind, a microdrive clings to do the door. Sebastian takes it and plugs it into his phone.

"What is it?" Cole says.

"Codes. Decrypted codes." Sebastian studies the small screen in his palm, strokes his beard with his free hand. He begins to mumble under his breath. "Goddammit. If this is synchronized, I don't know if we can organize this kind of manpower."

"I'm sure it's classified," Cole says. "But is there anything I can do?"

Sebastian bends at the waist as though he's been hit in the stomach. Still he mumbles quietly, like he's processing information. "There are fifty coordinates."

"For each state?" Cole asks.

"But when? Election Day? Thanksgiving? Christmas?" Sebastian straightens and pulls on the handle, but the door doesn't budge. He slams his palm against the metal door. "Renner! Renner, goddammit."

The moment feels private, like Cole doesn't belong. He has no idea what he's just stepped in. A tone sounds on Sebastian's phone. From a few feet away Cole can see Agent Renner's face. He knows him from their hospital visits to bombing victims. It's a prerecorded video. "It's over, Sebastian. I have new orders and they include eliminating you. We had a good run, though. You got so close. Too close. And you should know the truth when you die. I confirmed Dash is Carter Benson, deputy campaign manager to

Richard Hensley. At least you have some resolution. Blame President Clark, Hensley, and the government for taking Kate. Looks like they were also the ones who tried to run down Taylor in the alley that night. She's bad press. Seb, I'll miss our two A.M. coffees. Good luck. You have five seconds left."

Without hesitation Sebastian turns in the direction of the alleyway and with full force hurls the phone, drive still in it, so that it disappears over the edge. A tremendous explosion shakes the building, the sheer power knocking Cole and Sebastian over. Cole checks his torso, his hands run down his legs and arms. His whole body is shaking. He looks over to Sebastian. There's no blood, no contorted limbs, just a thick layer of dust covering him.

"Good friend?" Cole says.

The slightest gasp-laugh sound escapes Sebastian. "In this business, one minute you're friends, the next, well."

"You're dead."

"He'll have to keep trying. But he wouldn't have warned me about the blast if he really wanted me dead."

"Why bother at all, then?"

"He has orders. Appearances are everything."

Sebastian is the first to his feet. He offers a hand to Cole. "Get home to Lily. There's a fire escape on the east side."

Descending the rusted staircase, Cole takes each step slowly as he fights to regain the practiced calm that has gotten him through years in emergency medicine. At the bottom the asphalt beneath his feet is hard, immovable. Pleasing. Sebastian lands next to him. His hair and beard are wet and gray with dust. Cole knows he must look the same.

"Stick to being a doctor," Sebastian says. "It's safer."

"Not anymore." Cole looks around at the crumbling building facades around them. "Remember when you used to argue the merits of this government?"

A flash of anger, a flush in Sebastian's checks. "When we're ill-informed, we make bad decisions."

Time to go. Cole offers his hand and Sebastian shakes it.

"I'll look for the kid, see what I can do," Sebastian says.

"Thanks. Let me know if I can help in any way."

"There's a hit out on me, Cole. Stay as far away as possible."

That, Cole can't argue.

Chapter 53

WITH THREE WEEKS to go in the election, Richard has given in to being shuttled around like a child. His team schedules him for ninety-minute visits in one state after another. He pumps hands, spews rhetoric, grins until his face hurts, and drinks so much coffee it hardly has an effect anymore. After he gives his stump speech on the lawn of the mayor's sprawling estate in West Chester, Ohio, he escapes into the mansion.

With the mayor still outside shaking hands with constituents, the house is empty. His footfalls echo off the high ceilings as he wanders, slipping into a formal living room filled with stiff, ornate sofas. The din of voices outside reminds him time is of the essence. He pulls out his phone, touches his thumb to unlock the screen. The live feed of Taylor's home fills the screen. He pulls up Sienna's room. A fairy in the sunlight dances on a pink tufted rug. He breathes easier, catches himself smiling. Such a lovely little creature. If anything happens to Taylor, Sienna will come to live with him. A little girl's dream—to live in the White House!

But his thoughts quickly darken, turning to the threat over

his girls. Despite his blood pressure medicine, the stress is getting to him. Since receiving the text with the bribe, he's been out of breath, sweating profusely, not sleeping. The money isn't ready yet. The Cape house remains on the market, though the Nantucket property sold. Still, the paperwork takes weeks. Even if he cleared out all of his savings accounts, he doesn't have five million dollars to hand over to Charles Mitchell. There must be another alternative.

The door to the room opens. Richard wheels around, drops the phone and fumbles for it. When he looks up, he sees it's only Carter. "Five minutes, sir. We need to get to the airport or we'll be late to Wisconsin."

"Yes, yes." He's under constant watch, everything he says and does, everywhere he goes. By Reverend Mitchell and by his own people. After days of debating how to handle this extortion for the safety of Taylor and Sienna, he's had to admit to himself that he can't do it alone. But all his close friends are mired in politics with a web of strings attached. Old family and friends are dead, out of touch, or have emigrated. He has to take a chance on someone.

The door begins to close.

"Carter?" He steps back into the room. "I need help with something."

"Of course."

"It's quite unorthodox." Richard takes a seat on one of the couches. "It needs to be handled quietly. With the utmost confidentiality."

"We've known each other two years, Senator." Carter sits in an adjacent chair. "I hope you know by now that you can trust me."

The weight on his chest eases as he explains the situation with Mitchell.

"So, you want me to do the swap?" Carter asks. "The money for your daughter?"

"Not exactly." Richard leans in, elbows on his knees. "I can't get that kind of money. Not this fast. So, we need to get Taylor and Sienna out. Transport them somewhere Mitchell can't find them."

"Excuse me for saying so, sir, but it's only money. Why take chances? Can you just ask for more time so you can pull it together?"

"If I thought that would be the end of it. But even if I hand over the money, Taylor won't leave Mitchell. My granddaughter will still be in danger. And when I'm in the White House they'll come back with more requests, more demands. I need to put an end to this."

Carter hesitates briefly, then nods. "Thank you for confiding in me, sir. I'll help you however I can."

The door to the room swings open and Kendra stomps in, breathless. "What's happening? You two sitting down to a formal tea?"

"That sounds lovely, actually," Richard says.

"Wheels up," Kendra says. "Wisconsin here we come."

Richard follows his team back down the hall and into the Town Car. Sharing his burden with Carter is a relief. Together they'll come up with a viable plan. And goddamn if he's going to let Mitchell win.

Chapter 54

IN THEIR EYES, Charles sees salvation. From the podium at BASIA HQ he soaks in the enormity of his efforts. In this building and via monitors around the country, God's Army of thousands stand at ease awaiting instructions at their final training session. Glory be. They will pave the way for the Second Coming.

"On your way out tonight, each of you will pick up your mission pack," he says. They hang on his every word. "Each pack has the necessities on which to live for three days. All you'll need to get in and back out to a safe location."

Out is open to interpretation. These fine men and women have been trained thoroughly and believe in their mission, in the word of God. No need for his meaning to be overt.

"In the coming days you will be measured and fitted for clothing appropriate to your mission," he continues. "You will complete your training. And finally, you'll receive your assignment and specific instructions. Flights and hotels will be arranged and paid for. There's to be no contact with your families once you leave home. You don't want to put them at risk."

Heads nod throughout the crowd and on the monitors. He says, "We have over five hundred targets. Clearly they're outnumbered."

Laughter erupts. The joyous sound lifts him, his eyes fill. These people are his beloved family. He moves his hand to his heart, then opens his palm in the air. In unison, his soldiers do the same.

"Armed with His blessing and strength, you will deliver us from the present evil age, according to the will of our God and Father. Go with God."

The screens go black. The soldiers in the room stand and a hum of voices begins, indecipherable words, a fusion of vowels and consonants. Henry follows closely behind him as they exit the stage.

"I need to see Anderson," Charles says. Henry veers into the mass of people gathering near the door.

In the Command Center at the control panel, Charles relaxes, rests his head on the soft leather of his chair. His fingers press into his right palm, his nail tracing the cross. What a beautiful, perfect plan God has revealed. Years of work finally coming to fruition. There's a knock at the door. He sits up straight.

"Come in."

Henry enters with Will Anderson, who salutes and stands at attention.

"At ease, Sergeant. Thank you, Henry."

Henry closes the door behind him.

"Please, sit." He motions to a chair and Anderson sits.

"Thank you, sir."

"Your sharpshooting skills have been brought to my attention."

"My father took me hunting from a young age."

"He would be proud, then." Charles appraises him. A good find indeed. "You've proven your commitment to God and our cause with the earlier matter you brought to my attention."

"Yes, sir."

"There's a special, sensitive matter I'd like you to handle."

"I'm ready, sir."

"A member of our brethren needs protection. I believe the two of you have become close recently."

Anderson cocks his head. "I'm not sure who you mean."

"Taylor Hensley."

The light dawns. Anderson's his eyes widen. Clearly, he's surprised to find their relationship is not secret.

"I'm afraid she's in danger. You must know, her very existence threatens her father's political aspirations. She's part of her family here and she needs us now. So, continue your . . . friendship with her. In fact, I encourage you to become entrenched in her life. For the safety of her and her daughter."

"Of course," Anderson says. "Is there anything in particular I should be watching out for when I'm with her?"

The senator's money should be coming through any time now. "As it happens, Richard Hensley is about to make a considerable donation to the church. He's trying to buy back his daughter. For a smart man, he should know love can't be bought. So as we wait for the transaction to go through, we need to ensure that Taylor and her daughter remain here, in their hometown. Not taken by Hensley's men in the middle of the night."

"Is Taylor aware of any of this?"

"No. We shouldn't worry her. She should lead her normal, day-to-day life, utterly unaware of our protection. Is that clear?"

"Yes, sir."

"This won't be a challenge for you. The trust between you and

Taylor is already there. It should be more of a reward than an assignment, really."

Behind the beard, Anderson grins. "Thank you."

"You've met my chief technology officer, Huan Chao? He'll provide you access to video feeds into Taylor's home. You need to get in deeper, faster. Figure out what she wants, and give it to her. Enjoy yourself, but don't forget this isn't a dating service, it's your job."

"I appreciate your trust," Anderson says. "If I may ask, is this my role in our mission? To protect Taylor Hensley?"

"No. This is like extra credit, Sergeant. Play before work. Yours will be a key role in our Holy War."

"Thank you, sir."

"You're dismissed, Sergeant."

Anderson stands and leaves. Once again Charles rests his head on his chair, kneads his palm. Anderson's a good man. He couldn't ask for more in a soldier. But should he be placed in the center of the action, where he can handle himself deftly? Or assign him an easy target, one with little risk that will ensure he returns home? Either way, God wins.

Chapter 55

"HOLD HER STILL," Dr. Westin says. She positions the MedID injector over the translucent skin of Talia's forearm. "Just a pinch. It'll all be over in a second."

A burn, Lily remembers. It's more of a burn than a pinch. Five-month-old Talia squirms, never happy when her body is restrained. Well who would be? Lily holds down her arms, kisses her forehead. Cole stands opposite, his hands gripping Talia's legs firmly but gently. The pediatrician injects the MedID into her arm. Talia's high-pitched screams tear at Lily's insides and she blinks back tears. It's hard to know if it's empathy for Talia's pain or the disappointment of knowing the end result.

"You're okay, little one." Dr. Westin deposits the injector on the counter and takes the MRS. With a wave over the site, the MedID is activated. The doctor calls up the chart and the smartwall illuminates a screen with details from Talia's DNA. In seconds Talia's MedID number, 74, appears in red next to her name. Her pediatrician says, "All done."

Lily picks up the sobbing Talia and holds her close. The three of them stare at the screen. To be one number away is cruel.

"I'm sorry," Dr. Westin says. "Do you have any questions?"

"If I'd done the in-utero screening—" Her cheeks are hot, her shirt suddenly damp under her armpits. She buries her head in Talia's neck. "This is my fault."

"There's no way to know, Lily." The doctor stands and disposes of the injection needle, stores the MRS.

"Her whole life is on a different track because I was too stubborn."

"You did what you thought was best for your child," Dr. Westin says.

"She's perfect." Cole stands abruptly, pulling on his jacket. "Talia's exactly who she's supposed to be."

"Of course she is." Dr. Westin gives a conciliatory smile. "Call me if you have questions."

"Thank you." Lily's fingertips caress the soft folds of Talia's legs, she inhales her scent. Cole swoops over and takes their baby, buckles her into the car seat and they leave the pediatrician's office.

They haven't spoken for weeks. After all these years, he's like a stranger to her. This movement of theirs, this Project Swap, is treason. Her momentary relief that he's not having an affair with Dr. Riley has been replaced by anger at his willingness to put his family in danger. They could be torn apart by this, the children taken away. He could be imprisoned, and God knows what would happen to her.

Back in the car, she slams shut her passenger door as Cole powers the ignition and shuts off automated drive. Shifting gears, he tears out of the medical practice parking lot, down the street.

Not in the direction of home. Holding her tongue is the last thing she has control of, but she can't do it any longer.

"Where are you going?" she demands.

"It's time. You need to see what we're doing."

"I've heard and seen enough."

"Please Lily, I need you to trust me."

"Forgive me if I don't trust you after watching you burn a crime scene. You've put your entire family on the line. You could destroy us all, Cole. And all we have is us."

"I understand. But I want you to see it for yourself. And then make up your mind."

Soon they're in Cambridge. The once quaint neighborhood is just like the rest of them, ruined, unrecognizable. "I want to go home."

"We're almost there."

One hundred, ninety-nine, ninety-eight, ninety-seven . . . Counting backward helps her to calm down. When she hits sixty-two the car stops. Before her is a slightly off-kilter Victorian painted a bright lilac color with shutters that hang off the windows. Long curls of paint give the building a shaggy look. Cole retrieves Talia, who now sleeps soundly after her MedID ordeal. Reluctantly, Lily gets out. An oak tree shades the front yard and rains a steady stream of leaves in the breeze, acorns hitting the pavement with an infrequent, dull beat.

"What is this place?" she asks.

"Our headquarters."

She follows him inside. The air is musty, mixed with a strong antiseptic scent. There are holes in the wall and patches of rotting floorboards. It's quiet, no one in sight. Then a door down the hall opens and closes. A man wearing a surgical mask passes them on his way out. He doesn't make eye contact or acknowledge them in any way.

"Next," a male voice calls from the same doorway.

From an adjacent room—what used to be a living room—two women also wearing surgical masks emerge, quickly disappearing into the room down the hall. Lily notices Dr. Riley—Karen—sitting at a desk in the living room. She's talking in hushed tones to what looks like a teenage boy, also with a mask.

"Why is everyone wearing masks?" she asks.

"Anonymity. The process is quick and we ensure privacy to anyone who comes."

With Talia's car seat in hand, Cole leads her through the house as he talks in depth about Project Swap. It's a lot to take in. Slowly her animosity—for his lies, his secrets—dissipates. He's helping these people. They're all desperate with diminishing hope, just like they were when they were turned away in London. She watches him talk to his team members and her chest aches for him, for her.

In Sean Cushing's room, she wears a mask and watches as he wipes a MedID clean. Just like that, a life is changed, restored. A family is whole again, they can move around in the world without predisposed physical barriers to employment, home, medical access. With both hands, the person envelopes Sean's hand, shaking it with pure gratitude. Lily imagines that behind all these masks there are smiles. Perhaps determined looks of hope.

Cole sets the car seat on the floor and rocks it with his foot. "I'm sorry I didn't tell you from the beginning, Lily. But what we're doing is dangerous. I guess I just wanted to keep you and the kids safe in the district, as long as I could."

"No more secrets."

"No more secrets." He wraps his arms around her.

"Will all these people leave the country?"

"Some will." He looks around. "But many will stay and try to make a better life here. We're building an underground network. Eventually this group will make a difference. We'll take positions of power in the government. We'll have a say in our own lives again."

"A new political party?"

Cole nods.

"How many people are you talking about?"

"We're growing quickly. Sean's brought in associates with his skill set and they're planning to expand our reach. In the Northeast alone we've helped hundreds in only a few weeks."

"The government will kill you, Cole." She squeezes his arm. "They'll either kill everyone here or put you all in prison for life."

"We're being careful. It's a calculated risk."

"I don't like any risk. Especially when it might affect Ian and Talia."

"I'm trying to give them options. To give them a future."

"But what if you're arrested?" she asks. "What if we're arrested? The state takes the kids? They go into foster care?"

"I won't let that happen."

"We could lose everything."

"Family is everything," he says. "If I woke up tomorrow and our house was gone, the hospital was gone, all of this." He gestures to the Project Swap headquarters. "If I was with you, Ian, and Talia, I would still have everything."

"There are no guarantees." That's what she wants. It's why she stays at home most days, where she makes decisions that are confined to the life inside the four main walls of that house.

"Let's give ourselves a guarantee," he says.

Lily and Talia slide into the schedule, between Sean Cushing's appointments. Still, she can't shake the uneasy feeling. Sean takes the MRS and punches in a few keys on the computer. A red light emanates from the scanner and in one fluid movement he brushes it over Talia's MedID site. Instantly, her medical record appears on the screen.

"What number do you want?" Sean asks, his fingers hovering over the keyboard.

"Safe but not obvious," Cole says.

"Eighty-two," she says. Safe, clean.

"Eighty-two. Keys to the kingdom." Sean types away and in minutes Talia's medical record is rescanned, her MedID updated to reflect the change.

"Your turn, Lil," Cole says.

"Me?"

"Sixty-seven doesn't cut it," Cole says. "Imagine how well you'll sleep at night with, say, a seventy-eight."

She'd been so focused on Talia, on all of this, that it hadn't occurred to her that she might want to have her own MedID cleaned. Since stepping through the threshold of this place, her entire world has been challenged, and changed. In this room, as everyone stares expectantly at her and Sean dangles the MRS in wait. She realizes she's been fighting alone. It's time to join the others.

Chapter 56

THE GRAY SUV speeds under the streetlights of Route 9. A few cars behind, Steven drives his favorite hearse. As conspicuous as it is, it's an unlikely vehicle to use when following someone. The thought makes him grin vaguely. He'd waited in his car all afternoon, into the evening, until he saw Reverend Mitchell and his bodyguard leaving Patriot's Church. Twenty minutes later they're west of Boston and he has no idea where this ride will end. It's a dangerous errand. If this religious zealot was truly behind the Planes, he's capable of anything. And if Mitchell was the one who took Kelly, Sam, and Georgia from him, goddamned if he will let him take Jonathan. It's been a week since that hulk of a man, Harry, Henry, whatever, showed up and demanded three million dollars. Steven doesn't have it, won't have it. The most he could pull together is a little over a million in cash. Hell, he'll throw in the hearse.

The SUV veers off the highway and onto a dark stretch of road. After several turns it heads down a gravel drive, thick with trees. Steven can't see the house from here. His mouth is dry, his stomach in knots. The hearse kicks up a funnel of dust behind it as he presses on. About a mile in an enormous mansion appears, surrounded by a wall and a gated security system. At the gate, he begins to reach his arm out the window to press a call button when the gate suddenly swings open.

"He knows I'm here," Steven mutters to himself. "Shit."

The gates close as he pulls inside, around a circular drive, coming to a stop behind the SUV. Waiting for him at the front door are Reverend Mitchell and his bodyguard.

Deep breath. Steven eases himself out, careful to appear confident, chin up, his right hand firmly gripping an old leather briefcase.

"Mr. Hudson," Reverend Mitchell says. "Welcome to my home."

He shakes the Reverend's extended hand. "Was I too obvious in my hearse?"

Mitchell laughs. "It's a pleasure to meet the man behind Hudson's."

"I'm not sure anything about our meeting is a pleasure."

Gesturing to the door, the Reverend says, "Please. Come in."

Crossing the threshold, Steven's grip tightens on the briefcase. Inside, the house is alive with voices. Children of all ages, but mostly teenagers, roam about or lounge in a living room playing video games. What is this? Are all of these kids being held for ransom? They look content, certainly not under any duress. He searches their faces. No Jonathan.

A circuitous route ends in a wood-paneled office. Reverend Mitchell sinks comfortably into the leather chair behind his desk. Steven takes the rather stiff one across from it, placing the briefcase on his lap. The bodyguard closes the door, staying inside, annoyingly mute.

"Where's Jonathan?" Steven asks.

"He's here," Mitchell says.

Without explaining the contents, Steven slides the briefcase across the desk. He swallows. It's impossible to guess what his reaction will be. Coming here with less than three million was a risk. But he's run out of time.

Mitchell peers inside the case briefly, then closes it. "Where's the rest?"

"It's what I have. It's not unsubstantial. A million dollars goes a long way these days."

"Indeed. But that wasn't the price."

"It's all that I have."

"We're both businessmen, Mr. Hudson. You can't expect me to believe that with your nationally successful chain the most you can come up with is one million dollars?"

"As a businessman, I'm sure you're aware of the ebbs and flows of business. The constant need to reinvest, to grow the business. Currently most of my savings and the profits from the past few months have been funneled back into the business."

"Hmm. How unfortunate." Mitchell pushes the briefcase aside. The man's hands clutch together, hard, until his knuckles are white.

"Take the million dollars." Something inside Steven is unraveling. "Please let me take Jonathan. And we'll be out of here."

Mitchell clears his throat. "Come back when you have the rest."

The bodyguard appears at his side. Sweat soaks Steven's back. His head begins to throb. He locks eyes with Mitchell and strains to keep an even voice. "The way I look at it, Reverend, I've already paid. Again, and again, and again."

Mitchell doesn't flinch, doesn't register that he understood Steven's meaning. Is it possible he wasn't behind the Planes? Is someone else responsible for the deaths of Kelly and the kids?

"I'll go to the media," Steven says. "The police. FBI. Tell them that the famous Reverend Mitchell extorts money to fund his so-called Armageddon and—" He flounders, gestures to the door. "Recruits young children that he brainwashes into spreading his insidious words."

Mitchell's smile reveals perfectly straight, polished teeth. He leans his elbows on his desk and leans closer.

"The media would eat it up, Mr. Hudson. The FBI would be on my doorstep within the hour to reunite you with your stepson. But we're all programmed with self-preservation, aren't we?" From his jack, the bodyguard retrieves a tablet and hands it to Steven.

A video plays. Shaky footage, from someone entering a building. Steven narrows his eyes at the screen. The rooms, the people. It's Project Swap HQ. Holy shit. *Holy shit.* A BASIA mole pretended to need a MedID, was wiped by Sean Cushing and released back into the world. Steven swallows back bile that burns his throat. He sets the tablet on the desk.

"As I said, self-preservation. We wondered why on earth Jonathan would want to steal the clean MedIDs from our soldiers. So we did some research of our own and what we found was so interesting. Don't you agree?"

"No one's innocent anymore. But we're not hurting anyone."

"I think the U.S. government would disagree."

Behind him there's a creak. Steven turns to see that the bodyguard has opened the door. He turns back to Mitchell. "I'm not leaving without my son."

"I'm afraid the deck's not stacked in your favor, Mr. Hudson. You've committed treason. Your son is an accomplice. And with a slight reach, I think you could even be implicated in the death of your lovely wife."

Steven leaps up and dives across the desk. He grabs Mitchell by the throat, watches his face turn scarlet, his eyes bulge. Mitchell grips his wrists and tries to pry them away. When that doesn't work, his fists fly at Steven. Suddenly, hands latch onto Steven's arms and jerk him up and back like he's a puppet. The guard holds him, unaffected by his struggling. Mitchell coughs, pushes up from his chair and rubs his throat. Then he straightens, his hands smoothing back his mane of hair. His smile is gone, a flush remains in his cheeks. He walks around to the front of the desk where Steven dangles from muscular arms.

"That wasn't very smart." Without warning, Mitchell slugs him in the stomach.

Doubling over, pain radiates through Steven. *Son of a bitch*. He can only gasp as he watches Mitchell pace in front of him.

"I'll let Jonathan know you dropped by. Please do visit again soon. Don't let a little money stand in the way of a future with your family." He leans in closer now, so that his mouth is almost touching Steven's ear. In a whisper he adds, "After all, if you could bring back your dead wife and kids for a mere three million dollars, wouldn't you?"

The guard releases him. He crumbles to the ground, his knees weak, his tongue failing him for any kind of response. An admission! As close as anyone could get. He'll kill Mitchell. He'll kill him before this is over.

Roughly gripping his arm, the guard escorts him out. Steven hardly registers the soles of his shoes making contact with the ground, going from the polished marble tiles of the hallway onto the front porch, down the stairs, brushing across the pea-stone driveway. His whole body shakes. For ten years he's wanted to know who to hate, who to blame for the death of his family. Now he knows.

As he opens the hearse door, Steven is overcome. Vomit spills from him, along with a gust of emotion. He wipes his face with the back of his sleeve and gets in, starts the car as he replays the conversation with Mitchell. As the gates close behind him, he vows to rescue Jonathan. But first he's got to warn Cole and the others.

Chapter 57

TAYLOR OPENS HER apartment door to see Will, grinning beneath a newly trimmed beard.

"Hair cut?" she says.

"Didn't want it to interfere with my wind speed."

She laughs. He carries his bike over his shoulder and a bouquet of daisies in his other hand. No one's given her flowers in years. As she puts them in a vase, he plays with Sienna. Lying on the floor, he scoops her onto his feet, playing airplane. He's so good with her. An ache in her chest tells her how badly she's wanted someone in her life. These past few weeks with Will have brought such comfort and happiness into their world. Sometimes being with him makes it difficult to breathe. It's fear, she knows. She often wonders if it's fair to bring a man into their lives, to expose Sienna to someone she could lose. But this feels good. It feels right.

The three of them eat dinner together, though after ten minutes Sienna departs, opting for toys over food. Taylor grins at Will as he drops spaghetti sauce onto his T-shirt.

"Can't take me anywhere," he says, dabbing a napkin at the spots.

"It's good to know you're not perfect."

"Far from it."

She studies him. He's a good listener, always asking her questions, interested in what she has to say. It occurs to her that she hasn't done the same for him.

"So, where's your family?" she asks. "Are your parents still around?"

"It's just me. My mother died in childbirth. My father died a few years ago."

"I'm sorry."

"We've all got stories." He shakes his head. "No one's walking around unscathed."

She glances at his ring finger. "You never talk about your wife."

He hesitates, looks at his plate. "It's not the best dinner conversation."

"There is no best time for such topics."

The air changes, his shoulders hunch. Finally, he says, "Rose was a lieutenant in the army. During the L.A. Riots of 'twenty-four she was out fighting with her squad. You remember the fires? How they burned for days?"

She nods.

"They couldn't get her out. Didn't find her until days later."

"I'm so sorry."

"A shame we have so much in common." His lips press together, a thin, sad smile.

The other night she'd told him about Mason. He'd known some of it, of course, through the news. But it felt good to tell her version. How she'd spent her life blindly following her father, how she still feels responsible and guilty for Mason's death. Just sharing it with Will had lifted her spirits.

After dinner the sitter arrives. Taylor kisses Sienna and she and Will depart with their bikes. Outside, they strap on their helmets and prepare to ride. No press waiting for her on the lawn tonight. She breathes easier.

"Where're you taking me, woman?" he teases.

"Don't worry. We'll take it slow."

They glide down the street in the direction of the waterfront. The bitter October wind licks her cheeks, makes her eyes tear, though weather is never a deterrent to her art. And riding alongside Will makes her feel content, as though everything is in its place.

They wend through Boston's Seaport District, nearing her destination. Their tires on the pavement create a comforting sort of music. Will is just a few feet behind her. She wonders if he's watching her hips hovering just above the bike seat as they move. It's hard to believe she's doing this, bringing him. Not once in her career as a graffiti artist has she invited someone along.

"Here we are." She slows her bike and hops off. Will pulls beside her and the two stare up at the remains of a convention center that overlooks the harbor.

"Why here?" he asks.

"Remember the World Convention on Peace they held here? Look at it now, in ruins. I love the irony. The ocean side will be the canvas. Asian cargo ships dock at Southie's Conley Terminal. And depending on flight patterns, planes should be able to see it either departing from or arriving to Logan."

"A guaranteed audience."

"Exactly. Let's get started."

A narrow passage on the side of the building leads to the waterfront. The wall is four stories high, pure and clean and perfect. Taylor visualizes the piece, inspired by the Declaration of Independence. She considers how to approach the structure while considering the dimensions of the work. Will watches as she pulls out tools and accessories from her bag. Within seconds she's rigged a pulley and finishes by strapping on a safety harness.

She hears the hum of a car engine rising over the white noise of the wind and ocean. The rotation of rubber on asphalt is jarring.

"Dammit." She closes her eyes a split second. "Goddammit."

"The press?"

"Has to be."

"Okay. We have three options." Will lowers his voice. "Go back down the alleyway and confront them. Go around the building and ride out of here to try and ditch them. Or jump in." He glances behind them at the black ocean water. "I didn't bring a wet suit."

"There's one more way." She places suctioning attachments on her feet and tosses a pair to Will, along with another harness. "Follow everything I do and you'll be fine. We can travel along the rooftops."

A car door slams shut. Soles scratch the pavement as she begins to climb.

"Too late," he says, dropping the harness.

She moves quickly, doesn't turn to see the intruder. In seconds Will is only inches tall below her as she waits, hanging, at the top of the building.

From around the corner a man appears. He wears a suit and walks confidently, carrying no camera or video equipment. In the dark, she squints to see if she recognizes him. He's tall and lean, with black hair and dark features. Is that her father's aide?

"Will!" She can't just unharness herself and take off without him. Her numbed fingers fumble to unclip the latch on her courier bag but she can't quite do it, her phone is just out of reach. She looks down. Will is aiming a gun at the man. Why does he have a gun?

The man stops, raising his hands slowly into the air. "Sorry to interrupt," she hears the intruder say. His tone is friendly but cool. "I see you take your art seriously."

"You need to leave." Will steps toward him, his gun steady.

"This is public property, unless I'm mistaken?" He gestures to the gun. "Please. There's no need for that. Name's Carter Benson. And you are?"

"Not your new friend," Will says.

The man looks up and waves at her. "Taylor! I need you to do some of that—rappelling, is it? And come with me."

"You're my father's assistant," she says, recognizing him.

"Deputy campaign manager, actually. He's asked me to come on behalf of Sienna."

A wave of nausea hits as she grips the rope tighter. "Where is she?"

"She's fine," Carter says. "Didn't you get the text?"

Steadying herself, she shifts her bag and releases the clasp. Her head is dizzy with thoughts as she finds her phone. Sure enough, a new message is waiting for her. A video plays.

A close-up of Sienna stares back at her, cherubic and smiling, wearing her princess pajamas exactly as Taylor left her. "Mommy, look who's here! It's Grandpa!" From behind Sienna, Taylor's father leans into frame. "Taylor, honey. I thought it was time we had a little family reunion." The clip ends.

"She's five years old!" Taylor shouts. "Does he have so little power he has to involve a child?"

"He's about to be the most powerful man in the world," Carter says. "Perhaps he wanted a moment alone with his granddaughter before the madness starts."

"I'm pretty sure the madness has started," Will says, his voice surprising Taylor. His gun is still aimed.

Carter cocks his head. "Have we met?"

"I don't think we run in the same circles," Will says.

As the men stare at one another, Taylor considers her options. The truth is, if she died right here, right now, her father's problems would be solved. Hell, he'd probably look heroic, raising his orphaned granddaughter in the White House.

"You need to come with me," Carter calls up to her. "I'll take you to Sienna. She's safe." He puts a finger to his ear and appears to be listening to an earpiece, then looks up again. "Actually, right this moment she's having hot chocolate with her grandfather."

The rooftop is just a couple feet up. She can touch it with her fingertips. The urge to run is powerful. They'll leave Will alone, won't they? It's her they want, her silence, until her father wins the election. She waits, dangling in indecision.

ABOUT FORTY FEET away Sebastian focuses on Carter Benson, a.k.a. Dash. Dark eyes, a brush of stubble on his olive cheeks and chin. A slightly different shade of skin and they could be brothers. Adrenaline courses through him, every muscle taut. Maybe Benson didn't release the sarin himself, but he sure as shit helped arrange it. It doesn't matter that he's a middleman. In the end, we all have choices. Sebastian's index finger strokes the gun's smooth metal trigger.

"You okay, Taylor?" He glances up at her.

"How did you find us?" she asks Benson.

"Your father wants to ensure you're safe," Benson says. "Please, come down. I'll take you to Sienna."

"Despite what he's done, my father won't hurt Sienna."

"You're right about that," Benson says. "But have you wondered exactly why Will—it's Will, right?—is so interested in you? No offense, you're perfectly attractive and all that."

"What's he talking about, Will?"

Utterly confused, Sebastian is momentarily speechless. How does Benson know his name? His alias? Maybe he's been watching the senator's video feeds from Taylor's apartment. That has to be it.

"I wouldn't know." He stares at Benson. "How do you know my name?"

Under his breath, so only Sebastian can hear, Benson says, "We're on the same side, brother. Go along. That's a direct order."

"I don't take orders from you."

Benson's voice is a growl. "But you do take them from Mitchell. So stand down." He looks up and shouts to Taylor, "He's an errand boy. The Reverend's puppet. He's been around a lot lately, hasn't he? Has barely let you out of his sight?"

Glancing at her, Sebastian can tell from her face that she's buying it. Goddammit. With one quick move he could shoot Benson in the leg, just to shut him up. But these pieces don't connect. If he shoots him, is he shooting Hensley's man? Or Mitchell's? Or both?

"Don't listen to him, Taylor," Sebastian says.

"Do you know that Reverend Mitchell is currently extorting a great deal of money from your father to keep you safe?" Benson continues. "This here is your bodyguard."

"He's full of shit." But he recalls Mitchell saying Hensley would be making a donation to the cause.

"Will?" Taylor's tone is unsure, with an edge of anger. "Is it true?"

"I don't know anything about extortion."

"But Reverend Mitchell is having you follow me?"

He searches the ground. His time with Taylor has been special. Not what he expected, certainly on assignment. It's more than he wanted, more than he's ready for. It's so soon after Kate, guilt is ever-present. But he can't tell her the truth, can't endanger the mission. Most important here is maintaining his status with Mitchell.

"The Reverend knows we're friends," Sebastian says. "He asked me to keep you safe. But I'd be here anyway, Taylor. You know that. Clearly, Reverend Mitchell was right, your father's agenda is threatened by your involvement in the church."

"Asshole!" she shouts.

"Put the gun down, Anderson," Benson orders.

A subtle zipping sound from above draws their eyes. Taylor's gone. There's a frozen moment between him and Benson. Their shared asset has just disappeared.

"If she gets away, this is on you." Benson backs up slowly until he's at the narrow passageway that leads to the street. He turns and breaks into a sprint.

Wouldn't Mitchell have told him about Benson? Maybe this is a test. Losing her is not an option. He tucks the gun into his belt and grabs the discarded harness. He straps it on, along with the suctioning fittings for his shoes. Though he hasn't done this since basic training, it comes back easily. Using Taylor's pulley, he swiftly makes his way up to the roof, where he rips off the equipment. There's no sound, no evidence which way she went. It's a maze of rooftops.

He runs at full speed toward the city skyline. Benson must be doing the same on the ground. There's no sign of her on the fire escape or in the alley below. She's not on the building ahead as he bounds between them and lands roughly on the next roof. Again and again, no sign of her. The buildings are dark, the streetlights, long since shut down in this part of town, leave only moonlight as a guide. The white noise of the Atlantic is constant. He studies cracks in the buildings, crevices just big enough for a body to hide.

A soft patter of feet. Yes—he sees her—a silhouette on the next building, like a hunchback with her courier bag. He leaps onto an old brick foundry as she descends a fire escape. So close now. He skips stairs, glides between landings. He lands next to her in an alleyway. Nearby, an engine revs.

Taylor backs away. "Stay away from me, Will."

"Not a chance."

"Apparently I can't trust anyone anymore."

"You can trust me, Taylor. Please, come with me. We'll get Sienna back."

"She's all that matters. I don't care anymore. About the war, the church, the election. You."

"That's fair. Smart, probably." He moves closer. "But I'd never hurt you."

"Too late."

She sprints toward the street. He follows as tires screech somewhere up ahead. At the sidewalk, she stops abruptly. He's there now, beside her, as Benson emerges from a Cadillac. There's one more thing Sebastian can try. From behind, he wraps his arm around Taylor's chest and aims the gun at her head. Her body tenses, she gasps. This is not what he wanted.

"That doesn't look much like protection," Benson says.

"Leave now," Sebastian says.

"In the end, we want the same thing." Benson rubs the palm of his right hand with this left thumb and looks pointedly at Sebastian. "The very same, Sergeant Anderson."

That's Mitchell's move, rubbing his tattoo. And how does Benson know his BASIA rank?

In a swift move, Benson pulls a gun from inside his jacket. He aims it at Taylor. "Ever met an orphan, Taylor? It's heartbreaking, really."

"Fuck you."

"See, Will?" Benson says. "We want the same thing."

When Sebastian makes strategic decisions on assignment, they're usually clear, obvious. This is anything but.

"Sienna's waiting," Benson says.

"Let me go," Taylor whispers. Her shoulders move, her body wriggling from his grasp. Reluctantly, he releases her, lets her go to him. His aim shifts to Benson.

"And what is it 'we' want?" Sebastian asks.

"One nation," Benson says, opening the driver door. "Under God."

Holy shit. Renner was right. Benson is Dash. And he's with Mitchell. And Richard Hensley? As Taylor slides into the passenger side of Benson's car, Sebastian wants to say something to her, but there's no time. The Cadillac speeds off. Taylor doesn't look back as they drive away.

Renner predictably walks his Labradoodle between 11 p.m. and midnight. Sebastian waits in the shadows at the dog park. It's a gamble. But this has to be done in person, outside, where it's unlikely anyone is listening. For a decade he and Renner have had the same training, the same beliefs. So despite the fact that Renner's new assignment is to kill him, he also knows Renner must be plagued by the evidence that their own government is corrupt. And that he's—they've—been working for the wrong side.

The door on the chain-link fence creaks as Renner and his dog enter. Sebastian knows he'll have his weapons on him. But so does he.

"Like clockwork," he says, emerging from behind a large oak tree.

Renner drops the leash and has the gun in his hand, expertly aimed, in two seconds. "Sebastian. Jesus Christ you scared the shit out of me."

"We need to talk." The big fluffy dog lopes over and nudges him in the crotch. Sebastian scratches his ears.

"You shouldn't be here." Renner lowers his gun. He gestures to Sebastian's ankle. "I noticed you removed the locator chip. Why serve yourself up on a platter?"

"What reason did Satterwhite give you for my termination?"

"The evidence against you is classified. But he claims that BASIA turned you. Says you're an enemy of the state now."

"Did you tell him that's ridiculous?" He pushes the dog away and sits on a bench.

Renner holsters his gun and strolls over. "He wasn't hearing any of it. Gave me the kill order and sent me on my way."

"Can we have a brief moratorium on your assignment?"

"If I'd wanted you dead, you'd be dead."

"Well that's one piece of good news." He organizes his thoughts from the evening. "I have new information on Carter Benson."

"A.k.a. Dash." Renner sits on the other end of the bench.

"Tonight he forced Taylor into a car with him. Richard Hensley kidnapped his granddaughter and they threatened Taylor with Sienna's safety. So, Taylor left with Benson."

Renner digests the news. "Okay. Hensley doesn't want his daughter to interfere with his presidential race. Benson helps to distance Hensley from Mitchell and severs any potential terrorist ties."

"At first glance, yes."

"What more is there?"

"Two weeks ago Mitchell asked me to protect Taylor. Said her father was a danger to her and Sienna. He also told me that Hensley would be making a sizable donation to BASIA. Which of course is impossible."

"And?"

"And tonight Benson—Dash, whatever—told Taylor that Mitchell is extorting money from her father."

"That adds up." Renner shakes his head. "What am I missing?"

"When Taylor was out of earshot, Benson said some things to me. First off, he knew my name—my alias. I never introduced myself. He said that he and I are on the same side, that we want the same thing. He said Mitchell was ordering me to stand down and let Taylor go with him. He even knew my BASIA rank. And he pointedly said that we all want 'One nation, under God.'"

Renner kicks at a patch of dirt. "You're saying Carter Benson is with Mitchell?"

"I think he's Mitchell's key to the kingdom." It's tangled, he knows.

"If that's true, Mitchell's been inside the White House via Benson for about ten years now."

"After Benson's mother martyred herself, maybe Mitchell stepped in as his benefactor. Maybe even as a parent figure. He does have that habit of collecting orphans."

"All right." Renner closes his eyes. "That would mean it was Benson who told Mitchell the White House was behind the State House attack and Gardiner's assassination."

"Exactly. So what's Richard Hensley's role in all this?"

"Hensley could have orchestrated all of it. Maybe he was behind the State House attack. Killing James Gardiner automatically positioned him as the next President."

"Risky." Sebastian nods. "But plausible."

"Or maybe he's a pawn."

Nervous energy courses through Sebastian. He stands and walks aimlessly. "President Clark and the Liberty Party want Hensley in office to prop up the MedID law. After years of working with Clark, Benson's now keeping company with Hensley. Maybe Benson's playing both sides. Helping Clark get what he wants. Helping Mitchell."

"This shit is making me dizzy."

"And if the FBI is behind our dead State House suspect, Michael O'Brien, there's another goddamned tie-in."

"That order would've had to come from President Clark," Renner mumbles.

"Quite a theory."

"For fuck's sake." Renner turns to him. "That's only half of it!"

"There's more?"

"Mitchell and BASIA." Renner's usual calm demeanor deteriorates. "According to you, he's preparing to attack all fifty states! It makes the most sense for him to execute that plan on Election Day. And is it possible we can't even trust our own people with this?"

"You've got to work that end, the Bureau, the administration." Sebastian remembers that he'll have to tell Mitchell he lost Taylor tonight. "I'm close. Mitchell's starting to trust me. But it's late. We're ten days out from the election."

"Can we stop it?"

"I don't know."

They sit in silence watching the dog wander around the bushes. Proving any of this seems insurmountable. But Sebastian remembers Mitchell's cache of MedIDs from his militia. He explains it to Renner, tells him it could be the only physical proof to tie the Reverend to both the Planes and this future attack.

"If anything happens to me, get your CI to find those MedIDs," Sebastian says.

"If anything happens to me, take care of Harry."

Hearing his name, the dog trots over and leans into Renner for a scratch. Their theories and words float like mist between them. There's nothing left to say.

Chapter 58

STEVEN HUDSON BURSTS through Cole's front door. He's mumbling, his face is pinched. In the living room, he paces.

"I went to see Mitchell," Steven says. His hair is a wild mass of tangles as though he's slept on it for days. He grabs Cole's arm. "He knows about us. One of our Project Swap patients was sent by Mitchell. They know about Cushing and our method. They saw our headquarters. He showed me video footage."

Cole can't speak. His heart races, he mentally goes through the steps of their emergency exit plan. Clean MedIDs for the project founders and their families are in place. It shouldn't take more than twenty-four hours to arrange transport for Lily, Ian, and Talia out of the country. And then they run. He loosens his collar and sits down heavily on the couch. "So Mitchell is blackmailing us?"

"He doesn't care about Project Swap, but he knows we do." Steven runs his hands through his hair. "He's got his own agenda. All he wants is money. Money I don't have."

"You should have told me you were going to see him."

"What difference would that have made?"

"Maybe no difference. But my contact who's at Patriot's Church—the one I told you is looking for Jonathan—I wonder if he could have helped."

"Still could. I need all the help I can get. Who is this, your contact?"

Sebastian's face flashes into Cole's mind. "I can't tell you that. But he's someone we can trust."

"I don't trust anyone anymore."

If someone took Ian or Talia, Cole would lose it, too. There's got to be a way to help Steven. Should he share what Sebastian told him? The only one he's told is Lily, after he'd promised her no more secrets. But maybe this information could help get Jonathan back.

"There's an attack coming," he says, swallowing.

Steven shrugs. "There are always attacks."

"No. It's something monumental."

"Mitchell and BASIA are behind this attack?"

"My contact believes so."

"What is it?" Steven sinks into a chair.

"The little I know is that all fifty states are involved. It's got to revolve around a major event. Maybe the election."

"Christ. Does anyone else know? The FBI?"

Cole shakes his head. "Look, I didn't learn much. But it sounds like the current administration is focused on getting Richard Hensley into the White House, at all costs. I don't think they're paying enough attention to Mitchell's militia."

"They'll goddamn care if it has anything to do with the election." Steven springs up and begins pacing again. "What if it went public?"

"What do you mean?"

"Viral. Got word out that an attack is coming. That President Clark and his administration don't give a shit. They'd be forced to check into it."

"I like the idea of warning people. But we have families, Steven. We light a fire under this and they'll arrest us immediately. Secondly, they'll think, or at least claim, that we're somehow accessories involved with the purported attack. They could charge us with conspiracy. Detain our families. And, it would put Jonathan in even greater danger."

"No one has to know it's us. Thousands could die, Cole."

"There have to be people other than us who care, and who have actual power to stop Mitchell. Plus, we have a good thing going with Project Swap. If we stay the course, we could actually make a difference."

"If there's anything left, that is."

There are only a few options left, as far as Cole can tell. "I'm in this as far as I can go. Our MedID movement is risky but calculated. People want what we're offering. I can't endanger my family further by outing a terrorist and pissing off the government. But what I can do is help you get Jonathan back."

"How do you propose we do that?"

"Our network has grown substantially. I'd bet those we've helped would be willing to contribute, if they're able."

"What are you getting at?"

"We've saved these people's lives, haven't we? Up to this point we've only asked for a donation to keep the project going. So let's reach out. Tell them we need their help. Maybe we can raise the rest of your ransom."

"Half these people will be out of the country by now."

"Money can be transferred from anywhere, to anywhere. Privately. And every one of them is thankful to us for whatever problem we helped them resolve by cleaning their MedIDs."

"There's not enough time, Cole."

"I haven't slept in weeks. You'd be amazed at what can happen in twenty-four hours." He beckons for Steven to follow him to his office. "Let's send out an S.O.S. to our database."

Lily delivers a pot of coffee and sandwiches as they connect with Karen and Sean. Hours later, as dawn spreads over Boston, they finally shut down the encrypted communications. Thousands of families have been contacted, a network now reaching across the globe.

A grateful Steven thanks Cole and heads home. Buoyed by his mission to secure Jonathan's safe return, Cole can't imagine going into work. Instead he calls in sick and stares at a newly established savings account, refreshing the page every half hour. By noon the balance has climbed to more than half of what they need to get Jonathan out.

Chapter 59

BELOW, THE MAZE of the Grand Canyon cuts deep into the earth, its beauty now guarded by an electronic fence to prevent suicides. Richard and his campaign entourage rest in cushy seats aboard a private plane, flanked by U.S. Army fighter jets. It's a justifiable expense paid by the Liberty Party, to protect the future leader of the United States.

He glances toward the rear of the plane, where Taylor and Sienna sit. For two days, since Carter delivered Taylor from the grasp of that lunatic Mitchell, she hasn't spoken a word to him. She should be thanking him. But the politics of family are more complex than any election, or the labor of pleasing constituents. He knows with every thread of his being that he's saved his daughter's life, done it for all the right reasons. So many times, children just don't understand parents' motivations.

A tablet is placed in his hands. "What's this?"

Kendra takes a seat across the aisle from him. Despite her makeup and impeccable hair, dark circles underscore her eyes. "We're in L.A. for the night." She gestures to the screen, displaying points on a map of the United States. "Tomorrow is Utah, Illinois, Wisconsin, and we end in Florida."

"Ten more days," Carter chimes in from an adjacent seat. "Hard to believe."

Richard's phone rings. An image of the White House appears on-screen and he answers right away. A woman tells him to hold for the President. There's a click on the line.

"Richard." President Clark's tone sounds stern.

"Good afternoon, Mr. President."

"I hear you've gotten yourself involved with BASIA."

"Just the opposite, actually. I'm distancing myself entirely."

"We discussed this. I thought I was clear. If you were distancing yourself, your daughter wouldn't be in that plane with you."

"All due respect sir, she was in danger."

"This was a power play. And you went against my direct order."

Richard's face grows warm. He unbuckles his seat belt and heads toward the front of the plane for the most privacy he can hope for. "I didn't negotiate with Mitchell. I don't negotiate with known terrorists. Or has our policy changed?"

"You kidnapped a terrorist. You want brownie points for not paying Mitchell's price?"

"Taylor isn't a terrorist."

"The entire country knows she's a member of a terrorist group, Richard."

"She's my daughter."

"Get her out. I don't care how you do it, but get her out of the country before you lose the election on one bad decision."

"Fine. That's fine, I'll get her out." He'd thought getting her out of Mitchell's cult would solve things, keep her and Sienna safe. Now he has to talk her into leaving the country. Will she go? She's hasn't done a thing he's asked in years. Wait a minute. "Sir, how did you know about the extortion? How do you even know we have her?"

"With the state of the country, it's imperative that I know everything going on inside your campaign."

Richard glances back toward the cabin at his campaign staff, including Carter and Kendra. There's a mole in his team. He focuses on each one of them, willing the truth to come. But only one person has been in on his Taylor plan. *Son of a bitch.*

"Carter Benson."

President Clark sighs. "Dash was with me long before you, Senator."

"Dash?"

"Carter's nickname he's had since Exeter. Kid almost went to the Olympics."

Leaning against the wall just outside the pilot's cabin, his head rests on the hard surface. A wave of nausea surges. His one confidant has betrayed him.

"Get it done, Richard. Dash is at your service. He's quite resourceful."

Click. Richard finds an empty restroom and slides the lock closed behind him. A dim light colors him in a greenish hue, his reflection more ghostly than presidential. Has Carter lied to him about everything? What about the Cadillac that chased Taylor? Carter had admitted to taking a Liberty Party car. Was President Clark behind the attack on her? Random thoughts cycle through him. A flash of the State House attack, of hearing Carter tell him to "Duck." President Clark had ordered him to attend the State House event. My God, did they have something to do with the chemical attack? Clark wanted Gardiner out, that much was clear.

Richard presses his hands against the tight walls for balance. Good Lord. Did they set him up to play the heroic presidential candidate?

Sweat beads his forehead and seeps through his undershirt. He splashes water on his face, pats it off with a towel. When he steps out, Carter is waiting for him.

"Sir, your daughter wants a word."

He leans in close. "Tell me, who do you work for?"

"Excuse me?"

"At whose pleasure do you serve, Carter? Or do you prefer Dash?"

Carter's black eyebrows knit together. After a moment his face relaxes. "I serve at the pleasure of the President."

"And all this time I'd thought you were working for me."

"We all have the same goal, sir."

"Do we?"

Carter's eyes flicker to the back of the plane. "Your daughter's waiting."

Though he'd love to fire him, he obviously doesn't have that power. President Clark strategically placed Carter, who will see this election through. Richard's legs are weak and shaky as he follows his deputy campaign manager. He concentrates on remaining calm, breathing deeply. Though his impulse is to thrash this lying bastard who has made him the fool. Why didn't he see it? All of it, laid out plainly in front of him. If he'd paid more attention, he would have understood that he was a pawn. Nothing more.

NEXT TO TAYLOR, Sienna wears cushy headphones and escapes into a movie on her seat back. Taylor unbuckles her safety belt as her father and Carter approach down the aisle. What now? She stands to meet them, trying to shield Sienna from their conversation.

"We'll be landing in L.A. in a half hour," her father says.

"That's when we'll be leaving," she says.

"Charles Mitchell will find you."

"He won't. I'm done with all of you. Your agendas. This war of yours."

"You need to leave the country." He grips her arm and his voice is almost a whisper. "They'll kill you."

Something in his tone is different. She pulls away. How desperately she'd wanted to believe in the Reverend and Patriot's Church. She'd gone in hoping to be convinced. Instead, she'd enjoyed sticking it to her father and the Liberty Party. And she unexpectedly found herself caring about the first man she'd been with since Mason. After all that, she's back where she started.

"Your father's right," Carter chimes in. "You'll be killed. And if Charles Mitchell gets his hands on Sienna, she'll be indoctrinated into his child militia."

"What are you talking about?" She and her father stare at him.

"Mitchell has a group of children he raises in his residential compound," Carter says, his demeanor nonchalant. "Supposedly they're orphans. Probably the result of suicide missions or other attacks. God knows what he does with them."

The air is suffocating. Taylor grasps the empty chair beside her. Truth or more bullshit? She can't tell anymore. Maybe she never could.

Her father's face is flushed and his eyes are intense. He leans closer to her. "We'll arrange to have your MedIDs cleaned—yours and Sienna's—and you can disappear. We'll change your names. You can go anywhere. Be anyone you want to be."

"Am I here because you actually care?" she asks. "Or because you didn't have it in the budget to pay the ransom?"

"Despite our history, I love you and Sienna," he says. "But that aside, the U.S. government doesn't negotiate with terrorists."

"Why would Reverend Mitchell risk blackmailing the future President and possibly indicting himself when he already has so many supporters?"

"Because he can." Her father sounds tired, his energy waning. "Men like that, organizations like his, always need money. And he knows the right way to ask."

"The man you were with in the alley," Carter interjects. "What do you know about him?"

"He's a friend. Was a friend." Her chest aches.

"The man with the beard?" her father says, more to Carter than her.

"How do you know about him?" she asks.

"It's safe to say," Carter says, "all parties involved know how you take your cereal and coffee in the morning. And who you dine with."

"All I've ever asked for is privacy!"

"It was the only way to protect you," her father says. "The Reverend's watching you to protect his interests. We're ensuring that you're safe."

Tears sting her eyes. "I lead a normal life. I take care of my daughter. Go to work."

"But you're my daughter. And there's nothing normal about that."

She stares at the geometrical pattern on the seat. "Can't we forget about the MedID and just go back to letting people live their lives? It's all anyone wants."

"It's not that simple."

"Isn't it?" she asks. "I just want to raise my daughter."

"That's what I wanted."

For so long, she's fought to keep her home, her life, under her control. To what end? She won't change the government, or her father. It's all gone too far. She looks at him and he nods, perhaps for the first time in years understanding what she's thinking. For once he's right. She and Sienna could disappear to some faraway, secluded place, and start over again.

Chapter 60

IN THE OFFICE of Mitchell's mansion, Sebastian stands at ease. In his mind, he sees Taylor being driven away by Benson. A gnawing sensation tells him she's in danger. There's no way to know where she is or what her father's plan is. Hell, what Mitchell's plan is! Benson implied that his orders to take her came from Mitchell. Time for some answers.

"Sergeant." Mitchell leans back in his chair, eyeing him from behind the desk. "Your assignment was to protect one woman, and you end up here without a scratch of evidence that you fought for her."

"I could have shot her. That would have kept her from going."

"Why didn't you shoot Hensley's man?"

"He had the ace. Sienna. To Taylor, he was the only way she would see her daughter again."

"Powerful bait."

"Exactly. If I'd killed him, she wouldn't have left with me. I would have lost all the credibility I've been building with her."

Mitchell rubs his tattooed palm. As he waits, Sebastian considers Richard Hensley. The presidential candidate can't be in bed with Mitchell. It's impossible. But the link that ties Carter Benson to Mitchell—and President Clark—remains a mystery.

"There's one more thing, sir," he says. "The man who took her was Carter Benson, Hensley's deputy campaign manager and formerly President Clark's aide. Benson told me he was there on your behalf."

"And you believed him?"

"He was pretty convincing. I went with my gut."

Mitchell grins slightly. "Yes. Well, luckily your instincts were correct. This is a win-win outcome, Sergeant. And a test."

"I don't understand."

"The money is secondary. We have other means we can tap into. But Taylor Hensley needed to be returned to her father. Strategically speaking."

"You're saying I was supposed to let her go with Hensley's man?"

"Yes. Benson's one of us. A true believer."

It takes everything in him not to react to this confession. He lets the words solidify. Mitchell is pulling strings in the highest office. "Sir, at the risk of sounding bold, is Richard Hensley working with you as well?"

Mitchell roars with laughter. Finally, he says, "Bold, yes. But the answer is no. Let's leave it at that."

"But that's how you knew." Sebastian wants more, needs more answers. He can see Kate lying on the steps, blond hair lifting in the breeze. "You told me that President Clark was behind the State House attack. You knew because Carter Benson told you."

"And as I said, everyone has their agendas."

Not a confirmation, but close enough. Jesus Christ. It was all true.

"Onward." Mitchell gestures to Henry, who stands silently at the door, as always. "Your next assignment is to step in for Henry for a few days. He has a family situation to attend to."

"It'd be an honor."

"He'll be back in time for our mission." Mitchell stands. "Meanwhile, your training will continue. According to my ballistics squad leader, your sharpshooting skills are unmatched by your peers. So, in the remaining week, you'll train daily at the range and on a special outdoor course."

"Yes, sir." *Remaining week*. The words reverberate through him. A week plus the three days Mitchell said they'd travel and prepare. Election Day. There's no doubt now. "May I ask what my target will be?"

Rarely has he seen Mitchell surprised. It lifts his mouth and eyes, wrinkles his forehead. "Eager, are we?"

"Excited. Eager, yes."

Turning, Mitchell strolls to the window overlooking his vast property. "All will be revealed, Sergeant. On the chosen day, BASIA will spread its wings and fly. Fifty coordinated missions choreographed to create the most breathtaking and historic battle in this nation's history."

He should kill him. Right now. But Henry has his weapon, which is always confiscated before he's in Mitchell's presence. But he's quick. Strong. He could snap the Reverend's neck. And then he himself would die. And it would make no difference at all.

"Anticipation is a gift, Sergeant Anderson." Mitchell turns to face him. "The electrifying moments prior to the act are a major part of the enjoyment. The act . . . well, it will be quick and then over. And then anticipation begins anew."

All he can do is nod.

"I'll tell you this." Mitchell walks over, stopping inches from his face. "Of all our targets, yours will win us the prize."

"Thank you, sir." Sebastian's heart palpitates. Good God. They're going after the President. Future or current? Both? He swallows hard.

"But before the glory, the work." Mitchell pats him on the shoulder. "Do me a favor. Before weapons practice, tell the cook to prepare the boy's meal and take it downstairs."

"The boy?"

"She knows." Mitchell returns to his desk. "Dismissed."

Sebastian closes the door behind him. His soles click-clack on the tile as he heads to the kitchen. Time to take action, to use his nervous energy to his advantage. He's got to reach Renner, tell him he's confirmed Benson's tie to Mitchell and that Benson was involved with President Clark's State House attack. Someone at the Bureau had their only State House suspect killed. Did President Clark himself make the call to Satterwhite? There's no one left to trust.

For now, he'll go along. In the kitchen, he conveys Mitchell's request to the cook. At least there's one piece of good news. He's finally found Jonathan Hudson.

Chapter 61

COLE PULLS INTO the Mass General parking lot for the night shift. The cement structure is dimly lit and filled with cars as he backs into his reserved space. He powers off the Land Rover at the same moment wheels screech and a sedan pulls directly in front of him, their headlights almost touching. He blinks against the brightness. *What the hell?* He squints to try and make out the driver's face, the make of the car.

"Doors lock," he commands. A click sounds and he reaches under his seat, unlatches his gun. Images of Lily, Ian, and Talia run through his mind.

The sedan's driver door opens. Cole releases the safety on the gun as a dark figure approaches. Ten feet. Five. *Shit, it's Sebastian's partner, Renner.* He tightens his grip on the pistol. The last time he saw Renner, he'd tried to kill Sebastian. And, incidentally, him.

Renner raps on his window, gestures to him to roll it down. The bulletproof car is his only protection. Persistent, Renner knocks again. Cole lifts his gun—doesn't point it—and shrugs.

Renner takes out his piece and walks back to his car, placing it on the hood.

Despite Renner's issues with Sebastian, there should be no reason he'd want to kill him. Setting his gun on the passenger seat, Cole clicks the safety on. "Doors unlock." He steps outside.

"Forgive me," he says. "But the whole bomb experience made me a little wary of you."

"All for show." Renner extends a hand and they shake. "I needed certain individuals to think I was following orders. Sorry you were there."

"What're you doing here?"

"The Bureau knows about you, Doc. About your project."

His stomach seizes. "And you're here to arrest me? To shut us down?"

"I should be." Renner glances around. "But I made it disappear. I erased the file."

"Why?" Can he trust this man? He barely knows him. "I don't understand."

"Look, Sebastian's been my partner for a decade. Our targets are terrorists, anyone who threatens the safety of this country. This MedID thing you're doing isn't terrorism. It's self-preservation. And I get that. But technically it conflicts with my job responsibilities."

"Okay. What happens now?"

"I came to tell you to be more careful. Watch your back. Stay off the grid. And screen your patients thoroughly."

"Of course, absolutely." His curiosity gets the better of him. "But you could get in trouble just for being here. Not to mention erasing evidence."

"You were on the roof with Sebastian when I shared intel with him."

How could he forget? He's hardly slept since, knowing another attack is imminent, not to mention the government had a hand in the State House attack.

"Corruption from the White House on down." Renner sniffs. "I won't serve a country that's turned on itself. But I can do more from the inside."

"I guess I should tell you to watch your back, too. You want a free MedID wipe?"

Renner smiles. "Thanks, I'm clean. An eighty-six."

"I could take out your locator chip. Change your name."

"Thanks. But I need to appear as though I'm still on board with the Bureau. I can't make a difference if I leave."

"So you're not really trying to kill Sebastian?"

The slightest shake of his head. "Just keeping him on his toes."

"Thanks, Renner. I appreciate the warning."

"Go underground. No centralized meeting place. Good luck."

They shake hands and Renner leaves. Forgetting his shift, Cole hops back into his car and heads to Cambridge.

At Project Swap HQ, Steven and the team review their plans. The mood is upbeat, so Steven tries his best to put on a good face. It's hard to feign positivity when Jonathan is being held prisoner. Every hour that passes is more painful, and less hopeful, than the last.

"As of this week, our associates are wiping MedIDs in Denver, Orlando, Minneapolis, Dallas, and Seattle." Karen beams. "We're a national movement, everyone. Congratulations."

The tight-knit group applauds. Suddenly the front door swings open. It's Cole.

"We've had a warning," Cole says, out of breath.

"From who?" Karen asks.

"Doesn't matter. But it's legit. We need to vacate right away. Destroy anything incriminating. Wipe down surfaces for fingerprints. We were never here."

"That puts a damper on our celebration," Steven says. One more threat. The weight of it presses down on him. Everyone stands, unsure where to start.

"We'll work off-site until we can figure out a plan," Cole says.

"Are we in danger of being arrested?" Karen asks, standing.

"We're always in danger." Cole looks around, surveying the room's contents. "The warning is a gift from a friend. But it only buys us a little time."

"It'll be fine," Sean says. "We're all clean. Our families, too. Plan B is in place."

"There is some good news." Cole puts a hand on Steven's shoulder. "The outreach to our network worked in spades. We have more than enough to free Jonathan. Check the account we opened. You'll find what you need."

Relief washes over him, his whole body loosening from the tension that's held him for days. *Finally.* Emotion bubbles up and he coughs it away. "I should stay and help—"

"Go," Cole says. "Get Jonathan."

"Be careful," Karen says.

"Thank you." His tongue fails him. Words are not enough. "Thank you so much."

Since his meeting with the Reverend, he's been plagued by dark thoughts. He'd always imagined feeling a sense of closure in finding the person responsible for murdering his family. Instead, the news unearthed a powerful grief. Jolts of anger seize him without warning. Revenge, or justice—perhaps both—are the next logical step. It's time to share what he learned with his friends. And so he does. He tells them that Reverend Mitchell admitted he was behind the Planes. Heads nod, long held suspicions confirmed. He leaves them with a final thought. If the Reverend single-handedly arranged the murder of thousands, what would he do for an encore?

The mood in the room plummets. He shakes hands and hugs each of them, thanking them again for everything they've been through. Just in case.

Finally, he comes to Cole. "You're a good friend. It's all we can hope for these days."

"Mitchell is unpredictable." Cole lowers his voice. "You need a gun?"

"Just moral support."

"We're all here for you. Good luck."

Steven gathers his things and leaves. As he crosses the lawn to his car he repeats a mantra, *Don't think, just do.* There's no choice here. If he wants a future and to bring Jonathan safely out of this, he has to face the Reverend one last time.

Chapter 62

JONATHAN HAS LOST count of the days as he sits in his windowless cell. To keep sane, he devised a routine. For two hours a day, without access to a computer, he works out complex codes and hacking strategies in his head. He refuses to lose his edge—it's the one thing that makes him feel useful, powerful. To keep alert and in shape, he does crunches, push-ups, and runs in place. The endless hours are interrupted daily by a monitor that turns on whenever the Reverend is preaching or addressing BASIA. Hannah gave him the New Testament Bible to read, and she brings him his food, three times a day. At first he wouldn't even look at her. Her betrayal stung, he'd been used. He'd been foolish. But with all the time to think, he's worked out two things. One, she's scared. And two, Mitchell is the only family she's known for most of her life. She hasn't had a choice. And if he can plant doubts about the Reverend in her mind, she may be his only way out.

Down the hall, locks snap open, sneakers rub against the cement floor. It's dinnertime. Hannah appears at his door. Through the window panel, her pale skin glows, as though she's been infused with light. Rather than sliding the meal through a slit, she unlocks the door and comes in. She offers him a tray with a sandwich and a glass of milk.

"Eat up," she says. "You're free."

"What?"

"I don't know details." She doesn't look at him, just stares at the open door. "But Charles is asking for you. Hurry, eat."

He does. *Why are they letting him out?* As he eats, she talks in a random, nonstop stream. He can't follow it; all he can concentrate on is staying alive and getting the hell out of here. He barely chews his food, finishing quickly. As he stands to follow her, he realizes he may never see her again. Not if the Reverend is letting him go.

"Hey." Gently, he puts his hand on her arm and lowers his voice to a whisper. "I know you feel indebted to Reverend Mitchell, I know that's why you pulled the alarm that day."

"Things are so complicated." She tucks a strand of red behind her ear. "I'm sorry I did that to you."

"It's okay. I'm fine. But you're not. You don't want to marry him. I see the way you flinch when he touches you."

Her eyes glisten. She blinks and looks at the floor.

"Come with me." His hand slides down her arm to her hand, holds it in his. "I'll find your sister and brother. We can get out of here. Leave the country. You can make your own choices. And it doesn't have to be complicated anymore."

"Jonathan." She squeezes his hand. "You're so good to me. But I have to stay. I've made promises I need to keep. I hope someday you'll understand. I'm sorry, for everything."

Her response isn't surprising. His energy deflates as she releases his hand and leads him upstairs, through the maze of corridors. The windows reveal nothing, only darkness. From a hall closet, she hands him his jacket he follows her outside, onto the deck. Suddenly, security floodlights are switched on, illuminating the grounds.

"I'm sorry, Jonathan," she whispers.

He doesn't have time to ask why. Outside, a frosty breeze travels between the layers of his coat and shirt, chilling him. He sucks it into his lungs, savoring the fresh air. A memory of his first day on the compound and the Reverend's party comes to him. He's been so naive.

"It must be good to stretch your legs." It's Reverend Mitchell's voice.

He whirls around. "Am I free to go?"

"Short sentence, wouldn't you agree?" The Reverend strolls past him to the edge of the deck that overlooks the vast moonlit lawn. "For stealing from your employer?"

"I didn't think you needed the MedIDs."

"And you know people who do?"

Fucksake. He can't expose Steven's MedID business. Excuses circulate in his mind. Screw it. He doesn't have to say anything. He presses his lips together.

"That's okay, Jonathan. I understand you want to protect your stepfather. But his project isn't as secret as you might think."

"It doesn't affect you."

"Doesn't it? A mass of people utilizing the government's own weapon against them? Against the world? Imagine the potential. Might take only a few years to formulate a plan. A new party. I'm not interested in a new group joining the mix. Patriot's Church and BASIA serve God. We fight for eternal salvation. Your father's plans complicate our mission."

Glancing over his shoulder, the Reverend beckons to someone

with a wave. Jonathan expects Henry, but instead another man joins them. The man's wavy hair and beard are in contrast to Henry's clean-cut look. Jonathan's eyes dart to Hannah as she quietly disappears back into the house.

"Sergeant Anderson, this is Jonathan Hudson."

"I'm sorry for trying to steal the MedIDs," Jonathan says. "But I'm done with all this."

"You have a job to do, Jonathan," the Reverend says. "You're done when I say you're done. A few more days isn't a big sacrifice in the lives of you and your family."

He knows he's not in a situation to bargain. Acceptance settles in his stomach like a brick. "Fine."

"Good. Sergeant, let's get Jonathan's shooting skills up to par."

"Yes, sir," Sergeant Anderson says.

"Wait—I'm not a soldier. That wasn't the deal."

"New deal." Reverend Mitchell's face is rigid, emotionless.

From inside his jacket pocket, the soldier pulls out two semi-automatic guns and hands one to Jonathan. "Let's get to work."

"You'll find plenty of moving targets out there." The Reverend gestures to the land. "I'll leave you to it."

As Reverend Mitchell turns to go inside, the gun in Jonathan's hand draws his energy. One second to lift his arm, one second to pull the trigger. Would all of this be over? Would the world change in an instant if he killed this one man?

The glass door shuts. The moment over.

"There should be some wildlife out this time of night," Sergeant Anderson says. "Deer, usually. And the moonlight is good." He motions with his weapon to figures moving at the far end of the land, where the grass meets the woods. The floodlights from the deck cast a glow, helping visibility.

Shadows move. Deer, moose maybe. He follows Anderson off the deck, onto the grass.

"What are we practicing for?" he asks.

"Life."

Without warning, Anderson raises his gun, aims and pulls the trigger. The sound shatters the air, makes Jonathan's ears ring. In the distance, something falls and lies still. The shot scatters the animals, shadows moving into the trees.

"A deer?"

Anderson nods. "Your turn."

He takes a deep breath and raises the gun, holding it steady at eye level. He waits. Perhaps the shot scared them off. And then he sees something, follows it with his eyes as it walks into the open. But it's standing on two legs, not four.

"Hold on." He squints, strains to see. "I think it's a man."

Anderson clears his throat. "It's your target."

"What?"

Softly, Anderson repeats, "It's your target. Aim low."

"No." His heart pounds in his ears. "I'm not ready."

"It's you or him. And the Reverend is watching. "Aim low," he repeats.

Jonathan's hands tremble, the gun wavers. The man—is it a man or a woman?—moves across the lawn slowly, too far to see clearly. *Shitshitshit. I'm not a killer!* Who is it, out there? Do they know what's coming?

"Goddammit, Jonathan, aim at his legs and shoot," Anderson whispers. "Now."

The blast almost knocks Jonathan off his feet. The figure in the distance falls, and with it, a cry. *Oh God.* He reaches out for a solid surface and finds only Anderson, who lends his arm as Jonathan vomits violently into the grass. Afterward, he gives back the gun and wipes his mouth with the back of his hand.

"Good," Anderson says. "You did good."

"What happens now?"

"We survive another day."

He squints to make out details of the man on the ground, but he's too far away. "Is someone going to get him?"

Anderson nods.

THE FROST-COVERED GRASS is like needles against Steven's face. The drugs must be wearing off, whatever that bastard Mitchell gave him when he first arrived—he's able to concentrate now, control his body more, though he has no idea how long he's been lying here. He'd passed out from the wrenching white-hot pain in his leg. The drugs lessened the initial impact of the bullet, but now it radiates through him. If he lies here much longer, he knows he'll die.

With tremendous effort, he attempts to crawl. The Reverend's residence looms in the distance. He knows the driveway leads to the main road and so he pulls himself toward it. He can get to it through the woods if he can bear the pain. Somewhere in that compound, Mitchell has both Jonathan and his money. Just the thought gives him enough energy to go another several feet. But then darkness hits him once again.

TELLING THE KID to pull the trigger on his stepfather was on par with any torture training Sebastian's experienced. But he'd quietly instructed Jonathan to aim low, and luckily his aim was good. Any higher and it would have killed Steven Hudson.

Pasty white and wild-eyed, Jonathan follows behind him

as they make their way toward the body in the field. Sebastian wishes there was something he could say to prepare him. The biggest shock is yet to come. Mitchell wants Jonathan to discover the man's identity himself.

The sky is beginning to lighten. For most of the night, Sebastian stood quietly in a corner of the room watching Jonathan, tied to a chair in Mitchell's office. The kid's defiance drained right out of him. Even for Sebastian, it was excruciating to listen while Mitchell pontificated on the state of the world now and the world as it will be in a matter of days. Mitchell gave Jonathan options. Opt out of this "job" with BASIA and face death. Opt in, and a new way of life begins. Or, complete the assignment and be set free. Though Sebastian isn't sure what role Jonathan is meant to play, clearly, Mitchell wants to harness his hacking talents for a very specific task. And Mitchell doesn't like to be told no.

In the field, with about twenty feet to go, he glances back at Jonathan. For once, he wishes he could tell the kid who he is and what he's doing there. But this has to play out.

"He's breathing." Jonathan rushes forward, points to Hudson's back as it rises and falls.

"We need to get him inside."

Suddenly, Jonathan stops. "Steven!"

On his stomach, Hudson's head is turned to face them. His skin is a bluish-white, his eyes are closed. Sebastian goes to him, crouches down and places two fingers against his neck. The pulse is faint. Jonathan drops to his knees and begins shaking his stepfather.

"Get his legs," Sebastian says.

"I shot Steven?" Jonathan's voice cracks. "I shot Steven."

"He's alive. You're a good aim."

"You motherfucker!" Jonathan stands and with both hands shoves him forcefully. "You knew it was my stepfather?"

"I had my orders."

"Fuck orders." Tears run down Jonathan's face. He kneels again at Hudson's side, rocking back and forth.

"Do what you're told, and both of you can go home after all this." He's got to get them into the house. "Let's go."

Together they stumble and strain carrying Hudson's body back to the house. He watches Jonathan. His tears are gone now, replaced by a mask of restrained anger.

"You're valuable to the Reverend," he says.

"My skills are valuable."

"Just do your job and you'll get out."

"How about you? Why're you so valuable, Sergeant?"

"I'm a trained sniper."

"You should shoot that asshole, then."

Up the deck stairs and into the house they carry Steven Hudson. In a small room Mitchell calls their infirmary, a doctor cares for the wound while Jonathan sits stoically at his stepfather's side. Sebastian's only directive from Mitchell had been to keep Hudson alive, if barely. It's leverage with Jonathan, and it looks like it's going to work.

Chapter 63

RICHARD STANDS CENTER stage, grinning effusively at the last audience he will address before Election Day. The roar of the crowd is deafening. He soaks it in, their loyalty and support. Five days and it will all be over. The world will call him President Hensley. He'll be his own man, not President Clark's pawn. Richard raises his hands in thanks and as a signal to quiet the voices.

The words pour easily from him, as always. He is warm but firm, inspirational and on point. As the teleprompter guides him, he thinks of Carter, listening backstage, ready to report back to President Clark. If Clark had his way, Taylor would have disappeared by now. But Richard has different plans, a final act of defiance. It wasn't easy to convince Taylor, but in the end she acquiesced. Not in support of him, but in exchange for a new life with her daughter.

It's time. He pauses mid-speech, pressing a thumb on the button of the podium to halt the teleprompters. He affects a more solemn tone and loses the infectious smile.

"My friends and fellow citizens. I know that the most important thing to each and every one of you is family." Cheers. "As you know, I've had a very public struggle in my own family after losing my beautiful wife, Norah. But instead of being a devoted father, I've been a devoted public servant. I wasn't as available to my daughter, Taylor, as I should have been, in her own hour of need. Our damaged relationship is no secret. My friends in the press see to that. You've also probably heard that as she struggled to keep her own family whole, Taylor fell into the grasp of suspected terrorists. I won't name names—why give them what they want most? Instead I want to tell you that finally, my own family is whole again. I'd like to ask you tonight to accept my daughter, Taylor, despite her past choices. We've all made mistakes. She'll be by my side in these last few days before the election. So, any issues or differences you may have had with her based on rumor or fact, she and I would like to ask for your forgiveness."

On cue, Taylor emerges from the side of the stage, wearing a conservative dress with her cropped hair brushed neatly back. Seeing her, sharing this moment with her, is heartening. Somewhere, President Clark is cringing, along with other party leaders. And Reverend Mitchell is no doubt fuming wherever he is. He won't have his money or his daughter. There's a rumbling through the crowd as Taylor arrives at his side. He puts his arm around her. Her body stiffens.

"What matters is, she's here now. She supports us. She supports our causes. And she knows that family—and country—comes first."

Slowly, applause builds until they are all cheering. He looks down at her and they nod at one another. He takes a step away and she leans into the microphone, her face open and earnest.

"Thank you, Dad. Thank you, everyone, for being here in support of my father. In my grief after the death of my husband, I made mistakes. Several of them. I drifted from the beliefs I'd held true my whole life. For years I've sought to live a life in opposition to my father. I'm eternally sorry, and thankfully, he's forgiven me. But I've returned to the Liberty Party stronger and infused with renewed passion for the principles that are our foundation. From this day forward, I will devote my efforts in support of our party and my father, your future President, Richard Hensley."

Richard steps forward and grasps her hand, raising it in the air as though grasping victory itself. This is a proud moment for him, even if she is forcing herself to say the words. The noise from the crowd is thunderous. He must savor this. Having Taylor this close is fleeting. Because once Election Day has passed, with their cleaned MedIDs, she and Sienna will disappear to God knows where.

Chapter 64

JUST AFTER MIDNIGHT, District 149 Security calls Cole and announces that a man named Sebastian Diaz is at the gate. Next to him in bed, Lily moans softly as he gets up, finds his pants on the floor and pulls them on. Padding in bare feet down the hall, he opens the door, inviting a blast of chilly air. It's a relief to see Sebastian alive.

They shake hands. "Sebastian. Come in."

"I'm sorry to show up so late."

"I'm just glad you showed up."

In the living room, they sit in adjacent chairs. Light from a single lamp illuminates Sebastian's disheveled hair and circles under his eyes. Cole says, "You don't look so good."

"Least of my worries." Sebastian leans in, elbows on his knees. "Listen, I don't have much time here. Your friends, the Hudsons, are in trouble."

Sebastian tells him that Steven's been shot in the leg by Jonathan, who's being forced to work for Mitchell. Cole searches the floor, trying to make sense of it. The Reverend has the money now, so why not release them? He should have made Steven take the gun.

"Why does Mitchell need Jonathan?" he asks.

"You were right about his hacking. Kid's a master at cyber warfare."

"And Mitchell's letting Steven live?"

"If he kills Steven, he'll lose his hold over Jonathan. So while Jonathan cooperates, Steven's being cared for by one of Mitchell's private physicians. But as of tonight, I can't watch them anymore. I've been moved into another role."

"What can I do?"

"The attack will happen on Election Day. Mitchell should give the order today. He'll ship all of the soldiers out to key locations."

"Can't you just shoot Mitchell?"

"It occurred to me. But it's not that easy. He doesn't work alone. I don't have the identities, but he's got a board of advisors. Probably very powerful people strategically positioned. I'm sure he's made arrangements in case of his assassination. Capable hands will pick up where he left off."

Four days. He's got to make a plan for his family.

"Then what?" Cole asks. "Mitchell takes over Washington?"

"This is their Armageddon. For all I know, they think the world will end after the attack and they'll all be saved."

"Saved." It's ludicrous. An idea occurs to Cole. "You need a MedID, Sebastian."

"What good will that do?"

"I'll give you a clean one. When this is over, you can get out. Escape all this."

"I can't have a MedID because I'm in BASIA. And if I have a MedID, the government can find me and they already want me dead. Anyway, where the hell would I go?"

"Wear long sleeves. The government won't know to look for your new identity. Mitchell won't look for a chip he thinks he already extracted. And go anywhere but here."

"How can you get me a clean MedID?" Sebastian's eyes narrow. "It was you. You were behind Jonathan's attempt to steal Mitchell's MedIDs."

"He did that all on his own. Steven tried to stop him but he didn't get to him in time."

Without holding back anything, he explains Project Swap. There's nothing to lose now, with the world on the edge of chaos. He tells Sebastian about Renner's warning, and that their MedID clients are now met one-on-one, in preplanned, wire-swept locations.

"Where's Renner?" Sebastian asks.

"He's still at the Bureau. Appearing to be doing what they want him to do."

"Shutting you down, killing me."

"Sounds like he's planning to try and change things from the inside."

"Always on the side of right."

"Sebastian?"

They both turn at the sound of Lily's voice. It must be a shock—she hasn't seen him since Kate's funeral. She goes to him and they embrace. Cole doesn't need to see her face to know Lily's weeping. At last she pulls away. "I'd like to say you look well."

Cole watches as they catch up, savoring each other as though they're seeing Kate again, or a piece of her, at least. Eventually, Lily asks why he's come.

"I'm helping a friend of Cole's."

Her face falls as she looks to Cole. "Is someone in trouble with the FBI?"

"No, no," they say simultaneously.

She looks back to Sebastian. "Are you okay?"

"Of course. But I should go." He hugs her one last time, kisses her on the cheek.

"Take care of yourself." She heads back to the bedroom.

As Cole walks him out, Sebastian says, "I'll be in touch about the Hudsons."

"Is there a chance you can get them out before the election?"

"I'll do what I can."

"If you decide you want one . . ." Cole taps his own forearm.

"Thanks, Cole. Stay safe."

"You, too."

They shake hands. There's a finality to it that doesn't sit well in Cole's stomach.

A BUZZER SOUNDS at the door of Jonathan's cell. It's probably Hannah. He hopes she feels guilty. When the door slides open, he doesn't acknowledge her, just stays on the floor, doing sit-ups.

"Hi," she says.

Though he's tempted, he won't look at her. So much shit has gone on, he can almost forget the way he felt for her before. Almost. He doesn't want to be drawn to her, or to forgive her. The night of the shooting plays on a constant loop in his mind. He wonders what she knew, if she had any idea what the Reverend had planned. She was quiet that night. Guilty conscience.

"Steven's doing better," she says. "Getting stronger."

This soothes his stomach, gnawed at by regret and anxiety. He flips onto his palms and the balls of his feet and pushes up, fighting gravity. Fueled by Mitchell. He's probably planning to kill both him and Steven when all this is finished.

"You called, right?" Hannah asks. "Pressed the button?"

"You've moved up to bathroom monitor now?" No need to hide his anger.

"Go on." She gestures to the door.

He jumps to his feet and passes by her. As he does, a black device in her hand draws his eyes. A stun gun. Nice touch. He sniffs, shakes his head. Cameras watch him as he crosses the hall, into the bathroom. As far as he knows, this is the one place he has privacy. Then again, that sick fucker Mitchell might even be watching him take a piss. But before he flushes, he stands on the toilet seat and reaches his hands to the ceiling, fingertips feeling around the edge of a vent. For seven days he's been working on the screws, using a broken edge of a plastic fork from one of his meals. It's nearly impossible, but he was able to get one screw out. Three to go.

Sweat beads on his brow as he works. Finally, the second one begins to twist. He gets it halfway out and stops. No need to remove the whole thing, wait until the other two are loose and then take them all out at once. Progress. But it's time to go before they get suspicious.

Back in his cell, Hannah stands in the middle of the room, holding the Bible she gave him. It would be easier to hate her if she wasn't so beautiful. He crosses his arms and glares at her. She blinks and he notices her eyes are red.

"You can go now," he says.

"I'm sorry," she whispers. Then she talks normally again. "I hope you'll forgive me one day. You should read Psalm 32. If you forgive, it might open some doors in your life."

She hands him the Bible and he hesitates, but takes it. When she leaves, she takes with her a flowery scent that he imagines is just her, not a perfume or soap she uses. He lies down on the hard mattress and stares at the ceiling. The Bible rests heavily on his stomach and he drums his fingers on the cover. *It might open some doors in your life.* Brainwashed Biblespeak bullshit. Out of sheer boredom, he sits up and thumbs through the pages until he finds Psalm 32.

There, between the pages, are two pieces of paper. As discreetly as possible, with the Bible as a shield to the cameras, he unfolds them to reveal two hand-drawn maps, clearly marked. His heart races. One shows an escape route from the residence grounds. The other an escape route from BASIA HQ.

Chapter 65

"AT LAST, THE hour is upon us." Charles's voice echoes in the cavernous training space. Dressed in his black BASIA uniform, he peers out into the crowd, acknowledges the soldiers on the monitors, lets his gaze drift over the room. "God is watching. And we are ready. Today, each of you will receive your assignment. Tomorrow you'll relocate for the next seventy-two hours. At your temporary base, you'll find what you need to carry out your mission. You'll work in teams, with a designated leader. Each team has specific targets. We're not interested in mass casualties. Protect each other, do your duty to God, and we will prevail. We'll unshackle our fellow Americans, throw open the gates of possibility. Anyone who doesn't see the truth of our way may leave our country, for it was never theirs to begin with."

Wild applause erupts, the energy so palpable that it alights on his skin, prickling the hair on his arms. Praise God. Over the noise, he raises his voice. "When you rise up on that fourth and most glorious day, you will walk on christened soil. The soil of the United States of Christian Patriots."

They can't hold back any longer. The soldiers rise from their seats and in unison hold their hands over their chests, then raise them, palms open, to Charles. He returns the gesture. "Thy will be done!"

On the way out of the final BASIA meeting, each soldier is handed a bone-conduction headphone with a personalized message. Sitting in his car, Sebastian places the band around his head and activates the file. The sound waves penetrate immediately. He closes his eyes. With each word uttered by an automated female voice, his chest tightens.

> *"Sergeant Will Anderson you are team leader of Operation POTUS. You will lead nine men and women in your mission. Your identities will not be revealed to one another until election night. As team leader and prime target terminator, if for any reason you are unable to complete your assignment, there is a designated replacement soldier who will take command. Sergeant Anderson, you will eliminate the newly elected President of the United States during his acceptance speech. Arrangements have been made to grant you unlimited access to the event. There will be other teams in the vicinity with other targets, but you will not interact. Focus on your task. Once it is complete, return home."*

Sebastian takes off the headset, stares unseeing out the windshield. Confirmation, finally. Years he's spent protecting this country. But this administration was behind Gardiner's assassination. They murdered Kate. And all for what—their MedID agenda? They're no better than Mitchell. Still, killing a president? Taylor's father. God help me, he thinks, out of habit. A cough rumbles up through him and it feels as though he's choking.

Time to move. He shifts into gear and peels out of the lot. He has twelve hours to get his things together and get on the plane. Within minutes he connects with Cole and arranges to get a new MedID before he leaves. His thoughts are scattered as he drives to his apartment. In D.C., maybe he can get Taylor and Sienna out. A part of him—a stale part of who he used to be—considers calling the Bureau. The director? Or maybe Homeland Security? They can't all be corrupt. And Renner's still there. But if Mitchell's hand reaches all the way inside the White House, can anything be done to stop this?

At last he reaches his apartment building and sprints inside, up the stairs. Instantly his eyes are drawn to the dingy beige carpet in the hallway. Scarlet drops, smears of blood. He slows, draws his gun, quiets his breath. At the end of the hall there's one final turn. He presses his back against the wall. With his gun held firm, he jerks his head around the corner to see his apartment door. His knees go weak.

Renner is sprawled in front of Sebastian's door, blood pooling around him. He pauses, listens. The blood trail indicates the shooter is gone. He rushes over to Renner. His face is almost unrecognizable.

"Jesus." He kneels, his grip still tight on his gun. He feels Renner's neck for a pulse. Nothing. Tears sting his eyes. Someone at the Bureau was here to clean up loose ends. Maybe they left Renner as a warning, or maybe they came for him and found Renner here instead.

A creak comes from inside his apartment. He raises the gun, dives over Renner's body just as a shot shatters the bottom half of the door. Firing two shots blindly back through the hole, he turns to face a dead-end hall. Heavy footsteps are approaching. There's a window and a rusted fire escape. Shielding his face with one arm, he smashes his gun against the glass, leaving a jagged hole. He kicks out the rest of the window as his apartment door opens. A shot is fired. He ducks as the shooter fires again. It grazes his arm. Glancing back, he aims and shoots, just missing a masked figure dressed in black.

Sebastian leaps through the window onto the landing. He skips stairs down to the next level when another bullet slices the air above his head. Footsteps thud above him on the first landing. He stops, plants his feet, and points his gun skyward, aiming precisely as the shooter glances down at him. Direct hit. The shooter's body arches backward and crumples. Something wet drips onto Sebastian's face and he wipes it away. His hand is smeared with blood.

With his gun trained on the body, he climbs the stairs to the first landing. There's no movement. It was a clean shot through the head. He holsters his gun and leans down, rifles through the man's pants and jacket pockets. There's only a phone, locked, no identification. But there's one more place to look. He pulls up the right pant leg and pushes down a black sock to reveal the pale skin of his ankle. There, as he knew it would be, is the Bureau locator chip.

Climbing back through the broken window, his breath catches when he sees Renner again. He goes over, kneels next to him.

"I'll finish this." He forces himself to look at his partner. In this fraught moment, he realizes Renner may be carrying useful intel. Sebastian leans over him and runs his hands over his body, through his pockets. Nothing, except his phone.

He stares at the locked screen that prompts for fingerprint recognition. Taking Renner's right hand, he touches his thumb to unlock the phone. He pores furiously through the email, the apps, the contacts. He finds several notes. Dates and codes going back eight years. Some notes include Mitchell's initials, CM. It has to be correspondence with Renner's informant. Sebastian's best guess is the bodyguard, Henry.

Swiping through the list of contacts, only one stands out. Instead of a name, there's a number—a date—061515. The day of the Planes. Below it is a phone number. He checks the call list. There are numerous incoming calls in the past week from this number. Renner has—had—no life outside the Bureau. Never dated, no family. The one person he was faithful to was his informant. Not knowing what he's going to say, he presses the call button.

Three rings and then, "Where have you been?" It's a female voice, and for a moment Sebastian is so surprised he can't speak. She asks, "Renner?"

"This is his partner," Sebastian says. "Renner's down."

"What do you mean he's down?" There's an edge of panic to her voice.

"He's dead."

Silence. He can hear breathing.

"You meant a lot to him." Sebastian has only seconds to make her trust him. He remembers one of the conversations he overheard with Renner on the phone to his informant. "I know he was determined to help you find your siblings."

Still, nothing.

"Please, this is important—"

Finally, she says, "I only talk to Renner. I can't do this anymore."

"I can help you," he says.

"What happened? What happened to him?"

"Someone shot him."

"I don't know you."

"I don't know you either."

"Maybe you killed him."

"Listen." He stares down, his friend at his feet. "Renner was like family to me. He had a dry wit that always left you wondering if he was serious. The scar on his chin came from when we were in basic training together in 'fourteen from a bar fight when a guy didn't get his humor. He was devoted to his dog, Harry. His job. And from what I heard on the other end of the conversations, he was also devoted to you." He waits.

"What's your name?"

"Diaz. What's yours?"

There's a brief hesitation. "Hannah."

Hannah. He pictures her. Red hair. Always near Mitchell. "I'm sorry I'm calling under these circumstances, Hannah. But we can still help each other."

"How?"

"Where are you? And where's Mitchell now?"

"I'm at the house. He just left for church."

"Do you know the man being held there?" he asks. "Steven Hudson?"

"Yes. I take him meals."

"Good, that's good. On the night of the election, Mitchell will be at BASIA headquarters. I need you to let someone into the house and take him to Steven Hudson. Together you'll get him out of there."

"What if Charles wants me with him?"

"If he does, can you act sick?" She doesn't answer. "You know, he's about to change the world again. People are going to die."

"I know." A brief pause. "I can act sick."

"I'll get you the details."

"Why aren't you getting him out yourself?"

"I'm on a tight leash right now."

"Renner was making plans for me after this." It's a whisper.

"Do you want to leave with Hudson?" he asks. "Can you?"

"I don't know."

"We can arrange a new identity. Get you out of the country."

"I'll think about it."

"I'll text you my number. Hang in there."

"Be careful, Diaz."

"You, too, Hannah."

He hangs up and stares at the peeling paint on the hallway wall. Cole asked for his help to get Steven Hudson out, but this is the most he can offer, now that he's heading to D.C. Hannah's face surfaces in his mind. He wonders what her angle is in all this.

Digging his own phone out of his jacket, he dials Cole. Whatever else may happen, at the very least he can help save Cole's family, along with Steven and Jonathan.

Chapter 66

IN THEIR BED, Lily moves closer to Cole, straining to hear Sebastian's voice on the other end of the line. One phrase is clear: *Get out.* She sinks back into her pillow. Another long journey lies ahead. This time, with Kate gone, there are no goodbyes, nothing left behind. And this time they have science on their side. False science, yes, but the scanners won't reveal the truth. Tears stream from the corners of her eyes, dampening her hair. Let this be the last time. The end of living in limbo. The end of living in fear.

There's no time to waste. She bolts up in bed. They'll bring only what they can carry. Luckily, their belongings have been pared down, most items forgotten in boxes. Rushing through the house, she gathers the necessities. A change of clothes. Toothbrush. Kate's watch. A tablet. She packs one bag for each of them.

Cole finds her near the front door, hunched over their luggage. "Sites are down," he says. "Central News, Washington Online. Two of the network sites. All offline."

"You think it's related to Sebastian? To what he said?"

He nods. "It's too much of a coincidence. Someone's afraid of leaks. Especially three days before the election."

"The terrorists are powerful enough to shut down the news sites?"

He doesn't answer. The air is electric, sparking her nerves. Suddenly, he grabs his jacket.

"Cole?"

"Could be the terrorists. Could be the government." He takes her hands in his and tells her that someone in the government orchestrated the State House attack. Her head swims.

"The government was behind Kate's murder?" She feels disoriented.

"The Liberty Party wants to strengthen the MedID system," he says. "To make us more reliant on government systems. President Clark is strongly pro-MedID. And Richard Hensley, of course, since it was his idea. But James Gardiner wasn't a supporter."

"So they killed him?" She shakes her head.

"It's a theory."

All this time, they've never been safe. From anyone, on any side.

"We're going back to London?" she asks.

He nods. "We know what to expect now. And we have your family there."

"Thank you." She wraps her arms around him, buries her face in his neck.

"For what?"

"For keeping our family together." Her hand glides down his arm and rests on his MedID. For one quiet moment it's the two of them, safe, in their house. Sleeping soundly, Ian and Talia are innocent, unaware of any danger. This may be the last peace they'll know for a long time.

Chapter 67

Jonathan is sure the world has gone completely mad. Seated next to the Reverend in BASIA's Command Center, they study a wall-sized monitor. A digital map of the United States details state lines with stars denoting capital cities. Countless lines representing airplane routes crisscross one another. Alongside Jonathan at the board sit two other techs. Via the FAA tracking system, one cross-checks soldiers with their assigned flight numbers, confirming they are en route. The other stands by to take all phone networks and carriers offline nationally.

"The Great BASIA Migration," Reverend Mitchell says. "Our birds have taken flight."

Incessant thoughts of Steven interrupt Jonathan's concentration. In the basement of Mitchell's house, his stepdad lies handcuffed, recovering from the gunshot wound. In such close proximity to the Reverend, Jonathan has ongoing fantasies of attacking him in some way. Perhaps it will need to be less obvious than lunging at him with a crowd of witnesses.

"Jonathan." The Reverend swivels in his chair. "Give me a status."

He glances behind them to the two security men that have been at Mitchell's side since Sergeant Anderson left on his mission. "We have access to and control of power grids in forty-eight states. For each grid, I've conducted tests that created outages in off-peak hours. I restored power within minutes to minimize suspicion."

"Did you say forty-eight?"

The door opens and Hannah enters, carrying sandwiches. She passes them out to everyone in the room. He watches her, tries not to make it obvious.

"Sit, Hannah." Mitchell pats an empty chair so that he sits between her and Jonathan.

Jonathan chews the inside of his cheek as he watches him run a hand over her back. The asshole is probably keeping her here as a silent threat. His feelings for her must be obvious.

"Back to your status," the Reverend says. "What's happening with the remaining two power grids? Where are they?"

"D.C. and Virginia. They're impossible to test. Any outages will raise a red flag in seconds."

Mitchell's neck blooms red. "Unacceptable!" His hand slams down on the control console. Hannah and the other techs jump in their seats. She shoots a worried look at Jonathan.

"It'll be fine. I'm almost in." Jonathan's tone carries an edge of impertinence. "But their firewalls have firewalls. It's D.C., after all. The NSA, CIA, Air Command are all in Virginia. The security is solid."

"Nothing's solid." Mitchell's voice is a growl. "That's why you're here. It's the only reason you're here."

Breathe. Just breathe. He glances at the men with guns blocking the door. Swiveling to face the monitors, he says, "I just need another few hours."

In silence, they eat while the techs work. Though he's familiar with Huan Chao's dream team of hackers, they function separately, working on different aspects of the mission. That means he's the only one working to control these power grids. The only one. Jonathan lowers his sandwich. He has leverage here.

"Hannah," he says. "Is this hard for you?"

"What do you mean?" she asks.

"It must be like watching the Planes." She blinks. Reverend Mitchell shakes his head, opens his mouth to speak as Jonathan adds, "Is it hard being with the man who killed your father?"

A smack across the face knocks him from his chair to the tiled floor. His cheek burns and a trickle of blood escapes his nose. Inexplicably, the pain feels good. Maybe it just feels good to see this bastard lose his shit. Jonathan wipes the blood away with his hand, stands up and returns to his chair. The guards haven't moved. Hannah's hand covers her mouth.

"These men and women volunteer their service," Mitchell seethes. "They're heroes. Ours is a mission that won't be won without bloodshed. Because without sacrifice, there can be no change."

Hannah places a hand on the Reverend's arm. In a steady voice she looks at Jonathan and says, "My father went by choice. I'm here by choice."

"Amen, Hannah," the Reverend says. "Shut your mouth and do your job, Hudson. Perhaps you'll get out alive. Don't forget your stepfather is counting on you."

"Yes, sir." Asshole-mother-fucking-bastard. He should have killed him that night on the deck.

Mitchell stands and moves to the monitor. One by one his fingers touch the plane icons, prompting faces of the BASIA soldiers flying those planes to pop on screen. "Hannah, please leave us."

She gathers the dishes. When Jonathan passes his plate to her, their fingers touch, and she sends him a quick squeeze. *Yes,* he wants to say. *I found the maps. Memorized the exit routes. Thank you, Hannah.* The door closes behind her.

Mitchell doesn't look at him when he speaks. "Hudson. Tell me your plan for Tuesday."

"I've set up an alarm clock of sorts. Using a complex algorithm that ties all the grids together, at precisely midnight, Eastern Standard Time, they'll simultaneously shut down for twelve hours."

"And backup generators?"

"Buildings have backup generators that we can't control. But the outages will cause mass havoc across every major facility and system for miles. At least that's the hope, right?"

"Hope is irrelevant. We have faith." He breezes by as the security team opens the door for him. "Complete your assignment, Hudson. Get a handle on D.C. and Virginia."

They can make sure he sits here, but they have no idea what he's doing. He purposely left D.C. and Virginia off his list. All he wants is to survive and save Steven. Maybe even take Hannah out of here. Is there a way to cause a malfunction in Mitchell's plans and still go free?

Chapter 68

THE FLIGHT TO Washington, D.C., had felt like an eternity to Sebastian. Too much time to think. Now his taxi cruises alongside the National Mall, along with the commuters who make their way into the city during morning rush hour. Not since Bureau training has he been here. The government has spent millions in defense of the capital. It's as though a protective bubble lies above the historic structures. In contrast, the outskirts lie pockmarked and charred from numerous attacks.

His eyes sting. Somewhere in D.C., his BASIA team is preparing, though they've been instructed not to make contact. Typical Mitchell, controlling everything down to the last second. Nerves and lack of sleep have left Sebastian feeling shaky. Visions of Renner's bloodied body come in flashes. He rolls his head, cracks his neck. He needs distraction. And maybe some food.

At the hotel, he checks in under another false I.D. The lobby is a blur as he rushes through, taking the elevator to his room on the fifth floor. Tossing his bag on the bed, he empties his pack and combs through the BASIA supplies: ballistics skin, addresses, coordinates, event schedule, a semiautomatic and a disassembled long-range rifle, ammunition, contact lenses, and latex gloves. He studies the lenses, the gloves. The fingertips on the gloves are imprinted. The prints must grant access to high-security areas inside the convention center. Mitchell has planned for every scenario.

Sebastian pushes open the drapes on the window. A spectacular view spreads out before him, sun glinting off the U.S. Capitol. He's spent his career in pursuit of justice. But serving a murderous government was not his intention. Turns out no one is actually protecting the country. He flexes his hand and stares at the cross that stains his palm. He's got nothing to lose now.

November, 2032

Chapter 69

IN AN ABANDONED school cafeteria in Cambridge, Cole sits across from Karen and Sean on long benches attached to tables. A random location, far from the eyes and ears of government agents. As good a place as any for saying goodbye.

"We should feel proud," Cole says. "Project Swap has a life of its own now."

"Never thought I'd be part of a revolution," Sean says.

Karen shakes her head, smiles. "A revolution."

And it is. Cole couldn't be more proud. Across the country, their people are cleaning MedIDs in homes, at parks, in cars. In turn, many with cleaned chips are meeting, either for support or for political reasons. In time, another political party will rise.

"But you called us here to say goodbye?" Karen furrows her brow.

"I need to take my family away. Our flight is tomorrow night." After Sebastian's visit, he didn't need time to deliberate. They're all packed, ready to go. And in the past day, he's devised a plan to rescue Steven. "But I need to ask your help one more time."

"Whatever you need," Sean says.

There's no time to sugarcoat it. He dives into the details of freeing Steven. Reverend Mitchell's residence should be near empty on election night. An associate of Sebastian's on the inside will smooth the way. Without her, this rescue would be impossible. It's simple, in and out. But the plan requires one more person.

"I grew up in front of a computer screen," Sean says. "My only weapon is a keyboard."

"And you've been fierce with it," Cole says.

"I'll do it," Karen says.

"Can you shoot?"

She straightens. "You wouldn't guess it to look at me, but I grew up going to a shooting range every weekend in New Hampshire."

"Eternally surprising me." He remembers his first impression of her, the mousy, obstinate resident he almost fired. "This is good. A man and woman will raise less suspicion."

"What will Steven do when he gets out?" Sean asks.

"That's up to him," Cole says.

As they leave, the sun is slipping into the horizon. Cole wonders if he'll ever see his partners again. He pulls his scarf snugly around his neck as he gets into his car. Time is surging, unstoppable. And there's not enough of it.

Chapter 70

TAYLOR WATCHES THE red light brush her daughter's forearm, eliciting a beep from the computer. As Sienna goes back to drawing on the floor, the tech rotates his chair, his back to them as his fingers rapidly tap the keyboard. Thanks to her father's private hacker, Sienna's DNA has been purified, her MedID number raised to a safe 84. And after much thought, Taylor is changing their last names. To Mason. It's the only option that feels meaningful. She leans down and kisses the top of Sienna's head, breathes in her scent. No matter what, home is right here, with her.

At first she couldn't stomach the idea of faking their MedIDs—lying and giving in to this hierarchy of numbers. But with both their numbers under 75, they'd never gain citizenship in another country. And they can't stay here with her father in power. Now, more than ever, people would want the Hensleys dead. She imagines herself and Sienna in a new life, far from politics and war. Cleaning their MedIDs is the only way out. It's hard to imagine leaving the United States forever. Back home in Boston her bed is unmade, breakfast dishes are still on the table.

Pieces and parts of her life abandoned. Returning is impossible now.

The conservative suit they chose for her feels like a straitjacket. Tomorrow is Election Day. The collective energy of her father's staff, the press, and the world is electrifying. On their way to this office, they'd passed campaign chaos throughout the mansion, with people checking off lists and making final calls. Her imagination stirs, whipping up a black-and-white room with bars on every window and door. Then even bigger—the outline of the United States with bars running vertically across it.

She can't stop thinking about Will. Carter's accusations peck away at her memories. But after hours of debating with herself, she's made a decision. Believing in someone doesn't come easy for her. Regardless of the Reverend asking Will to "protect her," her feelings for him are real. Now that she and Sienna have clean MedIDs, maybe there's a chance for the three of them to escape all of this.

The tech's jacket is draped over an empty chair. She eyes it, locates the pockets. When she'd left with Carter, he confiscated her phone with the excuse that Reverend Mitchell could track her.

She rolls the wheels of her chair a few inches over the carpet, until the jacket is within reach. She leans forward, eases her hand into one pocket and then another. Nothing. The tech concentrates, doesn't move from his work. Slipping her hand inside the coat, she finds a breast pocket. Bingo.

She stares at the phone. Little good it will do her without the fingerprint to unlock the screen. There's only way to do this. Glancing at Sienna, she hesitates, considers their options one last time. But it has to be done. Silently, she begs Sienna to keep drawing, eyes on the ground.

Quickly, she scans the room for potential weapons. There, on the bookcase, is a trophy of her father's. Metal, solid. Casually, she stands and wanders the room. Glancing back at the tech, she sees he hasn't budged. And Sienna is deep into her project. Taylor picks up the trophy.

"All set." He picks up the scanner. "Can I get your arm please?"

Luckily, he's still turned to the screen. She sets the trophy in her chair and offers her arm. The scan is over in an instant.

"All set." He taps a few more keys. "You're now officially a seventy-nine."

"Thanks." Her hands shake as she picks up the trophy and holds it just behind his head.

"So—" Suddenly, he swivels in his chair to face her.

The trophy held high, she swings it and hits him on the side of the head. The impact shocks her. *What did I do? Holy shit.* He falls to the floor, unconscious. Blood trickles from his hairline. She drops the weapon.

"Mommy?" Sienna screams. "Mommy!"

"Shhh, keep drawing, baby. Don't look." Taylor locks the door.

"Mommy you hurt him! Why did you hurt him?"

Sienna's questions are a running stream, but Taylor needs to focus. She presses the man's index finger to the screen and it opens. The phone keypad appears. What's Will's number? It's a faint memory. Frantically, she tries one after another, to no avail. Finally, "Hello?"

"Will?"

"Who is this?" a male voice says.

"Taylor."

"Taylor! Where are you? Are you in D.C.?"

"Yes, my father's making us stay with him until the election's over."

"Listen very carefully, Taylor." His grave tone makes the hair on her arms stand on end. "You need to stay far away from your father tomorrow night."

"I'm supposed to be by his side at the acceptance speech."

"Break your arm. Faint. You can't be there."

"Why? What's going to happen?"

There's a knock on the office door and someone on the other side jiggles the doorknob. A male voice shouts, "What's going on in there?"

She whispers, "What is it, Will?"

"BASIA has a mission. Mitchell's soldiers will be there."

The knock on the door turns into pounding.

"Are they going after my father?"

"Please, just stay away from the party. I can't stop—"

A great slam against the door, one after the other.

"Please find us, Will—"

A forceful shove swings the door open as a Secret Service agent storms in. He aims a gun at Taylor.

"Is that necessary? It's a phone, not a weapon."

"Depends how you look at it."

The agent snatches it from her, leans down and checks the tech's pulse. Using a voice-activated sensor on his uniform, he calls a medic. Sienna's mouth hangs open, too stunned to speak or cry. Breathing heavily, as though she's run a mile, Taylor sits on the floor and wraps her arms around her daughter. The guard was right. A phone can be a powerful weapon.

Election Day

Chapter 71

"IT FEELS ESPECIALLY important to exercise one's civic duty today, don't you agree?" Charles asks Jonathan. The boy shrugs, tosses his head to shake the long bangs from his eyes. It's a quick five-minute drive to the library where they will cast their votes in this historic election. Of course, no one knows just how historic it will be.

"Paper ballots are so ancient," Jonathan says as he stares out the window.

"Don't be daft. You of all people can understand the threat of hacking into the election process."

No response. He's so young, and sadly integral to their mission. A shame he won't perform voluntarily. It will be good to be rid of him. After today he'll let the boy go with God.

National Guardsmen are posted at every corner of the ramshackle library, their loaded weapons strapped into holsters for all to see. It's early enough that people are trickling in and there's no wait to vote. Charles leads Jonathan, Henry, and two militants. Each checks in at the front desk and receives a ballot. With customary foresight, he had each of them change their residence to his address so they could vote together in the same district. One by one they move into the booths and close the curtains behind them.

Charles smoothes his hand over the long sheet and closes his eyes for a moment in silent prayer. *God bless America.* He prays for his people, the thousands around the country who are unified in this movement, in this moment. The thought sends a shiver to his core. In a matter of hours, perhaps a couple days, the theological state he's dreamed of will be a reality. With his strategically placed soldiers of God, he and the board members of BASIA will take their rightful place as leaders of this country. The United States is weak. With God's help, they will make it strong once again.

Charles guides his pen down the line of circles, filling in the empty spaces that will ensure the future he has worked so hard to build. He waits, savors the one that matters most. And then, as he instructed all of his flock, he casts his vote for Richard Hensley.

Dressed in a standard-issue black uniform, Sebastian approaches the security checkpoint allowing access to the event space. One guard ushers him through the body scanner that immediately detects his ankle and side-holstered firearms. Another guard greets him with a retinal scanner. Sebastian stands straight, confidently. His BASIA contact lenses are his gateway. The guard types something on the keypad and nods.

"Sergeant Smith," the guard says. "Apologies, sir, I'm sure you know it's just a formality. It's an honor to have you on-site, sir."

"Thank you." He scans the man's name tag. "Corporal Connor."

"If you need anything, let us know. We're at your disposal."

"I appreciate that."

Breathing easier, he passes the checkpoint and enters the cavernous space in the Walter E. Washington Convention Center. Security and Liberty Party volunteers swarm the floor. It's easy to blend in.

Scanning the area, he assesses the exits and points of vulnerability. A stairway that leads to the grid above catches his eye. He takes the stairs in twos. On the narrow walkway, he edges past camera teams and strides the length of the room, stopping above the platform on which Richard Hensley will stand in victory. Here the light is dim, good for cover. He works methodically. From hidden compartments in his uniform, he pulls out button-sized explosive devices that he attaches to the railing. At the end of the walkway, in fire extinguisher housing, he hides several rounds of EXACTO bullets. He's tested them a few times; the remote optical guidance system helps him adjust—mid-flight—for moving targets. He'll need the extra help in the chaos. His smartwatch vibrates. It's Renner's CI.

"Diaz," he says.

"It's all set." Hannah whispers, making it difficult to hear with the crowd noise echoing off the convention center walls. "We'll get Steven Hudson out tonight."

"Good." It's a relief that Cole won't be working alone. "Do you have any questions? Need anything?"

A long silence.

"Hello?" he says.

"If I want to leave, can I go with them?"

"That's what you want?"

"I want the option."

"Tell Dr. Fitzgerald if you want to go with him. He's a good man. He can help you."

"Okay."

"You all right, Hannah?"

"Nervous."

"That's going around."

"Good luck tonight."

"You, too. 'Bye."

Gripping the handrail, he peers below at the Liberty Party minions. It's hard to know how this will go down. But he won't assassinate the next President, nor will he allow anyone else to. In a matter of hours the platform will be filled with Hensley and his entourage, bright lights illuminating them. And in the shadows, nine of his team members will be watching Will Anderson. Waiting for him to succeed. Or not.

Chapter 72

Cole isn't sentimental as he walks through their sterile, Safe District house for the last time. Their next house, wherever it is, they will make a home. He finds Ian is in his room, reading. Cole sits beside him on the bed. "I'll see you in a couple hours."

"Where are you going?"

"A few last minute errands."

Concern fills Ian's eyes. "What if you get back late?"

"I won't. Listen to your mom and do whatever she asks."

He wraps an arm around Ian, kisses him on the top of his head. Lily appears in the doorway and as he goes to her, walking away from Ian, a twinge of terror seizes him. The thought he may never see his son again.

"I'll see you at ten?" she asks.

"Yes. If you don't, go to the airport. I'll meet you there."

"Be careful." She blinks back tears. "I love you. We love you."

"I'll see you later." He kisses her, then leans his cheek against hers and whispers in her ear, "I love you, Lil. This is not goodbye."

At the door, he adds his own bag to the other four, all straining at the seams. Medical kit in hand, he steps out into the frosty air and walks to the car. The rub of his ballistics skin makes him hyperaware he needs protection tonight. And though he's far from religious, he says a prayer under his breath.

As the numbers trickle in across the country, Richard Hensley savors each state victory. The concrete evidence that the people want him in office gives him an overwhelming high. Beside him, Taylor stares out a window. At his feet, Sienna amuses herself with a doll. He feels quite alone in the moment.

"Sir." Carter appears at his side and hands him a tablet. "A call from the Oval Office."

The room is too loud. Richard escapes into a quiet nook in the hallway and holds the device up to his face. He hasn't spoken to the President since their conversation about Carter. On screen, the presidential seal disappears, replaced by Clark's face.

"Good evening, Mr. President."

"It is indeed. And it's fortunate that the stunt with your daughter resonated with families. It was quite the gamble."

He can't help himself. A satisfied grin lights up his face. "Yes, well. It's hard to believe this night has finally come."

"It's a proud moment for the party." President Clark's face falls, the creases in his skin deepening. "But the challenges don't end here, I'm afraid."

"I'm not naive, Mr. President." Richard's grin falls, his body tenses. "I'm well aware of the state of the union. And my place within it. I understand the danger."

"It's crucial that you stay the course. Despite any unforeseen issues or threats to our soil."

"Do you have any doubt that I will?"

The slightest pause provides the answer. "We've placed all our chips on you, Richard. There's no room for doubt."

"So you're just calling to prematurely congratulate me?"

"I received a call from Director Hardy. They don't have concrete proof, but there's chatter coming through that indicates a potential attack tonight."

The FBI is hardly reliable. For all he knows, they could have worked with the President to assassinate James Gardiner. "Chatter and threats are a constant."

"This one seems different. Wear your skins."

He pats his chest, feels the snug fit of the bulletproof material. "Always."

"Your men have been made aware of the threat. Be cautious. But enjoy this night, Richard. There's nothing like it."

"I will, sir. On all counts."

The screen goes black. Mere chatter won't ruin his night. It's *his* night. He can already see it in his mind. In just two hours he'll be on stage, addressing thousands in person and millions throughout the country and the world. Taylor will be at his side. But a memory flashes, of him on the State House steps next to James Gardiner. The manic dancers. Sarin. He shakes his head, shakes off the unease. Carter pokes his head in.

"New York, Pennsylvania, and Georgia announced. We swept them all!"

"Fantastic." He checks his watch. "We should get ready. I need you to double-check that everyone's wearing skins. Including Taylor and Sienna."

"Yes, sir." Carter rushes off.

Returning to the living room, Richard settles back into his chair. Taylor doesn't acknowledge him. Sienna plays on her tablet while she sings softly. Her voice eases the tension, distracts him from the overpowering information coming at him from all sides. He closes his eyes and for at least a minute forgets all of it, drifting with Sienna to a sweeter place.

Chapter 73

Five guards barricade the BASIA Command Center door, while Reverend Mitchell observes with Huan Chao from the back of the room. Jonathan works at the control console, with multiple screens displaying maps, grids, and corresponding codes. Every keystroke he makes is filled with a heavy dose of guilt over helping this lunatic with his plan.

"Systems ready?" Huan Chao asks.

"Phone systems are a go," one tech announces.

"All soldiers are on the ground and in place," the second one says.

"Power grids ready," Jonathan says.

"Check again," the Reverend orders. "There's no room for error."

One by one he runs through all fifty states. The power grids are compromised by his codes, ready to be taken over at the Reverend's command. Simultaneously tonight, when the voting booths have closed, a power outage of historical proportions will occur. Under cover of darkness, every elected official will be assassinated.

Rendered blind, motivated by fear, citizens will scatter like mice, find their way home, and wait. When power is finally restored, they will learn there's been a movement, swift and absolute.

Unless Jonathan doesn't press these buttons. But if he refuses, Steven will be killed. Tucked into his waistband, the maps Hannah left him press against his skin. He can only hope he has a chance to use them.

A BALLISTICS SUIT stretches from Sebastian's neck to his knees. The tightly woven shield will be tested tonight. On top of that is his black guard uniform. He wears the BASIA contact lenses and carries the fingerprinted gloves in a pants pocket. For the last time, he enters the Walter E. Washington Convention Center under the identity of a high-ranking security official.

It's early evening as he and the security officers perform an official walk-through. The cavernous room has been transformed from a bland empty space to a festive red, white, and blue party venue. Over the main stage, enormous screens will display Richard Hensley during his acceptance speech. Food and drink stations line the walls. And in another corner there's a stage on which a band is doing a sound check. The chaos is perfect cover.

Several Liberty Party volunteers gather in a corner to watch live election results as they stream in. For the first time in his life Sebastian didn't vote. He didn't sleep all night, his imagination running with every possible outcome of tonight. Will Mitchell himself take over in the White House? Or maybe one of his board members? Mitchell can't possibly think he can commandeer the country and force his religion on the entire U.S. population. This country would never stand for a dictatorship. Unless it didn't have a choice.

Within the crowd, someone brushes against him. It's a volunteer, a young woman, attractive, wearing a dress and heels. She's looking intently at him, unblinking. Cold. Ever so slightly she nods at him, then continues her task of hanging streamers. Yes, he recognizes her. She's changed her hair color from black to blond. He knows that under her dress is a ballistics skin, and God knows what else. It's the first time he's recognized someone here from BASIA.

They must all be here now. Acting casual but moving at a good pace, he goes on a mission to find the others. They'll all be disguised in some way. With his hair cut and clean-shaven face, he's probably hard to spot as well. But the woman knew him.

If he can get rid of his BASIA team, he can at least put a dent in Mitchell's plan, derail Hensley's assassination. Sebastian finds the woman again. This time he catches her eye, nods toward an access door nearby. He nonchalantly walks to the door, which leads to a stairway, and waits on the other side. In a matter of seconds she pushes the door open. Before she can say a word, he grabs her by the shoulder and spins her into his arms, holding one hand over her mouth. She struggles, kicks at him. He drags her to a space under the stairs, dark and filled with boxes. In one swift move he twists her neck. Her body goes slack, her eyes stay open in a blank stare. He buries her under the empty boxes, soon to be refilled with paraphernalia from the party.

One down.

Chapter 74

COLE STEERS THE Land Rover down the driveway, just a sliver of night sky visible through the canopy of trees. He and Karen haven't said much. Both know what's at stake, their plan is tight. Still, nerves gnaw relentlessly at his stomach. One last time he mentally goes over the details from his conversation with Sebastian. But before he can finish, the security gate appears, and behind that, Mitchell's sprawling estate.

"Here we go," he says.

At the intercom a female voice says, "Hello?"

"It's Doctors Moore and Coleman. Here to check on the patient."

The massive iron gates groan to life, opening before them. Beside him, Karen coughs. He notices she looks white as a sheet.

"We're doctors, Karen. Doing the job we do every day."

"Right." She nods. "Just with guns."

They trade anxious glances as he parks. Medical kits in hand, they get out and head for the front door. It opens before he can press the bell.

"Come in." A young woman gestures them into the foyer, closing the door quietly. She must be about eighteen, striking, with a rope of strawberry blond hair running down her back, just as Sebastian had described. She motions for them to follow her.

They make it down one corridor unnoticed. But around the bend a hulking man dressed in black appears from an adjoining hall. He nods to Hannah but slows, clearly checking them out.

The guard blocks their path. "Who are they, Hannah?"

"Doctors. The Reverend asked for them to check on the patient."

"At this time of night?" he says.

"I didn't make the appointment." Hannah cocks her head. "Do you want to call Reverend Mitchell to verify their visit?"

Cole can't breathe, doesn't move.

The guard eyes them. His hand rests on his gun. "Go ahead."

At the end of the hall, they descend a stairway that leads to an underground bunker. There appears to be several rooms.

"It's quiet down here," Cole says.

"Most of the guards are on assignment tonight." Hannah continues walking. "But a handful are patrolling the house. There's one in the patient's room, too."

"We were warned," Karen says. "We're ready."

Hannah stops suddenly. "This is it."

She places her hand against a wall sensor and the door opens. The scene is surreal to Cole. Steven lies handcuffed to a bed. In a corner of the room, a guard rises from his chair and reaches for his gun. Steven's head jerks up, his eyes wide, mouth agape.

Doing his best to act unfazed, Cole announces, "Doctors Moore and Coleman, here to check on the patient."

The guard withdraws his hand from his weapon and sits again, now bored with their arrival. Understanding the situation, Steven rests his head on the pillow, stares at the ceiling. Cole avoids eye contact with him and, as Hannah watches them, he and Karen set their medical kits on a bureau and take out enough medical paraphernalia to show they're serious. They are across the room from the guard, their backs to him. Karen reaches inside her kit. In one swift motion she pulls out a dart gun, pivots, aims and fires. The needle sinks into the side of the guard's neck. One hand on his neck, the other on his holster, he slumps back into the chair and is out in seconds. Karen walks around the bed and retrieves his gun.

"I can't believe you're here," Steven says. "Have either of you considered a career in the FBI?"

"Too corrupt these days." Cole goes to Steven and puts a hand on his shoulder. "You all right?"

"The food was actually quite good."

Karen smiles as she tucks the guard's gun into the back of her waistband

"And you, with weapons!" Steven says to her.

"Physician is my day job." She pulls down his blanket and checks the wound in his thigh. "Looks like it's healing nicely."

"We need to move fast." Hannah points to a glass bubble in the corner of the room, housing a video camera. From a key chain, she selects a small key and opens Steven's handcuffs. He thanks her and rubs the raw skin around his wrist. Glancing at the sleeping guard, Cole is just about to ask, but Hannah anticipates his request. She pushes him into a heap on the floor and handcuffs his arm to the bed.

"We can use these." She pulls the guard's walkie-talkie from his belt.

"Who are you?" Steven asks.

"Hannah."

"Jonathan's friend," Steven says. "You've been to my house."

She glances at her watch. "We need to go!"

"Why are you doing this?" Steven asks her. "Aren't you very close to the Reverend?"

"We don't have time for my history." She doesn't make eye contact.

Cole pulls the tape off Steven's arm and extracts the IV. "Let's get out of here."

Taking a retractable metal brace from her kit, Karen reinforces Steven's leg. He drapes his arms around Cole's and Karen's shoulders and stands, his weight on his good leg.

"Follow me." Hannah heads to the door.

"Are you leaving with us?" Cole asks.

She hesitates, then nods.

"Can you shoot?"

"I've been preparing for Armageddon for a decade. Yes. I can shoot."

Karen tosses the guard's gun to Hannah, who leads the way. Supporting Steven makes for a slow departure. After great effort to climb the staircase, they reach the main floor of the house. They move quietly down the corridor, ten feet, then twenty. The main door is just around the bend. Sweat beads on Cole's brow. He wonders what time it is, wonders if Lily has left for the airport yet.

Suddenly, up ahead, they hear voices. The corridor is stark, there's nowhere to hide. From around the corner two guards appear. They pull out their weapons.

"Hey!" one of them shouts. "What is this, Hannah? What are you doing?"

She aims at them, and they at her. Karen runs up to join her as Cole pulls Steven out of the line of fire.

The shots are deafening. One of the guards is hit. The other guard stumbles as a needle from Karen's gun takes effect. At the same time, Hannah groans and falls to her knees, blood streaming from her left arm.

"Shit!" Steven says.

"I've got her!" Karen tucks the dart gun into her waistband and helps Hannah to her feet. "Go!"

"The others are coming." Hannah's voice is quiet. "They won't let us leave."

"We're not asking," Cole says. "Move!"

Blood from Hannah's arm spatters the floor, revealing their path down the hall as they flee out the door and into the Land Rover. Cole and Karen hoist their wounded accomplices into the backseat, then scramble into the front. Cole's hands shake as he grips the steering wheel. The front door of the residence swings open and four guards storm out, guns drawn.

"Go!" Karen screams.

Bullets ricochet off the glass and metal. Cole jams his foot on the pedal. The wheels spin the white gravel into a wall of dust as they rip around the circular drive. The bullets *ping ping ping* nonstop. The guards run after them. Holding his breath, Cole has a split second to debate ramming the closed security gate. But just as he presses the pedal to the floor, the gate opens. Glancing in the rearview, he sees Hannah holding a remote control. He exhales.

"Never underestimate a pretty face," Steven says.

A slew of bullets spray the back window, the sheer force of them spreading a web of cracks. Hannah presses the remote again, closing the gates behind them.

"Your car has bulletproof glass?" Karen asks, her breathing labored.

"We got all the bells and whistles. Lily's a little paranoid."

"Not paranoid," Steven says. "Aware."

"PHONE CALL, SIR." One of the BASIA soldiers in the control room holds out a phone to Charles.

"Not now." Next to him, Jonathan focuses on the monitors. On the wall-sized screen, fifty zones are lit up throughout the United States, latitudes and longitudes noted along with codes that mean nothing to Charles. Nothing, yet everything.

"I'm sorry, sir, but I think you'll want to hear this," the soldier presses.

Swiveling in his chair, Charles reluctantly takes the phone. "What is it?"

A security guard from his residence tells him that they've been compromised. That people disguised as doctors infiltrated the compound and took down three of their men. They escaped with Steven Hudson. And Hannah left with them.

Blood rushes to his face. *Hannah*? "Tell me again."

Charles closes his eyes. He envisions the moving parts, the way things are supposed to fit together in his plan. Hannah is—was—a part of that. Breathing deeply, he fights the urge to shout or physically attack something. This must be kept secret. Jonathan cannot learn that his stepfather has been freed. Without a word, Charles stands and strides out into the empty corridor, shutting the door behind him.

"How did this happen?" he seethes into the phone.

But all he hears are vowels and consonants, nothing that makes any sense. He interrupts the guard's excuses. "You're on

God's time tonight. The most important moment in our history, and certainly in your life, and you were what? Having a snack?"

The man starts to speak again, but Charles won't hear it. "And Hannah? They must have forced her. Did they hurt her?"

"No, sir. She let them in. Used our keys to free Hudson, accessed the security codes. She shot at our men and stole the remote for the gate."

Impossible. He leans his back against the wall for support. He's devoted years to her, been her only family, given her everything. It's unimaginable she would turn on him. Maybe she was blackmailed. Perhaps someone promised to reunite her with her sister and brother. It's the only answer.

"Who's following them?" he asks.

"They were too fast, sir. Hannah shut the gate before we could get into a vehicle."

"Unacceptable. Gather a team and find them. Now!" He hangs up and straightens, sniffs. He works to relax the muscles in his face. He will exude calm and confidence.

Back in the control room, he finds Jonathan adjusting something on the board. *Hannah, sweet Hannah.* Was Jonathan part of this rescue mission? Many times she brought him dinner in his cell. Before that, Charles allowed her to visit Jonathan's home. He shakes his head at the thought. This pierced, gangly kid may be technically savvy but his charms end there. Charles pushes an image of Hannah from his mind and reminds himself that God's mission is all that matters now. By this time tomorrow they will have seized power. And unless the Lord Himself appears in the morning, it's his duty to take back this country in God's name.

"Where are we?" He reclaims his seat.

"The codes are set." Jonathan points to glowing red dots in

each of the states. "That means the systems have been hacked. In two hours they'll turn green, indicating a blackout within those grids. Government and utility generators, too. It'll last twelve hours. Then things will return to normal."

"*Normal.*" Repeating the word, he lingers on the sound of it, feeling its vibration on his tongue. "Thanks to our Lord, Jesus Christ, *normal* is about to be redefined."

Chapter 75

At Logan Airport in the massive parking structure, Lily eases the car into a space near the International Departures Terminal. Cole just texted; he should be here any minute. Talia is asleep in her car seat. Quiet all night, Ian stares out the passenger-side window. Lily reaches over and tousles his hair.

Nearby, wheels screech on concrete. She checks the time, chews on a fingernail. Three hours until their flight departs. Finally, Cole's Land Rover pulls into the spot next to them. Lily and Ian jump out. Countless fingertip-sized indentations mar the car's body and the back window is a web of cracks.

"What happened?" On shaky legs, she gapes at the SUV.

Cole rushes to them and they embrace, cheeks and hair and coats mashing against one another. Relief washes over her and the fear drains. Everyone is here in one piece. Pulling away from her, Cole turns back to the others.

Steven rolls down his window as Karen gets out and opens the rear passenger door on her side. She takes vitals on a pretty young woman sitting next to Steven. Eyes closed, the girl's head rests on the seat back and a dark cherry-red stain on her arm makes Lily cringe. A makeshift tourniquet has stanched the bleeding. *My God, it looks like they were almost killed.*

"Where were you?" she asks Cole.

"I'll tell you everything, I promise." He gestures to her pristine car, barely driven. "Karen, you take Lily's car. It'll raise less suspicion."

Without questions, Lily removes Talia in her car seat, setting her out of the way.

"Hannah's stable for now," Karen says.

Together Cole and Karen unstrap the wounded girl from the backseat and place her into the Land Rover, securing the seat belt around her.

Lily goes to Steven's window. "Are you okay?"

"I'll live." He grins while Cole and Karen help transport him into the front passenger seat of Lily's car.

"What will you do?" she asks.

"Wish I knew," Steven says. "Once we have Jonathan, we can make some decisions."

"Who is she?" Lily nods to the girl who's been shot.

"We aren't sure," Cole says. "But she risked everything to help us. Karen's going to take care of them."

"I will." Karen sets a hand on Cole's shoulder. "You should go. Be safe."

"See you," Steven says, shaking Cole's hand through the window. "I owe you."

"I'm sorry we didn't find Jonathan."

"Look at our hardy group!" Steven gestures to what remains of their team. His face becomes serious. "We'll get him out."

"I know you will," Cole says.

Everything's happening so fast. With a final round of waves, Karen hops in the driver's seat. They watch as the Land Rover drives away. The sudden quiet makes Lily aware of her shortened breath, which appears in a fog before her.

"Let's go, Fitzgeralds," Cole says.

Lily picks up the car seat with her sleeping baby girl, as Ian and Cole manage the bags.

Briskly, yet as if it's any other trip, the family heads toward the terminal.

Chapter 76

On the limousine's soft leather seats, Taylor sits next to her father on their way to the convention center. Across from them, Sienna lies stretched out in a deep slumber. Taylor wishes she could feel as peaceful as her daughter looks. Will's warning has her stomach in knots, but it's impossible to avoid the party. Her attendance is buying their freedom, their future.

"Please stay," her father says suddenly. "You and Sienna move into the White House with me."

"So we can be a constant target? No, thank you."

"No one is more protected than the President of the United States."

"That's naive." Out the window, the blur of streetlights draws her eye.

"Do you and Sienna have your skins on?"

"Of course. But what's to stop them from aiming at our heads?"

"Enough!" The muscles in his neck tense. "This is my night. Our country's night. Don't ruin it."

His tone snuffs out her idea to share Will's warning. Never mind. She'll do whatever it takes to keep Sienna safe.

Chapter 77

FROM THE WALKWAY grid, Sebastian watches the action on the convention center floor. Under the lights, the crowd shimmers in elegant evening wear, waiting for the future President to take the stage. The man he's been assigned to kill.

On the side stage, a band plays standard party tunes. The festivities are in full swing. His phone vibrates with a text. An anonymous number displays the code signifying that Cole's attempt to free Steven was successful. *Thank God.* Under that, an alert from CNN declares Richard Hensley the clear winner in the election. He shoves the phone back into his pocket.

Through his earpiece comes the voice of the lead security officer for the event. "Stations everyone. T minus five minutes."

Throughout the floor, convention center security guards scatter to their assigned positions. But the one who catches Sebastian's eye is a man moving just as quickly and purposefully, although he's dressed as a party guest. He's smoothed his hair into a more refined look, but his buzzed military cut is still obvious. So far,

Sebastian has identified and dealt with two from his BASIA team. Below, the man with the buzz cut disappears into the stairwell.

Holding his XM3 rifle behind his leg, Sebastian waits. The metal of his handgun, strapped to his ankle, presses into the ballistics skin that stretches down his legs. The weapons are a solid, weighty comfort. In seconds the grid walkway door opens. Buzz Cut steps onto the passageway and strides past the camera crew busy setting up their shot.

"T minus sixty seconds," comes over the line.

Buzz Cut stops about ten feet away. Smirking, he nods to Sebastian. "Great view from here."

"The best." Sebastian glimpses the stage. Sweat dampens his skins.

"Showtime, people," the voice on the line announces.

"In the name of the Father." The man makes the sign of the cross from his forehead, over his chest. "The Son and the Holy Spirit."

Sebastian stares at his fellow assassin and joins in. "Put on the full armor of God, so that you will be able to stand firm against the schemes of the devil."

In unison, their voices rise over the cheers of the crowd below. "For our struggle is against the rulers, against the powers and against the forces of darkness in the world."

"Amen, brother," Buzz Cut says.

A sudden silence draws their attention below. At the podium, the Liberty Party chairman is beaming, his arms spread wide as he addresses the crowd. "This is a proud moment. A moment not just for the President-elect, but for the people. A moment that solidifies our country and our purpose. A moment that underlines our priorities and concerns, and most important, a moment that will define our collective future."

The revelers cheer, raising hands that hold flags, signs, and drinks.

"Without further ado, ladies and gentlemen, it's my honor and privilege to present your next President of the United States, Richard Hensley!"

The band strikes up a victory song as a blizzard of red, white, and blue confetti obscures Sebastian's view of the stage. Next to him, Buzz Cut reaches into his suit and pulls out three pieces of a rifle that he expertly assembles in seconds. There's no doubt he's there both to take out a target and to back up Sebastian, if his mission is unsuccessful.

A parade of people make their way on stage as Sebastian readies his XM3. Positively effusive, a smiling Richard Hensley waves both arms while he crosses to the podium. Behind him trail the vice president–elect, and a bit farther behind, both men's families. *Goddammit, Taylor.* Upon seeing her, Sebastian's heart pounds faster. Through his scope, he watches her carrying Sienna in one arm and waving to the crowd with the other. He shoots a glance at Buzz Cut, who is either gunning for the vice president–elect or Taylor. Perhaps both. The whole room is a sensory explosion, but the soldier beside him has unwavering concentration.

"Hey," Sebastian shouts. "Private."

Buzz Cut's eyebrows furrow, his annoyance clear. "It's sergeant."

"Forgive me. She brought the child."

"It's not a concern."

"No one likes dead children."

"Thanks for the tip. But my aim is tight."

"So is mine." Sebastian pivots, points the XM3 at Buzz Cut and shoots. The bullet hits the man's neck, and as he crumples, his gun clangs on the metal walkway. Swiftly, Sebastian drags him into the shadows a few feet away. His phone buzzes, announcing that it's thirty seconds until midnight. He pulls on his night-vision glasses.

A triumphant Richard Hensley gestures to quiet the crowd. The band plays the final notes as the shower of confetti tapers off. Then the lights go out.

Silence. Then panicked screams.

It's child's play to pick off the BASIA soldiers once the lights are out. From above, Sebastian finds the others outfitted with the same night-vision eyewear, calmly aiming guns instead of running with the crowd. In seconds his bullets land solidly in three of them. They disappear on the floor, swallowed by thousands of feet. Three left.

BEHIND JONATHAN, REVEREND Mitchell paces back and forth in the control room. Except for his footfalls, the only other sound is the light tap of fingers on keyboards. Right to left across the map, the illuminated red dots in each state turn to green until finally they are all uniform in color. Abruptly, the pacing stops and hands rest firmly on his shoulders.

"You've done it," the Reverend whispers.

Holy shit. Single-handedly he's turned off electricity across the country and shut down communications. Huan Chao's team has enabled the Reverend's assassins to murder every elected official, starting with the President. And to ensure BASIA's domination, most of the elected officials' predecessors are also being killed. It's all happening right now, this minute. A lump forms in his throat.

He pulls away from the Reverend's grasp and glances at a portion of the screen that displays the BASIA social network feed, shielded by an encrypted code Huan devised for BASIA communications. An influx of messaging has begun, soldiers confirming that their targets are down. Jonathan imagines the unified scream of the country. What has he done?

Without warning, he bends with the pain in his gut, leans over the side of his chair and vomits. On Reverend Mitchell's shoes.

"Get ahold of yourself, kid." The Reverend laughs.

The joyous sound in this moment makes him gag again but he swallows it back. He wipes his mouth with the back of his sleeve.

"A little vomit won't ruin my moment." The Reverend kicks off his shoes and dispatches a guard to clean them.

But then, one by one, the green lights on the board turn red, starting in the east and moving west. Mitchell leans over, hands on the console desk, gaping. Jonathan watches him. He's speechless, if only for a second. It's priceless.

"What's happening?"

Feigning innocence, Jonathan shakes his head. He stares at the screen and punches a few keys. "It looks like backup generators are kicking in. I'm not sure why—"

"You said you took care of those! You tested the systems and there were no glitches!"

"It'll just take a minute."

"Minutes are all we have. A minute is everything!"

Yes, sir. He is well aware.

Chapter 78

"Go, go, go!" In complete darkness, Richard is swept away from the podium. Bodies envelop and move him in a swift, insistent current. He can't catch his breath.

"Move! This way!" It's the voice of his lead Secret Service detail.

Richard opens his eyes wide as though it will help, but it's futile. This is no fluke. President Clark was right about an attack. Gunshots ring out above the thunderous noise of the crowd. Where are Taylor and Sienna?

Hands still tightly guiding him, Richard stumbles down a short flight of stairs. He recognizes the path, knows they're heading behind the stage. A fiery nugget of anger lodges in his throat—they've stolen this glorious moment from him.

Beside him, one of the men in his detail grunts and stumbles. As the man falls, he clings to Richard's suit jacket, nearly pulling him to the floor.

"Keep moving!"

Richard doesn't recognize the voice but he isn't in a position to argue. Screams echo off the high ceiling. He trips over something—was that a body? The force of hands pushing on his back disappears even as the urgent tug on his arms pulls him along faster.

The hum of a generator cuts through the noise, and with it, a flicker of lights, dim at first and then pure, bright light. His men don't stop moving. Richard cranes his neck to glimpse the path they've taken. There, in their wake, the bodies of two of his Secret Service team, bloody and motionless. Turning back around, he spots the vice president also being rushed out. They exchange looks. In that moment, from somewhere behind them, a bullet rips into the vice president–elect's head. *Oh my God.* Richard's legs falter. His men adjust, wrapping his arms around their shoulders as they storm ahead. Ahead of them the exit sign glows red.

SEBASTIAN WHIPS OFF his goggles and squints to see. He wonders if Jonathan had anything to do with this glitch in Mitchell's plan. No time to dwell, though, with three BASIA soldiers remaining. And he no longer has darkness as a shield.

Shrieks and cries echo in the vast space. The crowd knows now, they see the bodies, slip on the bloodied floor. He clips one end of a rappelling line to his belt and the other to the railing. Leaving his sniper rifle behind, he swings his leg over the metal rail and lowers himself into the chaos. No one seems to notice or care. Handgun poised, he sprints across the room and behind the stage to find Richard Hensley and Taylor.

People stream out any door they can find. Up ahead, Sebastian sees two downed Secret Service agents. He scans the crowd but no one stands out as militia. Rushing forward, he passes a crowd of men and women huddled on the ground around the vice president-elect as someone does chest compressions. Mitchell's soldiers must be close.

At the door, the river of escaping crowd is thick and slow. He shoulders his way through. For the first time in months he uses his credentials, shouting, "FBI!"

Finally, the fresh night air hits him. He's on the back side of the building, yards from the main parking lot. Droves of people sprint away, around the convention center to their cars.

A muted explosion turns him toward a line of identical black SUVs, headlights and engines on. The VIP parking lot. He holds a hand above his eyes against the glare of the high beams. Shots pierce the air and a woman screams. *Taylor?* He runs toward the voice.

Reaching the nearest SUV, he crouches behind it, peers into the windows. It's impossible to see inside through the tinted glass, but next to him there's a large hole in the metal where the door handle was blown off. Gun ready, he slides his free hand into the hole and pulls the door open. A bloodied congressman lies unmoving on the seat. In the front, the driver is unconscious, maybe dead. More shots ring and ricochet.

Does the Secret Service still have Taylor and Richard Hensley? Sebastian drops to his stomach and puts his ear to the cold asphalt to glimpse under the car. At the SUV farthest away, he sees several pairs of feet. Crawling to the back of the vehicle, he creeps past the other vehicles one by one, using them as cover. He pauses as he hears shoes scrape against pavement. Slowly, he moves until he's only a few feet from the last SUV.

Abruptly, Sebastian is knocked backward and drops his gun. *Oh God, shit.* White hot pain lodges in his ribs. He can't catch his breath. His hand fumbles with his jacket, rips it open. Reaching through layers of clothes, he feels the ballistics skin, locates the bullet and pries it out with his fingers.

Car doors slam. Wheels screech. Searing pain radiates through his torso as he finds his gun and pulls himself up, leans against the back of an SUV and forces his legs to move. Whoever it was, they're gone, leaving bodies dumped in the parking spaces. Two sets of taillights betray their path as they head toward the Convention Center exit. More shots ring out as he hauls the next unfortunate driver from his seat and crawls in. The motor is already running. He slams the transmission into drive and presses the pedal to the floor.

The taillights in the distance lead the way. He knows exactly where they're heading.

Chapter 79

WRAPPED IN TAYLOR'S arms, Sienna trembles. Taylor whispers into her daughter's hair, "Everything's going to be okay." They huddle on the floor of the SUV as two BASIA soldiers hold their guns just inches away. The car swerves, the engine roars. She raises her head and peers out the window. They pass K Street, then a few turns later, Pennsylvania Avenue. They're heading to the White House. Where can Reverend Mitchell possibly think all of this will lead?

Another SUV pulls alongside them, and the two vehicles race neck and neck down a busy two-lane avenue. Shots ricochet off the bulletproof glass. Getting as close to the floor as possible, she hugs Sienna tighter, using her own body as a shield. *We're going to die. It's not time, it can't be time.*

Their driver swerves, brakes fast, the tires screeching on the asphalt. When Taylor peeks up for a split second, she sees they're behind the other vehicle, close on its tail. The soldiers above her barely speak and when they do it's in code. Is her father still alive inside the other SUV? Are his Secret Service agents loyal, or plants by the Reverend? When she was grabbed in the parking lot, she'd thought these men in black were their protection. When they'd aimed their weapons at her father, her shock had turned to sickening regret for not heeding Sebastian's warning. But her father had threatened to renege on his promises, to brand her a terrorist and to sue for custody of Sienna. She'd had no choice. After all, what judge would deny the President of the United States his granddaughter?

SEBASTIAN'S BODY TENSES behind the wheel of his commandeered SUV. The two identical vehicles ahead of him jockey for position, but one takes the lead. He knows one car carries Secret Service agents and Richard Hensley, the other Reverend Mitchell's BASIA. But in which one are Taylor and Sienna? He knows they're still alive. As long as Richard Hensley lives, Mitchell will keep them as currency. It's easier to control the president-elect that way.

The White House looms just a block away now. The two SUVs disappear around a corner, and he follows, keeping a short distance between them. And there it is. At the White House gate, a line of U.S. troops stand in a barricade, assault weapons aimed and ready. They dare not fire. With three identical SUVs approaching, how can they know which one holds the president-elect? Neither SUV ahead slows down. Closer, closer. They're almost there when hands appear out of one of the passenger-side windows, holding a rocket launcher. A blast sends a fiery comet at the guard station. Flames erupt as a second blast unhinges the White House gate. Guards are tossed like rag dolls, with no one left standing.

RICHARD GAPES OUT the window at the bodies of the wounded and dying guards. He's in shock now, he's sure of it. His SUV is only seconds ahead of the one that he thinks—he hopes—carries Taylor and Sienna. *Let them be alive.*

The car screeches to a stop as the agents strap on gas masks and ballistics hoods. The nearest agent slides a ballistics hood with holes for eyes, nostrils, and mouth over his head. On top of that, a tight-fitting gas mask is secured. It's disorienting, hard to breathe. He watches as they ready an arsenal of weapons. With their guns poised in the direction of the nearing SUV, bodies surround him. He's never felt more helpless.

"Where's President Clark?" he shouts.

No one answers.

"Carter?" Richard searches the masks.

Behind him, Carter fastens his own gas mask over a ballistics hood. His voice comes out muted and deep. "By now he should be either in the tunnel on the way to Mount Weather, or secured in the bunker."

"Get Taylor and Sienna! Save my granddaughter, dammit!"

"Our priority is you, sir," says the agent to his left. The door swings open and hands tug him from both sides. "We'll send a team for them once you're secure."

Richard is thrust outside, up the White House steps to the door. As the other SUV screeches to a halt, one of his men lobs a device at it. An explosion releases a cloud of tear gas. He jerks his head to see behind them but the cloud of chemicals obscure everything.

"Taylor!" His shouts are muffled by the protective layers. They wouldn't harm a child, would they?

Bullets pock the white pillars and pristine paint as they race over the threshold and down the historic hallway. Breathing hard, he slows, but the arms that guide him grip tighter, pull stronger. They're deeper into the West Wing now. Almost to safety.

Shots shred a painting a few feet ahead of them as they make the last turn. Just ahead is the elevator, where a guard stands with an automatic rifle aimed in their direction, his foot wedged against the open door.

The lead agent shouts to the guard, identifying them and confirming they have the president-elect. A hand roughly shoves Richard into the elevator, his face slamming into the wall. He turns back to see a member of his team systematically shoot each of his Secret Service agents in their only unprotected areas—the hands and feet. Weapons and bodies drop to the floor, their agonizing, muffled groans shaking Richard to the core. Despite the shooter's mask, he recognizes Carter's suit. *Impossible! Carter is President Clark's man. Why would he disable his own men?*

Wait—the guard at the elevator! Carter hasn't shot him, hasn't even looked his way. Richard leans forward, reaches the wall panel and hits the button that should propel him to safety. Instead, the guard glares at him and steadies his hold on the open door. Then he nods to Carter. *Oh Christ. Oh, God. They're all in on it. Are they with BASIA?*

"You can have the honor," Carter says to the guard, indicating the men struggling on the floor. "Finish it."

As Carter steps into the elevator, he aims his gun at Richard's feet. Pressing his back against the wall, Richard uses it to steady himself and stand. Saliva pools in his mouth. He desperately wants to spit at the traitor but he swallows it. The elevator descends six floors deep into the earth. Why hasn't Carter killed him? What could they possibly be planning? Through the protective headgear the familiar brown eyes blink at him.

Richard slides his gas mask up onto his head, rolls the ballistics hood up, revealing his face. "Why, Carter?"

Carter also removes the protective masks from his face. "Ben Franklin said, 'They who can give up essential liberty to obtain a little temporary safety deserve neither liberty nor safety.'"

"Ben Franklin didn't live in our world."

"The MedID goes against everything our forefathers believed. It goes against our God-given freedoms."

"What if I shut down the MedID?"

"It's too late."

"What are you part of? Are you with Charles Mitchell?"

"I serve God. Years ago in His name and for our freedom, my mother sacrificed herself. Then my father enlisted in the U.S. Army."

"As a mole?"

Carter nods. "After he died, Reverend Mitchell took me in. I was just a kid. He taught me everything. Gave me everything."

"But you work for President Clark?"

"That was my assignment. It's completed now."

The moment is surreal. His trusted confidant is a double agent, and Richard knows he's been a fool.

"You need to put your hood and mask back on." Carter pulls two pairs of earphones from his pocket. "And take this. Make sure they're secure in both ears."

"Goddammit, Carter, think about the enormity of this!" Hands trembling, he does as he's told, readjusting the face gear and plugging his ears.

"You've waited your whole life for this moment, but so have I," Carter says. "So have I."

Chapter 80

Down the White House hallway, Taylor digs her heels into the carpet to slow the men who yank her forward. The gas mask limits her vision to what's in front of her. Before the tear gas erupted outside, she'd seen her father being ushered through the entrance. No doubt they're heading for the Presidential Emergency Operations Center with the bunker, several floors below.

Sienna. The bastards left her locked in the SUV, screaming "Mommy!" as the door slammed shut. Knowing she's alone and scared makes Taylor struggle even harder. But maybe her daughter is safer there? If Reverend Mitchell expects her father to give up his life—or the presidency—in exchange for his daughter's safe return, he's sorely misguided.

They're about to turn down a new hallway when Taylor raises her feet off the carpet. It doesn't faze her abductors, who continue on, carrying her now. So she kicks. Wildly. The kicking stops them, but a sharp jab in her thigh makes her gasp. Her body goes slack. One of the men picks her up and throws her over his shoulder. Consciousness slips away.

REMNANTS OF TEAR gas cling to the air. Without a mask, Sebastian had to wait for it to clear. Now he ties his shirt over his nose and mouth and, with only the ballistics suit covering his torso, jumps out of his vehicle and sprints toward the entrance. His eyes burn, but he ignores it as best he can, squinting through blurry vision. As he passes the first SUV, muted screams come from within. He presses his face up against the window but he can't see through the tinted pane. Still, he recognizes Sienna's voice.

He works rapidly as he wrests the shirt from his face and tears a seam, ripping off a section of material. In seconds he ties the shirt back over his nose and mouth, then from his belt he pops off a metallic button. Attaching it to the rear passenger door, he yells to Sienna to turn away. A pop blows out the handle, leaving a hole. He wads up the piece of fabric and shoves it through the hole.

"Hold this over your mouth and nose," he instructs. "I'll carry you through the gas."

Silence.

"Sienna, It's Will!" He pulls the shirt down briefly so she can see his face. A moment's hesitation until finally she holds the material over her face. He opens the door, and she jumps into his arms.

"Where's Mommy?"

"I'm going to get her, but I need your help. Can you help me?"

She nods and clings to him as he races up the White House steps. Inside the foyer, he sets her down and draws out his gun. There are no voices, no sounds. No evidence revealing their path. Suddenly, Sienna wraps her arms around his legs. He bends down so he's eye level with her. They both take off their masks.

"We're gonna play hide-and-seek, Sienna. Okay?"

"Where's Mommy?" she asks again.

"She wants you to hide. She asked me to find you a good place."

"Okay."

Keeping a tight hold on his gun, with his free arm Sebastian carries her through the East Wing. He's read countless books about the White House, knows about the secret compartments and rooms. They enter the library and he searches for a leather-bound copy of *The Odyssey*. He finds it and pulls it forward. A door no taller than Sienna opens beneath it.

"Wow," she says.

From his belt, he frees a thumb-sized flashlight and hands it to her as she settles inside the space. "Remember, part of the game is being as quiet as you can. Only come out when you hear your mom's voice."

"I'm scared."

"You're safe here. And I'll be back soon with your mom. Think about those happy dreams your mom puts into your ears."

Finally she nods.

"Okay." He smiles reassuringly, then seals her inside.

Pivoting, he bolts back down the hall and rounds another corner, entering the West Wing. He stops and listens. Muffled footsteps come from up ahead somewhere. Gun poised, he slows at the next corner and peers around the wall. There, maybe twenty feet away, a BASIA soldier carries a limp Taylor over his shoulder.

Sebastian's on him in seconds. He lands a powerful kick to the man's back and hears a bone crack. The soldier groans as he and Taylor land in a heap. Ahead, another soldier turns and points his weapon, but Sebastian fires first. The bullet explodes the man's hand, sends the gun flying. He moves forward, rips off the soldier's gas mask and ballistics hood and shoots him in the head.

Disarming both men, Sebastian stuffs their weapons into his

belt and kneels beside Taylor, feels for a pulse. Relief fills him. She's alive, probably drugged. For a split second he doesn't know if he should run out with her and Sienna or finish this—whatever *this* is.

Indiscernible sounds echo in the distance. He stops debating and moves, stripping the bulkier man of his pants and jacket. The clothes fit over his own, and he slides on the ballistics hood and gas mask. He hoists Taylor over his shoulder and strides around the corner.

At an elevator midway down the hall, a man dressed identically to Sebastian is furiously waving him forward. Another BASIA soldier. Sebastian quickens his pace and watches as the man touches his thumb to a wall scanner, then leans in for a retinal scan.

"Who fired shots?" the soldier asks.

"Secret Service," Sebastian says. "We got him."

"Where's Murphy?"

"He was hit."

The man nods and hits the elevator button multiple times, as though that will hurry it along. Sebastian grips his gun tighter, shifts Taylor on his shoulder. The door opens.

"PEOC is the last button, all the way down. Carter's just ahead of you."

Swiftly, Sebastian shoots the man in his temple. He sets Taylor on the elevator floor and drags the man inside with them. The doors close and the car descends. He leans against a wall, catches his breath. Carter Benson is one step ahead, he thinks. Charles Mitchell's reach is truly stunning, the scope of his plan immense. At this point, Sebastian isn't even sure what he hopes to accomplish. All he can do is move forward.

Chapter 81

RICHARD ADJUSTS HIS earphones as he scans the concrete vestibule that leads into the bunker. There's no way out. He watches Carter, who pulls up his ballistics sleeve and presses buttons on a device fastened to his arm. With worrisome ease, he activates the retinal key and the fingerprint scanner. The door opens with a loud click and a beep.

Downed guards litter the corridor, weapons forgotten as they writhe and moan. At least they look like they're moaning, but Richard can't hear them with the earphones. He feels his jaw drop, he can't move. But Carter prods him forward with his gun. The guards don't notice as Richard stumbles over them and Carter walks confidently to the end of the hall.

The mask is suffocating. Richard's senses are off, his balance unsure.

At the end of the hallway, Carter opens a door with the presidential seal. A half second later, Richard follows him into the Executive Briefing Room. He gasps. Fifteen, twenty people are on the floor, all in apparent agony. Many are hunched in the fetal position, hands covering their ears. People are vomiting, hyperventilating, unconscious. *My God, my God.* Richard recognizes almost all of them: the current vice president, First Lady Shannon Clark, the Secretary of State, two counselors, the Chief of Staff, and the National Security Advisor. The others' suits give away their identity as Secret Service. In a corner, crumpled in a heap with his wife, is President Clark. Blood streams from his nose. *This cannot be real.* Richard looks over to Carter, who systematically checks bodies and removes weapons.

Richard is paralyzed. Inside his ballistics suit, his chest is tight, his body drenched in sweat. Carter dumps the weapons into a trashcan. Gathering the pulls on the plastic bag within, he hauls out the sack and slings it over his back, like a macabre Santa Claus.

THE ILLUMINATED DOTS in thirty-eight states remain green, with the remainder red. Charles isn't convinced Jonathan is doing as he's told, working to take control of the power grids. The kid's fingers press keys, but perhaps he's just doing it for effect. It's been an hour since Richard Hensley took the stage, yet there's been no confirmation on BASIA's critical targets, Hensley and Clark. Charles presses his thumb into the cross in his palm. Presses until it hurts. Though their goal is finally within reach, the wait is maddening. Pain stabs at his temple. From his pants pocket he pulls out a bottle, opens it and swallows one of the pills. He begins to pray silently. *Heavenly Father, who art in Heaven. . .*

"Sir, you have a call." Henry hands him a phone.

"Watch him." Charles gestures to Jonathan. He steps out into the hallway, holds the phone at face level. "Go."

Carter's face appears. The image is grainy, distorted.

"What's your status?" Charles asks.

"I can confirm Clark. If he's not dead, he's a vegetable."

"If? If isn't a confirmation."

"Sorry. I'll finish it."

"And Hensley?"

"We've moved into Plan B, sir. He's alive and with me now."

The camera shakes for a moment and stops, revealing Richard Hensley, red-faced and looking ill. If Hensley were here, Charles would strangle him himself. He suppresses the urge to hurl the phone. Will Anderson was his very best, and his team was up to the task. Charles breathes in through his nose until he is calm and focused once again. Hensley is inconsequential. This is not defeat, merely a detour. The camera pans back to Carter.

"Where is Taylor Hensley and her daughter?"

"In the West Wing. Should be here any minute."

"Are you near the subway?"

"Close."

"Continue on to Union Station. Don't get on the train. You'll need to exit the tunnel on foot. Use the network when you're back aboveground. Help is near."

"Yes, sir."

It's clear the Lord had other plans when his soldiers failed to kill Hensley at the convention. Their faith is being tested. "Put Hensley on."

The camera steadies on Hensley's face.

"Congratulations, Mr. President-elect," Charles says. "Quite a big day for you."

"What have you done, Mitchell?" Hensley's voice is ragged, desperate.

"God's work. I serve at the pleasure of Our Savior, Jesus Christ. And so will this country. It's long overdue, I'm afraid."

"You're mad."

"Mad or not, I hold your future in my hands. And it seems we have two options, rather black and white. You and your family can live or die. Which do you choose, sir?"

"I won't be your pawn."

"Let's be honest. You've always been a pawn, Mr. Hensley. The government's pawn, my pawn, what's the difference, really? You can still lead the country. Enjoy your granddaughter. Make a difference in people's lives. Change happens slowly, as you know. But now there will be swift, unilateral decisions, whether voiced by you or someone else. Or, if you'd rather meet our Heavenly Father, we are happy to oblige."

Chapter 82

THE ELEVATOR DOOR to the bunker opens. In the vestibule, Sebastian places Taylor gently on the floor. It's good she's unconscious, a relief she doesn't have to see the mayhem.

The guard's body is much heavier. Sebastian struggles with his bulk, finally propping him against the wall where another retinal key and fingerprint scanner blocks their access. He presses the dead man's thumb to the fingerprint screen, then forces the man's right eye open in front of the retina identification monitor. As he drops the body to the floor, a buzz sounds and a green light appears on the screen. The heavy vaultlike door opens with a sigh.

Bodies are strewn on the floor at varying angles. The stench of vomit is strong and none of the guards is moving. *What the hell is this? A chemical weapon? Biological?* Quickly, he heaves Taylor over his shoulder and hurries past them to the end of the corridor. The door to the Executive Briefing Room is ajar, no voices come from within. He sets Taylor down.

A swift kick from his foot slams the door open completely. He takes aim and steps inside. *Jesus Christ.* Bile burns the back of his throat. More bodies, motionless. Moving swiftly, he checks faces in search of Richard Hensley. Sebastian knows these people, has seen their faces, heard their names on the news. The vice president lies staring at the ceiling, clearly gone. Many hold their heads and cover their ears. Then it comes to him. Carter Benson used a sonic weapon. Mitchell thought of everything. It's a chess game with a madman.

On the far side of the room he finds President Clark huddled with his wife in a corner, unmoving. Looks like Benson wanted to be doubly sure—Clark's been shot in the head. Sebastian checks their pulses, closes his eyes for a moment. Mitchell has successfully assassinated the President of the United States and disabled the government in one night.

But something's amiss. Richard Hensley isn't here. Assuming Benson has him, why would Mitchell take the President-elect hostage? To make a public display of him? Sebastian leaves the tomb and scoops up Taylor, racing down the hallway in the direction of the underground rail system. At least the TSA Federal Air Marshals that guard the train will be on high alert. It's his last chance to find allies down here.

RICHARD PRIES OFF the gas mask and perspiration-slick ballistics hood. Cool air hits his face and he takes deep, choking breaths. Next to him, Carter does the same. Surely by now the U.S. military is en route. This will all end very soon, and badly, for Reverend Mitchell and his militia.

"Time to go," Carter says.

Exhausted—and unwilling to aid the enemy—he shuffles his

feet, despite the gun Carter shoves into his spine. Down the dimly lit corridor that leads to the rail system, they pass unmarked doors, access routes for the tunnel system. Richard has never been this far in the PEOC, never seen the train, but he knows members of FEMA await him and any other administration survivors at Mount Weather. Before that, they'll encounter armed troops that man the train cars in case of emergency. There's still a chance to defeat these goddamned terrorists.

A rhythmic clicking echoes in the distance. It's hard to tell if it's in front of or behind them. Their pace quickens as Carter holds his gun with one hand and pulls Richard's arm with the other.

"Run, Richard!" Carter shouts.

"President-elect, if you please."

Footsteps, yes, footsteps. Close on their heels. Up ahead there's a brightly lit opening—the platform. He squints to try and discern if there are soldiers waiting but he can't tell at this distance. The corridor reverberates as a train passes through the parallel civilian rail line on its way to Union Station. Abruptly, Carter stops at one of the unmarked doors. He rummages through a sack attached to his belt. From it he pulls a tiny device that he attaches to the door.

"Carter!" a male voice calls.

Carter pivots, twisting Richard into his arms, aiming a gun at his head. There, maybe thirty feet away, is one of Reverend Mitchell's men. A body is draped over his shoulder, arms akimbo. Female arms. A pang lodges in Richard's chest. Taylor! And where's Sienna?

"Identify yourself," Carter says.

Wearing the same uniform and masks they just removed, the stranger slows to a walk.

"Murphy was hit," the man says. He nods his head, indicating the direction from which they came. "Nice work back there. The Lord must be pleased."

"Whittaker?"

"At your service."

"Not another step." Carter presses the gun into Richard's temple. "There's no Whittaker on this mission."

"Whoa, hold on a minute." The man doesn't stop, nor does he slow.

Richard's eyes widen, silently pleading with the stranger. If he isn't with Mitchell, he must be Secret Service or U.S. military. Oh please, let it be. He asks, "Is she alive?"

"Sleeping soundly."

"Shut up!" Carter's grip on him tightens and he forces him to walk backward. "Who are you?"

"Why haven't you killed Hensley?" the man asks. "That was the plan. Mitchell must be very disappointed in you."

"You don't know the plan." Carter continues moving toward the station.

"They're waiting for you at Mount Weather." The man juts his chin in the direction of the light. Carefully, he lays Taylor on the floor, but he's quick to aim his weapon. Carter adjusts Richard, positioning him as a shield. "So which is it? Does Reverend Mitchell want the President-elect alive or dead?"

"It's win-win," Carter says. "We'll make it work."

The metal against Richard's head sucks his concentration. He's not ready to die, not ready to give up everything he's worked for his whole life. He stares at Taylor's limp body. If Carter doesn't kill him, is it possible to still lead the country? Even with Reverend Mitchell at the true helm, perhaps he can still make a difference. Maybe serving citizens will ease the transition to whatever lies ahead. At least they know him, elected him. Want him. That's better than dying, isn't it?

SEBASTIAN ESTIMATES HE has about thirty seconds to take action. There's no way to know if Mitchell's men await them at the station. By now they could have killed the U.S. military guards and assumed their positions. Carter genuinely doesn't appear to care if Hensley lives or dies. But there must be a plan, Mitchell doesn't operate without one. Decision time.

"This has been fun," Carter says, subtly shifting his weapon. "But people are waiting for us."

Sebastian aims, shoots. Carter fires back. Blazing pain shoots up Sebastian's arm. His hand is shot through, fingers shattered. Then, an explosion. Hot wind presses against him. Situated between them, a blown-out door opens into the tunnel.

Prostrate on the concrete, Carter lies with a bullet through his eye. No need to check his vitals. Richard's also on the ground, but unhurt. Figures emerge from the lighted station ahead.

Summoning the last of his strength, Sebastian leans down and with his good hand pulls Taylor up and over his shoulder. Adrenaline pumps through him, numbs the pain. He stumbles over to Hensley. "Get up!"

Slowly—too slowly—Richard unfurls, sits up and stares at his dead captor. Half a dozen men in combat gear are coming. Sebastian can't take the chance that they're not BASIA. So far Reverend Mitchell's men are everywhere.

"Get up, Hensley! Or you're on your own."

"Do you have Sienna?" Richard asks, his voice quiet and weak.

"What? Yes, she's safe. Goddammit, are you coming?"

"We can't outrun them." Richard shakes his head. "It's me they want. Save Taylor and Sienna."

Sebastian nods. The pounding of boots is loud now. He moves to the blasted door. "Good luck, Mr. President."

With Taylor over his shoulder, he races into the darkness, through the blown-out door. He thinks of the East Wing, the library. They've got to find a way back to Sienna.

Chapter 83

On his knees in the private chapel within the BASIA compound, Charles's heart swells as he thanks God and his Savior, Jesus Christ, for their victory. The pure joy of accomplishing this mission on behalf of the Almighty for the people of this great country brings tears to his eyes. He gazes at the cross in his palm, clenches his fist tight. Their work has just begun.

Returning to the Command Center, he regards Jonathan, who has barely moved from his chair in over twelve hours. The map on the enormous screen now displays red lights in every state, power having been restored to eliminate the need for looting or other antisocial behaviors. No doubt citizens are holed up in their homes, glued to news sources, waiting for any information to explain the political tsunami that just swept their nation.

"I'm free to go now, right?" Jonathan says. "And Steven, too?"

"You weren't on your game tonight." He's convinced the boy attempted to foil the mission. "There are still a few elected officials running loose out there."

Jonathan doesn't reply.

"No matter. We'll find them and finish it. So yes, you've officially completed your task. But perhaps you'd like to reconsider and remain with us."

"No thanks." Jonathan stands. The three guards stiffen at his movement.

This kid is either a genius or an idiot. "At least wait for my address."

"I'd rather—"

"Wait." Charles nods to the guards, who move to block the door. "Bring up the screens."

Sighing, Jonathan sits once again. He pings the keyboards until the map disappears, replaced by dozens of small screens. With a few more strokes, live videos with thousands of faces appear, Patriot's Church members and BASIA militia from around the country.

The energy is magnificent. Beaming, Charles looks into the camera lens. "The light of a new day shines upon us. Last night, our brave, faithful soldiers executed a triumphant and swift victory in the name of Our Lord."

Jubilant applause. Some weep openly, others embrace. It has been a long journey indeed.

"Yes! Our cup overflows. With His help we have taken the reins and we will steer our country on the path of righteousness once again. Where we all have a voice. And we will be heard. Indeed, the world is already listening. Goodness and mercy shall follow us all the days of our lives, and together we shall dwell in the house of the Lord forever." Affecting a less jovial tone, he continues. "Still, you must remain patient, vigilant. I ask your continued silence in the name of our mission. The plan has changed and will continue to change as we navigate these new waters. Right now, our country is blind, and probably numb. We must shepherd our friends and neighbors through this time. For those who have not yet embraced God, who have followed their government into a hellish landscape with decrepit morals, they will come around. But it will be a slow and evolving process. Fortunately, we've acquired an important asset that will prove instrumental to our cause. The Lord has ensured our success by presenting us with a spokesperson with whom we're all familiar. Someone the country already trusts, and who will usher in the changes we are so desperate for. He will speak on our behalf. He will be our voice."

He nods to Jonathan, who brings up video feed with the face of Richard Hensley. Mouths drop, murmuring begins, people turn to one another in question. Hensley stares blankly into the camera, his skin ashen, his handsome features drooping. The camera doesn't show the shackles around his hands and ankles as he rests in the vehicle that will deposit him at the BASIA compound in just a few hours.

"As we know, the Lord works in mysterious ways." Charles gestures to the sky. "May I present your new President—our new President—Richard Hensley."

The people are slow to react, sparse clapping throughout.

"Say hello, Mr. President," Charles instructs.

Hensley coughs, straightens. With little energy and less enthusiasm, he says, "Hello."

"Imagine how relieved the people of the United States will be to see their chosen representative alive and well in the wake of terror." He checks his watch. "It's almost time for our national address. Mr. President, we may need to get you some hair and makeup."

Laughter from his flock. No reaction from Hensley. That's all right, though. Once the cameras are on and Hensley's addressing the people, he'll cling to the hope that he can be their lifeline. And he will rise to the challenge. It's who he is.

"We are truly, once again, One Nation Under God," Charles declares, savoring those four words. "Thanks to all of you for your belief, your support, and most of all, your love. Our movement is a success because of you. We will continue God's work and be strengthened by Him in our quest to bring our beloved country to a more holy place. Freedom will be restored as we redesign the current systems until they represent all that we hold true, with the New Testament as our guide. Glory be to God. Amen." He places his hand on his chest, then holds his palm out to his people. Thousands of hands respond in kind. "Go in peace and serve the Lord."

Upon his gesture, Jonathan turns off the camera. The monitors go black.

"Am I done here?" Jonathan stands again.

"I'm a man of my word." Charles nods to the guards, one of whom opens the door. "These men will take you to Steven, and the two of you will be released. But before you go, tell me. How did you convince Hannah?"

Passing by him, Jonathan's brows furrow. "About what?"

Is it possible the boy doesn't know Hannah helped Steven Hudson escape? There's an earnestness, an openness, in his features. How very puzzling.

"Never mind." Charles waves him off. And with a subtle nod, the guards do as they've been told.

ONE GUARD LEADS, one follows behind Jonathan toward the compound exit. This duo has been with him for days. One of the men has white-blond hair, the other is big, solid as a brick. In his mind, he's nicknamed them Whitey and Horse. His heart pounds so loudly he fears they can hear it. *Please let this work.* He visualizes Hannah's map, the way through the forest, an uncut path that leads to the main road a couple miles away. Wiping his sweaty palms on his jeans, he glances behind him at Whitey. He's not an idiot. He knows they've been instructed to kill him.

Fortunately, Reverend Mitchell and his guards don't know code. Even Huan Chao will need time to solve the cyber puzzle he's left behind. Over the past week, when Jonathan was working on disabling power grids, he also hacked into the alarm system for BASIA HQ. It was hard to know when he'd be able to activate his escape plan, but moments ago, before he pushed away from the control panel, he'd slid his fingers over a few keys, engaging the code.

The exit door ahead is only a couple hundred feet away. His body is rigid, awaiting the click of a trigger. He counts silently. Without turning around, he knows Whitey has his hand on his weapon. Maybe it's even aimed at his head. Three, two . . .

Blaring sirens erupt from speakers all around. Red lights on the ceiling flash. An automated male voice instructs: *"Take your stations. The Command Center has been compromised."*

"What the hell?" Horse says, stopping abruptly.

"We gotta head back," Whitey says. "Now."

"We gotta take care of this." Horse nods to Jonathan.

"Doors lock automatically when the alarm is triggered. Kid's not going anywhere."

"I thought I was free to go," Jonathan says.

Horse shakes his head, reaches into a band strapped to his waist and pulls out plastic handcuffs. He forces Jonathan's hands behind his back, pulls the plastic noose tight around his wrists and pushes him roughly to his knees.

Over their radios a male voice commands, "All guards report to stations. I repeat, all guards report to stations."

"There are cameras everywhere." Whitey gestures to the various points in the hall. "There's nowhere for him to hide."

Little do they know that he's also compromised the security system. All video has been paused, creating the effect that the halls are empty. Jonathan slides toward the exit while they argue.

"Fine." Horse takes his hand off the weapon in his waistband. "But Mitchell is gonna be pissed this isn't finished."

"Stay here, kid," says Whitey. "If you so much as move we'll kill your stepfather."

It's a tired threat. Jonathan watches the men exchange glances, then quickly turn and run back toward the control room. As soon as they're out of sight, he slides his back up the wall, stands and sprints for the door. He slams his body against it and it opens, mercifully. Daylight!

Sirens pierce the air. He runs across the grass, into the woods. His feet fly over rocks, fallen branches. He knows he only has minutes before Huan rearms the system. The cold air wakes him up, feeds his body. Without his arms and hands to use for balance, he almost falls several times. But he never stops.

"Fuck you, Mitchell, you asshole!" There's no one to hear it, but it's music to him.

Crisp leaves crunch underfoot as he ducks branches, weaves around trees. The path he's taking should lead to the main road. It's hard to believe Hannah's behind this, that she risked everything to help him. He wonders what the Reverend's question was about. Did she escape? Will she be waiting for him?

The siren stops. Up ahead, sunlight streams in through the pine needles and twisted branches. A gunshot blast, a warning.

Faster, faster than he knew he could run, Jonathan pushes his body. The road must be close now. His eyes strain to find the pavement ahead.

STEVEN CHECKS HIS watch. Twelve hours have passed since the attack. They've been sitting here this whole time, waiting. The air in the Land Rover is soupy from three perspiring bodies. Karen's been a good sport playing doctor and driver, especially as she has nothing to gain from helping any of them. Despite his attempts at small talk, Hannah remains a mystery, though she must have her reasons for switching sides and leaving Mitchell. She's been vague with details, but she directed them to park here, a few miles from the entrance to the BASIA headquarters. Apparently, she left Jonathan a map that leads here. If they get him back, Steven won't know how to properly thank her.

"Where is he?" Steven asks.

"Should be any minute now," Hannah says.

Everyone stares in silence down the narrow two-way road.

"What if it doesn't work?" Karen asks.

"Have faith," Hannah says. "It'll work."

For the umpteenth time, Steven checks his gun. Loaded. Safety off. His fingers drum repeatedly on his good leg. He stares out the window at the gray asphalt that stretches west. In the backpack Hannah brought with her from Mitchell's home, she'd packed several thumb-sized explosives and a remote control stolen from the Reverend's arsenal. This girl—woman, he supposes—is a wealth of surprises. She and Karen placed the explosives strategically in different places on the one road that leads to the BASIA compound. Chaos and distraction will help them rescue Jonathan. It's the best—and the only—plan they have.

"I know it's cold but we should roll down the windows," Hannah says. "We need to be able to hear them coming."

Karen obliges, lowering all the windows. Somewhere nearby, staccato pops burst the silence.

"Shots." Steven sits higher in his seat, lifts his gun.

"They're coming from the woods." Hannah points. "That means Jonathan followed the map. He's heading our way."

The blasts ring out in an unpredictable rhythm. They're getting louder. Karen positions her gun, clicks off the safety. Hannah readies the remote control detonator.

"They're close," Steven whispers. Branches sway in the wind. He sees something—someone—heading in their direction. He aims his gun out the window. It's not an easy shot.

Suddenly, an engine roars. It's coming from the direction of the BASIA compound.

"It's him," Hannah says. "Look!"

Steven leans closer. Sure enough, Jonathan weaves through the last layers of trees until he hits the pavement. There, he pauses, only twenty yards away. Steven exhales as though he's been holding his breath for days. But with Karen's gun aimed out the window, a panicked look crosses Jonathan's face. He sprints in the opposite direction, away from them and the BASIA compound. In that split second, he realizes Jonathan must not see him or Hannah, must not recognize Karen.

"Jonathan!" He grabs Karen's arm. "He thinks we're with Mitchell. Let's go!"

"Wait," Hannah says.

Karen shuts the windows. Jonathan's body is getting smaller in the distance. From the opposite direction a dark SUV is heading toward them at high speed. At the same time, two men in black uniforms emerge from the woods with assault weapons. They're searching for Jonathan. Suddenly, they focus on the Land Rover, shifting their guns and firing without hesitation. Bullets ricochet off the glass, the hood, the side of the bulletproof car. The oncoming SUV is only a hundred feet away.

"Now!" Karen shouts.

Hannah presses a button on the remote, triggering all of the explosives simultaneously. Thunderous blasts, fire and smoke erupt. It's hard to tell what's happening within the billowing smoke. Steven turns to see Jonathan, stopped by the noise, watching this attack on his captors.

"Go, go, go!" Steven yells.

The tires screech on the pavement as Karen wrenches the steering wheel, turning the car in the other direction. Steven rolls down his window and waves to Jonathan, who stands motionless in the road. In the rearview mirrors the clouds of smoke are dissipating and there's no movement. The SUV is on its side, burning.

"Well done, Hannah," he says, glancing back at her. She stares out the window. Tears streak her cheeks and run down her neck. She makes no move to wipe them away.

Karen pulls the car to a stop alongside Jonathan. Upon seeing his stepfather, he bends at the waist, hands bound together at his back, and gasps for breath. If Steven could go to him, he would. Instead he leans his head out the window.

"You're not going to shoot me again, are you?" he says.

Jonathan straightens, revealing a face streaked with tears, but he's grinning. It's the most delightful vision Steven has ever seen.

Chapter 84

Sebastian glances into the rearview mirror. The glare of oncoming headlights reveals Taylor peacefully staring out the darkened window, Sienna nestled into the curve of her body. It was disturbingly easy to slip back into the East Wing of the White House. The quiet was terrifying, as though the world had ended. He'd found Sienna where he left her in the secret room. To his surprise, she was sleeping. Her body had probably shut down after the trauma.

D.C. was in utter chaos. Sebastian took the SUV he'd driven to the White House and blazed down the streets, passing U.S. military tanks and trucks filled with troops. They were frantically scrambling to set up barricades on roads leading from the convention center and the White House. If he'd been just a minute or two later, they might not have made it out.

An hour ago Taylor awakened, groggy and confused. When she saw Sienna next to her, her body shook as she gathered her into her arms and they embraced in a tangle of arms and emotion. They haven't let go since.

The country road they're on has little traffic. By now, he knows, all major highways have been shut down by the military, but there's not enough manpower to cover the side roads. He wonders if Cole and Lily got out all right, if they've landed already. A little while ago he told Taylor everything that had happened since she was drugged. She listened without comments or questions. And though she can clearly see they're heading south, she hasn't asked about their destination.

In his lap, Sebastian's right hand throbs from the bullet that pierced it. Wrapped tightly in a white T-shirt, it's now stained a rust color from dried blood. Despite the pain, a part of him is glad. Glad the cross tattoo will be obscured by the scar that will remain. A lifetime of memories in his hand.

It will be several hours before they reach the Outer Banks, and after that it shouldn't take long to find a willing captain with a boat to ferry them away. Plane travel will be suspended by now, but it should be easier to travel by boat. The coast guard and navy will be on alert, but they simply can't cover the expanse of the Atlantic. A small fishing boat should do the job. And money will speak volumes to a fisherman.

"Will?" Taylor's voice is hoarse, weak.

Their eyes connect in the rearview. *Will.* It's all still lies.

"Can we go somewhere sunny?" she asks. It's a child's question, a simple request based purely on want, not need.

"You read my mind." He grins. Given what they're escaping, they should be granted asylum. Not to mention they all have clean MedIDs. "British Virgin Islands?"

"Yes." Her head lolls back on the seat. "Virgin Gorda. Tortola. Anegada."

It feels like a dream to talk of such things. Too simple, that after everything that's happened they can be transported to a land without politics or terror, bullets or bombs. A twinge in his chest, a flash of Kate's face. She'd want this for him. A new life. Maybe even a family.

"I can sell my art to tourists." Taylor's eyes are closed now, daydreaming.

"There's something you should know." He positions the mirror so he can see her better. "My name isn't Will Anderson."

Taylor leans forward, rests her hand on his shoulder. "I've had enough truth for a lifetime. I don't need to know your real name to know who you are."

He stares at their headlights on the road ahead. His family in Buenos Aires must be watching the news, must think he's dead. In many ways, it's like Sebastian Diaz died along with Kate, died along with his passion to defend a country corrupt to its core. Will Anderson only existed as an assignment, someone who witnessed too much death and horror. Maybe she's right.

"I like the name on my new MedID," she says. "Starting now, I'm Cleo Mason. And this is my daughter, Sophie."

The name on his new chip, courtesy of Cole, is in honor of Boston and of his partner. Yet another identity, but this one he'll easily remember. "Nice to meet you, Cleo. Name's Logan Renner."

"Logan Renner." She reaches over the seat, lays her hand gently against his cheek. He kisses her palm.

Sienna stirs, restless. "Are we there yet?"

"Not yet," he says.

Taylor settles back on the seat and sings softly. The tune calms the little girl, and him as well. Logan Renner, he thinks to himself. Who is he, or who will he be? It's not a question he needs to answer now. Time will tell.

THE SUDDEN, JARRING motion of the plane's wheels hitting the tarmac make Cole grip the armrest of his window seat. He pushes up the oval shade to reveal a leaden sky, dampened asphalt, and green grass in the distance. It's been twenty years since he and Lily have seen her cousins and this city they'll now, finally, call home. London. He rubs his eyes, which sting from the stale air and the emotion of the past several hours.

Three hours into the flight, seat monitors displaying news networks had suddenly interrupted programming to report a large-scale terrorist attack on the United States. At precisely midnight, Eastern Standard Time, a wave of choreographed assassinations had swept the country, aimed at both newly elected and former administration officials.

Shrieks, cries, denials had filled the air. People frantically tried to call, text, or email loved ones. Cabin air grew ripe with nervous sweat, the space suddenly claustrophobic. Some passengers fainted in the commotion.

From what Cole learned, officials confirmed at least sixty deaths, but with updates coming hourly, sources said the actual number was likely to surpass initial reports. Shaky phone videos displayed footage taken at campaign parties where darkness fell, followed by gunshots and explosions. One reporter said the collective hope of the United States was with the Secret Service, who likely executed an escape for both President Clark and President-elect Richard Hensley, along with the vice president and the vice president-elect. Then the pilot disconnected all incoming plane communications in the cabin.

He'd tried to call Steven and Karen, but it was no use. Throughout the plane, voices shouted out names of known terrorists—including Reverend Mitchell and BASIA—along with conspiracy theories rooted in their very own government. His thoughts turned to Sebastian, where he was when it all went down. *If he's still alive.* And have Steven and Jonathan been reunited? Perhaps he'll never know.

Eventually, the crew turned down the lights and people quieted. Worry and his imagination kept him awake through the flight. The War at Home changed in one night, and left a revolution in his wake. There are no winners, not yet.

Beside him, Ian sleeps. In the aisle seat, Lily cradles Talia, her downy head resting against Lily's chest. He studies his wife. She's still beautiful, but something about her has changed. As though ten years passed in six months. Fine lines like parentheses curve around her mouth, and her ivory skin creases at the outer edge of her eyes, even when she's not smiling. He imagines she thinks the same about him.

"I love you, Lily."

"I love you, too."

They both smile weakly. A *ding* sounds as the pilot comes over the speakers and, in an English accent, welcomes the native citizens home.

"For those of you who are United States citizens, I'd like to extend our deepest sympathies on behalf of myself, your copilot, and your crew." The pilot's tone is grave. "All passengers need to be aware that flights originating in the U.S. will be met at the gate by military officers. It's standard procedure when an event like this takes place. They'll be interviewing everyone before allowing you to leave the airport. It's for your own safety, and for the safety of England. I'm sure you understand."

The plane taxis to the gate and everyone stands. Cole scans the cabin. It's the first time he's seen the faces of the passengers since the news. Cheeks streaked by tears, bodies hunched, eyes wide and alert with what he guesses is the universal look of shock. Fear hangs between them, connects them forever in this moment. The ache of it all settles in him.

He pulls Ian to him, kisses the top of his head. He has no regrets. His family is alive. No matter what was left behind, his world is right here.

Acknowledgments

To MY AGENT Laura Gross who took a chance on me and who worked with ceaseless energy and enthusiasm for this book until she found it a home. Thank you to my phenomenal editor, Emily Krump, who understood my characters as though they were her own and who helped me to make *Nation of Enemies* the best book it could be.

To my unflaggingly talented writer's group, Loren Schecter, Laurie Nordman and Karen Halil-Mechanic, who supported me throughout the journey beginning at page one. To my friend, Celia St. Amant, always honest, always true, who has never steered me wrong in my writing and my life. To my sister, Heidi Thielen. An early reader and champion of my work, her tenacity of spirit and determination can be found woven through my characters.

Also, to my friends at L'Aroma Café. It's impossible to calculate the number of coffees and curries enjoyed within the comforting walls of this gem I like to call "my office." Thank you for always saving me a seat.

To my eternally supportive husband, Ben, and daughters,

Amelie and Ivy, who understand my passion for writing and leave me with kisses and hugs as I go off to write each weekend.

And last but not least, to my father, who told me I could be and do whatever I wanted to in life. And to my mother, for the dreams she never pursued.

About the Author

H.A. Raynes was inspired to write *Nation of Enemies* by a family member who was a Titanic survivor and another who escaped Poland in World War II. Combining lessons from the past with a healthy fear of the modern landscape, this novel was born. A longtime member of Boston's writing community, H.A. Raynes has a history of trying anything once (acting, diving out of a plane, white water rafting, and parenting). Writing and raising children seem to have stuck.